I0648126

OPENING NIGHT,
Theatre Play Collection

By
Richard Mousseau

MOOSE HIDE BOOKS
imprint of
MOOSE ENTERPRISE PUBLISHING
PRINCE TOWNSHIP
ONTARIO, CANADA

cover illustration by Rick Mousseau

Opening Night
Theatre Play Collection
Copyright February 1, 2019

Published June 1, 2019
by
MOOSE HIDE BOOKS
imprint of
MOOSE ENTERPRISE PUBLISHING
684 WALLS ROAD
PRINCE TOWNSHIP
ONTARIO, CANADA
P6A 6K4
web site www.moosehidebooks.com

NO VENTURE UNATTAINABLE

ALL RIGHTS RESERVED, NO PART OF THIS BOOK MAY BE REPRODUCED, THIS INCLUDES STORING IN RETRIEVAL SYSTEM OR TRANSMITTED IN ANY FORM BY ELECTRONIC MEANS, MECHANICAL, PHOTOCOPYING, RECORDING OR OTHER, WITHOUT THE WRITTEN PERMISSION FROM THIS PUBLISHER.

THIS PLAY IS A WORK OF FICTION, NAMES, CHARACTERS, PLACES AND INCIDENTS ARE EITHER PRODUCTS OF THE AUTHOR'S IMAGINATION OR ARE USED FICTITIOUSLY. ANY RESEMBLANCE TO ACTUAL EVENTS OR LOCALES OR PERSONS, LIVING OR DECEASED, IS ENTIRELY COINCIDENTAL. PERFORMANCE RIGHTS AND FEES AND BOOK COST SHALL BE OBTAINED FROM THIS PUBLISHER BEFORE ANY PRESENTATION.

SOUND RECORDINGS – LYRICS AND MUSICAL SCORES FOR SONGS PRESENTED IN INDIVIDUAL PLAYS CAN BE OBTAINED BY CONTACTING THIS PUBLISHER.

CREATED IN CANADA

Library and Archives Canada Cataloguing in Publication

Title: Opening night : theatre play collection / by Richard Mousseau.
Names: Mousseau, Richard, 1953- author.
Description: Includes index.
Identifiers: Canadiana (print) 20190064994 | Canadiana (ebook) 2019006501X | ISBN 9781927393574
   (softcover) | ISBN 9781927393581 (PDF)
Classification: LCC PS8576.O977 O64 2019 | DDC C812/.54—dc23

INDEX

A FIRE SIDE OLD TIME RADIO SHOW
by
EDMOND J. ALCID
Copyright June 1999

STAGE:
THE STAGE SHOULD RESEMBLE THE INTERIOR OF AN OLD TIME RADIO STATION. MIKES, BENCHES, CHAIRS, MUSICIANS, ANNOUNCERS, ACTORS, SOUND AFFECTS AND SOUND AFFECTS PEOPLE ALL PLACED ON STAGE. OLDER LOOKING STAGE PROPS AND ACTOR'S ATTIRE SHOULD REPRESENT THE ERA OF THE FORTIES.

SOUND:
THE STAGE MUSICIANS SHOULD SUPPLY ALL MUSIC FOR BACKGROUND INTERLUDES, INTROS AND PERFORMED PIECES.

LIGHTING:
AN OVERHEAD LIGHTING SHOULD BE USED TO GIVE AN INTERIOR LOOK OF A SOUND STUDIO. LIGHTING SHOULD BE IN THE EARTH COLOURS TO GIVE AN AGED LOOK TO THE SET AND TO ACTORS ATTIRE. A SOFT SPOT LIGHT SHOULD BE USED TO HIGHLIGHT SEQUENCES IN PROGRESS.

NOTES:
LET ACTORS REACT BEHIND THE SCENES. LET BUD BE ANIMATED BUT SILENT. LET THE PLAY BE HECTIC, CALM, MYSTERIOUS AND JOYFUL AT DIFFERENT TIMES. PLAY SHOULD NOT BE STATIC.

CHARACTER LEADS:

THE ANNOUNCER:	BEN PHELPS.
MUSICIANS:	OUR ALMOST THERE ORCHESTRA.
POET:	MR. CHEEKS TOO SOFT.
BEST FRIENDS:	WOJO THE DOG AND YOUNG'IN.
VENTRILOQUIST:	DONALD KNOTS.
DUMMY:	KNOT HEAD.
THE CRABTREES:	WILBUR AND MILDRED CRABTREE.
SCIENTIST:	PROFESSOR E.D. UCATION.
STORY TELLER:	PENELOPE PEABODIE.
STAGE DIRECTOR:	BUD
MA:	YOUNG'IN'S MOTHER.
DOCTOR:	DOC GOOD.
SOUND AFFECTS:	WALDO.

BEN PHELPS:
Ben is a young announcer searching for his own distinctive radio voice. He is always dressed to the tee. In his mind he believes he is above the life standards of the other radio players. His intellectual ability far surpasses the others, so he thinks of himself. A bow-tie on his neck, pinstripe suite and his hair is greased back and black. He seldom acknowledges others, he seems to be in his own little world.

OUR ALMOST THERE ORCHESTRA:
Musicians are a mixture of country folk and well-polished musicians. The sounds they play are pigeonholed as country music. Slight mistakes are made but a good effort should be made of the performed songs. All instruments should be acoustic.

POET:
Mr. Cheeks Too Soft is an old down and out, a real-life cowboy. There is nothing said or done fast for this slow moving grizzled old man. His attire still carries the dust of the plains along with the smell. His cowboys' poetry is all of the memories he has collected of his life, when he recites his poems, he begins to live the life of his poetry.

WOJO:
Wojo is a man dressed as an old blood hound dog. Being so old, he has gained the ability to talk. Being old gives him the privilege to be sarcastic and irritable. Makeup and floppy ears would be enough to distinguish the actor as a dog.

YOUNG`IN:
Young`in is a forty-year-old bachelor who works the family homestead. Being a farmer, he dresses in coveralls and mopes around. A hard-working lazy farmer that is destined to be alone for the rest of his life. Wojo, his dog runs his life.

DONALD KNOTS:
A young up and coming vaudeville performer. He has all the drive to be good but is not. His lips always move at the same time as the dummy. He tries to dress well in a suite that seems to have been a size too small. A pleasant nervous performer.

KNOT HEAD:
Knot Head, is an actual dummy. He is a young boy with an oversized head, big eyes and rosy cheeks. He is scarey looking in an innocent way.

WILBUR:
A man between thirty-five and forty-five. He wears light red pajamas with red wool socks. He is always tired wanting to just sleep. A frustrated man who works hard for little money.

MILDRED:
A light brained blonde woman in her late thirties. She wears a head full of curlers and a long nightgown with a fur scarf. A typical nag who will not leave her husband alone. All she ever thinks about is herself.

PROFESSOR E.D. UCATION:
An absent-minded scientist dressed in a long white lab coat. Horn-rimmed glasses are balancing on the end of his nose. In a foreign voice he spouts as he points with a telescopic pointer. He always sounds as if he is teaching pupils.

PENELOPE PEABODIE:
A country bumpkin who was the prime reporter of gossip for the folks back home. Now she is in the big time of city life and out to be part of it. She still dresses in a puffy dress that is out of style. A good-hearted gossip.

BUD:
A stage director that wears head phones with a mile-long cord. Dressed in light pants, checkered shirt, spotted bow-tie and red suspenders. He moves about the stage moving mikes, props and points directions to the actors.

MA:
Young`in's mother. A nice little old homely woman, sweet and kind.

DOC GOOD:
He is an old veterinary.

WALDO:
An on-stage sound affects man.

SONGS INDEX:
I AIN`T GONNA SIT AROUND NO MORE.
Copyright April 29, 1986
OLD DOGS
Copyright March 27, 1989
GOING HOME SOON.
Copyright March 20, 2001
FORSAKE ME NOT.
Copyright April 28, 1987

WE DON'T DO IT THAT WAY NO MORE.
Copyright April 1, 1986
A COWBOY'S LULLABY.
Copyright January 21, 1994
FRIENDS' WE NEVER FORGET.
Copyright December 14, 1994
All words and Music
by
Richard E. Mousseau
A SOCAN Member
Song sheets and audio tapes are available to groups when agreement is made
for the production of this play.

SET AND PROPS:
STAGE SHOULD RESEMBLE AN OLD TIME RADIO STATION OF
THE NINETEEN-FORTIES. OLD BENCHES, TABLES, OLD STAND UP
MIKES AND SCRIPT EASELS, A SOUND AFFECTS AREA.
CHARACTERS SHOULD WEAR CLOTHES THAT RELATE TO THE
TIME PERIOD. MAKE UP SHOULD ALSO GIVE THE OLD LOOK OF
EARTHLY COLOURS. ORCHESTRA MUSIC STANDS SHOULD BE
CARDBOARD LOOKING WITH THE NAME ON THE FRONTS. PLACE
AS MUCH OF EVERYTHING POSSIBLE AND STRANGE ITEMS ON
STAGE, PLATES, CUPS, COFFEE-POT, WHOLE AND HALF EATEN
SANDWICHES, TOWELS, COSTUME CHANGES AND A LOT OF OLD
SCRIPTS SCATTERED AROUND.

PART ONE
A FIRE SIDE OLD TIME RADIO SHOW
THE STAGE IS DARK. ALL ACTORS ARE ON STAGE IN POSITION.
THE ORCHESTRA BEGINS TUNNING UP. THE MUSIC THEY PLAY
FOR BACKGROUND FILLERS SHOULD BE INSTRUMENTAL MUSIC
OF THE SONGS IN THE SCRIPT. AS THE ORCHESTRA BEGINS TO
PLAY THE INTRO MUSIC FOR THE SHOW THE STAGE LIGHTS
OVER HEAD OF THE STAGE BRIGHTEN. IN ORDER THE
CHARACTERS SLOWLY START TO MOVE. ONCE ALL THE ACTORS
ARE MILLING AROUND MUMBLING. ORCHESTRA BEGINS TO
SOUND BETTER. LOW SPOT LIGHT BEGINS TO FOLLOW BUD
AROUND THE STAGE AS HE SETS UP THE MIKE FOR THE
ANNOUNCER.

Bud: (After setting the mike up for the announcer wave arms to the actors
to become silent. Bring down the volume of the orchestra. Count to five, with
an open left hand hold it up to the actors, with a right-hand point to the
announcer. Music stops.)

Orchestra: (only a guitar softly plays in the background)

Phelps: (search for a voice) Do not touch that dial. It is now time for
A Fire Side Old Time Radio Show live on the airwaves from station W.R.I.K.
. . . Tonight we are pleased to present and feature Young`in, Wojo the dog,
Wilbur and Mildred Crabtree, Donald Knots and Knot Head, Mr Cheeks Too
Soft, Professor E.D. Ucation, Penelope Peabodie, Our Almost There Ochestra
and myself your announcer . . . Phelps . . . Ben Phelps. This portion of the
show is sponsored in part by Mousseau's fine line of pine furniture. If you are
in line for fine pine furniture but hate to whine standing in line to spend that
dime . . . well put that dime away and let your smile shine . . . you will find a
fine line of pine furniture at Mousseau's fine line of pine furniture located at
the side-line near the pipe line on Baseline by the coast line. But do not worry
for they have a streamlined guideline to give you a beeline to their shop of
fine pine lines of furniture.

Orchestra: (music of a guitar hits a sour note then is back to normal
playing)

Phelps: (an irritated look on face) If you do not like their fine line of
pine furniture, they also have oak, ash, walnut, elm, mahogany, spruce . . .
well you get the idea . . . they have everything you may wish for at Mousseau's
(drag out line) fine line of pine furniture. (Pause) Now to open A Fire Side
Old Time Radio Show we bring to you the down-home warmth of 'Our
Almost There Orchestra' with their rendition of 'I Ain`t Gonna Sit Around
No More.'

Orchestra: (guitar builds then fades, song begins)

Hand me down my walking stick, I ain`t gonna sit around no more.
At sixty-four, I ain`t gonna let these old bones get old no more.
Granny get your dancing shoes there's a real hot dance tonight.
Hand me down my walking stick, I ain`t gonna sit around all night.

Do they still do the two step and the Texas trot?
If we get old and tired, we will waltz the Tennessee waltz.
I will lean on you, Granny when the night is through.
On this hardwood sawdust floor, I'm as young as,

Hand me down my vitamins, doctor Baily's liniment.
Your nineteen-fourteen corset-waist will put my chest back in place.
I will be in real fine shape for all those pretty fillies tonight.
Hand me down my walking stick, I ain`t gonna sit around all night.

8

Bud: (As the music ends point to the announcer)

Orchestra: (only the stand-up bass player plays in background)

Phelps: (search for voice) Yes . . . yes . . . yes . . . Our Almost There Orchestra will be back throughout tonight's show. Right now, please welcome that renowned potentially prominent professor of prose and poetry Mr. Cheeks Too Soft. Tonight, he will recite poems from his new book titled 'Pioneer Poetry of Mr. Cheeks Too Soft'. (say off mike) What else would he call it? (back to mike) This book will be for sale after the show for our studio audience. Please give a warm hello to Mr. Cheeks to Soft.

Orchestra: (bass music builds then fades as actors applaud)

Phelps: The title of this selection is 'Week Old Soup'.

Orchestra: (bass player plays and plays as he waits for Mr. Cheeks)

Mr. Cheeks: (slowly take time walking to mike, the wrong mike)

Bud: (wave Mr. Cheeks to right mike)

Mr. Cheeks: (clear throat, adjust eyes to read script, act out lines of poem) (note, other cast members could recite other character speaking parts in poem)

"Hey, Cook what's a-simmering in your pot?"
"Something mighty special, enough for you lot.
When you taste this, it will hit the spot.
Now don't touch that, the handle is hot."

Sour Dough backed quickly before he received a swat.
One more inch and Sour Dough would have got shot.
Just-the-Cook was a mean tempered French-Scott.
When Just-the-Cook is cooking don't touch the pot.

Just-the-Cook looked like any other cattle man.
At forty yards shoot the label off a tomato can.
He'd always say, 'The road to good health is plenty of bran.'
Rumours where he learned cooking in a place called Japan.

I don't rightly recall what is his real name,
but he is renown, with world wide fame,
a genius at making a hearty meal out of any old wild game.

If you ever get sick, take my word, him you better not blame.

Just-the-Cook is might sensitive, he just loves favouritism.
He say's, 'Food should be devoured with candle light romanticism.
Close your eyes and let its taste remove any scepticism.'
No matter how fast a draw you are, don't offer criticism.

I know, for I was once warned not to speak my mind.
The boys all said, 'Cheeks-Too-Soft say something kind.'
When them words left my lips, I knew I was in a bind.
I felt rock salt from Cook's twelve gage hit my behind.

It was not that I didn't enjoy trail side gourmet cooking,
but swimming in my tin plate were critters, I ain't joking.
Mexican jumping beans with legs grabbed whiskers with their hooks.
Like a wild bronking horse I bucked and shook and shook and shook.

Cowboy profanity profusely rambled freely from my lips.
Just-the-Cook took exception to my literary verbal quips.
With lightning speed sprang up the shotgun from Cook's hip.
Stinging rock salt tingled the flesh of my butt as away I did skip.

Now when Cook asks, I quickly recite, 'Mighty fine.
There is no greater honour then to sit here and dine.
With campfire light, cowboy chatter and day-old cactus wine.'
Word spread quickly that Mr. Cheeks-Too-Soft has no spine.

Many a cowboy has wondered what kind of special ingredient,
Just the Cook adds to his daily soup to make eyes glow radiant,
or wonder what Cook is picking on the plains that are so nutrient.
No one will ever say to his face, 'That Just-the-Cook is deviant.'

Sitting around the campfire late at night we all contemplate,
if it is snake or worms or grasshoppers into the soup he grates.
Cowboys ain't scholars, some stutter but all join in on the debate,
and wonder if we are long for this earth or is it boot hill our fate?

Then one day the trail Boss said his son was a-joining the cattle drive.
We all thought the new Tender Foot was one we should want to deprive,
of ingredient knowledge of Just-the-Cook's cooking and see if he survives,
and if he asks what's in the pot, if no gun shots then Tender Foot's alive.

"Go on Tender Foot ask the cook what he puts in his soup?"
Us cowboys hid behind a sage bush in a tight little group,

like a bunch of old clucking hens afraid to come out of the chicken coup.
Tender Foot marched right up to Just-the-Cook, a typical nincompoop.

"I was wondering," said Tender Foot. "What makes your soup so delicious?"
We all cringed knowing that Just-the-Cook could become quite vicious.
Now what I am truly about to relate is not anywhere near friction-us.
A few more mumbled syllables then Tender Foot said, "It is nutritious."

Surely shotgun rock salt would be flying, but Cook stood there with a smile.
He sucked in his belly, brushed back his beard, for a cook he looked virile.
Cook seemed somewhat proud, almost pleased, no sign of being hostile.
"Sit down Tender Foot, let Cook explain culinary delights for awhile."

Tender Foot sat on a block of wood and held out a dented tin cup.
Cook grinned and poured black coffee for the kid, an innocent pup.
Cook rambled out tales of cooking for royalty. Tender Foot said, 'Yup.'.
Those stories were so good we decided to join them, from hiding we got up.

Just like little cowboys at bedtime we hung onto every word said.
A few tales were so heart felt that a few of us had tears to shed.
Just the Cook told us of a fellow who swallowed a goat's eye then dropped dead.
A lady that gave up wayward ways because of his cooking, him she wanted to wed.

Long into the night Just-the-Cook lamented, cattle were being lulled to sleep.
Sour sighed delightfully. We all felt that Just-the-Cook was not an old creep.
Tender Foot asked, "How do you make your soup." Silence, no one made a peep.
We held our breath, did Tender Foot make a mistake, we were ready to leap.

Cook scratched a critter out of his beard then proceeded to rub his nose on a sleeve.
"Well," Cook grumbled. "Plenty of experience is needed before one can happily achieve,
a great taste, smiles of satisfaction, applause and money you guys never leave,
but a great gourmet cook should always say, I am great, in myself I do believe."

"Then you get yourself a great big thick-walled cast-iron pot three feet round.
Build a good hardwood fire, use buffalo chips, there's plenty on the ground.
Use water, preferably swamp water, it has a bit of an edge, best I've found.
You need meat, so-what if it has been chewed up by a hungry blood hound."

11

"Throw in some wild root, wild rice, some noodles I picked up in Japan.
Keep the campfire going, we need really hot coals, use your hat as a fan.
Chop up rattle snake, pinewood grubs, Cheyenne pepper then fry it up in a pan.
Just keep cooking, add what-ever's at hand, there's no need to have a recipe plan."

"Every day just add something new, never ever let the pot go dry.
Add what-ever is left over from last month, any day that's gone by.
If need be wash out the coffee pot and tin plates in the soup, I need not lie.
It adds taste, you guys lack a sense of good taste, you'd rather see beans fry."

At about that moment there weren't a cowboy around to hear them words.
Every Tom, Dick and Harry scattered wilder then a stampeding cow herd.
I tell you the chirps us cowboys made weren't the sweet sounds of southern song birds.
To die of thirst or trampled by steers or snake bite us cowboys would have preferred.

Now I wouldn't say Just-the-Cook was a-trying to put every cowboy in Boot Hill,
but everyone came to the conclusion, that there was poison a-brewing in his swill.
Tender Foot said he was too young to have growing on his grave a bunch of daffodils.
"Tom, Dick and Harry you hold Just-the-Cook down, that pot of soup we need to spill."

Just as Cook's twelve gage hammers clicked up stepped the cattle Boss.
"Boys let the cook go, Cook, your speciality of pot soup will be your loss,
but after six weeks of your soup I'm filled to the brim, your soup we must toss.
I'm laying down camp law, don't cook anything that tastes like swamp moss."

For awhile things cooled down, I wouldn't say the cook was being mean.
Of his cooking, we all found tolerable, the flavour and substance a bit lean.
Around the campfire on cool evening nights our antics created quite a scene,
if you can imagine forty cowboys after digesting fired up beans, beans, beans!

Bud: (begin to clap, urge actors and audience to clap, rearrange mikes)

Orchestra: (drums beat fast then slow then fades, organ or violin begins to play in background)

12

Bud: (point to announcer)

Phelps: (low voice) Now it is time for the ongoing saga of Ma, Young`in and Wojo the dog featured in 'Young`in's World'. It is early morning on the old homestead. Ma is busy in the kitchen baking four of five dozen oatmeal cookies for Young`in. She figures that the cookies should last him for two or three days before she will have to slave, baking up another batch. Young`in is just now getting up.

Orchestra: (music fades)

Affects:(toilet is flushing, door closing, walking sound stepping down stairs, dog yapping in pain)

Young`in: Oh, sorry Wojo I . . .

Wojo: What . . . you did not see my tail wagging?

Young`in: I am afraid not.

Wojo: For the past twenty years I wait at the bottom of the stairs wagging my tail . . . and for one hundred and forty dog years you have stepped on my tail. You are pushing this man's best friends' thing a bit too far. (grumble)

Young`in: There goes a mighty fine old blood hound.

Ma: Is that you Young`in?

Young`in: I have lived here for the past forty some years . . .

Wojo: Forty-five point six.

Young`in: Pa is out milking the cows . . . Uncle Clyde and Aunt Bonnie have not been around since twenty-eight . . . who else would it be?

Wojo: Humor her.

Young`in: Yeah Ma, it is me.

Ma: I know son . . . who else would it be? You have been here for the past forty some years . . . when in tarnation are you going to leave home? I have worked my fingers to the bone for you.

Young`in: Mothers . . . when you are young, they say go out . . . meet girls . . . have fun. You do what they say and what happens. (act like an old woman) They say . . . you are always out late . . . you never stay home anymore, . . . we never see you.

Wojo: You cannot please her.

Young`in: I try to be a good son . . . stay home . . . do not stay out late . . . and for forty some years later . . .

Wojo: Forty-five point six.

Young`in: . . . she still wants me to leave home.

Wojo: You just cannot please Mothers.

Young`in: I am moving out tomorrow morning.

Wojo: Right on.

Ma: Oh, you will move out . . . meet a girl . . . then you will never come around anymore . . . I will never see you . . . I will have a couple of hundred oatmeal cookies made and no Young`in to eat them. (cry and sob)

Wojo: (growls) Man's best friend ha . . . you treat your mother just like you treat me . . . we give you everything . . . do you appreciate it . . . no . . . you step on our tails.

Young`in: Well if it makes you feel better . . . here bite my leg.

Wojo: (growl, bark, make slurping sounds)

Young`in: Do you feel better now?

Wojo: (pant) I would if I had teeth . . . do you think you could get me a store-bought pair?

Young`in   Ah . . . I do not think so. (Wojo sighs) You are looking a bit peeked . . . are you feeling okay?

Wojo: I have a slight bladder problem . . . it has been nagging at me at night.

Young`in: That explains the puddles on the floor. I thought the roof was leaking . . . but it has not rained for near on ten weeks.

Wojo: I think we should go see Doc Good.

Young`in: Okay Wojo . . . I think that is a good idea. I will give ole Doc Good a call.

Affects:(phone sounds of dialing and ringing)

Doc: Hello.

Young`in:     Hello Doc Good . . . this is Young`in.

Doc: Well hello Young`in . . . are you still living with Ma and Pa . . . You must be . . . oh, what forty?

Wojo: Forty-five point six.

Doc: I thought you were sweet on Gerty, the hog farmer's daughter?

Young`in: Listen Doc . . . I am calling about Wojo . . . he says he has a slight bladder problem. (talk away from mike) Slight is an understatement. (back to mike) He is leaking like a sieve.

Doc: Well Young`in, I think Wojo should have a simple operation to correct his problem.

Young`in: A simple operation?

Doc: I should be able to arrange an operation for the first thing tomorrow morning.

Young`in: How much will a quick simple operation cost?

Doc: Oh . . . with operation cost . . . my fee . . . hospital stay for one night and one day . . . oh . . . I would say about fifty dollars.

Young`in: Fifty dollars for a simple operation on a flea infested dog.

Wojo: (Growl and snap sounds)

Young`in: Doc . . . that is as much as I have saved up for a vacation on

15

a tropical beach with an exotic native girl.

Doc: What about Gerty, the hog farmer's daughter . . . I thought you were sweet on her?

Wojo: Man's best friend . . . I was there for you . . . but now when I am old and sickly . . . you would rather get sand between your toes and nibble on the soft neck of a beach bimbo . . . When I am gone, you will miss stepping on my tail each morning.

Young`in: I have not had a vacation or a girl in about . . .

Wojo: . . . forty-five point six years.

Doc: Well Young`in what will it be . . . Wojo . . . a vacation . . . or dumping sweet Gerty.

Young`in:       (fuming) I ain`t sweet on Gerty . . . and never was.

Wojo: (give a big sigh)

Young`in: Okay Doc . . . make all of the arrangements for the operation . . . goodbye.

Wojo: Young`in . . . a hospital can be a cold . . . dark . . . strange . . . did I mention a lonely place. Operations can be tricky . . . there is not always a guaranty . . . I . . . I . . . just might not make it . . . I . . . am starting to feel poorly . . . did I mention lonely. A strange place filled with irritating cats . . . birds . . . that talk too much . . . waiting behind turtles in the washroom line . . . rabbits all over the place . . . pigs squealing on each other . . . did I mention a lonely place to be.

Young`in: Yes, you did mention lonely . . . you are a DOG . . . snap out of it. I am taking you for an operation.

Affects:(sounds of feet walking doors opening and closing, a car door opening and closing, a car sound speeding down an old gravel road)

Phelps: Yes Young`in was taking Wojo to the animal hospital to have his leaking bladder plugged. In the caring hands of nurses Wojo was left . . . Young`in returned home to do farm chores.

Affects: (sounds of cats and dogs, feet walking, car door opening and closing then driving off, pause, then the sound of a phone ringing)

16

Young`in: Hello . . . yes . . . uh . . . ha . . . okay put him on. Wojo what is the matter boy . . . are you feeling okay . . . are they treating you well?

Wojo: I am a bit lonely in this big strange . . . cold . . .dark . . . did I mention lonely!

Young`in: Yes, you did.

Wojo: Do you think that you could come and visit me?

Young`in: Wojo, I just left you . . . it is a forty-mile drive.

Wojo: Oh, I am a little down . . . I just might not make it through the night.

Young`in: Are you feeling that poorly? . . . Well okay, I will be right there.

Affects:(faster sounds of footsteps, car doors, speeding car sounds, screeching to a stop sounds, running footsteps, hospital sounds of dogs, cats, cows, horses, pigs)

Young`in: (panting out of breath) What is wrong Wojo, are you taking a turn for the worst.

Wojo: It is just that I cannot sleep in a strange place . . . and . . . I thought you would please an old, old dog and sing me to sleep.

Young`in: You made me come all this way down here just to sing you to sleep . . . I traveled forty miles twice and you are not dying . . .

Wojo: I am a one hundred and forty years old in dog years . . . I have no teeth . . . I am going under Doc Good's knife tomorrow . . . I do not know if I will make it.

Young`in: Okay . . . Okay . . . I will sing you one of your favorite songs 'Old Dogs'.

Orchestra: (music begins on beginning of Young`in's last line)

Old dogs, ain`t nothing better than being old,
Hazy days, tales of past loves we have told,
Some-day, every old dog will have life made,

17

Any time roll over and snooze in the shade.

I'd rather be an old dog fishing at the fishing hole,
Then have a cat of a woman clawing at my mortal soul,
When young I prowled around nights for the female kind,
But the upkeep and maintenance blew my mind,

So, I'd rather be an old dog sitting on an old park bench,
Feeding hungry pigeons while looking for a pretty wench,
Then yonder comes a cackle of on the prowl old hen gals,
Out in search for an old dog to be a one-night stand.

So, I'd rather be an old dog cruising and going fishing,
Ain't wasting my time, rather be misbehaving.

Wojo: That was beautiful . . . just beautiful

Affects: (a duck begins to quack agitated)

Wojo: (sarcastic voice) We do not hunt ducks anymore. . . no teeth.

Affects: (duck quacks happily)

Orchestra: (build music for announcer)

Phelps: We leave Wojo and Young`in at the animal hospital where Doc Good will attempt a delicate bladder operation on a one hundred and forty-year-old dog. Will Wojo be able to hold his water after the operation . . . will Young`in go on his vacation . . . and what about his one-time girlfriend Gerty the hog farmer's daughter.

Orchestra: (build and fade music to background filler)

Phelps: (high voice) This portion of our show is brought to you in part by Uncle Mort's day-old manure. By the shovel full, bag full, wheel barrow or wagon full . . . you too can pick up, Uncle Mort's day-old manure.

Orchestra: (music change, banjo sound of hillbilly style)

Phelps: Uncle Mort proudly sponsors 'Letters from Home' with Uncle Mort's favorite niece Miss. Penelope Peabodie.

Bud: (frantically help Miss. Peabodie sit onto a stool in front of a mike, try to flatten out her fluffy dress)

18

Penelope: (giggle each time Bud touches dress)

Orchestra: (build music)

Bud: (give a cut sign, brings hand across throat, stage becomes silent, pause, roll hands to get Miss. Peabodie to start)

Penelope: Hello . . . friends, neighbors, cousins and Uncle Mort down at Uncle Mort's day-old manure factory. Speaking of manure . . . I have just received a letter from cousin Billy-Bob-John-Boy down on his horse ranch. Girls, Billy-Bob-John-Boy is an up and coming stage actor down at the community theatre. Well, he writes. . . (shuffle papers, pat down dress, adjust flowery cosmetic glasses) . . . 'Dear' . . . he calls me Dear, how sweet . . . 'Dear Penelope, my Cousin, I am writing this letter from inside of the outhouse behind the barn. During a fall afternoon I had just finished cleaning out the horse stalls when I decided to take a break and soak up the last of the afternoon's sun, just like my five horses were doing. On the south side of the barn a couple of horses were laying down snoozing, the others, just kind-of lazily stood around snoring'. . . Mama Peabodie snores just like cousin Billy-Bob-John-Boy's horses . . .(giggle) . . . 'Sitting up on a fence rail I leaned back against the barn wall. Feeling comfortable under the sun's warmth I also stretched my legs over the side fence rail. Cousin, did I mention that several weeks earlier I had joined a local theatre group and they gave me a small part.' . . . I told you cousin Billy-Bob-John-Boy was a famous actor . . . 'Sitting on the fence I decided to recite seven verses I had to memorize. Speaking in my best theatrical voice.' . . . His voice is as smooth as aged apple cider. . . 'I began reciting without mistakes . . . well, a few. One of my horses is named Cheyenne, a cross between a Clydesdale and a Palomino and Hackney, she is a big friendly five-year- old. Cheyenne always wants attention and a good scratch behind the ears.' . . . Don't we all. . . 'While I was reciting, she came over and rested her head across my legs. After I finished my moment in the spot-light, I nodded my head with pleasure knowing I had made it through my recitation.' . . . He is good. . . 'I asked Cheyenne what she thought of my performance. Turning and stepping away from me Cheyenne acknowledged my performance by raising her tail and filling the air with that ever-intoxicating barn yard perfume, 'Cattle Drive Number Forty-five.' This was my first review from a renown theatrical critic.' . . . Whooo . . . eeeh!

Orchestra: (build up banjo style of music)

Bud: (help Miss. Peabodie down from stool with comic interlude)

Phelps: Only at Uncle Mort's day-old manure would you be able to get the best manure fertilizer for miles around and only Uncle Mort would bring you Miss. Penelope Peabodie's Letters from Home.

Orchestra: (bass music builds then fades when Mr. Cheeks begins to speak)

Phelps: (talk away from mike) Who is next . . . who is up in this section?

Bud: (shrug shoulders as you look at all of the actors who are shaking their heads no, quickly point to Mr. Cheeks then rush to wake him and bring him to the mike)

Phelps: Him . . . (give voice a drawl) . . . from way out on the lonesome prairie please welcome back Mr. Cheeks Too Soft. . . (talk off mike) . . . Is he with us . . . Bud, keep things flowing?

Mr. Cheeks: (spit into a spittoon that Bud is holding) I was darn near fifty years old when I fell in love with someone other than my horse . . . she was a pretty sight to see . . . I will never forget 'Miss Anita'.

A pretty little gal, is Miss Anita the vet,
though not well endowed with a big set.
I was sure tickled pink on the day we first met.
"Not your type," the boys sassed, "wager a bet?"

Now old Doc Good use to come around,
that's when he was a virile young hound,
but I can't say that I miss the old coot.
Someone must have gave him the boot.

I must say folks, that I am a bit perplex.
This situation could become complex.
For you see, each year come early spring,
Doc Good, with some tools, he'd bring.

People doctors back in them good ole days just were not around.
With a youngin a-coming many a Pa rejoiced when Doc was found.
By-Joe, I think ole Doc was there when I was a-coming.
He sure done good, for I'm still here and still humming.

Let us not linger, that is another story.
When Doc's working, he is in his glory.
He checked Buttermilk my old mare.

20

I stood next in line somewhat bare.

As if nothing different he checked my withers,
then casually said, "fancy a game of checkers?"
Once a year, every year this was the ongoing situation.
For what ails me, Doc gave me caster oil for lubrication.

This spring it was pretty Miss Anita the vet.
I sure fancied her my type, I'd wager a bet.
I was tickled pink, I blushed, she said, "I'm glad we met.
Bring in them horses Mr. Cheeks Too Soft, I'm all set."

One by one, all in a row, in came a horse.
At the end of the line I stood of course.
The old timers watched intently from around the checker board.
Will she, or won't she, they wagered hoping to claim a reward.

Next came I, my teeth just a chattering.
In long-johns would she find me flattering.
"Open wide," said she. "I'll check your teeth."
Raising each bare arm, she checked beneath.

A hush fell among the menagerie in the barn.
I hope you all don't think this is just a yarn.
"You're in fine shape," smiled Miss Anita the vet.
My eyes were transfixed on this pretty brunette.

I could speak not a responsive word.
The other old guys, yes them I heard.
"Well make your move," they chimed.
Without spoken words, I pantomimed.

With love struck eyes my heart did pound.
Comments from the guys were sure to abound.
Flowers from behind my back to her I gave.
Rubbing my face, I realized I needed a shave.

"That's sweet of you Mr. Cheeks Too Soft."
My blood pressure rose, my heart was aloft.
"Here is some caster oil for whatever ails you."
This wasn't what I expected, this is surely true.

I spoke not a word as the sun began to set.
In the distance rode away Miss Anita the vet.

I sure fancied her my sweet Miss, and I'll wager you a bet.
Come next spring, I'll ask her to be my Mrs. Anita the vet.

Orchestra: (build music and fade to bass music for background for announcer)

Bud: (dab eyes with a hanky, actors sigh and applaud)

Phelps: (voice makes fun of sentiment of others and of poem) I am sure Uncle Mort from Uncle Mort's day-old Manure wishes to thank you for your heartwarming . . . poem. Waiting to entertain you is Our Almost There Orchestra with a song titled 'Going Home Soon' . . . (off mike) . . . More manure . . . (on mike) . . . take it away please.

Orchestra: (fumble with instruments then begin to fall in tempo with bass player)

Lone lonesome cattle get a-long home.
Lone lonesome cattle, no more to roam.
Never more wanting to wander under prairie skies.
Memories that we keep is a bond that ties.
A love of a wife longing to hold near.
Little wee ones their faces so dear.

Long lonesome nights where home fires burn.
Long lonesome nights where our hearts yearn.
Weathered voices sing to the restless cattle.
Horses ears listen for a winder's rattle.
Fire flames crackle between tall, tall, tales.
In the night's slumber a lonesome cowboy wails.

Lone lonesome cowboys whisper to the sky.
Lone lonesome cowboys sing a lullaby.
For a loved one a cowboy is searching.
In our dreams seeking, children's arms reaching.
Hold onto a cowboy she misses sadly.
Clinging to pant legs a child calls out daddy.

Goodnight cowboy going home soon.
Goodnight cowboy going home soon.

Orchestra: (music fades as a violin picks up the background filler,)

Bud: (Prompt actors and audience to clap)

22

Phelps: This portion of our show is sponsored by Moose Ventures, with locations in Moosonee, Moose Factory, Moose Jaw and Moose City Wyoming. Moose Ventures will guide you in your endeavors to seek the spirit of that ever-evasive northern moose. Moose Ventures disclaims any notions that one will vision the spirit of the great moose by drinking Moose-Head beer. But on every venture with Moose Ventures you will be supplied with Moose-Head beer. Moose Ventures guarantees a sighting of the majestic spirit of the great northern moose. Moose Ventures with locations in Moosonee, Moose Factory, Moose Jaw, and Moose City Wyoming. Moose-Head beer, imported from Canada's east coast where drinkers of Moose-Head beer have sighted the spirited northern moose walking upon water.

Bud: (direct orchestra to change style of music)

Orchestra: (heavy soap opera music builds)

Phelps: From Those There People Theatre Group we bring to you live on W.R.I.K. radio an original radio play. Tonight's production 'The Crabtrees On Butternut Corners' , featuring that charm-able couple Wilbur and Mildred Crabtree. Tonight's episode is titled, 'You Say It, But you Don't Do It'.

Orchestra: (build and go wild then bring down the volume)

Phelps: (give a frustrated face to the orchestra) It is late at night and Mildred is in bed waiting for Wilbur to come home. Mildred hears Wilbur come in, she lays down after hiding a fur scarf under the bed, she pretends to sleep. We hear Wilbur stumble in.

Affects: (door slams closed, a throat gurgling sound then spitting, door slams, foot prints then the sound of Wilbur Snoring and whistling)

Mildred: Wilbur . . . Wilbur . . . where have you been all night . . . for heaven's sake why do you snore and whistle like that? Who are you dreaming of . . .? I bet it is that Betty BOOBS Ohanlin over in the next apartment . . . Wilbur wake up . . . wake up. I cannot sleep . . . you are snoring too loud.

Wilbur: (snoring stops) Mildred I am tired . . . I worked all day . . . let me sleep . . . I am tired.

Mildred: You . . . never talk to me . . . you are gone all day and I do not see enough of you . . . You come home late at night and . . . and you never, . . . never kiss me or hug me . . . you never . . . we never do . . . you know what.

Wilbur: We do too . . . I fulfilled my husbandly obligations on a Saturday . . . six weeks ago.

Mildred: It was a Monday six weeks ago and you . . . you fell asleep . . . You do not care about me. (sob sound)

Wilbur: I care . . . I care . . . but I work hard Mildred . . . I need my rest . . . I slave all day so I can give you nice things . . . and Tuesday was another work day . . . (a somewhat sexy voice) . . . we will play love birds in the morning.

Mildred: You say it . . . but you won't . . . If Betty BOOBS Ohanlin offered, you would do it and you would not holler.

Wilbur: I holler all the time and she still offers. (raised voice) We never do it . . . leave Betty BOOBS out of this.

Mildred: Tell me you love me.

Wilbur: I do.

Mildred: How much do you love me?

Wilbur: How much do you need?

Mildred: Say you love me . . . tell me you will love me until the end of time.

Wilbur: I love you . . . (build in volume) . . . I love you . . . I will love you until I die.

Mildred: You say it, but you won't . . . if you meant it you would do it right now.

Wilbur: (exasperated) You want me to die?

Mildred: No, I don't . . . I am sorry . . . but it would be nicer if you thought of me once-in-a-while instead of yourself . . . Only two weeks ago you had your life insured for fifty thousand dollars.

Wilbur: What about it?

Mildred: You were only thinking of yourself.

24

Wilbur: What kind of fool talk is that . . . if I kick the bucket you get the money.

Mildred: You know perfectly well you have no intention of dying . . . you only had your life insured to tantalize me.

Wilbur: (angry and raised voice) I will drop dead in the morning.

Mildred: You say it . . .but you won't do it.

Wilbur: (pleading) Do you know what you are saying?

Mildred: I am sorry . . . I did not mean it that way.

Wilbur: For heaven's sake.

Mildred: I do not think you love me anymore . . . When we first met . . . you use to kiss me every time I turned around.

Wilbur: I never kissed you when you turned around.

Mildred: If you really loved me, you would make out a will

Wilbur: (raised voice) A will . . . you get my life insurance . . . and you want more?

Mildred: You do not want me at the mercy of your relatives . . . the minute you drop dead.

Wilbur: Don't talk like that . . . can't you say passed on . . . or something like that.

Mildred: You always say that.

Wilbur: Only when I am talking about your no-good mooching brother . . . You should be more delicate when discussing a will . . . especially mine . . . You make it sound like I could go any minute.

Mildred: Well Saint Peter doesn't deliver you a two-week's notice you know . . . Every man should make out his will for the loved ones he leaves behind.

Wilbur: Okay . . . I will make one out tomorrow.

Mildred: You say it . . . but you won't . . . get up and do it right now.

Wilbur: You are out of your mind . . . in the first place you need two witnesses and in the second place I have nothing in the first place to leave you.

Mildred: You are a stubborn man Wilbur Crabtree.

Wilbur: Why . . . why am I stubborn?

Mildred: It is the hardest thing in the world to make you admit I am right when you know I am wrong.

Wilbur: That's woman's logic for you . . . You get my life insurance . . . everything in my will and the first thing you do . . . (start to speak faster and louder) . . . is find a new no good bum . . . and he takes all of my hard earned money . . . drives by my grave in my brand new car . . . loafs around like a prince . . . never amounts to anything . . . make him get a job Mildred.

Mildred: I will . . . I mean I won't . . . I won't Wilbur I promise.

Wilbur: (relaxing with mumbled speech) I worked eight hard years . . . struggled, did without . . . and what do I have to show for it . . . a wife.

Mildred: I just need you . . . I never sleep until you are in bed with me.

Wilbur: You were sleeping when I came home.

Mildred: You said you would be home at ten after one drink.

Wilbur: Well I had ten drinks and got home at one.

Mildred: What other woman would put up with your antics, night after night . . . you snore and whistle like a bag of old bones . . . and you keep me up all night . . . Wilbur what do you think I am made of?

Wilbur: Old bones.

Mildred: (sarcastic) Thank you . . . You would rather stay out all night tom-catting around with your old cronies . . . It kills you to stay home with me.

Wilbur: It does not kill me.

26

Mildred: I do not need anybody . . . (turn away) . . . I am just satisfied to be with you.

Wilbur: You are in better company than I am.

Mildred: (pouting) I am sick.

Wilbur: (concerned) What is the matter?

Mildred: It is my head . . . the doctor said there is something wrong . . . I've had it on and off for the past three weeks.

Wilbur: Then take it off and let's get some sleep.

Mildred: How would you like to go through life with a pain in the neck?

Wilbur: I married you for better or worse . . . yet to come.

Mildred: You took advantage of my innocence and youth.

Wilbur: you were no spring chicken.

Mildred: I must have been to pick up a worm like you . . . I wish I had known you better before we got married.

Wilbur: You knew me plenty.

Mildred: What about that tattoo on your stomach? . . . Oh, that is a real indication of a man's character . . . I wish I had known.

Wilbur: I had that tattoo long before I met you . . . I was just a silly kid . . . it was foolish.

Mildred: You ought to be ashamed of yourself . . . A hula girl with a dimple in her chin.

Wilbur: That dimple was there before she was.

Mildred: Why don't you have that ugly picture removed?

Wilbur: I will have it removed in the morning.

Mildred: You say it but you won't . . . do it now.

Wilbur: IT IS TWO O'CLOCK IN THE MORNING.

Mildred: You would get rid of it right away if you were married to Betty BOOBS Ohanlin.

Wilbur: (fed up) Do not mention Betty BOOBS.

Mildred: She would holler plenty if you did not do what she liked.

Wilbur: I do what she likes, and she never hollers . . . I mean . . . do not mention her name in this house or else.

Mildred: Mother was so upset that we eloped and got married by the Justice of the Peace.

Wilbur: It should have been the Secretary of War.

Mildred: I want a real wedding . . . if you loved me, we would get married in a church.

Wilbur: I will arrange it in the morning.

Mildred: You say it, but you won't . . . get up and do it right now.

Wilbur: It is too late . . . the preacher is sleeping . . . he is dead tired too.

Mildred: It is unlucky to postpone a wedding.

Wilbur: Not if you postpone it long enough.

Orchestra: (build music)

Phelps: Will Wilbur ever do what he says he will . . . will Mildred ever let Wilbur sleep . . . and who is Betty BOOBS Ohanlin. Stay tuned for the return of that charm-able couple, the Crabtrees on Butternut Corners, in the second half of our show.

Bud: (cut the music of the orchestra, then bring up the volume)

Orchestra: (change the tempo of the music to suit the upcoming song)

28

Phelps: (change voice to be that of a western cowboy) It was early spring in the year of eighteen-ninety-six when a lone cowboy was making his way through Rogers Pass in the wilds of the Canadian Rockies . . . There in the bank of the mountain trail a cowboy was frozen in the remnants of a snow drift . . . there in the clutches of his clenched fist was his last love letter to his loved ones . . . After the poor old soul was buried the cowboy delivered the letter to the man's Misses and young'ins . . . His plea for them was 'Forsake Me Not'.

Orchestra: (build music up for song)

I am lonely as tumbling tumble weeds.
On lonely trails rustlers I heed.
I sing to sooth the cattle so wild.
And I dream of memories of my child.

Lonely nights in the saddle mile after mile.
I can't seem to recall your lovely smile.
If I could write a letter, I would entrust.
Delivery to you on forsaken winds of dust.

By our campfire skyward I stare.
To angels I tell a tale of woe I share.
Of ruthless rustlers and cattle so lost.
Your picture I hold they did accost.

Forsake me not, oh my love this harm.
To never return to your loving arms.
To my children give a loving touch in lieu.
Forsake me not if I bid adieu.

Lead burns deep into my flesh.
Still onward a hundred miles we thresh.
With cold winter storms the mountain pass may close.
A season may pass to find our bodies froze.

In defeat to the night I softly sing.
As if near my children I still cling.
Angels on high oh please hear my cry.
Bring to my love, my sad, sad, goodbye.

I no longer feel the burning pain.
Our campfire is doused by pelting rain.
Eyes search for loved ones I no longer weep.

Angels carry me home while I sleep.

Orchestra: (let the music softly dwindle)

All: (everyone on stage is silent, some women dab a hanky to their eyes)

Bud: (rub nose constantly on sleeve, forget what you are supposed to do)

Phelps: (be busy making notes on script, there is a lump in throat but keep it away from the others, clear throat several times off mike to hide emotion)

Bud: (realize time delay, rush to set up mike, call E.D. Ucation to mike, point to announcer to try and gain his attention)

Phelps: (refrain from looking at anyone, dab eyes behind script)

Ucation: (look bewildered to what announcer and Bud are doing)

Bud: (keep arms rolling to try and gain announcer's attention, give up and repeatedly point to E.D. Ucation)

Ucation: (take note of Bud, tap the mike before speaking) Good evening ladies and gentlemen . . . my name is professor E.D. Ucation . . . I study the phenomenon known as 'what it' . . . for an example . . . what if this happens or what if this happens . . . Tonight, we will consider blatant sadistic behaviors of dear sweet grandmothers . . . Take your typical grandmother . . . silver hair, sparkling eyes, always a smile and sticking a cookie in front of a child's face . . . as-long-as she can pinch the cheek endlessly and hug the life out of the kid . . . Many a kid develops what we call 'cannot breathe syndrome' . . . the face turns red . . . tiny feet and hands frantically try to escape . . . the mouth is crying but no sound is coming out. (pause) I investigated a situation of grandmother sadistic behavior just the other day . . . A four-year-old boy while visiting his grandmother was tortured from so much hugging that his little bladder would no longer hold in water created from two popsicle, one large glass of milk and half a cup of grandpa's tea . . . A four-year-old boy likes to be able to go pee by himself . . . but he has not been around long enough in his short little life to know that grandmothers booby-trap the house against innocent little children . . . This proud little boy stands in front of the toilet ready to pee . . . he lifts the heavy plastic covered artificial flower inlayed ugly looking lid then the peekaboo seat . . . standing close to the bowl he aims . . . his hands on his hips . . . lips smiling proudly . . . then suddenly without warning . . .

Affects: (a loud bang sound and a child's scream)

Ucation: Wham . . . in the prime of his young life a sadistic grandmother booby trapped the toilet lid and seat with an overabundance of useless coverings of flowers and plastic . . . just like a guillotine . . . chop . . . the poor little boy needs to pee but never will for the rest of the day and night . . . Mom, all the aunts and grandmother come to inspect the damage . . . inspired comfort from grandmother as she pinches his cheeks and says . . . (imitate old woman's voice) . . . 'that is okay . . . little boys should not have a wee-wee anyway' . . . for years to come the little boy never goes for a pee at grandmother's house . . . Beware of smiling grandmothers with a sadistic look . . . (point to grandmothers in the audience)

Bud: (quickly motion the orchestra to play music)

Orchestra: (play a death march theme though announcer's dialogue)

Phelps: (a squeaking voice change) Thank you professor E.D. Ucation for that insight study into human behavior . . . thank you . . . I remember my grandmother . . . (shiver with remembrance of childhood pain) . . . This first half of our show was brought to you by Mousseau's fine line of fine pine furniture and Moose Ventures with locations in Moosonee, Moose Factory, Moose Jaw and moose City Wyoming . . . After a fifteen to twenty-minute station break we will be back with part two of 'A Fire Side Old Time Radio Show'.

Orchestra: (build volume of the death march theme)

Bud: (go mad trying to get the orchestra to cut out the music)

Orchestra;   (music fades, only the bass player continues playing the death march until the house lights go down)

Lighting: (overhead lights go out, the soft spotlight is on the bass player, fade spot light)

INTERMISSION

PART TWO
A FIRE SIDE OLD TIME RADIO SHOW
THE STAGE IS DARK. ALL ACTORS ARE ON STAGE, EACH IN THE
SAME PLACE AS BEFORE THE INTERMISSION. THE BASS PLAYER

IS SLOWLY PLAYING THE DEATH MARCH. A SOFT SPOT LIGHT
COMES UP ON THE BASS PLAYER. THE OVER HEAD LIGHTS COME
UP. ONE BY ONE THE ACTORS BECOME ACTIVE, MUMBLING AND
SHUFFLING THEIR SCRIPT PAGES.

Bud: (move to stand in front of the bass player, with a hand moving
from side to side across throat give the cut-it-out sign, face is grinning in a
frustrated grin)

Orchestra: (begin to play background music of show)

Bud: (with left hand count to five, actors become quiet, hold left
hand open, with right hand point a finger to the announcer)

Phelps: (off mike say) . . . Testing . . . testing . . . 1 . . . 2 . . . 3 . . . (on
mike) . . . Welcome back listeners and our studio audience to 'A Fire Side
Old Time Radio Show' . . . live over the air waves from station W.R.I.K. . .
.featuring Young`in, Wojo the Dog, Mildred and Wilbur Crabtree, Mr.
Cheeks Too Soft, Professor E.D. Ucation, Penelope Peabodie, Knot Head and
Donald Knot, Ma, Our Almost There Orchestra and Myself . . . (drag out line)
. . . Ben Phelps . . . your dedicated announcer.

All: (Soft collective boo directed at the announcer)

Phelps: This portion of the show is sponsored in part because of an
outstanding account . . . on account of they have no money to pay the members
of this cast . . . but being members of the sponsor of this show we will
announce that the sponsor is hopeful that someone will hear our advertising
and hire us . . . We are members of local union . . . P.M.A.A.A.N.M.S.S. . . .
the poor musicians, authors, announcers, actors need money soon society . . .
now to open the second half of 'A Fire Side Old Time Radio Show' our
orchestra members of P.M.A.A.A.N.M.S.S. . . . will present an original
number titled . . . 'We Don't do It That Way No More' . . . (off mike) . . . who
came up with this dumb witted title?

Orchestra: (all stick your tongues out at the announcer, music begins)

Bud: (hold up a hand towards each party to stop any physical
action)

The night when we met, we waltzed across the floor.
High-stepped to the fiddle sound asking for more.
Double stepping in the old town saloon.
Longing to be under a blue, blue moon.

32

In our ripe old age when we reach ninety-four,
We'll not complain about life or say we're sore.
Crank up that old antique gramophone,
And waltz across the dance floor one time more.

The swinging Texas fiddle and the double bass swayed,
As sweet as I remember Bob Wills played.
Times seemed better, back when we were young.
We sure don't sashay that way no more.

In our dreams is seems to be yesterday's rodeo,
When we kicked up our heels to the Cotton-eyed-joe.
The Tennessee waltz made us dance so slow.
Longing to be one-another's first-time beau.

Orchestra: (overall music fades, only bass player keeps music beat in background for announcer)

Bud: (in rhythm with the music frequently point towards the announcer)

Phelps: (with an irritable voice begin to announce) A fine rendition from Our Almost There Orchestra . . . now back by popular demand with another tail of western folklore please welcome Mr. Cheeks Too Soft . . . (actors begin to applaud, Phelps cut them off) . . . Mr. Cheeks will be signing his book 'Pioneer Poetry of Mr. Cheeks Too Soft' after tonight's program . . . and remember that your purchases will help the P.M.A.A.A.N.M.S.S, Of which Mr. Cheeks is a member . . . that is the poor musicians, authors, announcers, actors need money soon society . . . reciting an original poem titled 'Mail Order Bride' please welcome back Mr. Cheeks Too Soft.

Orchestra: (bass player builds volume and speed as the actors applaud)

Mr. Cheeks: (begins to speak at a mike that is dead, only his mouth moves without sound)

Bud: (try to get Mr. Cheeks attention to move to the right mike, go and take him by the arm and drag him to the good mike)

Mr. Cheeks: (tap the mike with the flat of the hand, turn to Bud) . . . Does this thing work . . . do they hear me?

Bud: (frantically nod head)

33

Mr. Cheeks: Okay . . .

I was talking one day to the holy guy above,
about that day in May when I met my true love.
It was about this time I was mending my ways,
rejecting saloons and boudoirs where I would stay.

Abstaining from my fill of whisky straight,
rather those hangovers that I truly did hate.
After a night of gambling and dance hall girls,
a cowboy's mighty fist sent me flying in a whirl.

I sailed through the air, my head landing with a thud.
I sniffed an aromatic smell, dung not a pillow of mud.
I lay there contemplating an existence in this universe.
A stranger dressed in black said, "You need a hearse?"

You could say I saw the glow of hallelujah angels in the night.
It dawned on me I was laying in mud in morning's first light.
Whatever the reason I swore off liquor for the rest of my life.
That's about the time I became free of a drunkard's strife.

I stood tall as possible with my boots stuck in the muddy street.
Ladies of morals walked quickly by, me they would not greet.
For new clothes, a bath, a hair cut and shave, six bits was lacking.
Many nights were spent in a town jail, the walls needed shellacking.

"Not here to be incarcerated sheriff, I'm seeking meagre employment.
I'll polish the bars, paint the walls, mend curtains for your enjoyment."
He was apprehensive but I truly promised to be a new upstanding citizen.
With an oath on mother's grave, I swore never to be an inmate in this prison.

Quickly passing saloon doors a whiff of liquor filled the air, I hesitated.
'No,' I said, a hot bath is required, to Harry Woo's steam baths I gravitated.
Near on three years since I last soaked old bones, I requested a two-bit bath.
"Well Harry Woo, I have changed my ways, I'm heading along a new path."

"Where you go, what you do, you no cook?' Woo babbled, "You need a girl mate."
Soaking in that tub of hot water I did contemplate, what I first needed was a date.
"Take too long, too much work." Harry Woo pointed to an add in the daily news.

Lose your blues, a slightly used mail order bride, no guarantee, you can't lose.

Well to my arousal the idea was just dandy for alone one should not sleep.
A pick of a blonde, brunette or red head from back east did not come cheap.
With a thought of a mail order wife occupying my mind I now had a real-life goal.
Old man Barns offered a job, buck-board, a nag, and a winter fixing fence poles.

Winters can be mighty long and cold out on the Ontario Manitoba boarder.
Every night by campfire light I read that add and wished to place an order.
With the cold north wind blowing I hugged my Hudson Bay blanket a bit.
I'd try to cuddle up to Buttermilk the old mare, she thought I was a twit.

Not much body warmth from four spindly legs, not much to hug.
After moving from leg to lanky leg she stomped on me like a bug.
In dreams, I dreamt of a blonde, brunette and red headed vison of beauty.
I had six months to come up with one hundred bucks, this was my duty.

Springtime finally arrived, I was no worse for ware thanks to my old mare.
I taught her to lay down to keep me from freezing, warmth I would share.
I did not mind her big lips or even her tongue licking me behind the ear.
Several times she'd roll over me and wouldn't move until I called her dear.

We came out of the dry gulch rolling hills a pitiful sight in the early spring.
Old man Barns felt sorry, he gave me Buttermilk, pay and extra for a ring.
Though I smelled bad a bath could wait, I high tailed it to the telegraph office.
I placed my order for the only girl left, a plump dance hall girl from Memphis.

I ain`t much for dancing, maybe a slow waltz, they did say she was a red head.
Whispered word spread quickly that my bride was bringing a four-poster bed.
On a little plot of cleared land outside of town a small cabin I began to build.
'Ain`t big enough the fellows all said.' At beds and buildings, they were skilled.

Well not to get in the way I sat back and watched as the cabin became a house, with an entrance, parlour, social room with a piano, all for me and my spouse.
There on the boardwalk in front of the stage office I waited in my Sunday best.
By noon time a crowd gathered, mostly fellow men all waiting to be impressed.

There she was a vision of beauty, fifty mouths fell open, a lilac smell filled the air.

What a sight, the mayor declared a holiday, with all this attention did I have a prayer?

Did I mention the main street parade, eight men carried the bed on their shoulders?

She rode like a queen on a down filled throne, I hung to a post like a discarded bolder.

That night it was a gay affair, music, men dancing with men and my soon-to-be wife.

She was supposed to be my wife, but the preacher was a bit late, another fate in my life.

At about twelve o'clock my Memphis bell shocked all and happily gave a rousing speech.

I quote, 'There are too many men that needs a woman and the preacher ain`t here to preach.'

Come sun up I found myself with old Buttermilk as cozy as can be snuggling in the hay.

On the cabin door a freshly painted sign said, 'Madame May's.' Men were hooting hurry.

I was told to get in line, me, the man who had ordered a red headed bride to be.

There was no need for the likes of me to want to plea for thee on bended knee.

At about noon after Buttermilk nibbled behind my ear, I decided to hit the trail.

I realized you just can't buy true love or order a bride via the Canadian mail.

In my broken down old buck-board and Buttermilk leading the way,

the sun began to set on the prairie in eighteen-sixty, the month of May.

Oh, I love the smell of spring flowers, the wide-open spaces of the range,

northern lights, skies of blue, freshly fallen snow and no need for change.

I had me a long heartfelt talk with you know who, the holy guy up above,

and thanked him, Buttermilk neighed, for a cowboy's life is my true love.

Bud: (build up energy of the musicians)

Orchestra: (build up music of song 'Old Dogs', play behind announcer)

Phelps: Yes, it is time again to drop in on the old homestead where we listen in on the ongoing saga of Ma, Young`in, Wojo the dog and Young`in's new little brother Knot Head . . . did Wojo survive his operation . . . what about Gert the hog farmer's daughter . . . will Young`in go on his vacation . . . it is another early morning on the homestead . . . Ma is still in

36

the kitchen . . . this time she is busy baking five to six dozen peanut butter cookies for Young`in to munch on while he is out in the field watching the corn grow . . . listen . . . Young`in is just now getting up.

Affects: (sound of toilet flushing, door closing, walking sounds coming down stairs, Wojo is yapping in pain)

Young`in: Oh, sorry Wojo . . . I did not notice you laying there.

Wojo: What! . . . you did not see my tail wagging?

Young`in: I am afraid not.

Wojo: I am a hundred and forty-year-old dog in dog years . . . I may not be around much longer . . . do you think maybe just for one day you would not step on my tail.

Young`in: Well if I did not step on your tail, we would not have a good conversation each morning . . . Think about it . . . we may go through all of the day not communicating.

Wojo: I get your point . . . I must suffer pain just to fulfill a time worn slogan . . . man's best friend.

Young`in: I noticed that there were no water puddles in the house . . . that operation that you had must have worked . . . how are you feeling boy?

Wojo: The plumbing is working fine . . . may I note that you have gotten up a little late this morning.

Young`in: Yes, I did . . . last night . . . I . . .

Wojo: Well do you think that you could open the door and let me out to water the lilies before I have an accident on purpose . . . (growl)

Young`in: Yes . . . yes . . . of course.

Affects: (sound of screen door opening and closing, dog feet making their way out of the house)

Ma: Is that you Young`in?

Young`in: No Ma . . . it is just one of the neighbors checking to see if our door works.

Ma: Well invite them in . . . I have hot coffee and fresh peanut butter cookies to dunk.

Young`in: Great . . . now I have to run five miles to the nearest neighbor to invite them over for coffee and cookies before Ma thinks I am making fun of her . . . In forty some odd years you would think ma would have had time to give me a little brother . . . then I could send him to fetch . . . hey Ma . . ., did you and Pa ever think of having more children?

Ma: We are working on it Young`in . . . it takes patience and practice . . . We kind of rushed it when we had you . . . we want the next child to be perfect.

Young`in: I am forty some years old Ma . . . don't you think that you and Pa have been practicing long enough?

Ma: Now Young`in . . . your Pa is not as young as he use to be . . . so we have given up on having another child . . . we would rather just have fun . . . We . . .

Young`in: Ma! . . . I do not want to know the details.

Phelps: Young`in walks into the kitchen and is surprised to see a stranger sitting at the kitchen table . . . On the table in front of the stranger are two cups of coffee . . . A wooden ventriloquist dummy is sitting on his knee . . . Ma is talking to the dummy as if it was real.

Ma: Young`in this is Knot Head . . . he is a nice-looking little boy . . . this young man is down on his luck . . . he is in show business . . . Mr Donald Knots is willing to rent out his partner . . . how would you like a little brother Young`in?

Young`in: A wooden substitute for a brother . . . Ma he is not real . . . he is made of pine . . . probably knotty pine . . . where was he made . . . At Mousseau's fine line of fine pine furniture?

Ma: Young`in, do not go making fun of your new little brother.

Young`in: Me . . . not me . . . I would not make fun of a last meal for a south bound woodpecker.

Ma: Young`in, give him a chance . . . you are not too old to put over my knee.

38

Knot Head: Not too old . . . ha . . . ha.

Young`in: Hey, I am just on the sunny side of thirty.

Knot Head: More like the dark ages of forty.

Young`in: I know some hungry termits that would like to meet you.

Knot Head: Ain`t you kind of old to be living at home with Ma and Pa . . . what . . . can't find a girl to hitch up with.

Young`in: I am being patient . . . I am waiting for that perfect girl to fall into my arms.

Knot Head: Homely boy can't get a date . . . eh . . . ha . . . ha . . . ha.

Young`in;   I am not homely . . . and I can get a date anytime I want.

Knot Head: Give Gerty the hog farmer's daughter a call.

Young`in: Ma . . . did you tell him about Gerty?

Ma: Yes dear . . . she is a wonderful wholesome girl.

Young`in: Homely . . . she is homely Ma.

Knot Head: At your age you can't be picky.

Young`in: Age is only a state of mind.

Knot Head: At your age the mind is the first thing to go . . . When that happens, you forget what to do when you bring your date home.

Young`in: That has not happened to me . . . yet.

Knot Head: When was the last time you had a date . . . a girl . . . the female species . . . soft . . . curves . . . hubba . . . hubba?

Young`in: I know what a girl is . . . I was trying to remember if the date was on Friday or Saturday.

Knot Head: Of last week . . . longer . . . longer . . . nineteen-seventy . . . I think Gerty may be your last chance . . . if you wait any longer, she may fall into your arms at the retirement home. . . eh old man.

Young`in: Listen you son of a gate-leg table . . . you would make a nice ornament on a stairway banister.

Knot Head: Hey look . . . Gerty is coming up the driveway . . . oohoooh . . . she has been living with those hogs too long.

Young`in:     She ain`t all that bad . . . listen Knot Head be nice to her.

Knot Head: You really must be desperate . . . old age is fogging up your eyes.

Young`in: Look you sap . . . I do not need you around when I am courting . . . out you go . . . and you too Mr. Donald Knots . . . I saw your lips move when the dummy talks.

Knot Head: I do my own taking . . . you bachelor . . . you, lonely old man, . . . mamas' boy.

Young`in: Out!

Affects: (a kicking sound of a boot against wood, a crashing sound of a dummy falling down stairs and crashing into garbage cans)

Ma: Young`in . . . I smell Gerty a-coming . . . she is the last maid around . . . invite her in . . . I have coffee and cookies for dunking.

Affects:(growling sounds, a chomping sound of teeth against wood)

Young`in: Ata-boy Wojo . . . chew his leg off.

Affects:(louder growling)

Orchestra: (build music of 'Old Dogs')

Phelps: Will wedding bells be ringing for Young`in and Gerty . . . will they adopt Knot Head as their son . . . what will happen to Wojo, Ma and Pa . . . listen in next week for the continuing story of Young`in's World . . . (lower voice) . . . Now a word from our sponsors . . .

Orchestra: (change style of music to suit advertisements)

Bud: (standing between mikes with Penelope on one side and E.D.

40

Ucation on the other point back and forth as required for timing)

Penelope: Fresh from the annals of farm science . . . developed in the barns located on Dung Hill Farms . . . To be sold worldwide at a very low price because of the overhead . . . If you have a shortness of hair on your head . . . you should join the growing number of men seeking the cool paste treatment guaranteed to grow hair on the backside of a hairless pig . . . For nine dollars and ten cents . . . you too can order 'Hick Remedy Manure Paste' from Dung Hill Farms . . . City folks welcome.

Ucation: Our grand assortment of corsets is unsurpassed . . . We guarantee every pair for elegance of fit and wearing qualities . . . Every farmer's wife will be pleased to own a quality corset ranging from long waist to short waist . . . nursing . . . long waist medium form to extreme long waist slender form . . . priced to suit your pocket book . . . mail order price guaranteed . . . all corsets range from fifty cents to ninety cents . . . do not delay . . . order now for our nineteen-hundred and one fall fashion corsets.

Penelope: For just sixty-five cents you too can order a wonderful new hair tonic and producer . . . restores the natural colour . . . preserves and strengthens the hair for years . . . promotes the growth . . . arrests falling hair . . . feeds and nourishes the roots . . . cures dandruff and scurf and allays all scalp irritations . . . The only absolutely effective, unfailing successful, perfectly harmless, positively no-dye preparation on the market . . . Just sixty-five cents to order Princess Hair Restorer . . . If ordered by mail, please add two cents for postage and handling.

Ucation: The old reliable brand for infants and children . . . A purely vegetable remedy for regulating the stomach and bowels . . . promotes appetite . . . aids digestion and cures diarrhea . . . This remedy removes worms, overcomes constipation and relieves fevers . . . The old reliable brand is absolutely guaranteed to give satisfaction.

Bud: (quickly point to the announcer)

Phelps: The makers of all natural sweet smelling barn yard extract wish to thank the hundreds and thousands of horses, cattle, sheep and rabbits that spend hundreds of hours manufacturing the all needed substance all farmers need to help grow corn, carrots, peas, tomatoes, lettuce, broccoli, cabbage, string beans, potatoes, cauliflower, celery, turnips, beets . . . ummm . . . ummm . . . good . . . Uncle Morts day old manure presents Mr. Cheeks Too Soft and his poetry stories of the old west . . . Please welcome the only living cowboy that takes a regular bath on Saturdays four times a month . . . To night's poem is titled 'The Ballad of

41

Stuttering Slim Jim Sarns'.

Ben: (Point to the orchestra and Mr. Cheeks at the same time.)

Orchestra: (build music of A Cowboy's Lullaby)

Mr. Cheeks: (stand at the right mike) . . . Is this the right mike . . . this one?

Ben: (shake head yes then no with frustration)

Mr. Cheeks: This one?

I had been on the snake bite trail for days on end,
just me and four horses, a dog and an old friend.

Jim stuttered bad, each sentence started with but.
I figured his tongue was stuck in a wagon rut.

Eventually he said what he had to say, darn if I could figure the story out.
Then he began to shout, something about being a scout suffering the gout.

Now he may need a doctor but there was no way I was a gonna turn about.
"But, But, But," Slim Jim shouted with restrain. "This land is a drought."

I reckoned we was riding for three days under a scorching sun,
taking Jim near on seventy-two hours to get them words undone.

For a man that stutters bad, simple communication is a frustration.
When Slim Jim began singing, diction of words was a salvation.

I remember a time in ole Cheyenne and a high noon gun fight.
Jim was a-trying to tell the sheriff to head to the main street site.

Darn if Jim didn't start singing to the tune of 'Mary had a Little Lamb'.
Slim changed the words to suit the situation, the Sheriff said, 'Damn.'

Town folk began gathering around, not the gun fight but around Slim Jim.
"Mighty fine singing strange." Stuttering Jim decided to go out on a limb.

It didn't matter if it was a sad or happy song or a spiritual hymn,
Jim added fancy yodelling, thus generating a nick-name for him.

From then on folks began calling him yodelling Jim Sarns,

though not to be confused with old man Yodel Jim Barns.

Jim was tall and skinny, and became Yodeling Slim Jim Sarns.
Plenty of Folks around to ask, so don't think this is just a yarn.

Now come to think of it, I cannot recall the gun fight's outcome.
One guy was Billy, just some kid, the other Rango, Billy's chum.

That was just about the time I met up with Stuttering Slim Jim.
For a partner on the trail, I asked for his company on a whim.

I figured with him a singing, I wouldn't have to do all that much talking.
If complaining about my cooking, well his singing would be fine balking.

Once he found his voice, Yodelling Slim Jim never seemed to stop yapping.
He would rattle on for hours singing, I showed my appreciation by clapping.

The funny thing was, I recognized all of those fine old western tunes.
Words were slightly different, whatever he was thinking he'd croon.

Never interrupt Slim when he's a singing, I once made that grave mistake.
I thought he asked a question, I answered, he stopped and began to shake.

He just stopped singing for hours, stuttering his complaints, he was sore.
I was disappointed for I had become fond of his renditions of folklore.

"But, but, but, but, but." I reckoned that his words were stuck in a big deep rut.
In-between buts, Slim used profanity quite well, I figured that he called me a nut.

I pleaded for forgiveness between buts, in unison the pack horses tried to apologize.
Suddenly Jim slid off his horse and wandered into the sage brush, I began to theorize.

To be civilize one must not antagonize, one must surmise to compromise,
refrain from interrupting an artist's tune, for you, he may want to vulgarize.

The sun was setting on the horizon while Jim was wandering through the brush.
Tumbling tumble weeds tumbled on by and the air suddenly had a queer hush.

Slim Jim was way off yonder, I could no longer hear him stutter and cuss.

We were all in agreement, me, horses and dog that Jim was making a fuss.

We was on the trail for near on four or five days and I made only one mistake.
Who would figure that interrupting the singing would cause Jim a headache?

Observation is a big part of preservation of man's life in the wide-open spaces.
Villains, vultures, one could die of a lingering thirst leaving no tangible traces.

The pony express was a hundred or so miles north of the bad-lands locale,
and ain't no way to send a letter to kinfolk, no messenger pigeon to corral.

The sun was setting, and I was getting worried about Slim Jim wandering off.
It was getting late to make camp, I planned to cook his favourite, stroganoff.

Putting on my specs, I only use them when I need to see something important.
This was the time to observe any of Jim's peculiar irregularities of movement.

There behind a weather-beaten sage brush next to a dried-out cactus,
and what I am about to say is the truth and is truly real and factious.

Slim removed suspenders and gun belt and mooned the desert critters.
Some men have their morals when nature calls and Jim was no exhibitor.

Maybe he was a little constipated from eating my gourmet cooking.
I organized camp, Jim did not need an audience to keep a looking.

A fire crackled and the setting sun set the horizon a blaze in an orange hue.
Wojo the dog yawned, the horses neighed, I commenced stirring the stew.

Hours later from way out yonder came Jim with a hoot and a bellow.
I sensed some kind of pain in his voice, I felt sympathy for this fellow.
Why? I had no idea, Slim was jumping and hollering, his britches hanging
down.
He looked like a clown, he rolled on the ground, his face had a gruesome
frown.

"But, but, but, but, but what? You have a cut, you hate my mutt?"
"Gut, you hurt your gut, butt, butt, butt, bite your Lilly white butt?"

Well, I looked at dog, he looked at me, the horses turned away from us three.
Cowboys have a code of honour to oblige when a friend calls, but why me?

We could have been there all-night a-trying to make sense out of stuttering
Slim Jim.

For without a clear understanding of what he was saying, I wasn't a-gonna bite him.

"Sing it Slim, sing it out loud and clear, give me just the facts."
Jim yodelled that it was snake bit poison he needed to extract.

Well, I looked at dog, dog wandered off, Slim looked hopelessly towards me.
Jim got down on bended knee and to the tune of Amazing Grace began to plea.

"But, but, its your butt," now I began to stutter uncharacteristically.
Thinking I mumbled, "I am allergic to snake bite," said hypercritically.

There is a code of the west all cowboys do abide by from time to time,
and I am never one to take an oath or pledge to a lodge, it is no crime.

So, shoot me for leaving Slim Jim with a bite on his butt from a snake.
On his next birthday, if it comes, I will bake him a butter biscuit cake.

Ah heck, Jim's butt was swollen for a week, it was a little wee baby snake bite.
Not even one rattle, Jim rode side saddle, but this snake bite gave him a fright.

From that day forward ole Slim stuttered twice as bad, and as jumpy as all get out.
Every once in awhile when nature's call is necessary, into the brush he would shout.

Jim is a bit bashful and reluctant to give up his privacy behind the sage.
I guess battling a snake ain't worth betting the outcome of a yearly wage.

Over time Jim won a few hands and lost a few to the side winders.
He became immune to snake bite, but once in awhile got a reminder.

Slim Jim's singing is sweeter than ever on the trail, to Jim just wave.
Do not stop to talk if you're not needing some precious time to save.

It has been near on ten years riding the trails for days on end.
Just me, four horses, a dog and Slim Jim Sarns, my old friend.

Orchestra: (build up music softly behind announcer)

Phelps: Thank you Mr. Cheeks Too Soft for that little vignette into history . . . this portion was brought to you as fresh as Uncle Morts day old manure . . . Do not forget, if your manure is not day old then it is not Uncle Morts day old Manure . . . now to help all of those cattle to relax and produce more manure, Our Almost There Orchestra will play a song titled 'A Cowboy's Lullaby".

Orchestra: (intro music builds)

Ben: (give beat tempo with a foot and hand)

Orchestra:

Lonesome nights on forgotten trails.
To you I tell of a cowboy's tale.
Of loved ones left back on the farm.
Angels keep from the devil's harm.

Many a river we will cross.
A wandering calf will be lost.
A stampeding herd on a moonless night.
Do dare to hide this cowboy fright?

Saddle up boys it's time to ride.
Find those steers that want to hide.
Sing a soothing song, a lullaby.
Move them out the cowboys' cry.

Lonesome times out riding alone,
My heart so sad as the cattle moan,
Your face I see upon the moon,
Forsake me not coming home soon.

Ben: (walk to centre stage keeping the tempo of the music going, point to the announcer)

Orchestra: (fade music, build new music for the background music for the Crabtrees)

Phelps: What a soothing song for cattle everywhere . . . I am sure they are as appreciated as we are . . . remember to be sure to pick up a song book of original songs heard on this program . . . also for sale are original novels, short stories, poetry all from local artists and authors who are members of P.M.A.A.A.N.M.S.S. . . . That are the poor musicians, authors, announcers, actors need money soon society . . . (pause) . . . Those Crabtrees on Butternut Corners are still at it the second half of our show . . . is Wilbur asleep dreaming of Betty BOOBS Ohanlin . . . is Mildred still nagging Wilbur . . . we now enter the bedroom late at night when most normal people are sound asleep . . . hush . . . you can hear Wilbur snoring.

Orchestra: (build music then fade)

Mildred: (an angry raised voice) . . . It is unlucky to postpone a wedding.

Wilbur: Not if you postpone it long enough.

Mildred: (crying feeling) . . . You do not love me . . . you even hate the cat and the canary.

Wilbur: I love the cat, I love the canary . . . (raise voice) . . . and I even love you . . . I do not know which one I love the most.

Mildred: (with affection) . . . Am I the only wife for you?

Wilbur: I swear you are the only wife in the world for me.

Mildred: Do you swear Wilbur.

Wilbur: I swear I wouldn't have another wife like you as long as I live.

Mildred: Am I the last person you dream about when you go to sleep?

Wilbur: you are the last person I ever think about.

Mildred: You would not say that to Betty BOOBS Ohanlin . . . You would be a gentleman if you had her in your arms.

Wilbur: She has been in my dreams plenty of times and I have never been a gentleman. I hate Betty BOOBS, do not get her and I involved.

Mildred: (pleading) I cook . . . I clean . . . I sew . . . I do everything for you . . . Do I get any thanks?

Wilbur: Thanks.

Mildred: Thanks . . . is that all the thanks I get . . . You are so cheap . . . We can not afford it . . . leave it there . . . you are always looking for a bargain . . . When you married me, you did not get a bargain.

Wilbur: (elated) How well I know.

Mildred: You are lucky you got a cheap wife like me . . . If you were married to Betty BOOBS Ohanlin, you would have to pay her for kisses.

Wilbur: I am not married to her and I get them for nothing . . . Do not mention Betty BOOBS in my presence.

Mildred: (upset and distant) . . . I got a bargain last week . . . a dyed grey rabbit's scarf . . . for only ninety-nine dollars . . . Do you want to see it?

Wilbur: (in hysterics build emotion) . . . Ninety-nine dollars for a dead rabbit . . . bring it back . . . we cannot afford it . . . You spend our money foolishly and I do without . . . I sewed collars on your old bloomers and wear them as shirts . . . I have no new pants . . . last week I put a whisk broom on your old plaid skirt and went to work dressed as a Scotsman . . . and you spend ninety-nine dollars on a dead rabbit . . . Take it back.

Mildred: Okay . . . okay . . . I will . . . (sheea sound, pause) . . . If my Grand-dad were alive he would not let you treat me like that . . . I always took his advice . . . and if he were here, he would say 'keep that scarf' . . . When I get to heaven, I will ask him.

Wilbur: What if he is not in heaven?

Mildred: Then you can ask him . . . (pause) . . . It is my birthday next week . . . so is it too much to ask for a little close affection?

Wilbur: Nobody gives you as little affection as I do.

Mildred: And when you bring the car around . . . you could open the door for me . . . No . . . I have to fling the door open and jump in by myself.

Wilbur: I slow down, don't I?

Mildred: How could you?

Wilbur: How could I what?

Mildred: How could you forget that it is my birthday next week?

Wilbur: This is really getting silly . . . you had better see a shrink.

Mildred: That kind of talk won't help you . . . you are just trying to make me forget you forgot to remember not to forget my birthday.

Wilbur: What? . . . Coming from you that must make some-kind-of-sense.

Mildred: What did you get me?

Wilbur: A genuine imitation fake fur alligator traveling bag.

Mildred: A traveling bag . . . Last year you gave me a large print dictionary . . . and the year before that a beauty kit . . . You think I am ugly . . . stupid and you want to get rid of me.

Wilbur: I do not want to get rid of you.

Mildred: You think I am stupid?

Wilbur: I did not say that.

Mildred: You think it of me.

Wilbur: I never think of you.

Mildred: Never a kind work or a compliment . . . just work me until I am skin and bones . . . You hate my meals and you complain about my cooking.

Wilbur: I never complain about your cooking.

Mildred: Then why didn't you eat that pie I made for you last night?

Wilbur: I did eat it . . . I ate every bit of it.

Mildred: You did not like it.

Wilbur: I could not chew it . . . the crust was as hard as cardboard.

Mildred: Crust . . . there was no crust . . . I served it on a paper plate.

Wilbur: The plate tasted better than the pie.

Mildred: On our eighth anniversary you gave me an eight-dollar bathrobe.

Wilbur: We had no money then . . . we were just getting on our feet . . . we were poor.

Mildred: I figure that's a dollar a year for cooking . . . cleaning . . . sewing . . . and bringing up your children.

Wilbur: (confused) . . . Children . . . we do not have children.

Mildred: What do you expect for a dollar a year.

Wilbur: (dreaming) . . . She spends every dime I earn . . . I have nothing . . . what is a man to do? . . . If I had the guts, I would climb a building or a bridge . . . she would be better off without me . . . she will get the will and my insurance . . . There is only one thing to do . . . (begin to snore as if going to sleep)

Mildred: Wilbur! . . . Wilbur . . . I heard you in the kitchen when you came home . . . did you put the dishes away and clean the counter?

Wilbur: (moaning) . . . I was fixing the toaster and your curling iron just like you had asked me.

Mildred: Do they work?

Wilbur: (excited) . . . Do they work! . . . they work fine . . . only . . . the toast pop up with a permanent curl.

Mildred: Did you make sure the cat was in . . . he got out three times last week.

Wilbur: He won't get out.

Mildred: Where did you put him?

Wilbur: In the bird cage.

Mildred: Where is the canary?

Wilbur: In the cat.

Mildred: (cry) . . . Wilbur, how could you?

Wilbur: Don't worry . . . the canary is fine, and the cat is asleep in the oven . . . I set it on low.

Mildred: Don't scare me like that . . . Are you sure all the animals are alright?

Wilbur: I am sure.

Mildred: How about the fish . . . did you heat up the water for the new baby gold fish?

Wilbur: (begin to yell) . . . I heated his water . . . gave him his pablum . . . burped him twice and changed his diapers . . . Please let me get some sleep Mildred . . . I am tired.

Mildred: Wilbur . . . you may need all the practice you can get.

Wilbur: (sleepy) . . . Practice for what? . . . I am too tired to practice tonight.

Mildred: Call your girlfriend . . . Betty BOOBS Ohanlin.

Wilbur: Do not start again with Betty BOOBS.

Mildred: You would play mommy and daddy if Betty BOOBS Ohanlin was willing.

Wilbur: (soft) . . . She is always willing, and we never play mommy and daddy . . . (louder) . . . How in the heck do you play mommy and daddy?

Mildred: (whine) . . . Wilbur . . . I forgot to tell you that a letter came for you today . . . it was marked private and personal . . . I forgot to give it to you.

Wilbur: What did it say?

Mildred: You do not have to be so snide about it . . . I accidently steamed it open when I was pouring a cup of tea.

Wilbur: Tell me what it said . . . for Pete's sake.

Mildred: It . . . is from Doctor Hiron . . . he said . . . Mr. Crabtree . . . our tests confirm that there is nothing physically wrong with you as your wife insists that there is . . . There is plenty of action in your test tube sample . . . In order to have children . . . I suggest more intimacy . . . (softer, sexy voice)

. . . love . . . affection . . . cuddling . . . kissing . . . hugging . . . and SE . . .

Wilbur: I get the idea . . . The Doctor said that did he . . .well . . .

Mildred: Wilbur take me . . . ravish me . . .I am all yours.

Wilbur: All right Mildred . . . I should be ready in the morning.

Mildred: You say it, but you won't do it . . . do it right now.

Wilbur: All right . . . I give up . . . have it your way.

Mildred: (in a soft sexy voice) . . . Wilbur . . . Wilbur . . . OH WILBUR!

Wilbur: (loud snoring sounds that build)

Mildred: (speak through Wilbur's snoring, voice drags and becomes disappointed) . . . Wilbur . . ., Wilbur . . ., Wilbur . . ., Wil . . ., bur . . ..

Orchestra: (build the theme music quickly until Bud cuts orchestra off and points to the announcer)

Bud: (clap, motion to actors and audience to clap, carry on as-long-as possible then point to the announcer)

Orchestra: (begin to play background music for Penelope Peabodie, banjo music)

Phelps: Will Wilbur now get his needed sleep . . . will Mildred ever have a child . . . and what ever has become of Betty BOOBS Ohanlin? . . . If you care be sure to tune us in next week on the same location on your radio dial . . . This portion of the show has been brought to you by the members of P.M.A.A.A.N.M.S.S . . .that is the poor musicians, authors, announcers, actors need money soon society . . . now the president of P.M.A.A.A.N.M.S.S. . . . Miss. Penelope Peabodie with another letter from home.

Orchestra: (build and keep playing until Penelope becomes frustrated by being drowned out by the music and gives a hateful look, music stops instantly)

Penelope: (regain composure before speaking) . . . Sister writes . . . 'a typical letter from a Canadian family about Grandma and Grandpa Peabodie . . . big sister and hubby . . . Junior and niece . . . My folks live on a quiet street full of butter-nut trees and they live just around the corner from Mr. and

Mrs. Crabtree and the vivacious Mrs. Ohanlin . . . Oh Mercy! . . . Well . . . oh' Sister writes that Junior does not eat his spinach . . . Junior wants to be lazy and flabby like his Grandpa . . . Grandpa say's if he starts eating his vegetables now at his age it will mess up his constitution . . . 'Everybody knows that Grandpa's constitution needs drastic improvement . . .OH MERCY!' . . .Sister say's Niece wants to go out with Bobby instead of Billy, but Jerry may not like it because he told Mary who told cousin Jill to tell Niece he kind of likes her . . .so Niece decided to have a party and just invite boys . . . Well sister's hubby put his foot down on the coffee table and broke sister's favorite vase . . . In turn that got sister hollering at hubby who got on Grandpa's case about not showing a good example for Junior by not eating his vegetables . . . Then Grandpa gave Junior an ear-full . . . he told Junior to do as his elders say . . . not as they do . . . 'can you believe it' . . . Junior never understood a single word he said . . . you know Grandpa usually talks with his mouth full of mashed potatoes . . . Grandma cuffed a good one up along side of Grandpa's head for putting a pea in Junior's ear . . . Then Junior meant to kick Niece under the table for laughing but hubby ended up with a bruised shin . . . sure enough hubby accused sister who blamed Grandma who blamed Grandpa who blamed Junior who then blamed Niece . . . because we all knew that Niece wanted to have a party with only boys . . . Yes, sister said that Niece could have her party as long as she invited other girls and had some chaperones . . . There was Bobby, Billy, Jerry, Fred, Gilbert, Wendle, Steve, Jim, four girls and fifteen other boys on her list . . . sister, hubby, Grandpa and Grandma would chaperone like bear grease on an old wagon wheel that had summer flies wallowing in the goo . . . Sister say's that Niece would have more freedom in a convent . . . They should have been watching Junior . . . 'A true Casanova' . . . He and the four girls disappeared before the party began . . . The party was just pity-full . . . pity-full . . . say's Grandma . . . Niece sat alone on the parlor sofa with twenty-three boys scattered around the room watching sister and hubby doing something called a jitter-bug . . . even Grandpa and Grandma did a dance called the flapper . . . It says here that Grandma even had a few boys flapping . . . 'Whooo . . . eeeh! . . . sounds like a great old time . . . Wish I was there . . . I do a mean twist' . . . Well it has been quite a week say's sister . . . Junior is taking courting lessons from Grandpa . . . who is starting to eat his vegetables . . . Even though it is only one pea per meal . . . Grandma say's she wants to throw a party and invite some of those young boys . . . Hubby is set to have a talk with Junior about the birds and the bees . . . Niece has not said a word to anybody for over a week now . . . Our prayers have been answered . . . she gave us a note yesterday . . . it says she wants to be a Nun . . . Sister say's we will be shipping her to basic Nun training in a few days . . .' Mercy . . . Mercy' . . . Well that's the news from sister and hubby, Junior Grandma, Grandpa and soon to be Sister Aloysius . . . All our love to Aunt Penelope Peabodie . . . 'Mercy . . . OH MERCY! . . . It is so good to get letters from home . . . Living so far away

I seldom get to enjoy family life . . . With letters from kinfolk, I am able to enjoy the antics of everybody back home . . . Oh Mercy . . . I just cannot wait until sister's next letter' . . . (wipe a tear from eye)

Bud: (comfort Penelope by placing an arm on her shoulder, with a free hand cue in the orchestra to begin to play)

Orchestra: (start banjo music off with a sour note, play until Bud takes Penelope to her seat)

Bud: (sit Penelope on her seat, begin to build the orchestra up and then point to the announcer)

Orchestra: (softly begin to play the closing music of 'Friends We Never Forget')

Phelps: Thank you Miss Penelope Peabodie for that insight into domestic life . . . I would like to thank our sponsors . . . Mousseau's fine line of fine pine furniture . . . Moose Ventures with locations in Moosonee, Moose Factory, Moose Jaw and Moose City Wyoming . . . the P.M.A.A.A.N.M.S.S. . . . yes that is the poor musicians, authours, announcers, actors need money soon society . . . special thanks to Our Almost There Orchestra . . .sound affects by Waldo . . . Mr Cheeks Too Soft . . . Ma . . . Young'in . . . Wojo . . . Knot Head . . . The Crabtrees . . . Professor E.D. Ucation . . . Donald Knot . . . Doc Good . . . Penelope Peabodie . . . our stage Director Bud . . . and myself your announcer for this evening Ben Phelps . . . Our closing number with be performed by cast, crew and our orchestra presenting a tribute song titled 'Friends We Never Forget'.

Bud: (point to orchestra, motion for the actors and crew to gather around the mikes)

Orchestra: (build music)

Friends never forget.
Laughter never regret.
Your applause leaves us so speechless.
To you we toast a cup of kindness.

So, if you ever want to smile.
Just turn on your radio dial.
And listen to us clown around.
On your radio we can be found.

Kids from nine to ninety-four.
And crave for laughter ever more.
Our hospitality we extend.
On this radio of pretend.

Laughter we never regret.
Friends we never forget.

Lighting: (over head lights slowly dim, soft spot light covers complete stage, as the music closes the spot light narrows until it is focused on the top of a mike)

Orchestra: (music fades)

Lighting: (all lights go out, after a pause the spot light fills the stage)

Orchestra: (begin playing instrumental of final song)

Actors: (take group bow)

Lighting: (all lights go out)

Orchestra: (music fades)

THE END

A HOCKEY NIGHT IN CANADA
by Richard Mousseau
Copyright April 2, 2013

BASIC STORY:
One blustery winter of eighteen-eighty-six in the home of John Louie, and Isobel Stanley-Creighthon, a gathering of mostly men discuss the various games played on ice with sticks and a disc. Their concern is the various rules followed by different teams in different areas of the country and in that of the world. The men decide that a set of rules should be drawn up for everyone to follow. They also decide to define the way the game should be played. Of most importance is the name to be associated with the game. Beware of the influence and suffrage of women making a stand in society and evolution in history. Many a man, woman and child of Canada's landscape of snow and frozen ponds has contributed to the history in the making of a Hockey Night in Canada.

CHARACTERS:

John Louie Creightion:

Business man of thirty to forty years of age. Married to Isobel Creightion. A distinguished businessman. Slender build of six feet in height. A leader of men and of this group of men, of which all look to him for answers and guidance. Always polite and respectful. Wears a suit coat, white shirt, vest, pants, bow-tie with shot tails. A good skater and plays the Centre position on the team.

Isobel Stanley Creightion:

Woman of thirty to forty years of age. Married to John Creightion. A woman of sturdy, not fat, substance. Approximately five foot eleven. Tomboyish at times, yet women like at other times. Respectful of John but wears the pants in the home by speaking her mind yet can be one of the boys. Wears working household dress and appropriate attire. Is a good skater and plays the Rover position on the team.

Master Joseph Henry:

Man, of thirty to forty years of age. Solid build on a five-foot-eight-inch height. Wears a suite coat, white shirt, long tie and dress work pants. A master carpenter, business man. Always concerned about measurements and accuracy. Always firm with final answers. Can be stubborn at times. Plays Goal for the team.

Ri`chard:

A man of thirty years of age with a normal build and approximately five-foot to six foot in height. Wears fancy dress clothes. He does not work, he inherited wealth, plays sports, is flamboyant, a man about town, dances lightly and moves with exaggeration, always playful, confident, a tease. Plays Cover Point for the team.

Hugo (Smity) Smith:

A large man of strength, not delicate or agile in an average height of five-foot-five-inches and of twenty to thirty years of age. The husband of Mrs. Smith. He is a blacksmith and business man. Not dumb witted when it comes to his trade but slightly off when following rules. Uses his build to gain success in sports. Wears working business suite, a bit tight on his body frame. A pleasant man, a gentle giant except when pushed beyond a comfort zone. Plays Point for the team.

W.F. Murray:

Twin brother of F.W. Murray. An average man of size and height at twenty to thirty years of age. A lawyer in training. Dresses identically to twin brother in a business suite, though they are not facially identical. Sports minded and acts defensively. Plays Forward, right sided for the team. He is right handed.

F.W. Murray:
Twin brother of W.F. Murry. Same description as W.F. Murray. F.W. wears a moustache. Not as decisive as W.F., Plays Forward, left side for the team. He is left handed.

Constable Aloysius O'Hera:
A man of forty years of age in a large frame, a man of substance. Wears a suite representative of the police force, but not a uniform. He is the senior constable, strict, upholds the law, abused the law as a youngster, makes up rules as he goes, rarely backs down, tries to intimidate others, but subsides when others of importance scold him. Hobbles about on an injured foot. Uses a cane. Usually plays the Rover position for the team.

Mrs. Smith:
Wife of Mr. Hugo Smith. A small petite woman of twenty to thirty years of age, giddy, squeaky voice, full of enthusiasm, always cheerful, always encourages and praises others, even the opposing players.

Secondary cast characters:
Two sons of the Creightions between eight and twelve years of age.
Two young women, fiancées of W.F. and F.W. Murray.

STAGE:
Interior setting of upscale home of the eighteen-eighty-six era. A dining room - parlour atmosphere. Furniture and decor of the time period. Round dining table, rocking chairs, various straight back chairs, knitting basket and utensils, fireplace against wall, buffet against wall. Main door at centre back stage. Internal entrances to sides, coat rack by main door. Candelabras and oil lamps. Hockey sticks and skates at back wall location.

SOUNDS:
Winter wind sounds and various echoing. Music rendition of the 'Hockey Night in Canada Theme', and the 'Canadian Anthem'.

LIGHTING:
Aging light of heavy browns and greys to present an aged effect to characters and interior of home, reflective of oil lamps and candles.

COSTUMES:
Men and women's attire are that of fashions of the eighteen-eighty-six era. See individual character description for each person's description of attire. Hair and makeup reflecting era.

PROPS:
Hockey sticks and skates of the type used in eighteen-eighty-six. Hockey puck a six-inch diameter by two-inch-high disc of wood. Oil lamps, brass and glass candelabras of era. Wall paintings, chairs, tables, fixtures, decorations of era. Cricket shin pads.

FIRST ACT

DIRECTIONS
(Stage is dim, only a faint illumination of the room by the fireplace. The sounds of winter wind howls. Isobel Creighton enters the room, places tray of tea cups on table. John Creighton enters with a newspaper under an arm and begins to turn up wall oil lamps. Stage lights brighten to illuminate room. Both sit at table. Isobel pours tea. John unfolds paper on table. The sounds of two boys heavy into a ruckus sound from off stage. Their banter becomes louder, and Shinny play enters from hallway and onto centre stage. Boys display stick action of chasing a wooden disc about the room. Both parents watch the action and make similar moves of imitation of the boys' play. The game play exits out through an opposite entranceway. Isobel picks up knitting needles and begins to knit.)

ISOBEL
John . . . I do hope that a limited amount of snow falls tonight. I am looking forward to skating on the pond tomorrow.

JOHN
(mumble) Yes skating. (concentrate on paper)

ISOBEL
Are you and your gentlemen friends going to play a game of Shinny against the men from the Iron Works.

JOHN
(mumble) Yes skating.

ISOBEL
(hopeful) If you are a player short . . . I will gladly fill in as Rover?

JOHN
Yes skating.

ISOBEL
(frustrated) John Louie Creighton, you have not absorbed a single word I have said. John, what is of importance in that newspaper?

58

JOHN
You are the best skater in town Isobel. Out-skate the best of the men. But . . .
play shinny against the Iron Works team, never. They play with a very
animalistic nature.

ISOBEL
I do believe Mat Billings plays for that team as a Point.

JOHN
Billings is a seasoned Iron Worker. I do not see your intent of comparing
yourself to Billings.

ISOBEL
Mat Billings is Mrs. Matilda Billings, the widow of Mr. Billings. She assumed
his job after Mr. Billings' untimely death, and a position of Point on the Iron
Works Team.

JOHN
(shocked) Billings is female, a woman. My word, a woman . . . a woman! He
. . . she is a brute upon the ice. A woman you say . . . a woman?

ISOBEL
She is not a great skater, I am. I do not believe there are rules preventing
women from playing?

JOHN
That is the problem, no rules. Everyone makes up their own rules, often
changing rules to suit the situation on a whim. We, those of us of the business
class play a dignified game. Those of the working class play a rowdier game.
When we play in their backyard, it is their rules. When in our backyard, our
rules.

ISOBEL
Not always true, the Iron Works Team seem to use their rules no matter where
they play. Sometimes not playing by their own rules. So much for rules.

JOHN
Rules is exactly the discussion in this evening's paper. (look at paper) It says
here that in the previous year of 1885, that a game played on the clean ice of
winter with players on skates and using various sticks of variable designs to
move about an object is a common pastime, yet the game is as variable as the
weather. No consistency, no rules.

ISOBEL
We use skates, a stick and a disc and a code of decency and it is called Shinny.

JOHN
In Halifax they play Ice Hurley with a ball. Over in England they play Bandy. Some Scotsman play Shinty and some play Hookie. The Mi`Kmag Play Baggataway, and those Americans play Ice Polo.

ISOBEL
Ice Polo! . . . such a silly name . . . sounds like a game snobbish people play. They seem to name every sport Polo, Water Polo, Ice Polo, Field Polo, Horse Polo . . ..

JOHN
All games are similar, but no consistency, no defined description of play and definitely no rules written down, no singular rule book for all to abide.

ISOBEL
When you attended King's college in Windsor, Nova Scotia, you were on the boxing team. Did you not have rules of conduct?

JOHN
Yes, everyone that boxed in all civilized countries follow the Marquis of Queensbury Rules of Boxing.

ISOBEL
Then someone should write down the rules for Shinny.

JOHN
My dear, this is Canada. Never, ever will voting Canadians agree unanimously. This country will always be divided 50-50, not including the Separatists.

ISOBEL
When women have the right to vote, political matters will change.

JOHN
Absurd . . ., we my dear Isobel are always at odds and never agree a hundred percent. I shall prove my point. By which moniker would you label the game.

ISOBEL
Shinny of course . . ., by the end of the game everyone is rubbing their shins. Sticks constantly hit the shins. Makes perfect sense to me to name the game Shinny.

JOHN
I would prefer Hookie, because the stick is the most important object in the game. A curved stick having a hook in its' shape . . . hook . . . Hookie. One vote for Hookie.

ISOBEL
One vote for Shinny.

JOHN
We just need 98 percent of the rest of the voters to select one name to define a Canadian game played on ice.

ISOBEL
I see your point. A 100 percent agreement will never happen.

DIRECTIONS
(a rapping sound at the door, Isobel hurries to the door, boys enter from hallway, lose wooden disc under skirt of Isobel, Isobel dances about until disc is retrieved and boys exit, Isobel opens door)

ISOBEL
Master Joseph Henry, please, please, come in. (stare at the padding on man's legs)

JOSEPH
(waddle in) Good evening Mrs. (slightly bow and remove hat and remove coat) Evening John.

ISOBEL
(begin to close door) My word, have you injured your legs? (struggle to close door)

HUGO
Madame, Madame please! (stick arm and leg past door opening)

ISOBEL
(look away from Joseph's leg padding to man at door, open door wide to see Mr. And Mrs. Smith) Mr. Hugo Smith, my deepest apologies, please enter. Good evening Mrs. Smith.

DIRECTIONS
(small talk, actions among players, everyone is removing coats and hats and hanging on wall coat racks, Joseph is seemingly pushed toward hallway

opening, boys enter and play through, like a goalie, Joseph blocks the boys path, the boys take several shots, sticks repeatedly strike padding, disc passes by and boys exit, Mrs. Smith acts nervous, jumpy by sight of actions)

JOHN
Ingenious Master Henry, Padding. (approach to inspect) Did you feel any pain. I must say ingenious.

DIRECTIONS
(women talk, move to side cupboard for tea, Hugo approaches men to inspect padding)

JOSEPH
We are playing the Iron Works, bloody merciless men. If I am to play between the rocks, I need protection.

HUGO
(quickly kick pads) Did ya feel that?

JOSEPH
Blessed be my saviour, I did, but no lasting scars. Cricket pads with an extra layer of saddle felt.

ISOBEL
Rules John, the Iron Works Team may not abide the use of those pads protecting the shins.

JOHN
My dear Isobel, they have been invited to play at our pond . . . so . . . our rules take precedent.

ISOBEL
Then I request a rule to allow myself to partake in the game.

HUGO
The Mrs's wants to play? (shake head no)

JOSEPH
Prohibitive John, decency must prevail.

JOHN
Gentlemen, Matt Billings is none other than Mrs. Matilda Billing . . . a female . . . a woman playing for the Iron Works.

DIRECTIONS
(Mrs. Smith is shocked and giggles girlishly, Joseph and Hugo ponder the thought)

JOSEPH
A woman?

HUGO
Female?

JOHN
Yes both, a female and supposedly a woman.

DIRECTIONS
(both men shake heads in disbelief, Isobel and John nod yes, Mrs. Smith silently giggles)

JOSEPH
Matt . . . Mrs. Billings plays Point . . . with a wicked slap shot . . ., but lads I have . . . (head to door to retrieve a stick outside)

HUGO
What? A secret identity to tell us about. (deep self-laugh)

DIRECTIONS
(no one laughs, Mrs. Smith twists up mouth and shakes head, all watch Joseph with anticipation)

JOSEPH
Minding the goal that is ten feet wide, I will now have an advantage. (show new goalie stick) A cousin back home in England posted me measurements of a field Hurley Goalie stick. An advantage in stopping Matt . . . Mrs. Billings' wicked shots towards the goal.

JOHN
You are a fine Master Carpenter Joseph. (admire slightly wider stick) Exquisite craftsmanship. (test its' weight) What is it made of?

JOSEPH
Ironwood, Hornbeam to be exact. I ordered several slabs from Nova Scotia. Selecting a root and trunk section, I carved the stick in one piece. Ruined two draw plain knives. This wood is as hard as iron.

HUGO

May I? (accept stick, attempt to bend and break over knee, slap stick against Joseph's shin pads) Feel that?

JOSEPH
Mother of forgiveness, Hugo, yes that hurt.

JOHN
More padding Joseph.

JOSEPH
Yes, Yes, a must.

DIRECTIONS
(men mumble about pads, women whisper and shake heads, a knock sounds at the door)

ISOBEL
I must say, the pads are a good idea. John, actually wears my corset, supports his back when playing Shinny. (walk toward door while talking to Mrs. Smith)

JOHN
(hearing name called raise head) Isobel, please, that is a privet matter.

HUGO
Not anymore.

JOHN
I am tall, the stick is short, and having to bend over when skating takes a toil on my back. The corset supports my back.

HUGO
It does wonders for your mid-drift and hips.

JOHN
Do not look at my hips.

ISOBEL
Have Master Henry make you a stick with a longer handle.

DIRECTIONS
(men stare at each other, seemingly contemplating the idea, agreeing, disagreeing, shaking heads no, yes, shrugging shoulders, Isobel opens door to greet two men and two women)

ISOBEL
Mr. Murray, Mr. Murray and Ladies, please come in out of the cold.

F.W.
Madame Creightion, may I introduce my brother's fiancée, Miss. Kay and my fiancée, Miss. Key.

ISOBEL
Gentlemen, Miss. Kay and Miss. Key.

DIRECTIONS
(gentlemen nod a greeting, ladies curtsy, ladies join Mrs. Smith, men join men)

HUGO
Evening F.W.. (pat man on shoulder) My good buddy.

W.F.
Hugo, I am W.F.. The one with no moustache.

HUGO
Oh yes, you play left Forward. You, I am not partial to. (pat F.W. on shoulder) My good buddy.

F.W.
No, I play left Forward. W.F. plays right Forward, on your right side.

HUGO
(inspect hands, think about confusion)

F.W.
No Hugo, your other right.

HUGO
You twins, look alike. Now I cannot remember which one of you is my good buddy.

ISOBEL
Ridiculous Mr. Smith, they are not identical twins. W.F. is taller and wears a handle-bar moustache. F.W. has a soft baby face.

HUGO
They look alike to me. They should put personal names on their backs when

we play, or maybe numbers then I can say #1 Murray and #2 Murray.

JOSEPH
Ridiculous Hugo, but then again, on your broad back you have room for a double-digit number and your full name in block letters, 'Hugo Smity, Smith'!

HUGO
Yes, a great idea, I have an old wool sweater. (turn to ladies) Mrs. Smith, would you please knit the name 'Smity' on that old sweater of mine. (turn to men when there is no response from ladies) 'Smity' on the sweater is enough, do not want to overwork the Mrs.

JOHN
Gentlemen, do you not think we should concentrate on strategies for the upcoming game and decide on home rules.

W.F.
Every game we play we make up new rules.

F.W.
Depending on which team we are playing.

W.F.
Game rules agreed upon before each game from a selection of rules is a must. It would be mayhem otherwise. Imagine teams playing a free for all game.

HUGO
Won't happen. Teams like the Iron Works forget about rules once play begins.

JOSEPH
And what about teams in different countries or across boarders? All have their own home rules and style of play.

JOHN
And varied names to address this sport. May I ask for preference to a name of our game?

ISOBEL
(though talking to ladies, mindful of the men's conversation) Shinny!

HUGO
Shinty, from Scotland, a good rugged game played on grass. The hooked stick often used as a weapon.

JOSEPH
Hurling, similar to Shinty, but rather tamer, less drawing of blood. Hurling, meaning to hurl the ball toward the goal.

F.W.
I would back Mrs. Creightion, Shinny is the game.

W.F.
Shinny is played anywhere, anytime, any number of players and what-even rules they want to use.

JOHN
Well, Mrs. Creightion, I believe you now have 3 votes.

ISOBEL
So far John. I do have these ladies to convert.

JOHN
Gentlemen, I suggest the use of the word Hookie. The use of a stick with a hook shape.

HUGO
Won't go, hookie is what I did in my youth when avoiding attending school. Naming a game called Hookie will be a bad influence on the morals of children. They will be enticed to play hookie from school to go play Hookie. If I had stayed in school I could have been educated, maybe a lawyer, doctor, not a Blacksmith. See what hookie did for me.

JOHN
My man, you are suited for the Blacksmith trade, and an excellent tradesman. Hookie has no bearing on the game of Hookie.

JOSEPH
Smitty has a point John. This game should have class and merit, promoting decency and skills.

F.W.
I must agree, as W.F. will concur.

W.F.
I do not concur. Maybe a name that is not associated with any type of game played in winter or summer with a ball, disc, frozen potatoes of frozen cow-patties.

ISOBEL
W.F., I must demand that you stick with the name Shinny Mrs. Creightion.

W.F.
If no other conclusive option then yes, Shinny.

JOHN
If . . . I must stress the if. If naming a specific game and to have that game be distinctive, and superior to all other similar games, this newly created game must have specific and detailed rules.

JOSEPH
I agree, but John, if no one can agree on a name, it will be a factor of ten that it will be impossible for a hundred to a thousand men to agree upon rules.

JOHN
True. Rather though, if a small group of men . . .

ISOBEL
Women!

JOHN
(politely nod then whisper) Men . . . gather, develop a name and scribe rules, register and promote, then the majority may succumb and adopt, thus the new game and rules become the standard.

JOSEPH
We play the Iron Works on the morrow; a new name and rules cannot be formulated quickly enough to be adopted by those ruffians. They will not adopt.

F.W.
I must agree, I do not look forward to the Rugby tactics those hooligans use. There is no need for bumping, pushing and the curve of the stick is not meant to be used as a means of hooking skates to upend a man.

W.F.
The object of the game is to propel the disc forward and score by use of a stick alone. Often, I have witnessed feet kicking the disc, hands pushing and bodies covering the disc. Disrespectful tactics.

JOSEPH
Knees and elbows used to pummel opposing players.

HUGO
Definitely; I have been a victim of Mr. Sherri's elbows to my ribs and several times to my nose.

JOHN
Mr. Donald Cherry, the reverend Cherry's oldest lad.

HUGO
Donald Cheery has taken lessons from Patrick Sherri. Hooligans with intent to mangle a man into submission.

DIRECTIONS
(Hugo grasps the hand of Mrs. Smith and begins to waltz with elbows high, others back away from the exaggerated movements)

HUGO
The Mrs. and me were at the evening social and this is how Patrick Sherri dances with elbows high, hitting those in his way, and knees just a bouncing. Me wee wife receiving a knee to the bustle. (slightly knee Mrs. Smith's bustle)

DIRECTIONS
(Mrs. Smith slightly jumps and nervously giggles, places hands to face in embarrassment, joins women, they all mumble in silent gossip)

HUGO
I suggest a rule, in retaliation of Patrick Sherri inflicting elbows while playing. Opposing players may deliver matching elbows or knees. (slap a fist into a open palm)

DIRECTIONS
(women place nervous hands to cheeks, men recoil and shake heads no)

JOHN
If you are intending to suggest that fisticuffs would settle the matter.

JOSEPH
Donald Cheery is a rockem-sockem player. Hugo has had interaction with the hooligan.

HUGO
Heavy weight champion I am in sanctioned ring boxing for three consecutive years straight. Donald Cheery is no match for me, he is a feather weight.

JOHN
We would be required to include Marquis of Queensbury Rules.

HUGO
Acceptable. (dance about in boxer stance, throw short heavy punches)

JOHN
(dodge a wayward punch) No Hugo, this game must display the ability to skate, stick handle the disc, use multiple player plays, well defined strategies to outplay and out think the opposition. Out play lesser talented players as Cheery and Sherri.

HUGO
And when that don't work, and Sherri don't follow the rules, I will flatten him. (slap fist into open palm, show anger)

JOSEPH
Our families, women and children will be watching. We should not present immoral conduct and provide the seed of corruption to be planted into the children.

DIRECTION
(a loud rap sounds at the door, in bursts Ri`chard with exuberance, lively gestures)

RI`CHARD
Gentlemen, most humble apologies for my delay.

DIRECTIONS
(men offer greetings, Joseph and Hugo shake heads, concerned about the man's flamboyancy, W.F., F.W. seemingly admire the man, John is indifferent, Ri`chard instantly approaches women, gently taking hand and kissing W.F. and F.W.'s fiancées, they swoon, Mrs. Smith giggles, Isobel slaps his hand in a motherly way)

ISOBEL
Go talk to the men you cad.

RI`CHARD
My dear Mrs. Creighton, I shall pursue you until you swoon.

ISOBEL
A slap up-side of the head will make you swoon.

DIRECTIONS
(Isobel raises hand and attempts a slap, Ri`chard dances away)

RI`CHARD
Gentlemen, what have I missed?

JOSEPH
Rules of Etiquette.

RI`CHARD
I trust that you mean my affectionate adoration bestowed upon women.

JOSEPH
Quite . . . especially when forced upon married women.

RI`CHARD
Affection is never forced, it is offered and often accepted. I love women, women of all points in life and attachments. Women adore the affection I offer.

DIRECTIONS
(Hugo reaches large hands toward Ri`chard, Ri`chard ducks)

HUGO
I will force some etiquette into you the way I will on Patrick Sherri.

JOHN
(step between the men) Gentlemen, we are on the same team, we must focus on strategies to out-play the Iron Works with skills, not fisticuffs, and definitely-not amongst ourselves.

HUGO
Ri`chard can romance the Iron Works into submission.

ISOBEL
Mr. Hugo, Ri`chard is harmless, just a delightful tease to make us attached women enjoy the amusement.

DIRECTIONS
(ladies laugh and giggle, men nod heads in agreement)

RI`CHARD
(somewhat insulted) Women, please, my broken heart. (place hand to chest) You cast me into an oblivion of despair for without the affection I am . . .

JOHN
Playing Cover Point. Positions men, strategies of play.

DIRECTIONS
(men take up positions of play, [see ice diagram], Isobel joins in at Rover position, all assume actions of a game, John begins to narrate a game scenario, women hover like excited fans)

JOHN
A player shoots the disc towards the goal, Joseph deflects it to the Rover.

ISOBEL
I have it. (move about) Two players are after me.

HUGO
I'll take care of Patrick Sherri. (push an imaginary person against the coat rack) Okay, he is out of commission.

ISOBEL
A pass is deflected.

RI`CHARD
(dance flamboyantly around as if dodging all opposition players) I have it, I jump over sticks used to slash shins. I skate circles around the fumbling brutes. They cannot stop me. (pirouette then smile to the ladies)

DIRECTIONS
(players move about waiting for a pass, goalie is sliding back and forth between hats set on floor ten feet apart, the women smile and wave at Ri`chard, Mrs. Smith giggles)

ISOBEL
Pass the disc, John is open.

F.W.
I am closer, then I will forward to John.

W.F.
Hugo, join the play, help block the goal.

JOHN
Pass, pass, look for the open man.

HUGO
Take that Sherri. (elbow the coat rack)

W.F.
Too many men after Ri`chard, I got the disc, I pass across to F.W..

JOHN
No . . . no, do not pass across an open area, the opposition will intercept. Where is the Rover?

ISOBEL
I am too far away; the opposition has the disc. Ri`chard needs to cover for Hugo.

JOHN
F.W., W.F. fall back. Too late, they shoot.

DIRECTIONS
(Hugo wrestles with a coat and falls into the goal and pushes Joseph back, F.W., W.F. collide in the middle, Ri`chard stands near women, smiling and winking, John raises arms hopelessly)

JOHN
They have scored!

DIRECTIONS
(Mrs. Smith giggles and claps)

ISOBEL
(concern) Mrs. Smith, the opposition has scored on us, do not clap. (look at Hugo) I see you are cheering for Hugo, yes . . ., yes, he has Patrick Sherri in a scissor lock. Hugo is winning the fight, but not by the Marquis of Queensbury Rules of boxing, nor of wrestling.

JOHN
Exactly . . . no one is following rules.

JOSEPH
What rules? We have not decided what rules we are going to formulate, let alone present to the Iron Works that never follow rules.

F.W.
They never . . . ever follow their own rules.

W.F.
If I may say . . . this is but an observation, it does not matter how the Iron Works Play. It is how we play. Ice areas in our own zone are empty and other areas crowded.

JOHN
Yes . . . if Hugo is out of position then the goal is in jeopardy. We must lead and have the opposition try to follow our style and talent.

F.W.
Then a smaller goal width.

HUGO
Tell Romeo to play his position and not show off his fancy skating. (do an awkward attempt at a Pierrette)

RI`CHARD
Move toe Hugo, stretch upward. Sorry Hugo, it will not work, you are too top heavy for the art of dance. You are more adept doe a country Hoedown.

JOHN
Think gentlemen, think . . . if the opposition is unorganized and just skate willy-nilly and do not play positions then we should play zones.

JOSEPH
Yes, that is a great idea, move the Point position away from being directly in front of me. I can not see around Hugo. He is a brick outhouse equally tall and wide.

HUGO
(sulk, and physically shrivel) You guys need me. Not one of you has the muscle to go one on one with the Iron Works, not even Matilda Billings.

RI`CHARD
(interested) Who is Matilda Billings?

F.W.
There are no women on the Iron Works Team.

ISOBEL
Matt Billings is Matilda Billings.

W.F.
He is a woman?

ISOBEL
She is a woman.

RI`CHARD
My word, what a ruffian. You say, he is a woman, how can one tell?

HUGO
Exactly and you Ri`chard dance away whenever Matt Billings confronts you.

RI`CARD
Because Matt billings is not . . . (gesture to women) . . . a woman

JOSEPH
Then what needs to be done?

JOHN
Protect position areas. At the start of the game or when a re-start is required, we assume correct positions. Then once play begins we go into zones.

DIRECTIONS
(John begins to place people in a modern-day positions, except for Isobel, she is left in original position)

JOHN
Hugo, to the left of Joseph and a bit forward. Ri`chard, to the right of Joseph and back a bit.

JOSEPH
Good, now I can see what is happening, the barn door is open.

JOHN
Now Joseph can play the disc. If someone comes from the sides, Hugo and Ri`chard can cover. Hugo is the muscle, Ri`chard is the speed and can cover when Hugo is out of his zone.

F.W.
I see . . . I see.

W.F.
I move when F.W. moves and fall back.

F.W.
And cover the inside centre zones.

DIRECTION
(F.W. and W.F. move into position, John nods acceptance as if seeing the resulting play)

JOHN
Then I play the centre area and cover for either F.W. or W.F. if they are out of position. These same zone position can be used in the offensive attack.

ISOBEL
John!

JOHN
Passing will be easier, knowing a man will be in position.

ISOBEL
John!

JOHN
Yes dear.

ISOBEL
Am I to assume that playing the Rover Position allows me to rove about in areas not protected?

JOHN
Rather being a hindrance.

ISOBEL
(excited) A hindrance, John you know perfectly well that I am able to skate as well as you and Mr. Fancy pants, Ri`chard and definitely hold my own against Matilda Billings and any man of equal stature to F.W. and W.F..

JOHN
I would rather not allow you to participate.

ISOBEL
John! (annoyed) Allow?

JOHN
The position is redundant, actually; it is one too many a position on the ice.

ISOBEL
John Louie Creightion. (stern voice)

DIRECTIONS
(men turn their heads away, stare at ceiling, women lean forward, heads stern, Mrs. Smith cowers then joins others when Hugo is not looking)

JOHN
Maybe . . . the Rover position can be utilized for now. I would prefer that rules of play applied for all teams before women and men . . .

HUGO
Should not be playing in mixed company. A woman's place is in the home taking care that children do not play hookie. On occasions they may watch games.

DIRECTIONS
(men turn away, stare into emptiness, the women snort, Mrs Smith snorts behind the other womens' back so that Hugo does not see)

ISOBEL
We can take a hint Mr. Smith. In time we will achieve equality and supersede the mentality of the male Neanderthals. One day your insulting words will aggravate your digestive system.

HUGO
Never, men rule industry, politics and sports.

ISOBEL
I will assemble a team of women to play Shinny and disgrace men like you. On behalf of talented women, I challenge men to a game of Shinny.

HUGO
Shinty is the game.

DIRECTIONS
(in raising voices others add their game name suggestions)

ISOBEL
Shinny.

HUGO
Shinty.

ALL WOMEN
Shinny!

DIRECTIONS
(each say a notation that suits the character and repeat) Hurley, Shinty, Shinny, Hookie, Bandy, Shinty. (Constable Aloysius O'Hera bursts into the room, limping on a bandaged ankle)

CONSTABLE
(blow English style police whistle) What is this all about? I thought I was busting hooligans in the pub on a Saturday night. What is this all about?

ISOBEL
Arrest them all Constable Aloysius.

CONSTABLE
For what my dear woman?

ISOBEL
For disagreeing with logic.

CONSTABLE
Obvious I am at a loss.

ISOBEL
Aloysius, deciding on an official name of this Canadian game played by everyone on frozen ponds from coast to coast.

CONSTABLE
Back home in Ireland we call it . . .

DIRECTIONS
(all begin to blurt out names, women resounding the loudest) Hurley, Shinty, Hookie, Bandy, Shinty. (Constable blows whistle then hobbles to a chair pulled away from the table)

JOHN
Not only are we at odds in agreeing upon a common name, rules surrounding the variable versions of the game are inconsistent.

DIRECTIONS
(all begin to explain various styles of play, women cheering abstractly, Constable ponders situation)

CONSTABLE
We do play the Iron Works and they do not follow rules of decent play and

seem, to play in styles associated to Shanty, Hurley, Bandy and even the style of American play, swinging a stick as if playing Polo. (swing arm as if riding a horse and hitting a ball)

HUGO
And they play dirty.

CONSTABLE
I agree, it was Mat Billings who stomped on my foot.

F.W. W.F.
Matt Billings is a woman!

HUGO
Matilda Billings, the widow Billings!

CONSTABLE
Yes by-god a woman playing with the brutality of a man. Raising six children and doing a man's work. I do not agree with women playing a man's game, but do not begrudge her the pleasure of pursuing a bit of leisurely fun in playing a game.

RI`CHARD
Maybe these ladies should gussy the woman up a bit so she can find a man to take care of her and those ruffians she calls children.

HUGO
Joseph is single, maybe he could court the widow Billings, and forbid the woman from playing for the Iron Works. It will give us an edge in winning.

ISOBEL
No woman needs a man. A man needs a woman. We cook, clean, pick up behind them and mother them when they are sick, and what thanks do we receive.

RI`CARD
(say with childish emotion) Thanks

DIRECTIONS
Isobel slaps Ri`chard's hand, (men turn away, reluctant to acknowledge or confront the women, women back Isobel)

JOSEPH
(stress word as if thanking Isobel) Thanks, but no thanks, I would not like to

confront the widow Billings as to who will wear the trousers in the relationship.

ISOBEL
(scornfully look at Joseph)

JOHN
Isobel my dear, we are not here to be matchmakers or to debate an Adam and Eve comparison of obligations and superiority. Tonight, we are here to seek strategies in the playing of Hookie against the Iron Works Team.

ISOBEL
Shinny.

WOMEN
Shinny.

MEN
(each announcing their preference) Hurley, Bandy, Shinty, Shinny.

ISOBEL
(excited) F.W. said Shinny. That is now five preferences for Shinny.

CONSTABLE
(blow whistle) In the Police business, the government gave us the heading of the Commonwealth Law then gave us the rules pertaining to the law. So the assumption should be that a title associated to the game played on ice with a disc, sticks and players on skates should have a title first then rules affixed to govern the play of the game.

F.W.
Shinny is a most commonly used word.

HUGO
Hurley.

W.F.
Hurling.

WOMEN
Shinny.

CONSTABLE
Ladies and gentlemen. In order to agree upon rules of the game we must be

able to agree upon a name. A vote on the merits of a game after each name has been presented is a democratic way. I, being in the trade of law enforcement will preside over this matter. Ladies would you be agreeable to present your name for selection?

DIRECTIONS
(women muddle, mumble before Isobel straightens up and takes a position in the centre of the room, men assume variable places)

ISOBEL
This game, that women excel at should be called Shinny. The name suites everyone, a nice soft name, it floats off the tongue.

DIRECTIONS
(women agree, give praise, men shake heads no)

ISOBEL
Children already know the name and play informal games on the streets, ponds, grass and in the home. You men were once children and learned the game while crawling on the floor, dragging your shins.

DIRECTIONS
(men nod heads in agreement, boys play through on their knees, exit opposite entrance, men point and nod in remembrance)

ISOBEL
John Louie Creighton, see, they are playing on their shins. Do you recall teaching the boys and playing on your shins? Shins . . . Shinny. The shins accept slashing sticks, deflections of the disc. Everything about the game reflects on the shins, thus Shinny.

DIRECTIONS
(women clap, F.W. claps until stared down by the men, Isobel curtsies)

CONSTABLE
F.W., I take it you are in favour of the use of the word Shinny. Would you prefer to express further credit for Shinny?

F.W.
I am on the fence at-the-moment and would prefer to obtain information on other suggestions.

W.F.
I shall present. Being the decisive twin, it is up to me to forge forward clearing

the way for F.W..

F.W.
What audacity W. F., it was I that introduced you to a future fiancée. If not for I, it would be left up to Mother to be a matchmaker and take you by the hand to meet women.

DIRECTIONS
(W.F. and F.W.'s fiancées chant and nod heads in agreement, poking fun at W.F.)

W.F.
It is I that made a commitment to propose first and will marry first.

F.W.
First, first . . . must you always be first?

W.F.
Yes.

DIRECTIONS
(all mumble, chat, debate, point fingers)

CONSTABLE
So . . . gentlemen . . . who shall present?

W.F.
I . . . (step forward while a hand holds F.W. back) Hurling . . . is my suggestion. The word from a Gaelic dialect meaning to hurl a ball with a paddle shaped stick. Our grandfather made us Hurling sticks and we have used them to play the game on ice and we hurl the disc by slapping it toward the goal.

ISOBEL
And what pray tell do you call a game played on ice? The game you told your grandfather when searching for a descriptive word.

F.W.
Shinny.

W.F.
Yes Shinny . . . just because other kids called it Shinny. The point of this . . . (gesture to group with arms and hands spread) is to select a name of importance.

HUGO
Well it is not going to be a sissy Irish game that is prehistoric.

CONSTABLE
And your suggestion is Smity?

HUGO
A good rugged game of Shinty. I was introduced to the game on a visit to Scotland by me dear wife's father. A brutal game using a curved stick, not just used to hit a ball, but a player is-allowed to hook opposing players and check and even trip. Me dear wife's father repeatedly hooked me as did relations. The game only allows a strong, sturdy man to walk away.

DIRECTIONS
(silence builds. Mrs Smith nods knowingly and whispers to women)

JOSEPH
My dear man, has it ever occurred to you that the game was a means by which a Scottish family is able to test the muster of an Englishman that just happens to have married into the family without their approval or acceptance? An Englishman my good man, te Scottish resent the English, let alone marry into their clan.

DIRECTIONS
(Hugo shakes head then slowly stops after self reflection, looks over to Mrs. Smith who gently smiles, and giggles then looks innocently away)

HUGO
Bloody hell, me shins were cut to the bone and white leggings stained red and the Mrs.'s family proudly slapping me on the back.

ISOBEL
Another reference to shins. A Canadian interpretation of the Shinty is Shinny.

CONSTABLE
Objection, out of order Mrs. Creightion, no subliminal insertion of details to confuse each singular presentation.

ISOBEL
Noted Aloysius, but the obvious is obvious, I was just indicating the obvious, Hugo's bloody shins, a connection between shins, Shinty and Shinny, Shinny being the most rememberable name.

CONSTABLE
No rebuttals Mrs. Creightion. (notice Mr. Henry)
You have the floor Mr. Henry.

JOSEPH
As you may notice my shins are protected. If all players wore cricket pads, then injuries to the shins would be eliminated.

CONSTABLE
No references Mrs. Creightion. (hold up hand)

JOSEPH
Being the one protecting the goal, I attempt to stop every disc that is hurling toward me. Having the suggestion by W.F., the word Hurling being and action word, I would suggest naming the game Hurly.

W.F.
Both names derive the same meaning. I will side with Hurly.

CONSTABLE
Two votes for Hurly. Shinny may have a difficult time convincing Hugo to change Shinty to Shinny.

HUGO
No problem at all, I believe I have been belittled by my Scottish in-laws and their game of Shinty. Shinny it is.

CONSTABLE
Two votes for Hurley, two for Shinny.

F.W.
If I may. I have a strong association for Shinny.

ISOBEL
Bless you lad.

F.W.
My apologies for misleading you Mrs. Crighton, but I must be more assertive and rebut the notion that I am a follower, as W.F. has strongly indicated.
W.F.
Well, present your case.

F.W.
I shall, Bandy comes to mind. It has been played on ice for centuries and is

similar-to the game we play now. The European game is played on a larger surface with more players. I suggest that with a large surface area then both men and women could participate.

HUGO
Ridiculous, it is bad enough that Matilda Billings is-allowed to play. Her actions disrespect the decency of women.

DIRECTION
(women boo Hugo, men side with Hugo)

JOHN
Ladies, gentlemen, social debate should be left to the privacy of the households and only between a husband and wife. We should keep our focus on the matter at hand, Hookie.

ISOBEL
John, why are you so obsessed with that name? It is a bad influential word. Every child will play hookie from school, chores, church, meals and bedtime just to play Hookie.

DIRECTIONS
(all agree with Isobel, mumble, whisper, gesture their disapproval)

CONSTABLE
As a person sworn to uphold the law, I have difficulty as it is to track down delinquent children being absent from school. I do not need the extra burden of children not in school to play your inappropriate named game.

ISOBEL
And it will rub off on adults. John, every Sunday, I need-to constantly nag at you and the children to stop playing Shinny in the halls and get ready for church.

DIRECTIONS
(boys play through from entrance to exit, Ri`chard joins in to the delight of the sideline women)

ISOBEL
See John, the children are playing hookie from bedtime. (raise voice) Children, bedtime.

JOSEPH
John, I must agree with Isobel, Hookie is misleading, a corruptive name.

RI`CHARD
Hookie, Shinny, Shinty, Bandy, Hurly, Hurling, are all foreign names. We need a name that reflects a game unique to Canada, to Canadian people.

CONSTABLE
Hear, hear, I must agree.

RI`CHARD
If I say Ice Polo?

DIRECTIONS
(everyone boos, wave off suggestion, thumbs down, each person be different in response)

RI`CHARD
Exactly, everyone associates the name with the Americans. Not an original name, no deep traditional thought put into the name.

JOHN
Exactly Ri`chard, but I must clarify that Hookie is a name associated with the shape of the stick we use. In fact, most of the names mentioned must use a form of a stick with a curved end, or blade, or paddle shape. All make-contact with an object, a ball, disc, or a frozen road apple.

DIRECTIONS
(ladies squint at reference and inquire information from Isobel)

ISOBEL
For heaven's sake ladies, frozen horse poop, frozen road apples.

DIRECTIONS
(women blush)

JOHN
The stick hooks the disc or ball and is used to fling the object toward the goal, thus named the Hookie stick.

HUGO
I agree, and have been hooked repeatedly, (say respectfully) by warm loving in-laws. Master Henry, I would like to order one Hookie stick with a good curve and a one-foot long blade, (stamp foot out to show large foot) as-long-as my foot. I will hook Patrick Sherri.

JOHN

No, no, the Hookie stick should only be used to manipulate the disc, not be used as a weapon.

ISOBEL
Ladies and Gentlemen, there is now a double meaning for the word Hookie, thanks to John and Hugo. Children will play hookie to play Hookie with a Hookie stick to hook other hookie, Hookie players.

DISCRITION
(ladies, frown toward men, hands on hips, fingers shaming the men)

CONSTABLE
Now I will have to be breaking up hooligans fighting. My job is stressful enough. John, I do believe the majority of people here dislike the word Hockey.

ISOBEL
Aloysius O'Hera, your accent is lilting at times, though vowels in words that are close to consonants do sound harsh. (drag out word to express o vowels) Ho . . . okie.

CONSTABLE
(express first o as a vowel then the second o as a c as part of k consonant) Ho . . .ckey.

EVERYONE
Hooo . . . okie.

CONSTABLE
Irrelevant, the name is no good, won't work. There are thousands of Irish people about that have a problem with the bloody English language, so the word is banned from me vocabulary. No Hockey.

EVERYONE
Hoo . . okie.

CONSTABLE
(rap cane end on table as if a gavel) Mr. Ri`chard, I trust you will present a suitable name to distract us from the word . . .

EVERYONE
Hoo . . . kie.

DIRECTIONS

(Ri`chard slides quickly to centre with a flare of gaiety to distract the Constable from using the cane, women show a giddiness, Isobel moves a towel under the Constable's cane before it raps against the table)

RI`CHARD
Constable O.Hera, as I have mentioned earlier, the name of Canada's unique game should reflect Canadians and an originality in the name.

JOSEPH, F.W., W.F., HUGO
Which is?

RI`CHARD
Baggataway.

CONSTABLE
Bag a what?

RI`CHARD
Bag-gat-away.

JOSEPH
First Canadians play Baggataway, the French call it La`Crosse.

F.W.
I do not see the resemblance of La`Crosse and Shinny?

RI`CHARD
Oh contraire, every sport you have named from Shinny to Hurly to Shinty use sticks in games played on grass in the old country. This is Canada and First Canadians play year-round. The Mi`Kmaq are first Canadians, and they make the best sticks for our game on ice.

JOSEPH
Yes, they do. Now I do. I change my vote to Baggataway.

CONSTABLE
Now this is moving along nicely. Two votes for Hurly, two for Shinny, two for Bag-a-what-away, one for Bandy and one for that hook-stick name.

F.W.
I may have to change my selection.

W.F.
You have changed your mind three times. You are always indecisive.

ISOBEL
Mind your manners W.F., F.W. please take your time. Care for a sweet Canadian Butter Tart.

DIRECTIONS
(Isobel offers a plate of tarts with a broad smile)

F.W.
Thank you, no, I will savour one later. (pause) I am strongly in favour of Shinny.

W.F.
Are you sure . . . do you need more time to contemplate the facts?

ISOBEL
Do not hassle your brother W.F., F.W. has made up his mind. Constable add another vote for Shinny.

CONSTABLE
Three votes for Shinny, two for Hurly, one for Bag-a-what-away, one for Hockey, Hockey . . . Hockey. If you do not appreciate my pronunciation . . . too bad.

JOSEPH
This calls for an open vote, Gentlemen . . . those in favour of . . .

ISOBEL
(clear throat loudly and promptly stand, in front of the Constable) There are ladies present and we have intelligence and a voice with a right to vote.

CONSTABLE
Ladies and Gentlemen . . . those in favour of . . .

ISOBEL
A secret vote . . ., butter tarts gentlemen and ladies.

DIRECTIONS
(Isobel moves about with plate handing out butter tarts, John hands out pieces of paper and one pencil, all begin to mark votes, F.W. is last, boys play through as women dodge about and men use feet to play, Constable uses cane, the sound of the boys playing and the men and women keep the excitement up, John passes bowler hat around to collect ballets then stands by F.W. who is contemplating, slowly women become silent and stare at F.W., men begin

to stop, boys stop, house lights dim, howling winter wind builds)

END OF FIRST ACT

SECOND ACT

(Snow storm sound build, lights build, and boys begin to play out and exit. Slowly the sounds of laughter fade and the storm sounds fade.)

W.F.
F.W. are you changing your mind again?

F.W.
No . . . I am waiting for the pencil.

DIRECTIONS
(Isobel pulls pencil away from behind W.F.'s ear and hands it to F.W. who quickly marks down the name and puts paper into hat, John hands hat to the Constable)

CONSTABLE
(reach in, shuffle about and draw out, read the then shout out) Hockey . . .

DIRECTIONS
(mouths open attempting to say Hookie, Constable glares, all fall silent, as slips of paper are drawn out characters react in various ways suited to their characterizations)

CONSTABLE
Bag-a-what-away, Shinny, Shinny, Shinny. (build excitement) Shinny, Shinny, Shinny, Shinny. (pause, draw out last after searching) This must be F.W.'s vote. Shinny.

DIRECTIONS
(men talk accusingly, knowing that they all voted for Shinny except John and Ri`chard, women cheer)

CONSTABLE
(rap cane on table a few times, after moving towel to wipe lips) Canada's official game played on ice is to be known as Shinny. Now rules can be applied.

ISOBEL
Women must be allowed to play the game without bias.

JOHN
Isobel, that would be a matter for an organization of a league to decide. We are searching for rules of play. Remember we are about to play the Iron Works and rules of play are important at-the moment.

ISOBEL
My dear John, I will be playing in that game and yes rules must be agreed to, but who is going to enforce the rules upon the Iron Works.

DIRECTIONS
(heads turn to the Constable who is wiping his face after digesting another tart)

CONSTABLE
Seeing that I am unable to play the Rover position, I will be most suited to ring a hand bell when observing inappropriate play by the opposition.

JOSEPH
You must not be bias Aloysius, you must treat each side with equal scrutiny.

CONSTABLE
Master Henry, I shall and if need be, use a department whistle to halt play.

ISOBEL
Tradition has been the use of a hand-held school bell.

CONSTABLE
Those ruffians do not listen to a school bell, they do respect a constable's whistle.

JOHN
Rule one, six players per side.

JOSEPH
The disc should be a standard 3-inch diameter by 1-inch thick piece of oiled oak wood.

F.W.
The disc must not leave the surface of the ice.

HIGO
Plenty of hitting. (slam fist into palm) Body contact, especially on Patrick Sherri.

RI`CHARD
No fisticuffs, this face needs to stay unscarred for the ladies. (wink to women)

HUGO
Shoulders and good solid hip contact.

DIRECTIONS
(Hugo hips Ri`chard to the delight of Mrs. Smith, and the ohs from the ladies, Isobel is attempting to get a word in)

RI`CHARD
Okay, only shoulders and hips, no elbows.

HUGO
What about Patrick Sherri and his elbows? (begin to waltz with elbows up)

CONSTABLE
Rule number three approved, only hip and shoulder contact. Hugo, I will keep an eye on Patrick Sherri and that fighting hooligan, Donald Cheery.

ISOBEL
About rule number one, John mentioned number of players.

HUGO
Agreeable, eliminating Mrs. Matilda Billings from playing for the Iron Works. The widow Billings should not be playing. Seven players are too much, six is better.

W.F., F.W., John
Agreeable.

ISOBEL
Objection, seven players per side. I am the best Rover you have. The Constable is out with an injury.

JOSEPH
Mrs. Creighton, Ri`chard is-able to cover, if Hugo plays his position. Renaming the Cover Point and Point and calling them Defence-men makes perfect sense. It does give me a clear view with out a player directly in front of me.

HUGO
Agreed, having a Centre, two Forwards and two Defence-men is enough.

ISOBEL
Objection.

CONSTABLE
Rule number one deferred.

RI`CHARD
Thirty-minute segments with a fifteen-minute intermission for tea, and
interactions with my fans. (wave to women)

DIRECTIONS
(heads nod in uncertain manner, Constable sips tea and stretches out leg, picks
up pencil to mark down rules)

RI`CHARD
Change ends after intermission and change ends after each goal and play until
a tie is broken.

CONSTABLE
All in favour. (count nodding heads, be sure to count Isobel by an
acknowledged nod) Accepted, rule number four.

W.F.
Add to rule number two, face offs at centre ice should be fair, the way it is
done in Hurly.

DIRECTIONS
(while talking W.F. and F.W. grab sticks and a disc and demonstrate)

W.F.
Sticks on ice, lift and strike sticks over disc and repeat complete process three
times then play the disc.

RI`CHARD
May I. (take stick from F.W. and go through motion counting normal then
speeding up at end and cheat) One, two, three, onetwothree. (take disc away)

HUGO
Too complicated.

ISOBEL
Delays the game.

JOHN
Just reduce it to tapping sticks three times over the disc then play the disc.

CONSTABLE
Approved and added to rule number two.

JOSEPH
May I add a suggestion to rule number two. A ten-foot-wide goal is a bit much, especially with one less player to help defend the goal.

ISOBEL
We have not approved less players Master Henry.

JOSEPH
Whether or not a player is eliminated, I recommend an eight-foot-wide goal.

ISOBEL
In favour Master Henry, providing you endorse seven players.

DIRECTIONS
(Joseph looks about to see if anyone notices then nods head to Isobel, John paces out eight feet)

JOHN
Yes, ten feet is an extreme opening. Agreeable at eight feet.

CONSTABLE
(observe heads) So said, so agreed.

F.W.
What happens when Hugo takes out an opposing player now that hitting is allowed?

CONSTABLE
Once play commences there shall be no change of players. In the case of injury where a player is unable to continue to participate, a replacement must be allowed in for fair play.

W.F.
What if the player is faking and wants a fresh player to help boost the team?

CONSTABLE
I shall judge. (tap cane on wrapping of foot, wince) If the player cries out then the injury is valid. I accept rule number four.

94

DIRECTIONS
(all actors must be animated throughout, reacting to dialogue and participating in the social aspects of an evening visit, Isobel accepts stick from Ri`chard while he associates with women, Isobel plays with disc and is thinking until bumping into Hugo who does not move, Isobel begins to use stick on Hugo, Hugo reacts comically)

ISOBEL
The stick shall not be used to hook a player. (hook Hugo under arm) Nor for tripping. (place stick between Hugo's legs) Extensive slapping against shins not permitted. (slap stick against Hugo's shins) The poking of the stick not nice. (poke stick butt into soft belly and sides of Hugo) I would suggest that kicking also be banned. (draw leg back to kick) And no lifting stick over shoulders to clobber an opponent. (raise stick)

JOHN
Isobel . . . no need to demonstrate.

HUGO
(pull leg away) Please, a verbal description is enough. Constable, write down every word Mrs. Creightion said. I endorse rule number five.

RI`CHARD
I suggest that contact with the disc shall only be with the stick. No part of the body may be in contact with disc.

JOSEPH
Except for the Goalie, who uses the body to stop and deflect the disc.

RI`CHARD
That is acceptable, but the goalie must remain standing, no sitting, laying, crawling or kneeling, nor smothering. The disc must always be put back into play.

JOSEPH
Dignified play only. Rule number six Constable.

JOHN
We have forgotten about the stick. Since Master Henry has crafted a player's stick and a goalie stick, he should be trusted to set standards for sizes.

RI`CHAD
John, not agreeable. Each player crafts a personal stick to suit their style of play. Players do come in all sizes and talent.

JOHN
True Ri`chard, though the basic size should be adopted as is the disc. We cannot have each team selecting different size discs, then having sticks to suite the disc.

ISOBEL
Obviously, a disadvantage to visiting teams.

F.W.
Stick advantages will help us win if we keep ahead of the opposition.

JOSEPH
A standard height of 3 inches and 12 inches long for the blade then do anything else to enhance stick to suite the player.

DIRECTIONS
(Constable hesitates with pencil as Ri`chard and F.W. consider and accept with a nod)

CONSTABLE
So be it.

ISOBEL
Who shall govern the rules?

JOHN
A referee is a must.

CONSTABLE
Team captains must agree upon a referee and an umpire behind each goal. The referee having full authority over play and disagreements and all final decisions binding. And, everyone will bloody hell follow the rules or else.

ISOBEL
In this house I rule, and no profanity or abusive language shall be used as should also be applied to the rules of etiquette of fair play. Refined ladies and children may be present.

CONSTABLE
Most profound. Apologies dear Mrs. Creighton. Gentlemen and ladies, rule number seven shall govern the decent language used during playing of Shinny. All in agreement of adopting the combined rules of Shinny.

F.W., W.F., HUGO, RI`CHARD, JOSEPH, JOHN
Iye, Yes, agreed, Yes, Absolutely, Yes.

DIRECTIONS
(Constable continues to mark notes, women become silent and mumble to themselves, Constable begins to mouth words)

CONSTABLE
Being a representative of law, I confirm acceptance of said . . .

ISOBEL
(clear throat) Rule number one has not been verified by a unanimous vote. John . . . my dear, you were attempting to slip through a rule of six players, knowing well that I am a woman and playing the Rover position. Seven players per side. Ladies . . .

DIRECTION
(ladies agree and become aggressive, men begin to argue back, Constable rings table bell, no one reacts, frustrated, Constable blows police department whistle, everyone freezes)

CONSTABLE
Ladies and gentlemen, physical contact between . . . between . . . (gesture as if searching for a word)

ISOBEL
The sexes Aloysius, the male and female sexes. My god . . .women have been aware of the male anatomy since the birth of a male child, bathing and wiping butts from birth to old age.

DIRECTIONS
(W.F. and F.W.'s fiancées turn away with shyness, Mrs. Smith shakes a finger at Hugo in agreement with Isobel, W.F and F.W. and Joseph become bashful and turn away)

JOHN
Women are delicate, a man like Hugo will hurt a woman with just a bump.

ISOBEL
(instantly give a hip check to Hugo) Do you mean a woman cannot dish out equal contact?

HUGO
(stumble into Ri`chard) My dear woman . . . I . . . I . . . was off balance.

ISOBEL
Besides, there is no holding or grabbing mentioned in the rules so women can hip and shoulder check equally without sending men into a sexual frenzy.

RI`CHARD
I do not mind grabbing of innocent embracing.

DIRECTION
(Ri`chard approaches Isobel, Isobel frowns and places hands on hip, Ri`chard backs off)

CONSTABLE
Dear woman, since men and women are present, please refrain from innuendoes. This is not a debate of pros and cons of whether women and me should play Shinny together, rather it is a debate of requirement of six or seven players.

HUGO
A vote then.

CONSTABLE
All in favour of six players?

DIRECTIONS
(F.W., W.F. Hugo turn away from women and raise hands along with John and Joseph)

CONSTABLE
Five votes for six, those in favour of seven players?

DIRECTION
(all women raise hands, Ri`chard, hidden among the women raises his hand, Constable counts)

CONSTABLE
Five votes for seven . . . there are only four women among us, who raised two hands?

HUGO
Ri`chard . . . get away from my wife. You would like to have contact with women in a game. (grab Ri`chard and pull him back with facial anger)

CONSTABLE
Votes have been counted, thus a tie, thus I break the tie. (pause) Six it is.

98

DIRECTIONS
(men refrain from looking at women, women huff and mumble)

ISOBEL
Decided . . . fine, we will create our own league with our own rules and will challenge any male team to a game of skills. To make it easier for men to compete with women, no body contact what so ever.

JOHN
Dear, do not be like this.

HUGO
Mrs. Smith, do not partake, do not put such thoughts into your head.

JOHN
Such a game would not be suitable.

WOMEN
Chicken!

HUGO
Mrs. Smith, I am your husband.

WOMEN
(clucking sounds of chickens) Balk . . . balk . . . balk.

RI`CHARD
Balk . . . balk . . . balk. (move to join women)

HUGO
(reach out and choke Ri`chard) Chicken you say.

RI`CHARD
Ba . . . . lk!

DIRECTIONS
(women keep balking, Mrs. Smith begins to kick Hugo in the shins, Isobel hip checks Hugo, John wrestles with Isobel, W.F., F.W. cower to side, Joseph dances around the mayhem eager to jump in but never does, boys enter, walk about, shake heads then exit, Constable drinks tea then shakes bell then blows whistle, mayhem freezes)

CONSTABLE

A whistle is more effective than a bell, no, unsuitable, every constable in hearing range will respond then dilly-dally at the game and neglect their duties, and that would mean they are playing . . .

ALL
Hookie!

MRS. SMITH
Ba . . . lk, . . . Ba . . . lk, Ba . . . lk!

CONSTABLE
(blow whistle) Break it up. Do I need to call in reinforcements?

DIRECTIONS
(group disbands to opposite sides of the room)

ISOBEL
Ladies, all in favour of 'The Independent National Woman's League of Shinny'?

WOMEN
Yes, Yes, Yes.

JOHN
(frustrated) Gentlemen, all in favour of 'Canada's Royal Game of Hookie'?

MEN
Hookie, Hookie? (Shrug shoulders, shake heads no)

Hugo
We need a name that is stronger than the feminine name of Shinny.

MEN
(ponder)

CONSTABLE
Hockey, Hockey, Hockey!

MEN
(contemplate then nod yes as if a light of intelligence goes off in heads)

JOHN
Canada's Royal game of Hockey it is. Unless we register the name and publish the rules, no one will accept a unified game and rules.

ISOBEL

It will not last. Women will not be interested. Too mush hitting, no stress on skills. On the other hand, women will define the game with finesse. A bunch of hooligan men fighting over a Le-Rondelle has no appeal.

MRS. SMITH

May I explain the meaning of the French word Le-Rondelle being a disc. In reference to the object of the game, which has been transformed from various objects in different shapes from a round ball to frozen road apples, horse dung, a wooden disc, frozen cow patties can all be simplified to a single word from an old-world word being the name puck.

DIRECTIONS

(men linger to one side, women to opposite side, Constable continues to drink tea and eat tarts, boys play through as a simplistic rendition of the Hockey Night theme plays then leads into the 'Oh Canada anthem, stage goes dark)

THE END

Father
(Pa, Old Man, Dude, Dad, Donor)
by
Richard Mousseau
Copyright February 14, 2011

PLOT
Drama / Comedy
What if a man had fathered ten, twenty, thirty children?
How would ten, twenty, thirty children relate to a man that is their unknown birth father?
A man in his mid-thirties is told he has a disease that will eventually be terminal. As is Ed's character, life is what life is, and he does not bother to ask questions as to what the disease is, how it will become terminal, how long before father time is knocking on the door.
Ed decides that he should accept his fate and travel the world in a last effort to encompass life. He has a farm, no children, no wife, just a sister and brother in-law that farm the land and have a business that hires and jobs out pickers. Ed is not financially secure.
Through a pal, Haz, who handles all of his legal affairs and is his best friend, Ed lets Haz control his life. Haz suggests that getting laid should be an ongoing priority before death knocks down the door. Haz meets a female friend that has a friend that was ready to be artificially inseminated, but the facility burned down.

Haz makes an offhand remark that Ed could cut out the middle-man and the sperm bank and donate his sperm. This way the buyer would be seeing the man behind the donation. Besides Ed would not be around after kicking the bucket, so buyers would not need to worry about Ed intruding in their lives in the future. For Ed's caring cause he would enjoy the sex and be leaving a genetic part of himself behind to carry on in the jeans of ten, twenty, maybe thirty children.

So, deals are made, insemination in various ways, various women, various comical and dramatic situations, and payments are made. Haz handles legal matters, invests money, handles legal matters of the home and farm while Ed travels the world. Then Ed returns when in his late forties and not dead, seemingly in good health. Ed returns to find that all is well, farm is stable, sister and brother in-law working the farm. Because of Haz's investments, Ed is financially secure and stable. Haz is frazzled when Gwendolyn shows up, a first product of Ed's sperm donation. She is orphaned and has tracked down her birth father's name and location which leads her to Haz. Twelve-year-old Gwendolyn moves into the farm house and easily manipulates Haz into allowing her to stay and to help piece her existence together. Gwendolyn finds out about other possible children and insists that Haz help locate each and every one, a family of brothers and sisters she lacks.

This is where the story begins when Ed meets Gwendolyn and the many children, the many lives of each, troubles, and happy events, and the endless storied lives of all. Because of Gwendolyn, Ed reluctantly becomes involved in the lives of the children. Ed haphazardly learns to provide feelings, advice, affection and hard love. Each story segment relates to each child and how Ed is integrated into the child's affairs and the everyday events that a child has from a first crush, first date, first fight, new glasses, braces, girl problems, boy problems, all that Ed is unable to handle yet muddles through with comical success. Ed becomes friend, confidant, hated, loved and in ways becomes a father, pa, old man, dude, dad and donor.

CHARACTERS
Ed; Edmond Alcid Joseph Baptist
Haz; Hazelton Wentworth Bigg (friend of Ed)
Gwen; Gwendolyn Walls (daughter of Ed)
Grace; Grace Marie Baptist-Ramone (sister of Ed)
Jesús; Jesús Rodriguez Edward Ramone (husband of Grace)
Stella; Stella Boldrift (wife of Judge Rinhold)
Rinhold; Judge Rinhold Boldrift (husband of Stella)
Dr. R. Ginie; (doctor of Ed)
Jean; Jean Walls (mother of Gwen) (friend of Ed)
Betty; Betty Joe Snodgrass - McAlister (friend of Jean) (acquaintance of Haz)
Mother Rodriguez; (mother of Jesús)
Maria 7, Josephine 6, Carmen 5, (daughters of Grace and Jesús)

CHARACTER
ED
Edmond Alcid Joseph Baptist
Early thirties, progress to late forties, 185-195 pounds, average build, a worker, not afraid to try any type of job, has done all types.
Short greying hair, short to the skin type of beard also greying.
Not confrontational, easy going, accepting of life as is, lets troubles slide off.
A loner, shy, comical events happen around him but never slap-stick to him.
Owns farm house and farm, animals, rarely visits farm over the past years, an illness encouraged him to travel the world doing work that assisted others.
Of average intelligence, firm on commitments and of what is right and wrong.
Offers suggestions in little blurbs.
Has had relations but never commitments.

Character
Haz
Hazelton Wentworth Bigg
Early thirties, progress to late forties, 220 pounds, best friend of Ed.
Pleasantly chubby, always messed hair, well-kept beard, always dressed nice, lawyer.
Slapstick always happens to him.
Inteligent about the law but lacking knowledge about everything else.
Women like him, always several interested in him, dates and women cling but he is unable to commit.
Always has briefcase, but never seems to use it, always papers in hands, or left about, always has pens hidden in every pocket, when used never seems to remember to keep.
Handles all of Ed's legal affairs, but applications of carrying out affairs is a challenge, unable to handle, sometimes slapstick application, but in end all seems to work out.
Gwendolyn is his biggest nemesis, she rules and controls him, though in the end always lets him think it was his ideas and has solved problems.
A big kid at heart at times, unable sometimes to relate to adults in adult situations.

CHARACTER
Gwen
Gwendolyn Walls
(daughter of Ed and Jean)
Twelve years old, tomboyish when it applies, and a girl turning into a woman when it applies and before she wants it to, slender and tallish, blonde-ish brown hair, mostly worn with two pigtails to the side, intelligent beyond her years, neat and organised, always wants events to work properly.

Always the helpful person, regardless of obstacles, driving force behind story, likes people right from a first meeting, and hopes that everyone likes her.

If people resent her of have faults, she knows everything will get better.

Has had a lonely life, an only child, sick mother, child was caregiver, longs to have a big family now, and wants a big family of her own in the future.

Stubborn, clines to minute points, treasures the little stuff in life.

CHARACTER
Grace
Grace Marie Baptist-Ramone
(sister of Ed, wife of Jesús)

Mid-forties, married to Jesús Ramone, tomboyish as child, still is as an adult, works the farm machinery beside husband, three daughters.

Looks like Ed, facial similarities and mannerisms, slim, tallish, straight brown hair shoulder length, always happy, somewhat scatter-brained about knowledge, household and anything to do with ladies' auxiliaries, comfortable in labour world.

Usually calm until a crisis then peels off frantically.

Daughters are loved and doted over, mother in-law lives with them and cares for girls, girls are always well dressed, well mannered, heavily on the Latin influences of Grandmother Rodriguez.

CHARACTER
Jesús
Jesús Rodriguez Edward Ramone
(husband of Grace)

Husband of Grace, brother in-law of Ed, slightly shorter than wife, Latin American heritage and complexion, Canadian, no accent, perfect English, built for labour, inelegant enough to run farm and seasonal labourers, same age as Ed, they are pals.

Indulging in music, quiet at times, in discussions carries most of conversations, when wife is around, she dominates.

Short black hair, wares dressy work clothes suitable for labour and business, always has ideas for investments, no money for big ideas, yet their farm and labour business is successful.

CHARACTER
Stella Boldrift
(neighbour of Ed, wife of Judge)

Wife of Judge Rinhold Boldrift, late sixties, plump, not fat, lives next to farm, big spread of farm land that is not used for farmland, manicured fields and gardens just used to look at.

False smiles, always prim and proper, a busy-body, needs to know everything, wants to control everything, including the Judge, seems to know the law inside and out and forces the law to suit her, if it does not then it should bend to suit her.

Hair, make up and clothing stylish but two generations before current style.

Has binoculars of all kinds, hidden all over the place so that she can spy on neighbours,

drives own car, 1953 Hudson, obeys laws but drives according to her needs, others need to watch out for her actions, she thinks she has priority.

Happily married, behind closed doors, never in public, she is girlish with the Judge's advances and playful behind closed doors, snobbish debutante in public.

CHARACTER
Judge
Judge Rinhold Boldrift

(husband of Stella, friend of ED)

Husband of Stella, early seventies, career judge, honest and fair, yet his foil is wife Stella, seemingly frail but in good shape, enjoys the out of doors, fishing, hunting, hanging around the Baptist farm, hiding from Stella.

White hair, slightly hunched, five-ten, hides work clothes at the Baptist farm, hangs out with Jesús, hunting and fishing pal of Ed, invests in talk with Jesús, but Stella manages their finances, she gives him a weekly allowance, retired but still fills in as a judge, always gives free legal advice, always behind Stella's back.

Happily married, frisky at all times, with Stella behind closed doors, admonished for his conduct in public by Stella.

Always quoting statements but never finishes quote.

CHARACTER
DR. R. Ginie
(Ed's Doctor)

Female, specialist, Dr. Rose Ginie, Plump, happy, fifty-ish.

CHARACTER
Impersonator of Dr. R. Ginie
Man, late fifties, slight off-hand accent, of no known origin, compulsive liar, fabricates stories, is convincing, full of knowledge when expressing knowledge, falters when delivering false statements, likes to impersonate doctors, lawyers, detectives, business men, even the men of trades, plumbers, carpenters.

CHARACTER
Jean Walls
(mother of Gwen)

Full form woman, well proportioned, brownish hair, early thirties, well adjusted, prudish, does not try to be funny, yet funny events happen to her.

CHARACTER
Betty Joe Snodgrass - McAlister
(friend of Jean)

CHARACTER
Mother Rodriguez
(mother of Jesús)

INTRODUCTION Scene
Blurry scene of ocean and town from a distance.
Music builds, a lilting Celtic seafaring music, a soothing melody.
Scene clears, showing early morning of a waking town and busy fishing docks.
Camera begins to zoom in on Ed walking down a gang plank onto dock, common dock activities of fishing industry.
Ed is dressed in seafaring garb, Canadian Toque, felt coat, rubber boots, duffle bag.
Camera frames in on Ed, medium shot, at side of frame throughout is Haz, well dressed, somewhat plump, standing still, a lawyer with a briefcase at side and an abundance of legal papers in hand, hair is messed, face drawn and tired, he is constantly staring, bewildered.
Ed has a pleasing face, short cropped beard, a slight amused, innocent smile on face, he plops down duffle bag.
Title flashes onto screen in bold letters, first, (Pa), music is hard, different genre mingles with melody, then, (Dude) appears, (Old Man), (Dad), (Donor), and each time different music burts in interrupting and pouncing onto the melody, music clashes when title, (Father) overlaps other titles, then silence and melody carries on lilting.
Scene is frozen and framed by a picture frame.

STORY
After opening scene, camera shows wide angle of dock with Haz to one side and Ed standing beside duffle bag, mellow music playing, Ed looking skyward, shaking sea legs, getting use to try land, Haz slowly begins to approach, leaves brief case behind.

Haz
Ed, Ed, man where have you been?

Ed
At . . . (point to ship and ocean)

106

Haz
Man, you're supposed to be dead by now!

Ed
Not yet . . .!

Haz
(shake head, show papers)
Don't matter, you can die later. Right now, you got big troubles, big . . . lots
. . . in deep barn yard shit. Up to your (indicate neck), you're gonna drown in
shit . . . then you're gonna be dead finally. Then I'll be finished with your
legal matters.

Ed
(no worries on facial expression, pleased happy smile)
Good to see you Hazel.
(give hardy slap to Haz's shoulder)

Haz
(teary eyed, hugs Ed, drops papers)

Ed
I take it . . . because I am not dead . . . or that you messed up my legal affairs.
(shake off extended hug, pick up duffle bag and begin to walk towards car)

Haz
(pick up papers)
It ain't me Ed, I did everything you asked of me, and way more. It's all here
in these papers. No loop holes. Man, I've made your affairs airtight. No
lawyer could break in . . . because . . .

Ed
(standing at car, attempting to open locked door)
Hazel . . . you forgot your briefcase?

Haz
(looking over papers at ground)

Ed
Over there.
(point to briefcase)

Haz
Because you're supposed to be dead. Why can't you do what you said . . . and

die when you said you would die, back then, years ago. Now I Have to deal with you . . . your child . . . kid . . . daughter!

(camera slowly begins to spin around car, slowly gathering speed as Ed and Haz talk and as Ed reacts to Haz's body gestures)

Haz
She . . . she . . . this kid is at the farm, living there . . . telling me what to do . . . ordering me around! (become frustrated, red faced, Bloating)

Ed
(smile fading, then slowly returns, deep thoughts, not listening to Haz)

Haz
This wasn't supposed to happen. I don't need a kid telling me what to do. She's gonna open up a big can of worms. I'm supposed to welcome you home in a box, dead as a door nail. Why can't you kick the bucket like other people, be dead and stay dead!

Direction
(camera spins up above until a blur then spins down over the farm, camera stops on full view of Gwen standing on porch, happily smiling she begins sweeping porch, Stella enters scene walking on tip toes, avoiding stepping into any animal droppings)

Stella
Young lady, over here.
(come out from behind bushes)
Who are you and what are you doing on this porch, in this house, on these premises?

Gwen
(search for mysterious voice, lock on Stella, smile happily)
Who may I ask is asking?

Stella
(annoyed, step in chicken droppings, chicken squawks at feet)
I am asking, Mrs Judge Boldrift, Stella! Quit sweeping and answer me.

Gwen
Well, Miss Judge . . .

Stella
No, no, No, Judge is my husband.

108

Gwen
Mrs. Stella.

Stella
No, No, No, . . . No! The proper introduction of a person's name is to give last name first, with an indication of marital association preceding the last given first, then the first name given last.

Gwen
Oh, perfectly clear Mrs. Stella Boldrift, wife of Mr. Judge Boldrift.

Stella
Yes, (flustered) No, Judge is not my husband's name.

Gwen
No? . . ., then you should not give out your boyfriend's name by mistake. (frown as if scolding Stella)

Stella
Child, do not be obstinate. I do not have a boyfriend. Mr. Rinhold Boldrift is my husband, and he is a well renown Judge, thirty years on the bench.

Gwen
Miss Stella . . . (pause, wait to gain Stella's attention) then the proper introduction should have been, last name first proceeded by marital status associating, proceeded by husband's occupation then complete, followed lastly by person's first name. Thus Mrs. Judge Rinhold Boldrift, Stella. Is there a numerical lineage as to first, second, third? Are you Mrs. Judge Rinhold Boldrift the second, Stella?

Stella
Young lady, I am asking the questions under the authority that I am married to a judge.
(scrape shoe on grass before stepping onto walkway and puffing out chest)
Who are you and why are you here?

Gwen
(stand at attention with broom over shoulder, a soldier's stance, recite as would a soldier in ranks) My name is Miss Gwendolyn Walls. No middle name. Daughter of Jean, deceased, unknown birth father until now. I am the daughter of Edmond Baptist. I am living here and continuing my search for my father.

Stella
(waver on unsteady feet, blurt out)
Impossible!?

Direction
(sound of car door closing, Grace and Jesús exit car, kiss daughters in car, Mother Rodriguez fusses in driver's seat, waves and peels away, Grace, dressed in work clothes, ready for field work, Jesús shuffles through papers, they wave and approach Gwen and Stella)

Grace
Hi, Gwen, you've met Mrs. Boldrift, I see. The Judge's wife?
(puzzled, knowing what has occurred)
And Stella has asked you questions. Stella . . . Stella . . .
(reach to stabilize a weaving woman)

Jesús
Mrs. Boldrift, breath, breath, don't faint.
(struggle to hold her steady)

Stella
Impossible . . . Edmond has been missing for over ten . . . eleven years.
(Waver then gain some strength and stare at Gwen)
How old are you? Eight . . . nine? Ed is presumed Dead.

Gwen
(hands grip broom, smile on face shrivels, but stand firm)

Direction
(camera quickly spins around scene and draws up into blurred sky, camera spins down over city and street, slowly levels off at street level, all motion is in reverse, slow motion, Ed passes backwards with newspaper under arm, headline date is clear showing thirteen years earlier than present story line, camera picks up Ed, hair a bit longer, beard not as grey, fitter, Ed is followed by camera as he retraces steps backwards into medical building, speed picks up, action picks up through lobby, elevator, lobby, office, desk, doctor's office, seat, silent banter between doctor and Ed, camera slows to a stop, action stops, slowly movement advances and dialogue clears)

Impersonator / Doctor
(clear throat, clasp hands together, lean forward, a bearer of bad news, agonize, start, stop, struggle for words then just blurt words out)
You should be dead. I don't know why you're not. Maybe months, days, drop dead outside my office door. No don't do that, wait until you get to the street.

No need to distress my patients in the waiting room.

Ed
Excuse Me?
(lean forward with concern)
It was just a routine scope down the throat and up the wazoo. What did you find?

Impersonator / Doctor
In your condition you shouldn't be worrying about what it is, how it got there, how it is going to eat you to death. It is there. Death is inevitable. Forget about it, enjoy life, eat, drink, be merry, get laid, as much as possible, travel, see the world.

Ed
(become anxious)
You said I could drop dead outside your office door?

Impersonator / Doctor
I exaggerate at times. The importance of the matter is to live life to the fullest.
(sell like a used car salesman)

Ed
What about treatments?

Impersonator / Doctor
A waste of time. The medicine is worse than the disease.

Ed
You haven't told me what the disease is?

Impersonator / Doctor
The less you know the better, no need to worry about a long drawn out Latin name for a disease that will take a day to explain.

Ed
(slump back into chair, depressed)
What do I do?

Impersonator / Doctor
(point to name plate on desk facing Ed)
What does that say, right there.

Ed

Dr. R. Ginie, internal medicine, GP, IM, PHD, RH, MEGOOD.

Impersonator / Doctor
All of those letters there just mean I know what the hell I am talking about.
(rise, fold arms and stare at Ed over glasses, go to Ed, lift him out of chair)
As your Doctor, let me ask you. Do you feel fine?

Ed
Yes . . . I was before I entered this office.

Impersonator / Doctor
Eating well, sleeping well, strength good, bowel movements good, still have
your hair, eyesight good, no need for manipulative sexual arousal drugs?

Ed
(nod side to side, up and down, mumble)
No . . . No drugs, yes, no need for sex drugs!

Impersonator / Doctor
Getting plenty of sex?

Ed
(shake head, roll eyes)
A little off my game lately.

Impersonator / Doctor
Well then, take my advice. Put today behind, live life to the fullest, go forth
and sow . . . practice safe sex. Sexual disease will kill you. Not a pretty way
to go.
(Escort Ed to door)
There are a thousand ways to die before this disease kills you, so live each
moment as ifyour last.
(push Ed out of door)

Direction
(impostor fold arms and lean back against door, another internal door opens,
and the real Dr. Rose Ginie enters, looks about room, places hands on hips
and frowns at impostor, impostor shakes head in disappointment)

Direction
(camera watches Ed slowly turn to face closed door, reads names on door, Dr.
R. B. Ginie, Dr. R. A. Ginie and an endless attachment of monikers at the end
of names, Ed turns to patients sitting in waiting room, eyes connect to people)

Ed
(whisper)
The fancier monikers a doctor has at the end of their name, the more they know. These guys must be geniuses.

People
(begin to nod in agreement, various expressions)

Direction
(camera backs away as if attached to Ed's back, camera picks up all aspects of life unfolding on the street, good, bad, happy, sad, once Ed begins walking camera picks up headlines on paper being carried by a person walking by justifying the beginning when the scene was in reverse, camera follows Ed, who seems to be talking to self in thoughts, hand gestures, Ed passes a bar without seeing it, stops, backs up and enters bar, an afternoon happy hour business, Ed sits at bar, all types of people in bar)

Bartender
Good day sir, your pleasure today?

Ed
(work nervous hands together)
The strongest whisky you have, no mix, a triple.

Bartender
Straight.

Ed
(pause, questioning)
Yes, I am . . . is this a . . .

Bartender
No sir, you will have a whisky straight.

Ed
(nod)
Yes, yes, a whisky straight, thanks.

Direction
(bartender pours a triple shot, makes change from a bill Ed places on the bar, watches Ed stare at glass from all angles, turns, leaves, Ed inspects whisky and of the people in the bar, bartender returns, puts both hands on bar and stares at Ed and full drink)

Ed
May I use a bar phone, for a local call.

Bartender
Sure, a call to AA?

Ed
No, no, I didn't drive into town. Truck works fine, it's out at the farm.

Bartender
(shake head slowly from side to side)
Let me know when you would like a refill?

Ed
Yes, thanks.
(dial ancient black phone)
Hello, Hazel, I'm at a bar.

Direction
(sound of phone being dropped and picked up, camera jumps to Haz's law office, zooms in through door, Haz fumbling with phone and a finger indicating a moment to elderly clients)

Haz
A bar. What are you doing in a bar? What do you mean having a whisky? Ed, Ed, listen, you don't drink. You do not know how to drink. Drown what sorrows? I should be drowning my sorrows right now. I have two clients that have won a lottery and speak very little English. They don't want their kids involved. They think the kids will take the money and put them in an old folk's home. They're haggling about my fee. They say I charge too much. Ed, I need a drink. Don't drink that whisky. Where are you. I'm on my way.

Direction
(camera exits with Haz, turn back to watch the old couple gesturing as if to say Haz is nuts, useless, they sit back and argue between themselves)

Direction
(Haz bursts into bar, panting, out of breath, searches for Ed, spots Ed at bar, sitting, leaning, inspecting whisky glass, sniffing it, Haz dances through crowd, reaches bar, grabs whisky and downs it, places glass on bar in front of Ed, Ed does not move, Haz swallows, gasps, fights off burning sensation, bartender stops after double take, inspects empty glass)

Ed

(point at glass)
Another please.

Bartender
Yes sir.
(quickly fill glass, whisper to self)
It is about time.
(quickly make change, leave)

Ed
Life is so . . . life is like a shot of whisky, just enough for a taste then someone else enjoys the rewards of my labour.

Haz
Ed, you don't drink, why start now, besides, whisky burns the throat, reminding you how bitter life can be.
(down drink)

Direction
(bartender quickly returns, pours, makes change, leaves, Haz fights the taste and burn)

Haz
Why are you in a bar? Look about, only people with problems are in bars drinking their troubles away or trying to pick up a wo . . . wo . . . woman. I'm a lawyer with tension and no wo . . . wo . . . woman. I should be in a bar drinking.
(down drink)

Direction
(bartender arrives before glass hits the bar, one hand pours the other makes change)

Ed
Hazel, I've been to see a specialist, my doctor sent me to a internal medicine specialist. He said to live life, sow my seeds, but practice safe sex.

Haz
That sounds like good advice to me. My doctor says to lose weight, change careers. I'm too tense. I drink.
(sip drink)

Direction

(bartender advances then stops)

Ed
He said this after saying that I'm dying, sooner rather than later. So, I need a drink.

Bartender
(rush over)
Another glass sir, whisky straight.

Haz
He doesn't drink, bring him a tall glass of Canada Dry, iceberg ice.

Bartender
(disappointed)
Yes sir, Canada Dry over iceberg.

Haz
(sip drink, feeling loose, tear up, stroke hand over shoulder, head and attempt to hug Ed)
I'll miss you.

Ed
I ain`t gone yet. The Doctor didn't say when, just stressed getting laid as much as possible before I go.

Haz
Did you happen to tell the Doc that you ain`t having much luck in the getting laid department now. Dying ani`t gonna help improve your odds. You ain`t a player.

Ed
Yeah, women don't want a good man.
(sip drink through straw)

Direction
(Haz winks at girl, sip whisky with pinky extended, girl frowns, guzzles beer and walks on)

Haz
You need an angle, something to make women feel sorry for you, and beg you to ravish them.

Ed

I'm dying, maybe I should whimper and shuffle about.

Haz
No man, women don't like whoopsie men, and if you shuffle about, they'll think you'll give then your sickness. No, what we need is a drawing card, indicating something that they want from you. Maybe I'll get the overflow. (sip whisky) A drawing card. Man think, think. (tap temple with finger)

Direction
(two women walk by, see Haz's actions and keep going by, annoyed look on faces, in background is TV blurbs of news of closure of health clinic)

Direction
(scene of building on fire, smoke billows out of medical centre, camera focusses on Jean emerging in flimsy medical gown, carrying clothes, sees camera, hides face and tries to keep gown closed at back, tries to avoid camera, cameraman and reporter follow)

Announcer
Major fire in down town area, no injuries reported. We go live to channel 3 reporter, Susan Peel.

Reporter
Thankfully no one was injured.

Direction
(camera pans past reporter to get glimpse of Jean entering car, the bare buttocks of woman moons camera, reported steps into camera focus)

Reporter
No one was injured in this hour-long fire, but there are plenty of innocent victims that will never have a life. I am talking about the sperm and embryos held in the fertility bank. Potential donors and infertile couples wishing to have children are the victims also. The bank has failed.

Direction
(fire engine drowns out reporter, camera slips past reporter to focus in on Jean in the car, Betty enters the passenger side)

Betty
Jean, are you okay? (concern, brush hair from Jean's face)

Jean
Hell no, where's a dame firefighter with a blanket when you need it. My ass

117

is bouncing in the wind for all to see.

Direction
(Flash to bar, all see the TV clip of Jean mooning the crowd and camera, bar crowd sees except Ed and Haz, both hunched over their drinks, flash back to car)

Betty
What happened in there? Everyone was out and I waited for you. Where were you?

Jean
Spread eagle on the table waiting to be inseminated. The Doctor is standing there with the turkey baster and the fire alarm goes off.

Direction
(flash to examination room and to doctor holding long tube for insemination)

Doctor
This sample has been in dry ice for preservation. It has been warmed up a bit, but you may feel a slight chill and a bit of pressure. In and out and done, not like sex at all. Shall we begin?

Jean
Go for it.

Direction
(nurse adjusts covering over Jean's raised legs, doctor slowly lowers, and the turkey baster is last to fall below covering, then fire alarm sounds, doctor jumps up)

Doctor
Fire, Fire!!
(nervous, hold baster in air) Everybody to the fire exit.

Jean
Wait, wait, you said in and out, quick, done, pregnant. Do it, there's plenty of time.

Doctor
No, no, definitely no time. In and out quickly, but you must lay with legs up for twenty minutes. No time, there is a fire.

Jean

118

(stick leg out to side to prevent doctor from leaving)
I paid plenty of money for this quickie, so make it quick. I'll squeeze my legs together after so that the little hurrying tad poles don't escape. In and out quickly, job done.

Doctor
No, no, no, too dangerous. There is a fire and the whole building may go poof. (step to side when Jean's leg moves, push past to door holding the turkey baster high)

Jean
Leave the turkey baster with me, I'll perform my own quickie.
(reach out after escaping doctor, latch onto his arm)

Direction
(interior of car, Betty's mouth is a gape)

Jean
A thousand dollars a shot to create a possible life. A quickie he said, and the jerk runs away at the first sound of an alarm.

Betty
The building is engulfed. You were the last one out.

Jean
And the building is still standing, plenty of time for an in and out quickie.

Direction
(reflections of building collapsing is exposed in the rear-view and side mirrors)

Jean
See, ten minutes it took for the building to collapse. I could have been inseminated and laying in the back seat with my legs against the roof while a tad-pole and egg create a miracle.

Betty
There are other clinics and other options.

Jean
It takes thousands of dollars that I don't have, and the time I don't have. I am past my prime.

Betty

Jean . . .
(put a comforting hand on Jean's shoulder, comfort her)
there are always options.

Direction
(flash to bar, Haz sips drink and eyes catch news and hears the news report)

Reporter
Having only one clinic serving the greater metropolis, many women will not
have the option of artificial insemination, in vitro plantation nor selection of
available sperm housed in liquid nitrogen. There will be an urgent call for
sperm donors to fill the bank to its previous levels. So, listeners, if you are a
healthy male willing to donate your sperm for a future worthy cause, to assist
women to become pregnant, contact the number at the bottom of the screen.

Direction
(camera pans across the bystanders watching the fire and focusses in on the
Doctor holding the turkey baster in front, as if a candle burning brightly as a
symbol, Haz's eyes widen, he downs the drink, sucks in air and smiles)

Haz
That's what most women want to be, single, motivated and successful in the
business world. And they want children without a man hanging around the
house. They want it all, but without a man to deliver the goods, they're out of
luck. We give then what they want . . . for a price.

Ed
What! You're going to pimp me out?

Haz
No . . . that's illegal.
(think as you talk, think as you sip)
We provide them with a commodity the old fashion way. They get the seeds
for pregnancy and you get the pleasure and they in turn invest funds into your
pilgrimage around the world before you kick the bucket.

Ed
I don't know, this is all too much, too quick. You, the Doctor telling me what
I should do. It's just too much.
(stare at glass, twirl straw)

Haz
When was the last time you got lucky, snagged a quickie, romped in the hay,
made the truck bounce, got laid? (look Ed over, shake head in disappointment)

You need to get your mind off this dying agenda.

Direction
(TV in bar shows recap of woman's butt entering car, Jean and betty enter bar, Betty has blanket covering Jean, they head to woman's washroom, Betty pushes Jean in then pants and leans on the door frame, all of the bar patrons are staring from TV to woman)

Betty
(shake head knowingly) Yes, yes, that's her. (see TV segment) Give her a break, the clinic went up in flames and she didn't get inseminated. I need a drink. (Go to end of bar, sit, order two glasses of wine)

Direction
(Haz continues to think, make notes on pad, at same time begin to eye surroundings, notice Betty, takes a double take, recognises Betty, slides along bar toward her)

Haz
Betty Joe Snodgrass, you are looking fine, high school shape still impeccable. (hit on woman, make eye contact, take hand and pat it until feeling a wedding ring)

Betty
Hazelton Wentworth Bigg, yes I'm married, happily and not interested in an affair with you. And it is now Betty Joe McAlister. Brian J. McAlister is my Husband.

Haz
The chief of police?
(remove hand quickly, place hers on bar and pat it)
The second glass for the chief?

Betty
No, so relax Haz. How have you been?

Haz
Good, good, you? The glass is for a female, single, attractive friend?

Betty
Matter of fact yes, but you are definitely not her type.

Haz
(shake head)

Women need to get to know the inner me.

Betty
I know the inner you, since grade one you haven't changed.

Haz
Well, well, forget me. Why I'm asking is because of my friend. (point to Ed at bar, begin with sad face but somewhat sincere) He is not long for this mortal world and could go at any moment, a matter of . . .. The doctor just told him to go and live life each day, each dwindling minute. (lay it on thick then hit the line) He needs to get laid one last time.

Betty
Coincidence!

Haz
(look as if pleading, then perk up)
What, What!?

Betty
My friend, Jean has been trying to get laid, technically as in medically speaking for the past year.

Haz
(perk up, plan thoughts in mind, talk to Betty and self at same time)
Talk fast, we need to make events happen. Ed was just diagnosed today, terminal!

Betty
(talk to Haz and self at same time)
Jean, single, no prospects, wants a child.

Haz
Ed, still healthy and prosperous in the mechanical area.
(indicate groin area)

Betty
Jean, middle management, on the climb, no time for men.

Haz
Ed, won't be around long, will permanently stay out of picture.

Betty
Jean spent a fortune at a fertility clinic that just went up in smoke.

(point to TV)

Haz
(see butt of Jean on TV, and fire and Betty at car)
Ed mostly wants to offer his sperm, maybe a little enjoyment the old fashion way. A little cash to tide him over his dwindling days.

Betty
It will be a long shot to get them together.

Haz
We have to try for their sake.

Betty
A thousand dollars . . . for impregnation.

Haz
(startled by the offer, you were thinking more)
I'll draw up the legalities.

Betty
Deal.
(stick out hand)

Haz
Deal.
(sake hand manly, down drink)

Betty
(down half of glass of wine, see Jean coming out of washroom)
Beat it, go talk to your client. I need to talk to mine.

Direction
(Jean heads to bar, plops on seat, dejected)

Jean
Wine, you ordered wine. I can't drink, I'm trying to get pregnant. Not anymore! (point to TV) Hell. (down wine, motion to bartender) Something to take a bite out of reality. Tequila.

Direction
(bartender pour shot, Jean downs it, he pours another while Jean breaths in air)

Betty
Jean, . . . Jean.
(lean in seriously)

Jean
(pull back concerned)
What? What's with you? I know that look, and every time you're serious, I
become the subject of a prank, a set up that goes bad. The baby sitter of ten
kids while so-called friends go on vacation. A test dummy for some new kind
of makeup.

Betty
Jean . . . not this time, I promise. I was just wondering, thinking of your plight.
Have you ever thought of getting knocked up the old fashion way? Some nice
guy you like, maybe a gay guy, then there is no emotion involved.

Jean
I can't trick a guy. I would have to tell him. And, I am looking for specific
traits to be passed down to the baby. There is not a guy out there with those
traits. I tried the dating, visiting the parents, having a drawer at his place . . .
and the results . . . I'm still single.

Betty
Maybe you need to lower your standards.

Jean
I did, I went to a fertility clinic. No passion, no sex, just cold instruments and
a doctor that thinks he's a comedian.

Betty
What if, just a thought, off the top of my head. I know a guy who knows a
guy that is willing to donate his sperm. No attachment, no love, a bit of cash,
no long-term commitment, will never show up again in your life, is available
right now, just a quick old fashion wham-bam-thank-you-Mam and it's over.

Jean
Go back a bit . . . to a bit of cash. What are we talking about here?
(look interested)

Betty
If the price is right, you'll do it?

Jean
No! I'm not going to wham-bam-thank-you-Mam cold turkey with a stranger?

124

Betty
You were considering it, with a turkey baster, and you were just thinking it now if the price is right.

Jean
(nod almost yes then shake head no)

Betty
Then drink lots so you become easy, loose your inhibitions. Drink to the point that you can't remember. An easy night. Maybe knocked up in the morning, hung over and puking. A good experience of what morning sickness will be like.

Jean
There's this whole health issue. And the bit of cash that you didn't say the amount is.

Betty
Way cheaper than the clinic. I'll even cover the cost, you can pay me back later.

Jean
(nod again as if accepting, gulp tequila, indicate another, shake head no)

Betty
I can vouch for the guy who can vouch for the guy and I vouch for you for the guy who vouches to the guy in question. All hypothetical until you say yes.

Jean
You know a guy who knows a guy? What kind of deal did you make?
(start to look around bar)

Betty
Don't look, be cool. My guy is dealing with his guy.

Direction
(bartender pours another tequila, leans into the conversation, thinking, moves to end of bar, pours Haz another drink)

Haz
Look Ed, all men want to leave a part of themselves to carry on. Our species need to perpetuate. Have your jeans carry on from generation to generation? Just think, maybe doctors, financial wizards, inventors, jet pilots, boys, girls

all a part of you. Just think of the diversity, their mothers' a smorgasbord of beauty, talent, brains.

Ed
Smorgasbord? You've been watching the food channel and national geographic channel again at the same time.

Haz
What if, I know a woman who knows a woman that wants to get knocked up in a hurry. I can arrange it right now, make the deal, strictly cash, in and out, pok'er, leave a deposit, all done in ten minutes tops. I've got a contact working a deal right now.

Ed
Life isn't a porn story. I can't just randomly . . . you-know-what to a woman.

Haz
Ed, she's desperate, and you can't waste a moment of your limited life. She's here now, in the bar, I've brokered a deal and my contact is brokering a deal at her end.

Direction
(pan to women)

Betty
This guy I know is a lawyer, he can guarantee delivery and all legalities. No loose ends. Say the word and I can seal a deal right now. Just give me the word.

Direction
(pan to men)

Haz
Give me a yes.

Ed
(grin an interesting maybe, look over drinking glass at bar mirror reflecting people behind) It's a bit selfish on my part. It is a males' urge to . . .

Haz
Copulate . . . as often as possible!

Direction
(black out, scene change, present time, sounds of morning, Grace, Jesús, girls

126

giggling, Jesús speaking love words in Spanish, camera is dark, full scene is revealed when bed cover is thrown off, Grace is kissing Jesús, he has arms out welcoming daughters, a burst of girls climb in bed and kiss father, excitement erupts between all, Grace plops beside Jesús)

Grace
(panting)
Their your girls and they love you. I only carried them around for nine months each, that is twenty-seven months, that's two years and three months of not seeing my toes. (sigh, fake rejection) No one loves me.

Direction
(girls leap off Jesús and smother Grace with kisses, Jesús escapes)

Grace
Jesús, the north field needs to be ploughed today and the water system needs to be moved.

Jesús
I'll have the guys move it. The tractor is fixed, check the oil and don't break it this time.

Grace
It wasn't my fault, I didn't plant that rock in the middle of the field. (scream with laughter)

Direction
(girls tickle Grace, Jesús smiles from bathroom door, closes it and the sound of locking is heard, scene change, camera pulls out of house and skims across town towards field, traffic and peoples' action is fast, sun rising to show time lapse, camera pulls to a stop on Gwen's face)

Gwen
(sad face, almost to tears, firm up, be bold)
He is missing. They said so.
(Point to Grace and Jesús)
And the lawyer representing the legal affairs of Edmond Alcid Joseph Baptist is looking for him at this very moment.

Stella
That buffoon, Hazelton Bigg could not find a courthouse unless his mother leads him there by the hand.

Gwen

He is very competent. He has provided me information and brought me here to my aunt Grace and Uncle Jesús.

Stella
He is a stool pigeon, he could not keep a secret . . .

Gwen
He is an honest man.
(point broom at Stella)

Grace
Mrs. Boldrift, please . . .

Jesús
Please calm yourself, you look a little faint.

Stella
I don't need the hired help telling me what to do.

Grace
Mrs. Boldrift, Jesús is my husband. He is not the hired help.

Stella
(ignore Grace, struggle to stand)
This child is making me weary. I know what goes on around here.

Jesús
Yes, you do.

Stella
(glance angrily at Jesús)
This child should be told the truth. Any man that has been missing for seven years can be declared legally dead. I have not received one fact of information that would prove that Edmond is indeed alive.

Grace
None of us have, but having hope that Ed is alive makes us feel good, keeps us going, reaching for a miracle.

Stella
Hog wash. Don't kid yourself and don't pass that onto this child. What proof do we have that this . . . child is his child? Edmond was not seeing anyone, no one decent, never brought them home. This child's mother could have been a hussy, a gold digger.

Grace
Mrs. Boldrift . . . Stella, you have gone too far. Jean Walls was not a hussy.

Stella
Jean Walls, that scrawny little kid that use to tag around Edmond when he was seven?

Grace
Yes.

Stella
Makes no difference, never liked the child, too tomboyish, no refinement in that girl.

Gwen
(face growing angrily, lift broom, ready to strike)
Take that back, my mom was the best mom in the world, the best forward in the women's hockey league.

Grace
Gwen, Gwen. (hold up hand to stop the broom from striking, whisper) Mrs. Boldrift is elderly.

Stella
Elderly? I am right here. I can hear you clearly.

Directions
(camera focuses on Stella, in background the judge is seen sneaking past, dressed in farm clothes)

Stella
Judge, why are you sneaking past, (see judge's reflection in house window) and why are you dressed in . . . in . . . common work clothes? (do not turn around)

Directions
(Grace and Jesús meet Stella's eyes, Gwen stares past to see judge frozen in step)

Stella
We will discuss your discussing choice of clothing later. Get over here and preside over matters at hand.

Judge
(crumble emotionally)
Yes Dear.
(wave apologetically to Gwen, wink at girl)

Stella
(stare down at a slightly shorter man)
Judge, tell these people that a missing man can be legally declared dead after
seven years? Speak up.

Judge
(shrug shoulders, nod in agreement, eyes bounce from person to person)
It is true that family members can petition the court to declare a person legally
dead after seven years.

Stella
See, I just said that.
(cast eyes to all)

Directions
(Haz's car pulls up, Haz sticks head out of window)

Judge
But, I say this with the utmost conviction. Edmond Baptist is alive and well.

Stella
See! (Realize statement) What do you mean?

Directions
(camera jumps from face to face, Judge, Grace, Jesús, heads turn to car and
smile, Stella looks from face to face then to car, shade eyes, peer questionably
at passenger side, camera focusses on Gwen, she grips broom in shaking hand,
mouth drops, eyes water as they focus on car as Ed exits the car, Gwen slowly
backs up until pressed against door, Grace, Jesús, Judge all advance to greet
Ed, Stella stays put, discuss on face, Haz and Ed advance to house, pause at
Stella)

Ed
(polite, yet condescending) Good day Mrs. Boldrift, I trust you are well . . . I
am.
(smile, walk past, stop at foot of porch)

Haz
(stand in front of Stella, rise on tip-toes to look down on Stella) What!!

130

Disappointed. Last to Know?

Directions
(Stella's bewildered grin turns to anger, rise on toes and stare down on Haz, Haz withers and backs down, scurries to follow Ed, Ed and Haz step up on porch)

Haz
(clear chocked up throat) Ed, may I introduce you to Gwen, daughter of Jean and, I think that technically and according to Judge Boldrift, legally your daughter too. (gesture with arms for Ed and Gwen to greet each other) Gwen, Ed. (when nothing happens back away) Well, when you feel comfortable. (join others)

Directions
(Haz passes Stella, side steps when near, uses hand to block view of Stella, Stella grins, frustrated, she stomps away, yet watches from bushes at side of a shed, Ed nervously shifts from foot to foot, places hands in back pockets)

Ed
Hello Gwendolyn, . . . so sorry to hear about your mother. Jean and I . . .

Gwen
(tears flowing, drop broom, rush to hug Ed) Ed.

Directions
(Haz looks skyward to squint at sun, brush tears away, Judge and Jesús on either side of Grace, hug, each slapping the back of the other, Stella stares at watch, no tears, but pulls hanky from sleeve and dabs gently under nose)

Stella
Over seven years and he shows' up alive and well, and I am the last to know. Me against them.
(dab nose)

Directions
(Haz wanders off, briefcase at car door, papers in hand, Grace and Jesús go about farm work, the judge following to help, Stella continues to watch until a goat decides to approach and munch on her clothes, Stella shoos goat, Stella sneaks off home, Ed stands stiffly, unknowledgeable about what to do, slowly removes hands from pockets, gently taps Gwen's shoulder, looks about bewildered, eventually give hug)

Gwen

welcome home. (lead Ed by hand into home)

Directions
(camera backs away, overhead viewing of Haz wandering, Grace, Jesús and judge working and Stella tip-toeing from bush to bush on her way home with goat following, camera focuses on the house, penetrate through roof to living room, Gwen offers Ed a seat, sitting across from each other, each searches for resemblances and similar mannerisms)

Ed
Sorry . . . sorry for staring.

Gwen
Understandable. We both are searching for conformation that we are related. You're not what I envisioned. (become animated, confident) Not too many pictures about, only kid pictures. One of you and my mom playing hockey. In my mind you were tall, blonde, no beard and muscled.

Ed
Sorry to disappoint you.

Gwen
Oh, no not disappointed . . . well not yet, I mean you are quite handsome for someone of your age, but I haven't got to know you yet.

Ed
Thanks, I think! Yes, you need to get to know me. I could turn out to be a total failure as a father of a daughter.

Gwen
(lean forward seriously)
Father of, maybe several daughters and sons.
(Nod head as if revealing a secret)

Ed
(shocked, look about as if kids would seep out of the woodwork)
Haz is my best friend and is trustworthy. It would take a cunning forceful, self-confident person to extract information from Haz.

Gwen
Hazelton Wentworth Bigg is a pushover. (gesture with hand as if gently pushing over a candle) I know enough, probably more than you.

Ed

I take it you take after your mother. Jean controlled the neighbourhood and usually got what she wanted when she was your age.

Gwen
How come Mom didn't get you? You were friends as kids. What about a first date, first kiss, boyfriend, girlfriend, engaged, married, my father from the day I was born?

Ed
(back away, sink into chair as if being subdued)
It seemed that whatever I did, she did. I guess that in the end, your mom did get me.

Direction
(reminiscing, whatever Ed says is slightly different than what is displayed in scene, open field, Ed and Jean aged eight, wheat field is blowing, two children running, Ed leading, jean following)

Ed
Jean was tomboyish, always competitive. I could never figure out why. One hot summer day Wojo, my blood hound, and I are chasing rabbits through the field. Out of nowhere Jean comes shooting through the field after us.

Direction
(young Ed and Wojo are running, Ed turns head back to see Jean advancing, Ed begins to run faster, Jean gains)

Ed
Heck, I thought she was after me for something, so I ran faster. Jean was fast . . . for a girl. Competitive. A neck and neck run.

Direction
(Ed and Wojo are running full out, Jean is gaining, then is neck and neck then passes and keeps going, distance is major even though Ed pushes to gain, Ed and Wojo give up and stop and watch Jean going, going and going, Ed shakes head, Wojo lays down and covers eyes with paw)

Ed
Jean was fast for a girl.

Gwen
(with pride)
She played forward on a girl's hockey team and tried out for the national team.

Ed
(nodding with hidden pride)
She practiced with boys' teams. Back when we were young, in high school, Jean could skate, stick handle and score better than most second-string players.

Direction
(Gwen leans forward, interested, Ed beginning to relax, talk easily, eyes beginning to study Gwen and compare to Jean and himself, similar looks and mannerism)

Ed
But when playing with the first string, the guys where much bigger, able to crush her against the boards on a check.

Direction
(scene of hockey game when in high school, big guys have Jean pined at boards, puck is passed out back across centre line to Ed, Ed moving fast up other side is heading to opposing end, Jean recovers from check, sees Ed across ice, speeds with full force aiming to cut Ed off, just as Ed crosses opposing blue line, Jean collides with Ed, knocking him flat to the ice, Jean's face is asking if Ed is alright, did she hurt him)

Ed
Jean had talent, could have made the national team. (Nod, reminisce, a sense of actually missing Jean) I guess, as kids we were friends . . . friends.

Direction
(silence prevails, Ed and Gwen hesitate, reminiscing, camera circles the room, focussing on pictures, rooms, furniture, glancing out windows, seeing Jesús and the judge working on tractor, Grace on tractor out ploughing field, Stella at home with binoculars eyeing the Baptist home, wanting to know what's going on with Ed and Gwen, camera focusses on Ed and Gwen, Gwen sits on edge of chair wanting to reach out to Ed, Ed is becoming receptive, leans slightly forward)

Gwen
How did I come about?

Ed
(become uncomfortable, fidget)
Technically?

Gwen

Did you meet after years of not seeing each other and romantically fall in love? Then you had to leave because of your illness?

Ed
(waver head, nod, eyes wander) Kind-of. (eyes focus on Gwen then become misty and mind drifts to the past)

Direction
(camera circles up, goes black then open on fuzzy reflection in mirror of bar, clear to see Ed looking at empty glass that Haz places in front of him)

Haz
Just meet the woman. If it's a no-go, then no loss.

Ed
(give up, nod yes)
The day can't get any worse.

Direction
(camera jumps to Betty and Jean)

Betty
Just meet the donor. Maybe its fate and there may be instant chemistry. Just say fire as a safe word then we'll leave, and the deal is off.

Jean
Hell, the day has been a waste so far, may as well end it the same way. What do I got to lose?

Direction
(Betty turns head toward Haz for the confirmation nod, camera backs away to view the meeting of people, Haz stands and faces Betty approaching, Jean follows behind, an eye over Betty's shoulder)

Jean
Is that the guy? Too business like, hair's too messy.

Betty
He's the donor's lawyer, the guy I went to school with.

Jean
The broker, and what does that make you? My surrogate pimp?

Betty

Thanks!

Direction
(Betty and Haz step sideways away from the bar to introduce their clients, camera peeks between Haz and Betty and focusses on bar mirror to see unfolding meeting, Ed and Jean, their eyes focussed on the other's feet, then slowly advancing until eyes meet)

Ed
Jean . . . Jean.

Jean
You . . . You're the . . . you, Ed Baptist?

Ed
Jean Walls!

Direction
(Haz and Betty exchange bewildering glances)

Betty
Introductions were easy.

Haz
Not bad at all, a good start.

Jean
I threw myself at you since we were children. Now you want to . . . (gesture with hand, indicating poke-me sexually) I could have stood naked in front of you in junior high and still would have been rejected.

Ed
Da . . . maybe you should have, instead of trying to be the fastest runner, being stronger, showing off and lifting fat boys, being a better hockey player than the senior boy's team.

Jean
That . . . you notice, not my legs, my womanly shape, my boobs.

Ed
Oh, I noticed the boobs, but they came packed in a tomboy.

Jean
I ain't gay . . . I was beginning to think you were.

136

Ed
My parts work fine, and women enjoy my abilities.

Haz
Not lately . . . it has been awhile. Hasn't been laid in . . . a long while.

Betty
He . . . is still potent?

Haz
Well . . . they will need to get past their hostilities before we find out.

Directions
(Haz and Betty look back and forth between themselves and Ed and Jean, Jean is steaming with pent up frustration about her whole life, Ed seems at peace, unwilling to be angry and upset, Ed stands and affectionately hugs Jean as an old friend, nods hello to Betty, Jean just stands stiffly, unsure of self and emotions)

Ed
Well it is nice to see you again, you do look well, there is a glow about you.

Jean
(see drink on bar, down shot) Hormones . . . induced, makes the boobs inviting.

Ed
Well . . . yes, a fine pair.

Jean
(anger building, down another shot poured by bartender) They are boobs, required by babies for substance not for men to claim as trophies.

Ed
I've been informed of your dilemma and the options Haz and Betty are trying to organize.

Jean
(down another drink) Not with you, you had your chance years ago . . . free . . . and I ain`t going to pay you so that you can get your jollies. Ain`t going to happen.

Ed

No, I guess not.

Directions
(Jean wavers, Ed supports her, offers a chair, brushes hair away from face,
Jean does not resist)

Betty
(pull out cheque and begin writing) Well . . . the awkward introduction is over,
the drinks are reducing inhibitions, almost a done deal. (hand cheque to Haz)

Haz
(bewildered) I don't see it. Ed is being rejected. I should know. I have
experiences.

Betty
Maybe you should watch and learn.

Ed
Maybe I can be your sounding board, listen and try to understand, and
apologise for my past inconsideration. (comb Jeans hair behind her ear, stare
into her eyes, move hand down shoulder, arm, gently hold hand)

Haz
I see.

(Fold cheque and place in Ed's coat pocket without Ed noticing, at same time
patting a hand on Ed's back, turn to Betty, give companionate eye, reach out
to touch her shoulder)

Buy you a drink.

Betty
I'm married . . .
(show ring)

Haz
(back away)
Oh yeah . . . to a cop.

Direction
(camera flashes to present, focusses on Ed's reminiscent silence, Gwen tries
to get his attention)

Gwen

Mr. Baptist . . . Mr. Baptist.

Ed
Who . . ., please call me . . .? Ed . . . is fine.

Gwen
You were going to tell me how you fell in love.

Ed
Yes, it was great to see Jean after so many years. I came to realise that I had
missed our childhood years. Jean had become a beautiful woman, caring,
compassionate, very vocal, outgoing, always expressing her feelings. In the
middle of a crowded street she embraced me and would not let go. Very loving
and affectionate. The Perfect woman for any man.

Gwen
And you were the right man for her?

Ed
Kind of. (smirk on face)

Direction
(camera zooms in on Ed's grin then zooms out on Ed's face in the past, Betty
and Haz sneak away, leave bar, it is becoming night, camera enters bar and
focusses on Ed and Jean, Jean is talking, very animated and drinking, Ed
patiently listening, fast flashes of scene, Jean angry, happy, hitting Ed, gently
touching Ed, drinking, Ed listening, reacting to abuse, genteelness, never
drinking, never losing calm affection, when Jean is beyond stability, Ed
assists her out, search comically for Jean's car, find keys in purse to
questioning eyes of passer-by, try keys in several cars until finding right one,
stuff Jean into car, search purse for directions, struggle to bring Jean into small
home, once in door cradle Jean and search for bedroom, place on edge of bed
and remove outer clothes, just as Jean is standing and supported by Ed, and
dress falls to floor, Jean throws up, down the front of Ed, extending arms yet
supporting Jean at shoulders, Ed ties to back away, Jean continues to throw
up drenching Ed completely)

Direction
(camera flashes to present, Ed's face is smiling)

Ed
We sat on a park bench under a clear blue sky talking of our youth. So many
memories, fun times and our first date. She asked me to the Sadie Hawkins
dance. I was too shy to ask her out after that. I still thought of Jean as a friend,

a pal. She had changed so much from those childhood years. We both had changed and still realised that we shared the same thoughts and ventures.

Gwen
You both liked camping, cooking, long walks in the wilderness and all kinds of animals. Then you fell in love.

Ed
Love . . . yes, we loved each other all through our lives.

Direction
(flash back to bedroom, true to compassionate nature Ed walks Jean to bathroom, turns shower on, both get in clothes and all, comically shower with soap and wash clothes, out of shower Ed towels off Jean, seeing nightgown, puts over Jean's head and shoulders, at same time loosens slip off shoulders, in one motion slip falls and nightgown falls, quickly Ed removes her panties under the cover of the falling slip and covering nightgown, pleased with modesty of action Ed brings Jean to the bed and tucks her in, flashes, Ed cleans up bedroom, removes clothes, wraps towel around waist, finds dryer, stuffs clothes in, goes to bed, sits on edge, gently pats towel against Jean's face and wet hair, Jean opens eyes, smiles devilishly, suddenly Jean lifts covers, hugs Ed, draws him down under the covers, Jean smothers him, room goes black)

Direction
(camera brightens on smiling face of Gwen then turns on Ed in present)

Gwen
Then you really asked Mom out on a date?

Ed
A long overdue date.

Gwen
Then you made out.

Ed
What?

Gwen
Where? In the hay barn, on a picnic, in the back of a farm truck?

Ed
What? No . . . No . . . No . . . we did not just make out. Intimate love is not

140

messing around in a hay stack. Wow . . ., how old are you? You watch too much trashy television shows. Love is innocent, grows with compatibility. Your mom conceived by the emotion of love and for the love of you.

Gwen
Truly sentimental . . . but sounds corny. Grace told me that her children were conceived under a porch, in a row boat, and in a hay wagon under hay and the wagon was in motion, pulled by a tractor driven by the judge.

Ed
What do you women talk about, is nothing sacred. I never talk about personal matters like that to anyone.

Gwen
Grace and Jesús and the judge say that you are prudish.

Ed
I'm not a prude!

Gwen
Then tell me the truth. Where was I conceived or was I just the product of a one-night fling.

Ed
No . . . Jean planned for a long time to conceive you.

Gwen
Mom told me I was artificially created. I know better. Remember Hazelton.

Ed
Haz . . . is a lawyer, all lawyers askew the truth. The truth is . . .

Direction
(flash back to dark room, a towel is thrown out of the bed, followed by a night gown, bodies rumble under the covers, bed settles, Jean laying on top of Ed sticks head out from under covers, pleased smile on face, head settles, eyes close, body goes limp, camera focusses on Ed's face, a slight grin on one side of lips, camera goes black.

Direction
(camera flashes close up of Ed's lips in present, same grin is on face)

Ed
Jean and I courted, fell in love, shared a loving relationship, in a very

conservative normal way and you were conceived.

Gwen
I don't buy it. Boring . . . boring.
(make accusing expression)

Ed
Yup . . . that's me . . . boring.
(comical upturned grin)

Gwen
Then you just up and left because you were sick, dying, but you're not dead and my mother is. Why did you leave?

Ed
I truly expected to die, not your mom. I was told that my time was limited.

Directions
(dark room in past lightens, Ed is dressed, standing by bed, looking down at Jean, Jean is out, sprawled across the bed, Ed scribbles on a piece of paper then places it on bed side table, camera focusses on letter, 'Dear Jean. It is my fault that I never realized that possibilities in life should have been a relationship between us. I am dying and should not complicate your life. Love, Ed.' Ed feels cheque in pocket, takes it out and places on table, ink is faded, Ed scribbles a line across the cheque, camera focusses in on cheque until blurry)

Direction
(camera focusses on Ed's sad face, Gwen is sitting on edge of chair, stern face, arms crossed)

Gwen
Well . . . my Mom raised me for twelve years, and now is gone . . . so since you're not . . . you're going to raise me and take care of me . . . and all of the other children you help to conceive.

Ed
(act submissive, as a student being chastised) Inexperienced at raising children, and most . . . no, all of those women did not want me around, ever.

Gwen
Plenty of experience making children, so now you have to accept responsibilities. I'm pretty strong and the oldest. There is Travis., six years old and lives with two moms. He needs a male father figure to teach him how

142

to play hockey . . . and his moms are all for it.

Ed
Travis? How many children is there? (silently try to contemplate in mind how many were possible) Did Haz give you names? How many?

Gwen
Plenty, Father.

Ed
Father!!

Gwen
Yes, Father.

Direction
(camera focusses on Ed and Gwen leaning toward each other, Ed bewildered, Gwen confident, strong, smiling, camera pulls away, spins in a cork screw fashion then spins in on hockey arena and six and seven year olds playing hockey at one end, camera focusses on Ed and Gwen and two women, one woman has arm over other's shoulder, all are frowning and looking at other end of rink, camera follows stare to six year old boy doing figure skating moves on ice, goalie staring blankly, scene fades)

END Scene
Music crashes loudly with various genre trying to be dominant, camera is blurry on Ed's face, begin to pull away, face is tranquil with a slight amusement. Music begins to lose various genres, melody of Celtic seafaring song begins to be clearly heard. Camera clears at mid distance, Ed is sitting on a straight back chair in front of aged farm house, goats, dogs, cats, chickens, cows, horses oddly placed in frame. Camera begins to encompass a full framed style of a family portrait, beside Ed and at shoulder is Gwen at twelve years of age, smart, dressed conservatively, pigtails, smiling broadly.
To side at edge of frame is Haz, in same stance as opening, bewildering look on face, brief case on ground, legal papers in hand, hair mussed. Flash of camera bulb blinds scene, picture develops with title of Father at bottom, music lilts on. At each inclusion of a character, that character is added to portrait, various stances, various attitudes, emotions, other titles are added.

HO...HO...HOLD ON!
By
RICHARD MOUSSEAU
Copyright December 24, 2014

CHARACTERS
Santa / Nicholas / Nick.
Presenting classic characteristics of a Santa; appearing to be elder, slim in the beginning and plumper in the end of performance. Six feet tall with a happy face slightly rouge on cheeks, full head of white hair with a full trimmed white beard. Outside clothes are a dull red in the form of Canadian toque and Mackinaw coat of which is a bit large; pants are reddish and baggy and synched up with a wide black belt that matches boots. Inside clothes consist of red flannel shit and red suspenders, and fur lined leather Inuit slippers. Character always munches on oatmeal cookies, always has one in front shirt pocket of which he offers to people. Character is never anxious, always cool, insightful, smiling warmly and is social.

Molly Kickle-Berry.
A girl of approximately seven years old, of ethnic mix, is awe inspired of world and people and is smart for her age, seemingly smarter than her father. She is self aware, always neat and proper and speaks as if an adult and converses on an equal plain with adults. She is at a crossroads of retaining a child's innocence and a need to believe in fantasy. Does not have the typical girl dolls and accessories though communicates with a self as if having an imaginary friend. She wears dresses and attire on the fringe of sophisticated adult style and acts in an adult manner yet wants to experience the inner child.

Fredrick / Fred Berry.
A male of thirty-ish, of ethnic mix, short, plump is a loving father, husband and concerned of family well being. He is somewhat anxious, hyper and in a hurry to do things and aims to please then sometimes over reacts. He is a script writer for radio sit-coms. A top-rated show he was working for ended. He was unable to find a new job for a long time, thus family became homeless, so he decided to move family to the support of in-laws where he does not want to be. He is somewhat forgetful of manners though is down to earth. His basic attire is mismatched. He plays the harmonica.

Beth Kickle-Berry.
A female of thirty-ish and of ethnic mix has average features and is extremely pregnant. She is a writer and editor who is out of work though is writing a cook book but is unable to test recipes due to lack of funds and family situation. She is the rock of the family foundation though will play games and tricks and can be mischievous. She is always concerned about the well-being of family and those encountered. She is not a hateful person and looks for the good in all.

Burtrum / Burt Burton.
A male of British origin in his sixties and is a butler who is unemployed. He

is usually a live-in butler though is now looking for work. He is a staunch person and a perfectionist, and a true tradesperson dedicated to his profession. He is of average size and weight for age and dresses impeccably though attire is aged and worn. He has two sides, professional and a soft romantic side that shows through when singing.

Martha Burton.
A female of French stock, is in her sixties was a head house-hold cook. She is of mature figure and of pleasant demeanour. She is a strong woman of presence that easily shows a soft romantic side. She dresses in style though without the expense of extravagance. She is a person of family values that has lost a family and wishes to bring a family back together.

Jane Burton.
A female of average size, is in her late twenties and is of soft features and has educated herself and is willing to make her mark in society. She is not a pushover and pushes herself to stand out and control a business venture. Having been separated from family she is striving to bring her family back together. Her attire is of a classic woman in business though she does dress simple in a tom-boyish way and can be glamorous when acquired.

William / Bill Wentworth.
A male in his sixties is of mature weight and of common folk mentality that has worked his way into a fortune and is trying to fit in with his new social peers. He does not put on airs and is on the fridge and is never accepted by those of old money. He stands out for saying and doing the wrong thing at the wrong time. He is a family man with family values. Dresses well though plainly and does not want to be like the Jones. Likes music and plays the harmonica.

Elizabeth / Lizzy Wentworth.
A female in her sixties is always elegant and fits into the upper-crust of society though is a down home average person. She fits in well with everyone and is not afraid to get hands dirty or taking suggestions from anyone. She dresses well though does not flounces to the extremes with accessories. She is a woman that stresses family views and looks the part of a mother waiting to be a grandmother.

Richard Wentworth.
A male in his late twenties is tall and good looking and is able to fit into the life style of the rich of society. He dresses the part and mixes in the business and culture, though he holds the values impressed upon him by his parents. He has not found is place in society yet and is being influenced by everyone. He is searching to find himself even though a current girlfriend has planed out

his life.

Mildred Easthouseman.
A female in her late twenties is a classic rich girl with attitude and mannerism of a woman who has never had to work to earn a living. She is from a wealthy family of old money. Her attire is always fashionable and of great quality that includes all of the fineries and accessories. She is slim and tall and seems to be underfed, opinionated and pushy.

Robert and Louise Easthouseman.
Typical rich people of classic established old money and breeding.

SONG INDEX:
I Shall Return to Kintyre.
Copyright March 30, 2015
When Hearts Believe.
Copyright April10, 2015
Fred's Blues
Copyright April 6, 2015

SCENE
Music builds from a basic rendition of 'Silent Night' into a rendition of 'Jingle Bells' played by selected use of various bells building to suit unfolding scene. Various tempos of instrumental and vocal versions of songs, 'Fred's Blues', 'I Shall Return to Kintyre', and 'When Hearts Believe' to be used to accompany suitable scenes. Camera scans the night sky to see only the reflections of snow falling. Slowly the camera lowers to view the distant horizon; tops of snow-covered fir trees and bare branches of deciduous trees are focused bordering a narrow snow-covered highway. Distant dull headlights flicker. To the side is a cross roads and a bus stop sign wiggling in the cross winds. As the headlights slowly advance the camera moves forward to focus on the broad windshield of a converted 1930's truck modified to be a multi seated bus. A poor heating system fogs the windshield. From behind the fog a mitten hand wipes window moisture away as two small windshield wipers scrap snow from the exterior. The camera stops to focus on a woman's face turned to patiently listen to an animated man talking and gesturing while poorly attending to the technical aspects of driving. A young girl sitting in the middle of a second seat slowly turns her head from mother to father. Lips of the adults are conducting a conversation but only silence penetrates the windshield. Camera holds back until audience has sufficient time to try and read lips before penetrating the windshield to hear the conversation. Instrumental 'Jingle Bells' music plays soothingly below the conversation.

FRED

146

. . . your father hates me, BETH.

BETH
No, Fred, he . . . he . . .

FRED
Despises me!

BETH
Tolerates . . .

FRED
Tolerates!

BETH
Sorry, Fred, that was a wrong choice of a word.

FRED
You are just like him, BETH. You just tolerated my courting.

BETH
I grew to love you, and given time, Father will grow to like you.

FRED
You grew to love me? So, you did not like me in the beginning?
BETH
Fredrick Berry!

FRED
Beth-Anne Knickle!!

MOLLY
Molly Knickle-Berry.

DIRECTIONS
Fred and Beth turn to look back at Molly smiling. Both begin to smile then
smile at each other then Fred's smile weakens.

FRED
Your mother really hates me. Never liked me stealing you and Molly and
moving across the country.

BETH
We will be there shortly, and she will have Molly to hug and spoil. She will

thank you for bringing us safely to their home.

FRED
And resent me for free-loading on them. Despise me for not being able to provide a home for a wife and child. Tolerate me by providing an army cot in the cold dark dungeon of the cellar with the ghost of . . .

MOLLY
Santa Clause.

DIRECTIONS
Fred looks at Beth with a bewildered questioning glare. Beth squints and shakes an accusing finger at Fred then both turn to look at Molly smiling and pointing forward through the windshield.

BETH
No . . . no . . . Molly, Grandma does not have ghosts in the cellar. Daddy is just making up a story, that is what Daddy does . . . writes stories.

FRED
An unemployed writer going to live in your parent's cellar with the ghosts that haunted Ebenezer Scrooge not . . .

MOLLY
No . . . out there . . ., we are going to hit Santa!!

DIRECTIONS
Beth and Fred turn with wide eyes; Fred slams both feet onto the brake pedal. Beth attempts to block Molly's view by waving both hands in front. Camera instantly turns to view a tall skinny man with a large hobo style red sack on a stick stepping onto the highway beside the bus stop sign wiggling in the breeze. A gust of wind blows snow in front of the man's face. A slight smile creases the man's face and he winks directly towards Molly. Camera flashes to Molly who sees the wink from behind Beth's hands. The bus begins to fish-tail as Fred tries to handle the turning steering wheel. The 'Jingle Bells' song played by various bells begins to climax and at the sound of a church bell gong the music stops. A thump is heard, and a flash of a red toque and a reddish Mackinaw coat blinds the windshield. A rolling sound rumbles over the top of the bus. Molly's head follows the sound and looks out the back window.
The bus takes a slide action to the side and hits hard into a snow bank and ditch. A front wheel twists awkwardly. Fred's hands are griped to the steering wheel; one eye is closed tight and the other frozen wide open. Beth has one hand stretched back gripping Molly's coat, her other hand covering both eyes.

Molly and camera watch Santa sailing through the air then landing relaxed onto his feet with pole and Hobo bag placed correctly on a shoulder. Santa turns to look at the bus. A smile on his face dwindles when seeing Molly's wide eyes staring with wonderment. Santa awkwardly and comically attempts to fake injury and crumbles to the ground and tests several positions before selecting a sprawled-out position.

MOLLY
(blink eyes, hold closed then open to confirm what is seen)
Santa . . ., Daddy, . . . you killed Santa.

FRED
(in shock)
No . . . no . . . it is not Santa . . . it is just a Hobo.
(hysterical)
I killed a man!
(struggle to pull hands from steering wheel, fight to open door)

BETH
(force self to be calm)
No one is killed. Don't look Molly. Stay put.
(gently open the door then frantically wobble to the back of the bus)

FRED
Please . . . please be anything but Santa and not dead!

BETH
Like what . . . an Abominable Snowman?

MOLLY
(jump over seat and follow Fred out through the door)
It is Santa . . . he has a white beard and a sack full of presents.

BETH
No Molly, he cannot be Santa. Christmas is weeks away and Santa is busy up in the North Pole.

FRED
He better be! (pleading) I can't be the one who killed Santa.

DIRECTIONS
Beth and Fred stand limply looking down over Santa. A peaceful relaxed smile is on his face. Molly squeezes between Beth and Fred and stares down with a knowing smile.

BETH
There is not a mark on his clothes.

FRED
He is smiling . . . the guy is smiling.

BETH
And breathing; I see breath mist. He is breathing.

SANTA
(realize that the situation is not normal, grin and hold breath)

MOLLY
Santa has magic. I saw him float through the air.

DIRECTIONS
Suddenly bright lights illuminate the scene. Camera and the eyes of Fred, Beth and Molly lift to see a car's headlights. Fred begins to scream in a excited girl's voice. Beth hugs Molly and presses close to Fred. The car does not slow down and seemingly at the last moment veers to the side and bounces over a snow bank and across a small parking lot and heads directly towards storage bins beside a road side eatery. Patrons in the eatery rush to the windows. Heavy snow on the shed's roof and eatery begin to avalanche down to cover the 1930's coupe car.

FRED
It's my entire fault. I lost my job, can't support my family, ran a fake Santa down and caused a car to crash. Why me Lord? What penance must I do? Molly and Beth will be living on the street while I rot in prison for eternity.

BETH
Fred . . . Fred. (pull Fred along and rush toward the car) Fred, help the people in the car.

FRED
What about . . . San . . . (point at Santa) this guy?

MOLLY
Santa is okay, he is just holding his breath. (bend down close to Santa and with a finger touch the end of his nose and wiggle, when nothing happens then press a finger into a cheek until Santa blows out a breath) I know that you are okay.

150

SANTA
(open one eye, slowly smile, open both eyes and begin to rise onto elbows)
Hello Molly.

MOLLY
(eyes widen and mouth flops open) You know my name?

SANTA
I herd your daddy say your name.

MOLLY
You are Santa . . . I saw you float through the air.

SANTA
That was just a trick, a way to make people stop and then feel guilty and offer
to give me a ride.

MOLLY
We will give you a ride; we have lots of seats and Daddy will give you a ride
if I ask him.

SANTA
Well, thank you Molly.

MOLLY
On . . . one condition.

SANTA
You have conditions?

MOLLY
Yes. You must read my Santa letter. My Daddy does not have extra money
for a stamp, and I did not mail it yet.

SANTA
But, I am not Santa.

MOLLY
(stand up stiffly, confidently with hands on hips) I know you are Santa and so
do you. I will keep your secret if that is what you want. Just say that your
name is Nick.

SANTA
It is Nick, Nick for shot, my full name is Nicholas.

MOLLY
Sure, okay. (offer a hand to help Santa get up)

DIRECTIONS
Camera turns towards car accident and action in the eatery. Camera focuses
on an older man's face in the window of the eatery then it enters to follow
various people begin to gather at the windows. Man's eyes notice a woman
exiting the kitchen, moving past the counter then slowly walking past the
man's booth.

BURT
 (eyes sparkle, widen, begin to stand, reach a wanting hand towards the
passing woman, whisper) Martha . . . my love.

MARTHA
(suddenly hesitate, shiver with nervousness then reflective emotion) Burtrum
. . . Burt?

BURT
My love; years of emptiness has not lessened your beauty within my eyes.
You are as radiant as on the first day my eyes beheld you.

MARTHA
I never thought a butler could sweet talk as you did, and after forty years your
sweet talk still titillates my heart.

BURT
You have forgiven me? (approach Martha with both hands outward.

MARTHA
We are not lovers and it has been ten years of separation of our marriage
union.

BURT
Nine years, four month, three days and hours of missing your touch,
compassion, warmth and flavours of exquisite dishes to fill a hungry heart.

MARTHA
The special of the day is a leftover steak bone flavouring a pot of soup.
Twenty-five cents and it comes with a roll and butter.

BURT
Dinner for two!

MARTHA
(inquisitive glance to the booth and over Burt's shoulder)

BURT
Martha, will you kindly join an old fool, an old friend?

MARTHA
Burtrum . . . I, (begin to reach out towards Burt's outstretched hands) I am
working, I am the only cook. (turn away when hearing the bell above the door
ring)

DIRECTIONS
A commotion of people begins to enter the eatery.

BURT
Martha, please spend a moment, a gesture of a love we had, and I still have.

FRED
(attempt to take charge though accomplish very little) Please, step back, make
room. It was my fault, I mean running down Santa, not Santa, just a guy.

DINER ONE
(put hands over a child's ears) You killed Santa!

DINER TWO
What did you do to this woman?

FRED
No, no, not Santa and I did nothing to this lady. She swerved to miss the guy
I ran over on the road.
(turn as if to go back to guy on the road) She crashed her car. Give her
breathing room. Water, bring the lady water.

EATERY OWNER
(glance at Fred while holding out a glass of water)

FRED
(squirm while hesitantly reaching for glass, attempt to give to shaking woman,
keep eyes on eatery owner) I did not cause the accident nor the destruction of
that . . . (watch roof of shed fall onto the roof of the car) . . . shed. Termites
weakened the structure. Not my fault. (drink water)

BETH

Sit hear dear. (assist woman into booth, hover over and fuss about the woman's hat and hair)

JANE
I only saw those people at the last moment, and then the steering wheel spun free of my grip.

BETH
We . . . Molly and Fred and Santa, we were in the middle of the road. Hi, I am Beth, and this is Fred.

FRED
(hand empty glass to Jane)

DIRECTIONS
Jane looks into the empty glass, frowns then hands glass to Fred who smirks when questioning the emptiness when passing it back to the eatery owner; owner has a full glass ready and hands it to Fred.

JANE
I almost hit Santa?

FRED
No . . . no! Not . . ., he is just a . . . Hobo!

JANE
It doesn't matter; I could have hit all of you. You're . . . you're going to have a baby! I could have hurt you. Please sit.

BETH
You didn't hit anyone. Fred hit Santa.
(sit beside Jane)

FRED
(whisper to Beth) Why do you keep saying . . . you know what? (raise voice) Everyone is okay, spread out, back to your tables, back to your customers. (point at eatery owner then indicate a sleeping man with head on the counter) Not my fault.

DIRECTIONS
Crowd returns to their pervious actions prior to the accident. Eatery owner stares out through window at the destruction and begins to jot down figures while gesturing to a mechanic standing at the back door. Fred shakes head to indicate, 'not his fault'. As the crowd clears, Martha draws back emotion and

154

turns away from Burt. Her eyes open to stare at Jane. Jane lifts head and views the approaching woman.

JANE
(smile broadens, life returns, and the accident is forgotten) Mother . . . Mom, I made it, I am here.

MARTHA
Jane my dear.

BURT
(arms fall limply as shoulders slump, whisper in disbelief, step back as if looking for a place to hide)
My daughter . . . Jane, all grown up, a woman.

DIRECTIONS
Jane rushes into Martha's arms hugging with strength of possession. Martha becomes the fussing mother.

JANE
I am finally here, let me look at you.

MARTHA
I am the same old mother. It has just been a year and a half since you graduated . . . with honours I must say. How is work, are you alright?

JANE
Fine, just fine, I have an apartment and a car . . . had a car!

FRED
(eavesdropping) Just needs a bit of work; not my fault!

BETH
(cover Fred's mouth with hand) You started the chain reaction.

FRED
(mumble under Beth's hand) Santa popped out of nowhere.

JANE
The car is fixable. (shake head) Take that apron off, you no longer work here. You are coming home with me.

BETH
(hug Fred affectionately) Mother and daughter love. Will Molly love me the

same way when I am old?

FRED
(mumble under Beth's hand)

JANE
(return a hug, bury head with glazed eyes into Martha's neck, slowly open eyes to see a man shying away, whisper) Father? (stiffly back away from Martha and turn Martha to the side and step forward) Pa, Pa . . . OH PA-PA.

DIRECTIONS
Jane lunges forward without animosity and pounces onto Burt with a latching hug and repeated affectionate kisses. Burt does not know how to react and stiffly stands in a trained butler stance. Slowly Burt relaxes and slowly applies a lasting hug.

BURT
Jane, after all of these years, after I abandoned you and Martha, you do not resent me?

JANE
Oh, Pa-Pa, how could I not love my Dad? I understand why you left. I did miss you but never stopped loving my Father.

DIRECTIONS
Camera pans to take in the various reactions and emotions of eatery patrons observing the reunion of Jane, Martha and Burt. Camera passes and exits eatery through door as mechanic enters. Camera notices Santa and Molly walking along road. Molly is struggling to drag Santa's Hobo bag. While Santa brushes and adjusts clothing, Santa reaches back and lifts bag to assist Molly who continues to trudge with the lighter load. Santa and Molly sit on the bench at the bus stop. Snow is continuous and blows about and around as if encircling the pair.

MOLLY
(eye Santa with curiosity, truly believe that he is Santa, yet disillusioned by the clothes and his skinniness) Are you on a diet? My Mother says that Mrs. Santa Clause is a good cook. Your beard is nice and white though a bit short. You do have nice rosy cheeks and I saw the twinkle in your eyes several times. Did you fall out of the Santa sleigh? You and I truly know that you are Santa. I can keep a secret if you don't want other people to know. Not all people believe. Why didn't the reindeer stop and come back for you?

SANTA

156

(be jolly and pleasant but try not to be Santa, rather just a down and out Hobo just trying to get a ride to a destination, pull an oatmeal cookie from pocket, offer one to Molly, when she rejects then begin to nibble on cookie) Molly, there is no reindeer, no sleigh and no Mrs. Santa Claus . . ., I am just a Hobo that happens to look a bit like that Santa guy. Who would believe a skinny fellow like me could bring presents and joy to families? (become concerned when looking into Molly's hopeful expression fading into possible dismay)

MOLLY
(shake head no to offered cookie) I know; my best friend doesn't believe in you. She said that all of her dolls came from Sears and Roebuck's department store. She once pulled your beard and it came off. She said that proves that there is no Santa.

SANTA
Commercialism, each department store has to have the plumpest, rosy cheeked, massive curly beard and the loudest Ho . . . Ho . . . Ho! Macy's department store wouldn't hire me, too skinny, not jolly enough. (long pause, become sad, disappointed, look long into inner space, look deep into Molly's eyes) Children no longer believe . . . in the magical illusions of Christmas, the birth of a saviour and the newborn child's request, through Santa, to spread joy and share in gift giving is lost. Adults lose faith and do not pass down beliefs to their children.

MOLLY
You sure said a mouthful! (pause, think and ponder) Why are you so skinny?

SANTA
Economics, no job, less homes visited so less cookies and milk left by the chimney. Shrinking of the belly is in proportion to mankind's dwindling belief in the essence of Christmas. (drop head and sway, cast a side glance to Molly)

MOLLY
(slowly look down and lower head and sway, whisper) I believe.

SANTA
(begin the start of a growing Ho . . ., reach into pocket, unwrap handkerchief and offer cookie to Molly) Please have an oatmeal cookie with no raisins. I know it is your favourite. Ho . . ..

MOLLY
(accept cookie) Yes, it is, only half please. I will share with you. (break cookie, hand half back to Santa) I will make sure to leave warm milk and extra

cookies at my Grandparents home. We have to go live with them for awhile. Will you be able to find my Grandparents house in the dark?

SANTA
Oh . . ., I think so . . ., on . . ., (mumble) stree . . . ro . . .

MOLLY
Walls Road West, not East.

SANTA
Oh course!

MOLLY
(reach into pocket and pull out a folded letter) I understand that times are tough, and you may be out of work because people don't believe, but I don't need any toys or fancy clothes. Please read my letter and if you can . . ., maybe . . ., if I really, really believe in Christmas . . ., you might . . ., (gesture with open hands as if tossing magic powder) deliver just a smidgeon of Christmas magic . . ., not for me but for others in need. (shyly hand letter to Santa)

SANTA
(knowing magic is impossible, reluctantly accept letter, make excuses) Magic is not dished out willy-nilly . . ., a lot of factors need to align in the cosmos of the universe and the past, present and future must not be in conflict, or a magic spell could explode in my face like a cream pie splattering all over. (gesture, make face)

MOLLY
(snicker, become compassionate) I understand, I may be only seven years old but my mind is almost ten. Maybe you can try some Christmas magic.

SANTA
If I am stuck here in the middle of nowhere there is not much I can do. I am supposed to be at . . ., at a job . . ., I promised to help a friend. (turn to Molly) Performing magic for self gain is not permitted. I have to be human and accomplish matters in the same manner as everyone else.

MOLLY
We have plenty of room in our truck-bus; room for lots of people. Where do you need to go?

DIRECTIONS
Santa lifts head and stares into the blustery sky then turns to stare down the road that fades into darkness. Camera blends into the darkness and emerges

in the vestibule of a mansion. Camera seems to be circling and peeking into rooms and through windows. Trees are green, flowers are blooming, and a light breeze is blowing in through open windows. Camera turns towards the front doors and focuses on Santa's large Hobo bag lying on the floor before the door that is beginning to open. Before the door opens completely; the camera flashes to the outside. Luggage is being brought from a car to the front door by a chauffeur. William and Elizabeth Wentworth are conversing in small talk while casting an eye to their son Richard Wentworth who is saying goodbye to a love interest, Mildred Easthouseman. Camera focuses on the young couple.

MILDRED
(hold Richard's hands to prevent close contact) Just a light kiss on the cheek, I do not want you to mess up my make-up before I meet Mommy and Daddy.

RICHARD
We have been a couple for over a year; I would think that your parents know we do kiss.

MILDRED
We are not engaged, and a woman of my status must present an innocent presentation at all times. (fake a kiss onto Richard's cheek)

DIRECTIONS
Mildred disappears into the car as Richard slowly backs up the walkway. Elizabeth and William study the back of his head.

LIZZY
That girl is high society and is high maintenance. Her affection for our son is as cold as her home. (with an up gesture of head indicate the mansion next door across the manicured lawns, twist mouth in a disappointed manner)

WILLIAM
Old money; so old it is as stiff and stale as the generations that have occupied that mausoleum.

LIZZY
If I read our son correctly; that old money and our new money will be merging.

WILLIAM
What? Who told you that? Richard has not mentioned anything to me. I don't believe it. He is just socializing; testing the waters.

LIZZY
Testing, Dear, he is drowning and a woman like Mildred-Louise-Easthouseman knows how to seduce new money.

WILLIAM
You mean Richard?

LIZZY
No, new money; Richard just comes along with the money.

WILLIAM
Shameful . . .!

LIZZY
Yes Dear, lucky for you that I fell in love with you before you made your first one hundred dollars.

WILLIAM / LIZZY
We were penniless and in love.

DIRECTIONS
William unlocks the door and both William and Lizzy lug their own luggage into entrance and plop bags down past Santa's Hobo sack. Breathing in with satisfaction of being home they glance around. Entering the room, Santa is dressed in summer attire and greets the couple warmly.

SANTA
William and Miss Lizzy, welcome home. (heartedly shake William's hand, gently kiss Lizzy's hand)

LIZZY
Nicholas, it is delightful to be home for the summer.

WILLIAM
And away from the heat and crowds on the sea shore resorts; though I trust that you will welcome the warmth after being cooped up here through the long winter.

SANTA
As you see, I am dressed for the weather.

LIZZY
The beach house is ready and waiting for you to house sit.

WILLIAM
Bon-voyage; until our paths cross this coming winter.

DIRECTIONS
William and Lizzy grab luggage and climb stairs to upper bed rooms. Santa
heaves Hobo sack over shoulder and exits and sidesteps Richard who is still
backing toward the front entrance. Inquisitively Santa studies the love-
bewildered face of Richard.

SANTA
Lust for love can be fickle.

RICHARD
Hello Nick, do you think that I only lust for Mildred?

SANTA
It is possible. I do recall your childhood years. Miss. Easthouseman always
teased, and you always chased and often returned home shamed and rejected.
What about that other young girl . . . who . . ., Miss . . .?

RICHARD
Jane Burton, the daughter of Martha and Burt. That is an ancient memory.

SANTA
Yes, yes, the cook and butler's daughter Jane. Yes Jane, lovely child; your
best friend when you were children.

RICHARD
We were only twelve years old and just pals.

SANTA
Sometimes pals are more than pals.

RICHARD
The Burtons just up and left when Jane and I were still kids.

SANTA
Lifelong friends are gained when just children. It is a shame that snobbery can
force decent people to leave. (reach into pocket and retrieve an oatmeal cookie
and nibble on it)

RICHARD
One night they were there and the next the next morning gone, the house
empty of life. My parents are not snobs and they did not force the Burtons to

leave.

SANTA
Definitely not, if only they knew of the community gossip that shamed the Burtons. Burtrum and Martha left to prevent gossip from tarnishing the good name of this Wentworth household.

RICHARD
(stare towards the Easthouseman's residence then to Santa) The Easthouseman's are a bit stuffy but Mildred is different not like . . .

SANTA
Jane Burton . . ., I wonder how she is doing? She must be a beautiful young woman by now. Jane Burton . . .; well I am off young Richard, best of luck my boy. I will be back here before the cold of winter sets in to take care of the home while . . .

RICHARD
. . . we soak up the sun. You do enjoy house sitting?

SANTA
This is the best way to freeload the honest way.

DIRECTIONS
Santa walks down the walkway giving a wave to Richard who waves back. Richard glances toward the Easthouseman's mansion but his thoughts are somewhere in the past. As the scene fades the voice of Richard is heard.

RICHARD
Jane Burton.
(suddenly pat shirt pocket and take out an oatmeal cookie then turn to stare after Santa)

DIRECTIONS
Camera pans the eatery and pauses to see Jane and Burt continuingly in an embrace. Camera moves to Fred and Beth who is adjusting her belly into the booth's seat; while Fred tries to pull the table that is fixed in place. Several women oh and ah and offer womanly advice. Camera then pans toward the eatery owner who is listening to the mechanic and at the same time is answering the old basic wall telephone. Santa and Molly enter the eatery.

EATERY OWNER
(nod, look out window, nod to mechanic, look at the patrons) Thanks Willard, I will let these people know. (hang up telephone, turn to mechanic then to

patrons) Joe, try to clean up the mess and move the car into the garage. Attention please, Miss; it will be several days before your car can be fixed. And, unfortunately the overdue bus will not be arriving; maybe in a day or two. There is plenty of hot coffee and soup on the menu.

DIRECTIONS
Patrons continue to mumble and discuss options. Santa and Molly wink at each other. The eatery owner begins making a fresh pot of coffee.

JANE
Well now; this is a bit awkward for the two of you, but delightful for me. I get to share both of you at the same time.

MARTHA
Not awkward, just a surprise to see Burtrum here in the middle of nowhere. Our past was . . .

BURT
. . . my fault. I never stopped loving you Jane, nor stopped loving you Martha. Circumstances dictated that the family would be better off without my hindrance.

MARTHA
There is no need to be angry about the past. We can be sociable for the time being.

JANE
We are stuck here for the moment and must catch up.

DIRECTIONS
Martha seems to be a bit cold yet somewhat like a young girl avoiding the amorous eyes of Burt. Burt has not lost affection for Martha and wants to pursue a lost love and missed child. Jane is childlike in the presence of reacquainted parents. From a distance Santa notices the aurora of affection and the awkwardness when Jane pushes parents to sit side by side in the booth. The camera pans to Fred becoming anxious to leave.

FRED
Beth, dear, my love, you know how I detest having to be forced to live with your parents, and I am not anxious to arrive too early, but we need to get out of here before we're stranded. Too many people, too cramped to be stuck here for even a day.

MOLLY

Dad, we have room for Santa in the bus.

FRED
Santa . . . no . . . no, he is a Hobo stranger . . .

BETH
. . . that you almost ran down. Well you did hit him and tossed him into the air.

FRED
Bumped . . . he jumped . . . clear over the bus then slipped and fell down.

BETH
We will give Santa a ride.

FRED
He's in no hurry . . . are you Mr. . . . .

BETH
. . . Santa. We will give Santa a ride to his destination.

MOLLY
Thank you, Daddy. (hug Fred tightly around the neck preventing him from talking)

SANTA
Ho . . ., very generous of you Freddy.

BETH
Don't call me Freddy . . . no one has called me that since . . . (pause and look deep into Santa's eyes)
. . . my brothers and sisters . . . when I was on Santa's knee and he called me Freddy then everyone called me Freddy. (shake past memories out of head) My name is Fredrick.

SANTA
I remember. Your grandfather's name was Fredrick, and his brothers and sisters called him Freddy.

FRED
How . . . oh . . . you just took a guess and used some kind of magic trick!

SANTA
The Burtons surely need a ride to their destination.

164

FRED
Who are the Burtons?

SANTA
Jane, Burt and Martha.

BETH
She is the young woman who crashed her car.

FRED
Not my fault.

BETH
A chain reaction caused by your initial running down of Santa.

FRED
Bump . . . look . . . he is not hurt.

MOLLY
We have plenty of room in our bus.

BETH
We will invite the Burton family. (stare decidedly into Fred's eyes) Won't we
Fredrick Freddy Berry?

FRED
(whisper) Do not call me Freddy!

DIRECTIONS
Other patrons only perk up when hearing the word bus and then begin to
mumble. Heads begin to turn toward Fred who becomes nervously self-
conscious when feeling eyes staring upon him.

WOMAN 1
Do you have a bus? Are you a bus driver?

MAN 1
Will you accept my ticket? I am only going a couple of miles that way.

WOMAN 2
Is he going that way?

FRED

No . . .no . . . it is an old truck . . . just a truck,

BETH
that was converted into a bus.

MOLLY
The bus has plenty of seats.

FRED
(cover Molly's mouth with a fumbling hand) We don't use it as a bus. I do not have a bus driver's licence.

BETH
Fred, you do not need a bus driver's licence to give non-paying acquaintances a needed ride.

FRED
Non-paying, what if they pay then . . .

BETH
Non-paying.

FRED
I don't know these people.

WOMAN 3
Mrs. Mildred Huckerby, my husband Jack.

MAN 1
Zek.

MAN 2
Ed.

FRED
The bus . . . the truck is stuck in the snow bank . . . and there is not enough room in the seats.

MAN 2
We can push the truck out.

MAN 1
Let's go.

WOMAN 1
We will only be crowded in the beginning until we get dropped off. We are just going to the next town.

BETH
Fred . . . move . . . go . . . you have a purpose.

FRED
(grumble)
Why not . . ., it is my entire fault anyway.

BETH
(playfully agree) Yes, it is.

DIRECTIONS
Customers rush to the door, dropping money on the counter. Santa moves toward the Burtons with Molly at his side.

MOLLY
Excuse me.

MARTHA
Yes dear.

MOLLY
The bus is leaving, and you are welcome to join us.

SANTA
(present a smile) I recommend taking this ride for the destination will be a delightful surprise.

JANE
Yes please. (turn to parents with a hopeful plea) I can always come back later to retrieve the car.

MARTHA / BURT
(look at each other with mixed anticipation) Well . . . yes . . . we should.

MOLLY
Follow me.

DIRECTIONS
Molly leads the group out of the restaurant. Martha and the eatery owner exchange a hand shake and he hands over a final envelope with her earnings.

Santa trails then before exiting turns and withdraws a small gift from a pocket. Smiling at the eatery owner he gives an understated Ho Ho, and hands the gift to the man.

SANTA
Ho . . . Ho . . . Ho . . . merry Christmas.

EATERY OWNER
(with a blank look hold the small gift delicately in the air) Merry Christmas . . . Santa.

DIRECTIONS
The group of travellers mill around the bus while Fred begins to Rev the engine. Out of sight Santa stands near the back wheel slipping on the road ice. Just before the men attempt to push on the front of the bus, Santa slips his Hobo sack under the back wheel. The bus eases out leaving the men fixed in place in a gesture of pushing on air. Molly peaks to the side to see Santa pick up the Hobo sack. To her amazement the sack puffs back into the plump sack shape. Santa tosses the sack and pole over a shoulder. Inside of the bus, Fred becomes pleased with his success. Outside the group cheers and gather at the side door and begin to squeeze into the buss, each stating who will be getting out first and who will need to get in last. Fred, who is crowded, tries to turn around to inspect the placement of passengers.

FRED
Is everyone snugly in?

MOLLY
(from the back of the bus standing beside Santa, over look all heads then confidently announce) All aboard.

DIRECTION
Through the front windshield the camera focuses on Fred's grimacing face as he grinds the gear shifter into gear. The bus grunts, lurches, misfires and groans forward as the engine revs. Through the winter weather of snow falling and wind blowing the camera follows in a slightly sped up (very slight) film speed to observe the silent antics of the crowded bus stopping and starting as passengers exit at their destinations. In the darkness of night, the bus skids to a stop in front of the Wentworth's mansion. Through the windshield various faces express what they see. Beth and Fred are amazed by the size and grandeur. Jane reminisces of a past childhood memory. Martha recalls the joy of cooking in the main kitchen and the good times of life. Burt is a bit self-conscious and sad that he caused his family's break up and loss of a warm welcoming home. Molly and Santa are sound asleep in a twisted recline. A

grinding sound from the engine is heard then an explosion of sorts resulting in the engine hood denting up. All eye the hood then at Fred's startled face, all sigh, satisfied that they have arrived.

SANTA
(suddenly perk up) This is home sweet home for the duration of winter.

FRED
Are we at the right place? This is a mansion. You are a . . .

BETH
Do not say it Fred.

FRED
Well he is . . ., just look at his clothes . . . he is carrying a Hobo's sack, so he must be a Ho . . .

BETH
Do not say it Fred. Santa offered to share a home until the weather clears.

FRED
Maybe until this heap of junk recuperates. He must be a caretaker living in a shack way out back.

MARTHA
I wonder if the Wentworth's still live here? Elizabeth and William were more like friends than employers. Jane, do you remember Richard?

JANE
Oh . . ., that name; I have not thought of Richard Wentworth in years. We sure were pals and what adventures we had.

MARTHA
Mischief is a better description of you two hooligans. Poor Miss. Easthouseman, you my dear tortured her.

JANE
No Mother; oh, I have forgotten her name.

BURT
(bitterly say) Mildred Easthouseman.

JANE
Milly; she did not like me addressing her as Milly and she was too prim and

proper for our fun. After all, we were children.

BURT
According to the high and mighty, Mrs. Louise Easthouseman, domestic employees and their children should not mingle with the privileged class.

MARTHA
Burt, the Easthouseman's were good people, just set in their ways.

BURT
Class pressure has a way of forcing the separations of the subordinate class; us. We and our children should not associate with the privileged class on an equal basis.

MARTHA
The Wentworth's were not like the Easthousemans. They did not dismiss us; it was you, you Burt who forced us to leave.

BURT
If we stayed on, eventually all who associated with the Wentworths would snub them because of our lax relationship with Miss. Elizabeth and Master William.

JANE
Father! It sounds as if you care more about class distinctions and separation than the Wentworths.

BURT
I do. Eventually we would have been discarded by the Easthousemans. Mrs. Easthouseman had pre-designed a life for her daughter and Richard Wentworth; having their old money marrying the Wentworth's new money. You Jane were a thorn within her plans.

JANE
We were children, and Richard was just a pal.

MARTHA
They were children Burt, playing games; base ball, hockey, just what pals do.

BURT
Without Mildred; and Mrs. Easthouseman did not see Jane as just a tomboy, rather a possible future love interest of Richard.

MARTHA

Richard . . ., dear Richard would see through Louise Easthouseman's plans and class bigotry and not be trapped by class.

BURT
I saved us and the Wentworths from being the cause of any society gossip and shaming.

FRED
I agree, people should stick with their own kind.

BETH
Fred, you are one to talk. You are a contradiction; unemployed and poor who wants to be part of the working class yet expects to be white collar and who displays theatrics of being upper class and intent on living like royalty.

FRED
I am climbing the ladder of success from the bottom up. This is the correct way, not born with a silver spoon in my mouth.

MARTHA
Burt, because of your pride, our family and security faltered.

BURT
Yes.

JANE
Dad!

FRED
So . . . you folks once worked and lived here? How's the digs? Is this your home Mr. Nick.

SANTA
Oh . . . no!

FRED
What? . . . So, we are not staying here?

SANTA
Yes Freddy, we are staying here. I am the house sitter while the Wentworths are wintering in a warmer climate.

MARTHA
(turn to Jane, a hopeful glint in an eye)

They still live here. I wonder if Richard . . .?

JANE
I do not need a play pal Mother.

MARTHA
No dear . . . no!

FRED
Move it, all out, let's get inside.

DIRECTION
The bus doors fling open and people gather bags and rush through the blowing snow to the front doors. At the back-door Santa lifts a sleeping Molly. As Fred rushes by, Santa reaches out and latches onto Fred and pulls him back. Santa adds Molly into the luggage laden arms of Fred. At the front door Santa searches pockets for a house key. With slight of hand he goes through the motions of placing an imaginary key into the lock. With a shake and a twist, the door handle turns and the door opens.

SANTA
Please make your-selves at home. I trust that Burtrum will select respective guest rooms. Martha, you do remember where the kitchen is.

MARTHA
(with delight) Is the panty sufficiently stocked?

SANTA
Yes.

MARTHA
The cooler having suitable cuts?

SANTA
Yes.

MARTHA
Fresh produce?

SANTA
On a usual delivery.

MARTHA
Well then, dinner in the dining room promptly.

BETH
May I help?

DIRECTION
Martha nods. Beth and Martha help each other out of coats. Beth places coats in Fred's arms. They eagerly head to the kitchen. Burt removes coat and places over an arm holding single small suitcase. Seeing Fred struggling with Molly, Jane accepts the child.

JANE
Molly and I can share my old room off of the kitchen.

BURT
(finding self, become the butler of training, gain stance and mannerisms) This way Master Berry, I shall direct you to private accommodations.

FRED
(whisper and grin with snobbish pride) Master Berry, I can live with that. (begin to walk ahead) Great . . . please lead the way.

BURT
The bags sir.

FRED
(stop and glance down at the bags) The Bags? All of the bags?

BURT
Yes, my good man; all. I am a head butler not a luggage servant. (turn and lead the way up the curving stairs)

FRED
I guess that I am.

DIRECTION
Fred struggles to bend down and gather all of the bags. Santa assists by adding to Fred's load. Smiling with satisfaction, Santa takes in a deep breath, pushes toque to back of head he unbuttons his coat and heads to the lounging den. His red Hobo sack is left in the middle of the entrance floor in front of a decorative plant table. Camera backs towards room where Jane and Molly are. The camera's eye watches Fred lumbering up the stairs then pans to Santa turning on a gas fireplace and sitting in a lounge chair. Santa sticks a hand in a pocket and pulls out Molly's letter. As the camera turns to enter, sounds of pots crashing about then silence then laughter from Beth and Martha. The

camera slips through the bedroom door to see Molly struggling to wake. Jane is sitting at a makeup table studying face in mirror. Emotions are about to take over and eyes begin to mist. Molly notices the simple room, obviously untouched for years and still retaining the room essence of a young girl. Turning, she sees Jane's decline. Sitting up, Molly grunts a wake-up sound and pretends to stretch. Jane rushes to press hands to eyes to remove moisture.

MOLLY
Where's your husband?

JANE
(caught off guard, present a quizzical half smile as if to study Molly as a person older than she is, become assertive and turn the tables) Is there a boy in your life?

MOLLY
Not at the moment.

JANE
An ex boyfriend?

MOLLY
Yes, but he was a typical boy with no aspirations. I had to release him from further commitment.

JANE
Currently employed?

MOLLY
No, but I am in need of employment.

JANE
I see; your parents, Beth and Fred?

MOLLY
A result of the economy down turn. They are unemployed writers and we are homeless. We are going to live with my Mother's parents to the dismay of my Father. (put a hand to side of mouth and whisper) Father and Grandmother do not like each other and Grandfather has to take Grandmother's side.

JANE
I understand. It will be a few days longer before you travel onto your Grandparent's home. The bus made a boom sound and broke down.

MOLLY
Father will be relieved and will be in a happier mood. (look around room as if thinking) Where are we; is this your home?

JANE
No, I use to live here as a child. This is the Wentworth mansion. (pause, sigh, toy with table covering, slide out a small picture of two children)

MOLLY
(stretch to see the picture) Cute kids, they look like pals.

JANE
Yes . . . we were.

MOLLY
Okay, there is a story here, and, you better tell me everything.

JANE
(hand picture to Molly) That is me and Richard Wentworth. Pals. My parents were the Butler and Cook. We moved away when I was twelve. Mom and Dad separated. I had no more pals, rather I studied and studied and worked hard. No husband, no boyfriend, and as of last week no job, now no car, but after ten years I was reunited with my Father at the restaurant where my Mother worked. We are together and I am happy, despite what has happened previously.

MOLLY
And because of my Father we have met and arrived here . . . where Richard lives. Will you introduce me to your pal . . . your boyfriend?

JANE
I . . ., I, don't believe Richard is here . . . he could be married or living somewhere else.

MOLLY
Santa will know, I will ask him?

JANE
Molly . . . Santa . . . cannot, Santa needs to worry about Christmas not about finding Richard Wentworth.

MOLLY
You had a crush on him . . . and still do . . . I'll find Santa.

JANE
Molly . . . Molly . . . (turn back to picture, slump and sigh as if disappointed by a lost crush)

DIRECTIONS
Camera follows Molly exiting the room and entering various rooms as she misses Santa heading to the Kitchen. In the kitchen Molly scampers between Beth and Martha and exits one door as Santa enters another. Instantly Santa sniffs the air filled with stem and aromas.

SANTA
This house has not been filled with aromas of such grandeur in years. A cook Lizzy Wentworth is not.

MARTHA
No, she is not . . . though the good woman tried. I must say, Mrs. Wentworth is better suited as an organizer and executive purchaser.

SANTA
William Wentworth would agree. So . . . what is on the menu this evening?

BETH
From my Mother's recipe book, potato cheese soup and pumpkin pie with a whipped cream-cheese toping. Martha's beef and lamb stew and sour dough biscuits for the thick brown gravy.

SANTA
What a delight. No doubt unlimited generations of recipes to test, and, delightfully I will enjoy tasting each dish. I trust there shall be a variety over future days.

DIRECTIONS
Martha and Beth glance to each other.

MARTHA
I do have recipes that I have not prepared in years; restaurants tend to be basic meals.

BETH
I have my Mother's and Grandmother's and even my Grandfather's recipes that I would like to try, though I need someone with the skills of Martha.

MARTHA
All of my recipes are in my head, and not written down to pass on to Jane.

SANTA
Just imagine we have a multitude of recipes, a cook of renown and a writer of extreme talent. Just imagine the delight of collaboration?

DIRECTIONS
In mid action, Beth and Martha freeze as if a light bulb of ideas flash in their minds. Both turn to look at each other then turn to look at Santa's red form passing through the swinging doors. Turning back to each other and pointing utensils they begin to talk at the same time.

MARTHA
Forty years of cooking in a kitchen and not one recipe written down.

BETH
I have page after page of Mother's untried recipes.

MARTHA
And, you are a writer?

BETH
If only someone is able to test-cook these recipes?
(teasingly point to Martha)

MARTHA
I need to prepare and create a recipe from my mind; no time to write it down in proper order.

BETH
I am great at observing and I am a writer.

MARTHA
A new recipe to create is a challenge and a bonus for a cook's repertoire.

BETH
What is a pinch, and a smidgeon, and a dash of a sprinkle?

MARTHA
A dash of seasoning of herbs is different than a dash of salt or pepper, yet a smidgeon is important when building a flavour.

BETH
A pencil and paper; I need to take notes.

MARTHA
Bring out your books of recipes; we need to try something new for breakfast.

DIRECTIONS
Beth and Martha pause, heads tilting in thought.

MARTHA
Shall we combine our resources?
BETH
Delightfully!

DIRECTIONS
Daintily they both take a grip of their aprons and lightly wipe hands as flour residue puffs up. They shake hands daintily.

BETH
Shall we?

MARTHA
We do have hungry test subjects waiting.

DIRECTIONS
Camera instantly jumps to the sitting room to capture Molly rushing in. she anxiously jumps to the arm chair where Santa is reclining with socked feet wiggling on a stool in front of the fireplace. Molly relaxes as if nothing is important. She pays no attention to Santa other than studying Santa's puffy socks wiggling.

SANTA
There is nothing nicer than having warm toes; little piggies wiggling within warm wool socks. Pull up a chair Molly. Kick your shoes off and partake of the luxury of wiggling little piggies before a warm fire.

MOLLY
(squint face, ponder, pull a chair close to Santa and to the stool, kick off shoes and wiggle toes covered in multi coloured leg stockings beside Santa's big feet)
This is delightful!

SANTA
Isn't it so!

MOLLY
(lean on arm of chair and look at Santa)

I would like to add important details to my letter. Have you read it yet?

SANTA
Yes, I have. For such a young child your letter did not ask for one single toy or gift for yourself.

MOLLY
I figure that other people need assistance more than I need a toy.

SANTA
Not even clothes?

MOLLY
I help my Mom make my clothes from her hand-me-downs. I made my stockings from odds and ends. I like the colours.

SANTA
I must say, they are very fashionable.

MOLLY
Thank you.

SANTA
Christmas gifts usually are items, toys, ties for Dad, perfume for Mom, candy for Grandpa and even Grandmother's relish in receiving a broach, but . . . finding jobs for people is not quite Santa's forte of ability.

MOLLY
What about the magic aspect? Just one dose of magic can create a chain reaction that could affect others.

SANTA
Magic is rarely used.

MOLLY
My Dad is an unemployed radio script writer, so if a little bit of magic dust could find him a job them Mom could have more leisure time to write her cook book. And, then Grandmother will like Dad, because he is working and supporting his family, and not complaining. Then Grandpa will not always have to argue with Grandmother. (whisper) Grandpa . . . secretly kind of likes my Dad. See, it will all work out with just a bit of magic.

DIRECTIONS
Camera jumps to upstairs where Burt is preparing all of the rooms. Fred is

following as would a curious child, always questioning and in the way.

FRED
Is putting new soap in the bathrooms a part of a butler's job? I would think I can open a new bar of soap.

BURT
You may be able, though I trust that your loving, caring wife Beth makes sure that new soap is placed and that the discarded wrapper is disposed of properly. When was the last time you properly did this procedure?

FRED
(strain to think)
Never, Beth takes care of the domestic stuff.

BURT
A butler's job is to make sure a home is in a proper state.

FRED
So you are everywhere all of the time. There must be things that you see and hear?

BURT
A trained butler learns to be present yet immune of hearing and retaining the subject of conversations or seeing what should not be seen.

FRED
You must be human; all humans are curious. Gossip is ramped in the world. A writer needs gossip and juicy stories; it is the ingredient I need to build a story. You must have a story. What's your story; why did you leave a cushy job? This place is heaven. It is like you never left this mansion. Look; you are arranging the rooms as if you just did it yesterday.

BURT
(pause, think, recall) I must say; it is uncanny that I remember how Mr. and Mrs. Wentworth like the placements of their dressers.

FRED
Exactly; you even changed the way the toilet paper is dispensed. You have stories. What about the neighbours? There has to be something; a scandal, a murder. I sure could use a good story to get me back on top of a radio scrip writing team. I was there once.

BURT

And where was there? Why are you not there instead of heading to live with your in-laws? There must be a self-contained story that you can develop.

FRED
Nah, just plain bad luck; the show flopped, and the sponsor decided to back a famous actor and another show. I was there though, a top writer of the 'Cream Soap Theatre' staring Lance Rock and Betty Summers. They were famous sleuths of the city solving murder cases every Sunday night at prime time. The case of 'The Banana Killer', 'The Murder of the Cabana Boy', then the case of, 'Summer love and Murder in the Banana Cabana'. I was on top. I even wrote the sponsor's slogan, 'Be lustre clean, use Cream Soap the soup mix of natural soft ingredients of aloe bananas'. You must have listened to the show on Sunday nights at eight P.M. on CKCY 95.4.

BURT
No.

FRED
No?

BURT
No!

FRED
No!? well the show was up against Master Piece Theatre on the National network.

BURT
Yes, yes, enjoyed the theatre quality of their radio plays. Their presentations made one feel as if being there within the performed play.

FRED
Well . . . they had a national sponsor. With a good story I could be on top again, maybe with Master Piece Theatre. Burt, you must have a story; think, think.

BURT
(smooth bed covering, rise, walk to window and gaze out as if recalling a devastating story)
Once, from a distance, from this very room, from this window I . . .

FRED
(lean forward in anticipation, pull a pencil and notepad from a pocket)
Yes, yes, from this very spot?

BURT
... noticed a drastic occurrence, a strange case of bad taste; the master of the house confronted the grounds keeper in front of the entire staff. Mrs. Blackburn lay motionless on a lounge chair.
(pause)

FRED
Yes, yes, go on.

BURT
Mr. Blackburn was yelling, admonishing the grounds keeper; he said. 'The yellow banana colour of the covering of this cabana clashes with the purple grape colour of Mrs. Blackburn's swimsuit robe. Remove the cabana!' (drop head and sigh)

FRED
(pause pencil over page of notebook) Really, I get it, 'the Case of the Yellow Banana Cabana.'

DIRECTIONS
Camera pulls in tight on Fred's bemused face then whirls down to the kitchen where Beth and Martha are joined by Jane. Together they set the large dinning room table and place the meal. From various rooms, heads pop out when the aroma of food reaches their noses. Burt is standing at the table and as Fred, Santa and Molly arrive he seats them in butler style; Molly and Fred on one side and Santa at the head of the table. When the women enter, Burt seats Beth with Fred and Jane and Martha on the opposite side. Satisfied that the table is perfect and that all are seated he hovers at the edge as if waiting to carry out his butler duties. Among small talk and readying of cloth napkins, Fred breaks the moment.

FRED
Burt, you are not our butler, you are just one of us, take a seat.

MARTHA
Yes Burt, please sit. I do not mind you sitting beside me.

BURT
Of course, it is just ingrained old habits. I have not been a butler for three years.

DIRECTIONS
All go about normal mannerisms of partaking of a meal, small talk underlines main dialogue; example; 'Food looks delicious.' 'Martha's talent.' 'Beth's

Mother's recipe.' 'Santa could use a plumper belly.' 'Beth, your Mother's food is great.' 'Her attitude not so much.' 'Jane, learn to cook like Martha and grab a husband.'

SANTA
The Grand Hotel was it not, then . . .

BURT
How did you know . . .? yes, the Grand Hotel, I was a private butler to the Continental suites.

FRED
What happened?

BURT
Greed. With greed comes a decline in service. The hotel owner raised accommodation rates and reduced staff. His greed for profit filled his pocket.

MARTHA
Dear, what have you done in the duration?

BURT
Odd jobs, as a waiter, bus-boy and janitor; though, I have viewed the expanses of this beautiful country during long walking travels.

SANTA
There is always a sure position at the next destination; a guaranteed future is arriving on time.

FRED
Yeah, I have done the same thing. Remember Beth, Joe told us about a film job. We travelled a thousand miles only to arrive too late.

BETH
Then Millie, the secretary told us about another job opening.

FRED
Again, we were too late.

BURT
Always too late or excuses from the employer; 'you are too old' 'no need for a fancy butler' 'can you cook too'.

MARTHA

Burt, you could never cook.

BURT
True, thus no job.

MOLLY
But something made you travel to the restaurant where you met Martha and
we met Santa and then everyone met Jane and it is all because of . . .

FRED
Sh . . . sh . . . eat your vegetables.

MOLLY
But Dad!

FRED
Okay, okay it is all because of me. I ran down Santa – Nick and made Jane
crash her car and it is all my fault that the bus died and stranded us here.

DIRECTIONS
Everyone seemingly agrees and begins to nod their heads.

MOLLY
No Dad . . ., it is because of fate. There are specific reasons for leading
everyone to their destiny. There is a purpose for all of us being here. Just ask
Santa.

BURT
Quite a profound statement though I do not think that Nick is behind fate.

JANE
They were mostly accidental circumstances.

FRED
Maybe a miracle, no, it is a miracle.

BETH
No Fred, the bus is old and worn out. It was bound to die. And yes, eventually
we will be living with my parents.

FRED
Please let me enjoy the moment away from the old . . .

BETH

Don't say if Fred!

MOLLY
Santa, tell them that you arranged for everyone to meet. You have a purpose.

BETH
Molly dear, Santa only brings joy during the Christmas season and toys and pretty clothes for little girls.

MOLLY
Not this year. I did not ask for fancy clothes or toys.

JANE
All girls want nice clothes, even girls of all ages.

MARTHA
Yes, if only to have a gown for a Christmas dance.

BETH
Even if it is a hand made dress.

MOLLY
Mother, we can make clothes anytime. I asked Santa in my letter for more important things.

FRED
Like what Molly?

MOLLY
Oh . . . I cannot say. If I do, then the magic will not work; right Santa?

SANTA
Well . . . life has a way of creating its' own magic. In the strangest way circumstances can result in happy endings.

FRED
Until the owners of this place arrive and find us free-loaders eating their food. In short notice we will be residents of the city jail. No offence Nick, but I find it difficult to believe that the owners of this mansion let a Hobo house sit. Any minute the door is going to burst open and we are off the hoosecow.

DIRECTIONS
Fred pulls out a harmonica and begins to play 'Fred's Blues' instrumental song in the style of a jail house blues. Small talk and pleasant laughter hum

around the table until a door bell sounds, and sounds echo within the room then the full volume throughout the mansion. All around the table the characters freeze in mid action. The door bell continues to sound.

FRED
(whisper above the harmonica held in played action) I told you, the cops have arrived.
MOLLY
(grip Beth's arm, stare at and plead to Santa) Santa, is Daddy telling the truth? Do you have a plan!?

DIRECTIONS
Santa seems to act as puzzled as everyone else. Eyes dart about. Burt seems to relax, places folded napkin on the table and begins to rise.

FRED
Burt, don't move. If everyone stays put maybe they will go away.

BURT
I shall address the circumstances.

FRED
No, no . . . jail is worse than living with a hateful mother-in-law. Sit Burt, the ringing has stopped . . . see they have left.

DIRECTIONS
Santa dabs a napkin about his beard and winks at Molly.

SANTA
Dear Fred, you exaggerate, and you are frightening Molly.

FRED
(look nervously at Molly) It will be okay Molly. I will protect you. We will escape through the back door. (begin to rise)

SANTA
Relax Fred, you worry too much. Burt, please address the front door. Everyone, please relax.

DIRECTIONS
Worried eyes follow Burt to the double dinning room doors. Burt slowly slides open then closes behind. The camera withdraws toward the front door maintaining a focus on Burt who transforms mannerism of a butler meant to be employed in this household. First Burt turns on the porch lights then

reaches for the door handle. The camera passes through the door to see William laden with suitcases and bent over intent on pushing the door bell with his nose. At his side is Lizzy also laden with suitcases and bundled in winter coats. The door opens.

BURT
(with restrained surprise) Good evening Mr. And Mrs Wentworth.

WILLIAM
That voice, I know that voice. (confused, inspect address) What year is it, have we travelled back in time?

LIZZY
Burtrum, welcome home.

BURT
Welcome home Miss. Elizabeth. May I help you with your luggage? (accept and bring in luggage)

WILLIAM
Burt, Burt, are you here to stay . . . for good. I smell food . . . is it Martha's cooking?

LIZZY
Martha . . . and Jane? Burtrum, am I dreaming? (drop remaining luggage and hug Burt with a sisterly embrace after a long absent)

BURT
We . . . yes they are here, but we are not here to stay.

WILLIAM
Hog-wash Burt. (grab Burt's hand and shake) You are our gests.

BURT
You did not invite us.

LIZZY
I trust that Nick is here and if he invited you then you are our gests.

WILLIAM
Drop the luggage Burt. (pat Burt on back as luggage is dropped) Real guests, . . . we have real guests Lizzy.

DIRECTIONS

As William and Lizzy discard winter clothing and dropping them scattered among luggage, Burt attempts to be a butler and organize the clothing. Lizzy and William prevent Burt from doing anything.

WILLIAM
Stop that Burt . . . you are not my employee . . . you are my guest. Now let's go eat. I hope that there is plenty of food left.

BURT
Mr. Wentworth, the suitcases, the door.

WILLIAM
Not important. (with a backward kick, kick door closed, put a hand on Burt's back and direct him toward the dinning room) Lead the way Burt. How have you been? Where have you been? Everyone fine? Jane must be what sixteen —seventeen?

LIZZY
Bill, Jane must be a beautiful, full grown woman, not a child. It has been years since . . .

WILLIAM
Too many dam years. I miss our checkerboard games Burt.

BURT
Chess Mr. Wentworth.

WILLIAM
Oh yeah, chess played on a checkerboard, and call me Bill; my true friends call me Bill.

LIZZY
You don't have friends Bill. Burtrum, call me Lizzy, not Miss. Elizabeth. (take Burt's hand and pat it)

BURT
(overwhelmed, plod along and just nod) Miss . . . Lizzy, . . . Bill, I could not.

WILLIAM
You can.

LIZZY
You must.

DIRECTIONS
While William is pushing Burt toward the dinning room, Lizzy is halting him to ask questions.

WILLIAM
Fancy a game of chess checkerboard after dinner Burt? I've never won a game against you. I've practiced, but I think Richard lets me win. To win a game against you would be a challenge. Have you played lately?

BURT
No, no . . . no current opportunity.

LIZZY
Has the years been difficult Burt? When did you and Martha reunite and Jane? Martha's last letter did not mention . . .

BURT
Just a chance meeting recently.

LIZZY
Nick's doing . . . must have been.

WILLIAM
Lizzy, stop holding up our progression to the dinning room. Martha's cooking is beyond those doors.

LIZZY
What, my cooking is not worthy of such a rush to devour?

WILLIAM
You and I know and have agreed that your cooking is substance lacking taste.

LIZZY
Yes, true. Let's go, I am famished . . . means hungry, Bill.

WILLIAM
I know, I know the meaning of ten-dollar words too.

DIRECTIONS
Before But can reach for the doors, both Lizzy and Burt slide the doors wide and enter with childish glee leaving Burt frozen, slightly bent forward with hands reaching for invisible doors. With the sudden burst, the guests at the table rise. William and Lizzy enter and instantly rush around the table greeting those known and introductions made to the unknown. Lizzy hugs Martha,

Jane and Nick, even a reluctant Fred, a surprised Beth and Molly. William gives hardy, overly extended handshakes of childish eagerness. Rushing about Lizzy and William gather up place settings and place them on either side of Nick. William is tucked in next to Nick and Fred, and Lizzy between Nick and Martha. Burt is quickly behind to place chairs for Lizzy and William. Martha and Jane seem pleased and quickly become comfortable. Nick is at ease to fill in small talk of greetings. Fred and Beth is a bit shy and off guard. Molly is amazed by the reunion and the ease with which they are accepted, welcoming the warm large family feel, unknown in her young life.

WILLIAM
Sit, please, all sit and pass Martha's cooking. I have craved her meals for years.

MARTHA
Beth has created some dishes also.

WILLIAM
Then I must sample; please pass.

DIRECTIONS
With a random, logical flow hands pass and deliver pots, pans and dishes while Nick pours wine for Lizzy and William.

LIZZY
This table has not seen such warmth since . . .

WILLIAM
. . . ever, since Burt up and left us high and dry with no darn reason.

SANTA
Past events and due to circumstances a present reunion has occurred. Shall I offer a toast to this happy reunion?

WILLIAM
Here, here.

LIZZY
And to new acquaintances and most welcome guests.

WILLIAM
After what circumstances must we toast Fred, Beth and Miss. Molly as our newly gained guests?

DIRECTIONS
After a slight pause, everyone starts to add their version when Molly first utters.

MOLLY
My Dad . . .

JANE
My car skidded . . .

BURT
I saw Nick sailing . . .

BETH
My baby kicked and I screeched . . .

JANE
Snow was blurring my view . . .

MARTHA
Not until I came out of the kitchen did I know.

MOLLY
Santa planned everything.

BETH
The bus just skidded into the snow bank.

JANE
I didn't see them in the middle of the road.

DIRECTIONS
Lizzy and William bob heads back and forth to each person randomly. Nonchalantly Santa continues to nibble and nod occasionally in agreement.

FRED
(in a flurry stand up in anger and apologetic at the same time offering an abstract explanation)
Okay, fine, it is my entire fault. Beth is pregnant; she makes funny sounds that make me nervous then Bam! Nick, he just appeared, and I looked away and then he is floating among the snowflakes. Yes, I hit him, but he was okay, just faking it. Then I saw Jane's car speeding and I froze in the middle of the road, I didn't shoo everyone out of the way from danger. I forced Jane to swerve and crash. But . . . but, everyone is okay and . . . and . . . I was nice

enough to give everyone a ride then the bus broke down in the driveway . . . not my fault, I mean the broken bus. And, here we are stranded all because of me.

WILLIAM
No problem. Lizzy, we have quests. Welcome, pass the pie please.

DIRECTIONS
Everyone settles down to eat with arms passing food back and forth. Camera spins around the table as it blacks out intermediately to show time lapse. Moments of laughter with comical sadness by Fred; womanly scolding, men talk and Molly maintaining an audience. Camera slows to show everyone relaxing.

WILLIAM
This has been a most wonderful meal. (lean towards Nick, whisper) Nick, how can I entice Martha to return and cook. Even Lizzy would welcome not having to cook.

SANTA
I see. It would not hurt to ask. I do believe that Burtrum and Martha are searching for a place to call home. From the brief time I have spent with them, they have not lost a love for each other, though they present an indifferent front.

WILLIAM
Then what is the problem?

SANTA
It is the effects of being separated for so long. They need familiarity with each other and a welcome place to call home.

WILLIAM
Done, just offer them their jobs and resume togetherness as if it was the day before they up and left.

SANTA
Not as simple as that; there are emotions to consider and it must be their decision. Bill, you are just thinking with your stomach.

WILLIAM
(nod in agreement) Yes . . . yes . . ., you are right. Maybe you can do what you do . . . and make everything turn out hunky-dory. (move hands as if mixing and tossing up a solution)

SANTA
Magic . . .!

WILLIAM
Exactly, that is what you do. You solve problems.

SANTA
Not really. Are you in need of magic?

WILLIAM
Me, no.

SANTA
Lizzy?

WILLIAM
Lizzy, no.

DIRECTIONS
Gathered heads begin to turn and listen, stopping their own conversations.

SANTA
There must be a reason why you have returned in the cold of winter. It can not be the gathering of unexpected guests, for this gathering has been an impromptu occurrence.

WILLIAM
(shake head, mumble, search for an explanation)
Well, no . . ., but for this moment of time I and, from the glow on Lizzy's face, being here with such fine guests is the most . . . most . . .

LIZZY
. . . Fabulous and heart-warming experience we have had in years, but yes there is a reason.

FRED
You would rather endure cold weather and unemployed free-loaders scattered throughout your home than the aristocratic life in southern resorts and hob-knob with the rich?

BETH
Fred . . ., hush up . . . it is not your place.

JANE

There must be an important reason, for you did not know we were here?

MARTHA
Is there something wrong . . ., Richard . . ., is he sick, hurt?

LIZZY
No . . . no . . . not sick!

MARTHA
Oh, thank goodness!

FRED
The warm southern weather can not be depressing?

WILLIAM
No, I do like the warmth on my arthritis.

FRED
I know . . ., I know, I get it.

BETH
You know what Fred; Mr. Know-it-all?

FRED
Snobs!

BETH
Fred, Lizzy and Bill are not snobs.

FRED
No! all of the others are snobs. Bill and Lizzy do not fit in, not a part of the elite. Bill said it himself; being here with us no-bodies, poor, unemployed, and they are enjoying themselves. They are our type of people . . . just rich.

WILLIAM
Exactly . . .we don't fit in.

LIZZY
They do tolerate us because of our wealth, new money is somewhat welcome but wealth breeding we do not have.

WILLIAM
And I don't want to have their breeding, and now . . .

FRED
And . . . what? Go on.

SANTA
Magic may not be what you need, rather those gathered here may understand,
be compassionate and it may be the magic component you require.
FRED
Go ahead, bend our ears.

WILLIAM
Darn right; we don't fit in with the elite. We have tried to fit in, opened our
home and catered parties and only a scatter of them showed up . . . but Richard
fits in.

LIZZY
We need to be there for Richard and pretend to fit in for his sake. He needs to
be accepted and work among them.

WILLIAM
Richard . . . our son, born to poor folks . . . now is engaged to a daughter of
old money, and we have to back him up by having a big shing-dig engagement
party.

MARTHA
Lizzy, this is good news about Richard.

LIZZY
Yes, if we can pull it off and not embarrass Richard's Fiancé and her family.

WILLIAM
Miss. Mildred Easthouseman.

BURT
(suddenly burst up)
Mildred Easthouseman, your neighbours, the Easthousemans.

MARTHA
Burtrum, please!

WILLIAM
My sentiments exactly.

LIZZY
William!

WILLIAM
Well, they do not like us, and I do not like them. Richard is just blinded by Mildred's exterior looks.

LIZZY
They will be our son's in-laws whether we accept it or not.

WILLIAM
I choose not.

LIZZY
For Richard's sake we must be sociable and considerate.

BURT
At what cost must a person accommodate such class distinction?

JANE
Father, it is not your place to intervene with your views.

LIZZY
Of what concern is it of yours Burtrum? What have the Easthousemans done to you to make you so riled?

BURT
To us . . .yes to us . . . look at the state of our lives.

JANE
Mildred was a bit too prim and proper for joining in our play time as children, but she did not hate me.

FRED
It is not always the innocent children; rather their parents are prejudice and condescending.

BETH
Hush up Fred . . ., you don't know what happened.

FRED
I can guess.

WILLIAM
Go ahead Fred, do your guessing.

FRED

Burt is obviously upset by the mention of this Easthouseman name. Bill, if I may call you Bill . . .?

WILLIAM
That is my name, so use it Fred.
FRED
Bill feels a dislike for the Easthousemans, and they of him. Miss. Lizzy has tried to fit in, yet her gatherings are snubbed by them there up-turned nose people.

BETH
Watch your manners Fred.

FRED
Jane, a servant's daughter playing with the son of new money and the Easthousemans noticing that their daughter is not included is a big deal. So, Burt sees the big picture and concludes that if Jane and Richard become an item then the Wentworths would be treated like lepers.

DIRECTIONS
Heads and eyes are darting about, and faces are expressing ranges of emotion. Molly is spell bound by the in-depth subject matter. Burt is slowly sinking into self reflection and relief of a partial truth being revealed.

FRED
So, Burt leaves, his family separated by circumstances, love is lost, life is wasted, employment reduced, friendships strained and only the Easthousemans win.

WILLIAM
I will buy that.

LIZZY
Burtrum, is this true?

SANTA
(lean and whisper to Fred)
Quite a story with a possible plot for a future script.

FRED
(after a pause the idea registers, pat pockets in search of a pencil and paper)
Drama, intrigue, class distinction . . ., I need facts . . ., and an ending.

SANTA

No one is going anywhere. The bus is broken so you are stuck here as guests; the Burtons have nowhere to go, and the Wentworths just returned. There is plenty of time for events to unfold.

FRED
Burt . . . you are not denying my version?

WILLIAM
Is this true? You forced Martha to leave and made me suffer Lizzy's cooking?

LIZZY
Bill, food is not the most important fact. I may not be a wiz in the kitchen but give me a spread sheet and a party and I excel.

WILLIAM
That, my dear, is your greatest asset. If only you could have retained Martha.

LIZZY
I didn't have any idea that the Burtons were leaving. One day they were gone, and I could not find them. I inquired everywhere thinking they were working for our neighbours.

MARTHA
We would never do such an ungrateful thing as that to you. We loved our employment and uncommon friendship.

JANE
Father just told us we were leaving; he never said why.

WILLIAM
Burt, why? Is what Fred assuming, the truth?

DIRECTIONS
Silence prevails as all eyes turn toward Burt slouching in a chair. From a distance a clock chimes out the sounds of 'Silent Night' music. Molly leans on the table on crossed arms to stare deeply at Burt.

MOLLY
My dad is a good story teller; he makes up stories all the time. Did he make up a true story Mr. Burton?

BURT
(slowly raise eyes to look at Molly) Molly my drear child, I have missed important years of Jane's life because of my staunch class pride believing in

my place in class structure. I should have trusted in the humanity of the Wentworths and confided in them.

LIZZY
It is not too late Burtrum. We have not become the likes of those that consider class distinction secular.

BURT
Mr. And Mrs. Easthouseman hinted . . . no, they threatened to run this Wentworth household out of town if I did not contain our place and prevent Jane from associating with Richard and Mildred's social circle. They were no longer just innocent children; they were maturing, and Mildred was becoming smitten with Richard. Jane was in the way. So . . . I did what they demanded and ruined a marriage and family; mine.

JANE
Oh Dad!

DIRECTIONS
Faces sadden. Lizzy reaches for Jane and Martha's hands. Bill shakes his head in discuss. Fred secretly jots notes on a napkin. Beth hugs Molly with motherly affection. Santa slightly smiles with satisfaction, seemingly knowing that past and current circumstances will lead to a better outcome. Lights fade and the camera withdraws from room. A time change occurs as the lights come up and the camera moves about the house from the outside. Camera follows Jane, bundled up and walking about the snow filled walkways through the garden down to the small cottage. From a distance a man is advancing on skies from the Easthouseman's estate. Snow is lightly falling as the wind picks up. The Camera turns to the house to capture Santa looking out through the window, a slight smile on his face when seeing Jane and the approaching Richard, soon to meet. Molly squeezes her head between Santa and the window, though unable to see anything through a snow bank. Behind them a Christmas tree is in the stage of being decorated. Through another window the camera passes into the kitchen where Beth, Martha and Lizzy are looking over Beth's scattered recipes. Delightfully they visualize final products. Exiting the kitchen, the camera hears harmonica music of 'I Shall Return to Kintyre' song echoing hauntingly from the den. Camera enters. Fred is playing lead on a harmonica while William plays background harmony. Both men are concentrating on each other until hearing a low voice; they turn toward Burt adjusting the wood in the fire place. His voice begins to rise and the haunting lyrics of Celtic and blues music blend on the music of 'I shall return to Kintyre'.

BURT

(Song 'I Shall Return to Kintyre')

Send me a memory of lost years,
Of walking through the glenn,
Where hearts no longer fear,
The day when,

The snow of winter lay on meadows,
And clouds top the wee mull.
I left the day shadows,
On eyes tear-full.

I shall return someday to Kintyre,
To my bonny Gwenn, I desire.
From misty seas shall come I,
Returning from afar to justify.

That I am not worthy of embrace,
Until of me you trust.
In youth I once did chase,
The gold turned to dust.

I shall return someday to Kintyre,
To my bonny Gwenn I desire.
From misty seas shall come I,
Returning from afar to justify.

DIRECTIONS
Burt draws out the last line, his voice becoming melancholy. William holds a sustained note that fades on the last line. With wide eyes he studies Burt with compassion of not knowing the man years earlier. Fred is enwrapped in the music and faintly trails off a repetitive ending until noticing the silence of the two men. Self conscious, Fred looks down and slightly taps excess spit from the harmonica.

WILLIAM
Burt . . . your voice is so emotional, unlike the persona of being a butler. I envy not hearing such music throughout our earlier years of acquaintance.

BURT
In those years I separated my personal and employment lives. No longer do I hold such restrictions. I have been a waiter and have sung while serving romantic couples and thoroughly enjoyed myself. I am who I am and wish that others will accept me as I am.

200

WILLIAM
Burt, I always have. I wish you would have realized this and have been yourself and confided in me. All of that Easthouseman mess could have been nipped in the bud long ago. There have been wasted years, and years filled with Lizzy's inadequate cooking.

BURT
My sympathy Master William, concerning your digestive system.

WILLIAM
Bill to you Burt, and no further debate.

BURT
(contemplate) Yes, yes, Bill.

FRED
Well, all is easily settled, Bill, just hire Burt and Martha.

WILLIAM
Sounds simple enough.

BURT
It is not that easy. Martha may not be accepting of me within a joint employment. After all we have been separated far too long.

WILLIAM
Are you still legally married?

BURT
Yes; no divorce papers have been singed.

FRED
Do you still love her?

BURT
Yes; that has not changed.

FRED
Then no problem; you are still married, you love her, you got a potential job offer, so all you have to do is to get Martha to say she loves you.

WILLIAM
Then that can not be so hard to accomplish. Fred and I will help.

FRED
I will?

WILLIAM
Of course, it is your idea.

FRED
So, it is!

WILLIAM
Leave that part up to us. There is another problem we have not considered . .
. the Easthouseman situation.

BURT
Please consider the matter closed.

WILLIAM
You are the better man. But I do have a problem with the Easthousemans.
Richard is engaged to Mildred, and I must throw a big party. I don't know any
of the people in their social circles. My acquaintances are very limited; my
friends are my barber, baker and the guys at the automotive garage. Who am
I going to invite; it is winter, most families are in warmer locales?

BURT
It shall be a challenge, Bill. Leave matters to me. An occasion should be
enjoyed by all who wish to enjoy. An occasion should not be arranged to
impress only the Easthousemans. Should they not cater to Master Richard?

WILLIAM
Well said Burt.

DIRECTIONS
Fred begins to play an upbeat blues version of 'Fred's Blues'. Music drifts
into the main living area and the Christmas tree being decorated by Molly and
Santa. Molly begins to pull a string out of a box of decorations from beneath
assorted decorations from opposite ends of the box. Two ornaments begin to
draw together. Molly is mesmerized as the two objects move towards each
other. Santa peers over Molly. A smile beams and a twinkle reflects from an
eye. Molly is intrigued by a female figurine bundled up in fur and carrying
gifts, and a male figurine skiing with a scarf trailing in the wind, both
advancing toward each other. As Molly gives a last tug, the figurines collide,
and the strings entangle. The camera flashes to the out doors to catch Richard
colliding with Jane and tumbling in the snow. Richard appears out of nowhere

202

from around the back of the cabin. Jane had just stopped to face the cabin when noticing smoke rising from the chimney. In an awkward embrace the pair tumbles down a slight embankment into deeper fluffy snow. When the snow settles, and eyes blink away snow, the pair stare bewilderedly into each other's eyes. Faded memories of recognition puzzle their expressions.

RICHARD
Do I know you? Your face is so familiar; those quizzical eyes.

JANE
Yes, Richard, you should remember me, though we have never been so enwrapped in an improper compromising entanglement before.

RICHARD
No . . . no . . ., I am so sorry. (attempt to untangle legs and feet latched to skies stuck awkwardly in the snow) I did not expect to run into a stranger in front of my cabin. Yes, a stranger. What are you doing here, and who are you?

JANE
Circumstances are the results of being a stranger revisiting an old familiar place that holds many wonderful memories.

RICHARD
Jane . . . Jane Burton! (stop trying to untangle legs, with a hand brush snow from around Jane's fur hood) Behind the beauty I see the tomboy girl grinning and scowling when we played shinny-hockey.

JANE
And baseball; . . . and in every sport that I was as good as you in.

RICHARD
You were. (relax a bit too intimately)

JANE
Please . . . I am no longer a tomboy and wish not to wrestle Richard Wentworth at this moment.

RICHARD
UH!

JANE
(pull arms together over chest and pull coat tight around neck, narrow eyes)

RICHARD
(stare blankly into Jane's eyes) UH . . . OH . . . yes . . . my apologies.

DIRECTIONS
Richard struggles to roll away while legs kick at skies stuck in the snow. Like a fish flopping on snow covered ice, Richard buries himself in the snow. Rolling away, using the long coat as a barrier, Jane escapes, stands to watch Richard's comical struggle, her laughter hidden behind hands but is heard by Richard. Giving up, Richard relaxes on the snow.

RICHARD
Help . . . please help. Unlock me from these slabs of lumber imitating skies.

JANE
As I remember, I rescued you the first time you were learning to ski, and I am doing it again.

RICHARD
I was . . . what . . . seven years old?

JANE
And trying to impress Mildred Easthouseman.

RICHARD
Who?

JANE
Your fiancée, Mildred.

RICHARD
Yes . . ., Yes, Mildred!

JANE
Easthouseman.

RICHARD
Yes, Mildred Easthouseman; . . . how do you know?

JANE
Congratulations. (say sarcastically) I must get back before I freeze, it is getting dark.

RICHARD
You'll freeze; you must get warm first. The cabin is warm.

DIRECTIONS
Richard gently grips Jane's elbow and struggles to lead Jane up and over the

snow bank. Small talk of their childhood years flows throughout antics. Jane does not seem to have a problem; while Richard slips and slides and falls often because of smooth soled ski books. Once in the cabin, Richard adds wood to the open fireplace; clicks on a phonograph player and a song titled, 'When Hearts Believe' plays in background. He goes about madly to impress Jane; providing a blanket and warm slippers; hanging her coat, offering warm brandy, all the while shivering and standing as an awkward teenager would when fascinated by an older woman.

Song
'When Hearts Believe'

The north wind blows winter snows,
And warm hearts are aglow,
When lovers embrace beneath mistletoe.

Hear the bells ring,
Voices sing Auld Lang Syne.
Dreams come true,
When hearts believe on Hew Years Eve.

Give a kiss to your girl,
And a hug to your guy,
It's a love affair, young ones want to try.

Hear the bells ring,
Voices sing Auld Lang Syne.
Dreams come true,
When hearts believe on Hew Years Eve.

See the light of fire glow,
In a cabin wrapped in snow,
When young hearts whisper these words, all should know.

Hear the bells ring,
Voices sing Auld Lang Syne.
Dreams come true,
When hearts believe on Hew Years Eve.

JANE
Richard, you are staring, and shivering.

RICHARD
Yes. (shake out of stare, remove boots and coat, gather a blanket and sit

opposite of Jane in front of fireplace) Please tell me everything after the day you left me at the sand lot, one player short and no one to play short stop.

JANE
It was not by my choice.

RICHARD
We lost the game.

JANE
You should have gotten over the loss by now.

RICHARD
Not the loss of you, . . . a friend.

JANE
Life has a purpose and individually we do not have a say in changing life's time line.

RICHARD
You are here now . . . so what is the purpose of the new time line?

JANE
I did not plan anything beyond the moment I swerved my car and crashed into a roadside eatery and garage.

RICHARD
When; are you all right; who caused you to swerve?

JANE
Fred, Beth . . . little seven-year-old Molly, a cute little girl . . . and . . . oh yes Santa.

RICHARD
Santa . . . a department store Santa; a Santa bill-board cut out?

JANE
No . . . a Hobo Santa.

RICHARD
Hobo . . . a Santa that is a Hobo?

JANE
Yes . . . he brought us here with my Mother and Father.

206

RICHARD
A tall skinny man, short white beard, big red sack?

JANE
Yes.

RICHARD
You mean Nick . . . our winter house sitter. Okay . . . you had better start from the beginning and tell me everything about your life and including how Nick has changed life's time line.

JANE
Nick . . . Santa?

DIRECTIONS
Richard pokes the logs in the fire then moves beside Jane to pour more sherry. Settling down they awkwardly loose their adult persona and drift to their childhood closeness. Jane begins to tell about her life. The camera withdraws from the room, panning from the pair to the fire then instantly the camera pulls away from the fireplace and transforms into the fireplace in the main family room and then pulls away. Santa and Molly are continuing to hang decorations. Molly pauses to examine the tree and their decorating efforts. Her eyes are fixated on the two decorations; the woman in a fur coat, and the skier at opposite sides of the tree.

MOLLY
Santa, I do not think the woman in the fur coat should be by herself. The man skiing seems determined to ski to her.

SANTA
Let's name the woman Jane and the Skier Richard and see what happens when we bring them together.

DIRECTIONS
Molly selects the figurine decorations and places them on the same branch. Harmonica music of Christmas thymes filters through the house. The camera heads for the kitchen. Entering the kitchen, the women are chit-chatting while an abundance of cooking and exchanges of ideas and taste testing unfolds. A happy, equal camaraderie is unfolding as they also make fun of men, social status, neighbours and who eats what and when.

BETH
Fred loves Canadian Baked Beans. A man from the south, who loves Canadian Baked Beans; hot, cold, for meals and for a cold bean sandwich in

the middle of the night. He has never been to Canada, and he is not bashful when expelling gas. He say's it is a compliment to well made baked beans.

MARTHA
Now Burt would never, ever . . . he would clench up and turn blue before ever venting what is as natural among a herd of cattle.

LIZZY
Why do men hold the gas in until they are under the bed covers . . . then they have to vent by flapping the covers. Bill does it as a ritual.

BETH / MARTHA / LIZZY
Men! (laughter)

LIZZY
(suddenly become quiet, fall into deep thought, allow eyes to follow Martha spicing dishes and Beth making notes in her cook book) Ladies, . . . are we not talented women?

BETH / MARTHA
Yes.

LIZZY
Independent women?

BETH / MARTHA
Yes.

LIZZY
In need of jobs, a career?

BETH / MARTHA
(hesitate)
Well . . . yes.

BETH
Liz, if I may be so bold, you live in this mansion, you have stability, you do not need to seek a career.

LIZZY
No . . . the assumption would be no, but I am the woman behind the man and made the man that William is. I desire the challenge to create and be a career woman. To be honest, I hate hob knobbing and pretending to do a lot of nothing. I have an idea!

208

DIRECTIONS
Beth and Martha hesitate, shrug to each other then mindlessly attend to their tasks. Lizzy hovers on the edge of excitement, expecting enthusiasm from the ladies.

MARTHA
 Am just a cook.

LIZZY
Yes, yes you are, and Beth is a writer.

BETH
With a husband and a child to take care of.

LIZZY
You can do both. Please listen to my idea. I need to host an engagement party for Richard and Mildred, and I need help; your cooking abilities Martha, and Beth's recipes to impress the guests. We can become business partners and cater out our combined talents in the future.

DIRECTIONS
Beth and Martha become reserved as Lizzy continues talking. They begin to stir pots faster and begin to move in a cooking rhythm. Lizzy displays actions and movements of an orchestra conductor.

LIZZY
Equal partners, pooling our talents, I will take care of finances, after all fifty percent of William's worth is mine. Running accounts, inventory, sales, promotion, purchasing and dealing with clientele is my forte. Martha just tell me what you need to create dishes as you have in the past. Your mind holds a repertoire of culinary delights. Beth is the writer and holder of recipes requiring debuting. Beth can create our cook book and add in stories. We need stories; Fred's craving for Canadian Baked beans and William's positive critiquing of Martha's dishes. Promotion, promotion, promotion is needed. Three Ladies Catering . . . no, Ladies of Culinary Delights . . .?

BETH
Culinary Catering . . .?

LIZZY
Culinary Catering.

MARTHA
Classy Catering?

LIZZY / BETH / MARTHA
Classic Culinary Catering.

DIRECTIONS
Martha's Beams a wide smile and gives the pot an excited stir. Beth jots down notes and hands a tray of spices to Martha and watches how much is used and makes notes. Lizzy dabs a dry cloth to Martha's brow.

MARTHA
How many guests have you invited Miss Lizzy?

LIZZY
Liz; Martha we are partners.

MARTHA
Liz, sounds nice. How many picky eaters shall we need to impress?

LIZZY
Two-three hundred.

BETH
Three hundred?

LIZZY / MARTHA
That's a small gathering.

DIRECTIONS
Laughter erupts from Lizzy and Martha. Beth slowly builds and relaxes a tensed body. The camera fades then brightens on a new day forming through the main entrance's windows facing out through the back of the mansion. The sun's brightness is clouded, and snow is lightly falling. The camera turns to the staircase and watches Lizzy descending the stairs to greet Burt placing on an overcoat. Lizzy greets Burt and hands over a bundle of invitations.

BURT
Good morning Miss . . . (hesitate when Lizzy lifts a finger) It shall take me awhile to accommodate the ability to address you as Liz. I accept your presumption of equality.

LIZZY
Martha, Beth and I are equal business partners and having you address me as Mrs. Wentworth is awkward.

BURT

Martha and I are not . . .

LIZZY
Hog-wash; she is still in love with you. You just need to relax, be a man and court her. As far as I am concerned you two are together. You just do not realize it yet.

BURT
(ponder and glance to the kitchen) Well . . . we shall see. At the moment I have summoned a cab and shall deliver these invitations for the engagement party.

LIZZY
You may deliver, but I fear that RSVP's may be very limited.

BURT
I shall do my utmost to convince addressed parties.

DIRECTIONS
Burt exits and Martha heads for the kitchen. Burt's taxi leaves the driveway, the camera pans to the side to take in the panoramic view of the open landscape. Suddenly the camera halts then pans back and focuses on a woman's figure skiing toward the cottage. The camera zooms in on the woman approaching the front of the cabin. From the inside of the cabin the camera slowly revolves around the room to hesitate on coats on a coat rack by the door, the fireplace with ashes smouldering, empty wine glasses, the record player slowly spinning with the needle poised above the record, a candle flickering out above the melted remains of wax. When sounds of Mildred echoes through the front door, as she removes skies and stamps feet to remove snow, the camera zooms in on the feet of Jane and Richard. Toes wiggle and playfully play with each other's from a position of soles against each other. With a loud knock at the door from an external metal knocker, the feet freeze and toes cramp. The camera pulls back to see Richard and Jane awkwardly sleeping end to end on the rug in front of the fireplace. Heads move, eyes roll and arms stretch. Richard pops up and looks at watch then glances to the door then to Jane lovingly waking.

RICHARD
This is awkward! (wiggle toes against Jane's toes)

JANE
(draw feet away) Yes, indeed; inappropriate toe flirtation, shameful, what will mother and father say! (playfully tease)

RICHARD

What will Mildred say? What will she think?
JANE
Mildred?

RICHARD
She is at the front door.

JANE
Invite her in. we are all old friends.

RICHARD
My fiancée . . ., Mildred Easthouseman?

JANE
I see! (be understanding though insulted and put off)

DIRECTIONS
Jane rushes about gathering coat, boots, wine glass while straightening out
the sofa and rug before rushing towards the back door. She hesitates then turns
to Richard who is standing dumbfounded in the middle of the room.

JANE
There is no back door, and I am not some hussy fleeing from a man's wife.

RICHARD
Worse, this is Mildred we are talking about, a fiancée!

JANE
(rush to front door while whispering instructions) I'll hide behind the door as
you open it. Take her in your arms, kiss her.

RICHARD
Awkward!

JANE
Do it before she barges in and makes assumptions.

DIRECTIONS
Jane hides at the side of the door as Richard opens the door.

MILDRED
Richard! I was worried, you were supposed to meet me early this morning.
We have an appointment. Did you forget?

DIRECTIONS

From a corner of an eye, Richard watches Jane gesturing to speed it up as she pantomimes directions. Richard reaches out and grabs Mildred drawing her into the room and plants a kiss to smother further talking from Mildred. Through an open eye, Richard watches Jane escape and draw the door closed. The heavy door closes with a bank. Mildred jumps and turns as a shadow passes by a side window.

RICHARD

Awkward! The wind . . . no manners . . . interrupts at the most inappropriate moments. (repress Mildred's intent to resume intimacy) The wind . . . just ruined the moment.

DIRECTIONS

Mildred pouts then begins to mentally question Richard and the awkwardness of the situation. Wide eyes dart about the room while her body stays ridged. The camera is her eyes and focuses on the wine bottle, the one glass, the fire, the messed rug, the faint smoke rising from a wasted candle. She sniffs the air then leans over Richard's shoulder to look into the bedroom and notices the untouched, fully dressed bed and then to Richard's bare feet.

MILDRED

We must meet my parents for brunch.

RICHARD

Brunch, yes!

DIRECTIONS

The camera moves through the window to see Jane making her way towards the main house then it turns slightly and penetrates through the landscape and homes until finding Burt at the front door of a mansion. In fast clips the camera catches scenes of Burt at various doors while he attempts to hand out invitations. A slow draining version of 'Fred's Blues' plays. At one house Burt hands an invitation to a woman who instantly hands it back. At another an owner accepts then closes the door and drops it into the garbage can. The owner's butler retrieves it from the garbage can. At another, the lady of the house does not accept and indicates to hand it to her maid. Burt begins to pass the front doors and goes directly to the service entrances where he is greeted warmly, and silent conversations stretch out. Burt hands over invitations and adds names of the staff onto the cards. Burt approaches the service entrance of the Easthouseman's and is welcomed in for tea. While conversations continue between help about the past, servants pass in and out of the pantry doors. Voices are heard beyond the doors. Out of curiosity the camera and ears narrow in on the Easthousemans and Richard during brunch.

LOUISE
That Hobo man and the Burtons are back, and they brought uninvited guests; atrocious.

ROBERT
And the servant's girl . . . Jane?

RICHARD
Yes, the Burton's daughter. The guests I have not met yet, they are the good Samaritans that provided transportation for the stranded Burtons and Nick, who happened to be at the same location.

ROBERT
Yes . . . of course. That . . . that Mr. Nick; always seems to be present, about . . . under foot. My dear boy, he is not a character of our social standing.

MILDRED
Richard . . . you have not been home. You went directly to the cottage last night. When did you obtain information?

LOUISE
Rather from whom?

ROBERT
And when? Both questions must have a singular answer along with where this transfer of information occurred.

RICHARD
Well . . . well . . . Jane . . . Jane Burton!

MILDRED
Then you were not alone at the cottage? I sensed the presence of a person . . .!

LOUISE
(sigh with false arrogant surprise) An engaged man with a single woman all night?

ROBERT
I had told Louise . . . years ago that servants' off spring should not associate above their status.

MILDRED
Since when do you drink a bottle of wine by yourself, in front of a fireplace

214

with a fire and candle light?

RICHARD
Old friends . . . catching up . . . all is innocent . . . I can explain . . .

ROBERT
About what?

LOUISE
A fiancée and a married man should always have a chaperon when the woman of concern is not present.

RICHARD
We were childhood friends . . . even Mildred was a friend of Jane's.

LOUISE
The emphasis is on the past tense of were childhood friends. I believe this . . . this Jane person is no longer a child.

MILDRED
Is she still a child?

RICHARD
Well . . . no . . . but, she is still Jane, a friend from the past. I am engaged to Mildred.

MILDRED
You were in bare feet, exposed feet in front of a stranger. You have never been bare footed in front of me.

LOUISE
Heaven forbid . . ., you do know that servants' gossip?

DIRECTIONS
In the kitchen Burt is associating with the house servants while all tend to eavesdrop on the conversations of the Easthousemans. Heads of servants nod and sway as they make small comments.

MAID 1
Burt, the Wentworths are good people.

COOK
They started out like us, just normal everyday folk.

MAID 2
And Richard comes from that good stock.

BUTLER
He is the only good spice in the sewage pot of these . . .

COOK
Hush, they may hear you. They are our employers.

BURT
They are, and we must maintain our status.

MAID 1
Hog-wash, your Jane is as refined as any socialite, and with more compassion and sensibility.

MAID 2
Richard and Jane were meant to be together. I seen it when they were children. Without them knowing it then, they were in love.

BURT
It was not right then; a servant's girl and the son of the house master. That is why I decided to leave.

MAID 1
Big mistake . . . you interrupted true love.

MAID 2
And now that they have become reacquainted, that childhood connection will lock them together; mark my word.

BURT
Don't bet on it. I will not permit it.

BUTLER
A five-er says by New Years Eve.

COOK
Won't take that long. Five by Christmas. (pull a five-dollar bill from bra)

MAID 1
(draw change from apron pocket) They will be together before the engagement party.

BURT
Shame on you; the engagement party must take place for the sake of Mildred and Richard.

MAID 2
Missy, lend me a dollar. I am a sure winner. Richard and Jane will make an announcement on the night of the party.

GARDNER
(enter and hustle around asking, 'what is going on') What! Who you betting on! What's open? Five says today.

BURT
Ben . . ., you just like to gamble; you do not understand the situation.

GARDNER
Sure do; Miss. Jane and Richard; known since they were children. It is a sure thing. I can't lose.

BURT
(stand and back away to exit, show bewilderment and concern on face) I'll prove you wrong. (turn to look through swaying doors leading to outer dinning area)

SERVICE GIRL
(enter kitchen) They are ganging up on poor Richard, and fabricating a whole bunch of untrue stories; and him talking sweet talk about Miss. Jane.

DIRECTIONS
Camera pulls away from kitchen while focused on hands handing over money to the Butler to hold. Camera turns towards the dinning table. Stern faces are attacking Richard who is defending himself by praising Jane.

RICHARD
Jane, was like, like a younger sister. No, no, not a sister, a boy would not hang around a kid sister. Jane was a pal, a school pal, just a member of the gang. We just hung around together because we . . . lived in the same house . . . had lunches together . . . studied and played together . . ., nothing happened, we were just reminiscing about the past and catching up . . . a lot of years have passed . . . we . . .

LOUISE
. . . missed each other?!

RICHARD
(pause, begin to not yes, then glance at Mildred's stern face and begin to shake head no, but the movement turns into an awkward yes) Awkward!

DIRECTIONS
The camera closes in on Richard's face then opens behind two chairs near the Christmas tree. Nick and Molly are sipping hot chocolate and watch Jane approach the door and she enters holding a wine glass. Self conscious, Jane places the wine glass into a coat pocket and sits in a chair opposite of the inquisitive eyes of Nick and Molly. Molly picks up a tea cup as Nick pours hot chocolate. Molly passes the cup to Jane. All relax and sip their drinks. Music is soft and low then builds to a point then becomes instantly silent.

MOLLY
Santa told me that you once lived here?

JANE
Yes, I did, a long time ago.

MOLLY
And a boy lived here too.

JANE
Yes, Richard.

MOLLY
Was he your boyfriend?

JANE
A friend, yes, a good friend. He is engaged to Mildred Easthouseman. She and I were not the best of friends when children.

MOLLY
So . . . she stole your boyfriend?

JANE
No, yes! He was just a friend who happened to be a boy . . . and Mildred came between Richard and me. Yes . . . Mildred stole my friend.

MOLLY
Who was a boy . . . so in fact he was your boy friend? He could still be your boyfriend. You could steal him back away from Mildred.

JANE

218

(stare with bewilderment at Molly while contemplating the matter, slowly shake head no while Molly nods yes, turn to Nick) That would be unethical.

SANTA
There are rules in politics, rules in battles, rules in games, but when it comes to love it seems that rules constantly change and are often broken or disregarded altogether. Love seems to supersede and always triumphs.

MOLLY
If Santa says it is okay, then you can steal Richard away from Mildred.

SANTA
I did not say that Jane should . . . maybe she doesn't love Richard in a boyfriend, girlfriend way.

JANE
Maybe I don't want to steal Richard away from . . . maybe I don't love Richard.

MOLLY
You do.

JANE
(stare blankly at Molly then look at Nick)

SANTA
You always have. You still wear the small gold chain with a tiny pearl that he gave you on that last Christmas.

JANE
(clutch a hand to neck where the chain is hidden, slowly pull it out) How did you know?

MOLLY
(get up and move closer to see the chain) Oh . . ., Santa knows everything. You still love Richard.

JANE
(slightly nod) Richard may be in love with Mildred.

SANTA
(eyes twinkle, sway head slightly no) Rules are meant to be broken when love is at stake.

DIRECTIONS
The camera pulls away and turns to notice Fred standing at the top of the stairs and listening in on the conversation. On a little pad he is jotting down notes. Fred grins, smiles, makes wide eyes and sinister faces.

FRED
Real life drama. This will make a great script. 'Love Rekindled', 'The Assorted Affair', 'Jane's Christmas Romance', 'Breaking the Rules of Love'. I need more . . . more . . . more!

DIRECTIONS
The camera follows Fred as he sneaks down the stairs towards the kitchen door. Fred slightly leans on the door. Voices sound out. Burt, Martha, Beth and Lizzy are chatting.

BURT
I tell you, Martha . . . they would not accept the invitations. I had doors slammed closed on me.

BETH
Did anyone accept?

BURT
A few . . . those people that are outside of the Easthousemans' inner circle, those that are only acquainted with the Wentworth name. (frown, look down)

MARTHA
Well, we will make them welcome and dazzle them with a feast. (stare at Burt's down turned head) What did you do Burt? You did something, I can tell. Even after all these years apart, I can still read your face.

BURT
I . . . I . . . invited the servants and asked them to dress formal; to be surrogates of their employers, to be fillers to fill the room.

DIRECTIONS
Fred waits feverishly. Beth and Martha gasp and step back wide eyed as they look at Lizzy who is slightly twisting her head as an idea pops into thoughts and she begins to smile.

LIZZY
Ladies, who else would we impress, who else enjoys good food, and they will be our best critics. Regular people know how to party. Bill and I are regular people. Make some telephone calls Burt, invite more regular people. Ladies

we need more food, more dishes.

DIRECTIONS
Everyone begins to move about and chatter. Fred recoils and shakes a cramped hand as he wanders away. Without looking up or noticing, Fred passes Jane and Molly. Molly and Jane are giggling.

MOLLY
You snuck out of the cottage before Mildred saw you?

JANE
If Mildred is still as jealous as she was when a child, she might have hit me.

MOLLY
Girls should not fight, but if you need to, make a fist like this and put your thumb like this, then poke'em right on the nose. I had to punch Charlie Wilson the Third once.

JANE
Heavens why?

MOLLY
He tried to kiss me.

FRED
(suddenly freeze in motion with the pencil poised over the page)

MOLLY
I'm too young to be kissing boys. Did Richard ever kiss you?

JANE
Yes . . . and I did not poke him in the nose, I kind of liked it.

FRED
(without looking back begin to write again)

MOLLY
When . . . last night?

JANE
No, not last night; it was one Christmas when he gave me this gold chain.

MOLLY
If you didn't poke him then you really like him.

JANE
I do.

DIRECTIONS
Fred enters the games room and joins Nick and Bill standing by the fireplace.
Nick and Bill are in conversation.

WILLIAM
Old money seems to breed stale people. The Easthousemans' money is so old
. . .

FRED
How old?

WILLIAM
So old that the wrinkles have wrinkles.

SANTA
As do their owners.

FRED
I could use a few wrinkled bills, wrinkles don't bother me.

SANTA
Maybe a good story will be written. You have been jotting down ideas for a
story plot.

FRED
Yes . . .! how do you know?

WILLIAM
Nick knows everything. We have known each other . . . how long Nick?

SANTA
Seems like a lifetime.

WILLIAM
At least over forty years.

FRED
So, I take it Nick, you don't have old money and there are no wrinkles on
your face?

SANTA

Sharing and giving of one's self does not require winkled money.

WILLIAM
I would like to read your story, Fred.

FRED
No complete story yet, just ideas.

WILLIAM
Then, when you are finished, I may know a fella that knows a fella in the publishing business.

FRED
That would be great, but maybe you can help me now with some facts. What about this secret romance between Jane and Richard?

WILLIAM
First that I have heard of it, but that would be great. I envisioned them together when they were teens.

SANTA
Fred, I do believe that a few details have been missed when you were taking notes.

FRED
Oh, that's not important. A good writer is able to weave a spectacular story with the basics of information.

DIRECTIONS
The camera focuses in on the note pad and pencil poised over the page, then scene goes black. Scene opens as Richard enters through the back entrance. Molly is watching from the upstairs railing. Richard seems to be sneaking in as he tiptoes toward the kitchen door. Richard cracks the door and peeks in. the camera watches the back view of Burt and Martha leaning against the centre counter. Both are whispering and slowly and awkwardly moving closer to each other. Richard eavesdrops.

BURT
Martha, I have made a drastic mistake and ruined our lives. I should never have insisted on leaving.

MARTHA
No, you should not have, but your conscience had pride and class propriety.

BURT
I should have considered your concerns and Jane's.

MARTHA
Yes, you should have.

BURT
If I was not so stubborn and stayed, would we still be together . . . a family?

MARTHA
(inch closer, eyes seductively being shy) Despite the turmoil of the years, I have not thrown away the love we developed. It is only in a state of hibernation.

BURT
(inch closer, attempt to stretch a teenage adolescent arm around Martha, pull back) We have been given a second chance, I mean an opportunity for employment here . . . could we wake up from hibernation.

MARTHA
Well . . ., I am no spring chicken and an old rooster like you may not be up for the challenge.

BURT
(puff up and be cocky) I am in the prime of middle age, not ready for the retirement farm.

MARTHA
We can not just resume as if those years apart did not exist. I need to be romanced and have the passions of love rekindled. (inch closer, bat shy eyes)

BURT
(walk fingers along counter towards Martha, inch closer) I shall court you with the flare of the boy I was when I first saw your rosy cheeks on the moor.

DIRECTIONS
Burt looks dreamingly at Martha, though is afraid to advance closer. Instrumental music of 'I shall return to Kintyre' lingers in the background.

MARTHA
(lean against Burt) Burt, you may put your arm around me; I know that you crave to.

DIRECTIONS

Music builds. As Richard closes the door Burt puts an arm around Martha and hugs affectionately and places a kiss on Martha's cheek. The door closes. Richard smiles as he tiptoes towards the games room. Through the French doors he peeks through the glass where the curtains are slightly parted and watches strangers that Jane had described. Fred is teasing Beth by chasing her around the billiard table.

BETH
(squeal in whispers) No . . . no . . . Fred, someone may catch us.

FRED
Let them, them old folks may get a reminder of what young love is about.

BETH
No . . ., Molly may catch us.

FRED
She has caught us smooching before. She has got to stop acting like an old lady and stop lecturing us about being discreet. (grab hold of Beth and kiss her neck)

BETH
(giggle from the tickling) We need to act like adults, show a little respectability.

FRED
I will when you do.

DIRECTIONS
Beth grabs Fred by the ears and pulls his head in for a mushy kiss. The camera from Richard's eyes watches their heads sink beneath the edge of the pool table. The flames in the fireplace suddenly flare up. Richard pulls back slightly, nervously, and with a quick second look glances about to see if anyone noticed him. Music rises then softens as Richard walks to the library doors. At the doors he places an ear to the slightly parted sliding doors. Voices of Lizzy and William are heard. The camera peers through the parted doors to see Lizzy and William sitting side by side on a love seat and reading aloud lines from different books. The camera glances at the titles of the books, 'Joy of Cooking' and 'Mechanics for Beginners'.

LIZZY
. . . add two tenderly sliced succulent tomatoes, firm exterior with full malleable substance . . .

WILLIAM
. . . maintain a firm grip, remember that a loss of containment will result in the need to reform substance with hands . . .

LIZZY
. . . simmer, do not rush, the sensational flavouring should be savoured over time . . .

WILLIAM
. . . an over revving engine using an improper fuel mixture will falter and stall . . .

LIZZY
. . . let the firmness melt on the tongue, indulge by holding in the spices until every fibre had tingled all extremities of your being . . .

WILLIAM
. . . in case of needing to jump start for a second run, insert crank . . .

DIRECTIONS
During the recitations, Lizzy and William add physical animation and tonal inflections. Both begin to lean together then slouch. Heads touch, cheeks touch, lips touch and in reminiscence of teenagers in a rumble seat begin to make out. Richard's face expresses squeamish masks and he quickly backs away and then heads to the staircase and tip toes up with head lowered. Molly waits at the top landing. Richard reaches the top step and stops when down cast eyes fall upon Molly's wiggling toes hidden within big colourful knee socks.

MOLLY
Hello!

RICHARD
Hello?

MOLLY
My name is Molly, and you are Richard.

RICHARD
(extend hand and shake Molly's hand) A pleasure to meet you Miss.

MOLLY
I have been watching you sneak around. Are you looking for someone?

226

RICHARD
Oh, no, I live here.

MOLLY
Then why are you tip toeing about and peeking into rooms?

RICHARD
I . . . I . . ., did not want to disturb anyone.

MOLLY
I think that you are looking for someone, maybe my friend?

RICHARD
Is your friend around, upstairs maybe . . . downstairs?

MOLLY
Might be!

RICHARD
Will you tell me?

MOLLY
Well . . ., I will need to know what your intensions are.

RICHARD
My intensions?

MOLLY
You are engaged to Mildred Easthouseman. In order to be engaged you must
be in love with that person; devoted to that person, and not be thinking of
someone else; especially before an engagement party!

RICHARD
Yes . . . but . . . you see, your friend is also my friend.

MOLLY
Mildred Easthouseman is an engaged woman and will frown upon any
association that you may have with another woman.

RICHARD
No . . ., will she . . . even a close friend who just happens to be a girl?

MOLLY
(nod a long yes) Why do you want to see Jane? So, you have feelings for her?

You can't stop thinking about Jane.

RICHARD
(continue to think, ponder, nod head yes and no in the wrong order to Molly's questions. Become completely confused)

MOLLY
Is Mildred always on your mind, do you dream of Mildred or of Jane? Mildred and Richard: Richard and Mildred Wentworth? Doesn't sound poetic. Jane and Richard: Richard and Jane Wentworth? Now that is a good combination; rolls off of the tongue. I bet that both of you stayed up all night talking. I got a whole dollar that says that Mildred does all of the talking and you listen with ears closed.

RICHARD
Ah . . . ah . . . yes . . . no . . . no!

MOLLY
Red.

RICHARD
Green.

MOLLY
Sky.

RICHARD
Clouds.

MOLLY
Mom.

RICHARD
Dad.

MOLLY
Sister.

RICHARD
Brother.

MOLLY
Controlling.

RICHARD
Mildred.

MOLLY
Nagging.

RICHARD
Mildred.

MOLLY
Richard and . . .?

RICHARD
Jane!

MOLLY
Richard Loves . . .?

RICHARD
Jane!

MOLLY
(grin a big 'told you so smile', shrug shoulders)

RICHARD
Who are you; my subconscious mind disguised as a little girl?

MOLLY
If I may say; you were always in love with Jane, a love that was seeded early.
Few people get to experience and share a long life of friendship and love.

RICHARD
You are too intelligent and wise to be . . . what . . . seven years old. (attempt
to pass by Molly)

MOLLY
(block Richard's passage) You need to do a lot of thinking and make lasting
decisions before seeing Jane.

RICHARD
I see . . ., you are not going to let me pass? You will probably make a childish
scene if I do.

MOLLY

(smile intelligently) Yup.

DIRECTIONS
Richard and Molly dance side to side, each playing defensive – offensive moves. Molly continues to smile with a little girl innocence. Richard stares with double takes while making faces as if trying to see into Molly's mind. With rejection, Richard backs down the stairs and wanders the entranceway. From behind Molly, Jane exits a room with arms laden with towels. Jane glimpses a shadow of Richard disappearing around a corner.

JANE
Molly, was that Richard?

MOLLY
Yes . . ., I met your friend . . . who is a boy and we had a very interesting conversation.

JANE
You did?

MOLLY
And, you were the subject of our conversation.

JANE
Why would I be of such interest?

MOLLY
Because, Richard is in love with you.

JANE
No, that cannot be. Richard is engaged to Mildred Easthouseman.

MOLLY
When you woke up this morning; who did you think of?

JANE
Richard, but because we have just met after so many years of being apart! And . . . and, past memories are refreshed . . . that is all. I don't want to be the other woman, the person that comes between Richard and Mildred.

MOLLY
What about love?

JANE

Love is filled with disappointment.

MOLLY
And sometimes new growth! I saw Martha and Burt holding hands and hugging.

JANE
My Mom and Dad?

MOLLY
Yup! So, love can change and grow.

JANE
(walk hesitantly towards another room)
You saw my Mom and my Dad holding hands?

MOLLY
Yup.

DIRECTIONS
Jane smiles to herself while continuing about doing chores. Molly leans over the banister and watches Richard standing in the middle of the entrance room and slowly turning as if searching for a destination and at the same time seeking guidance. Nick enters from behind Richard and stands beside him. Richard does not seem to notice. Nick looks in the same directions but does not see anything of importance.

SANTA
Richard my boy . . . Richard?

RICHARD
(suddenly wake and realize the man standing beside) Nick, good to see you. How was your trip up north?

SANTA
Fine my boy. I brought a few guests with me. Delightful guests, and one in particular. I trust you have met and have become reacquainted?

RICHARD
I should have known that you would have had something to do with events.

SANTA
Always with good intentions, though I may have created a quandary for you.

RICHARD
(turn to face Nick, annoyance in facial expression) Do you think? I am engaged to Mildred Easthouseman. (continue to talk without really listening to Nick's responses)

SANTA
Mildred is a firm representative of social status.

RICHARD
Then, then I revisit childhood memories with Jane Burton.

SANTA
A wholesome girl, a pal, no hang-ups.

RICHARD
Mildred is refined, well mannered, fashionably dressed and prominent.

SANTA
Self confident, opinionated, high maintenance.

RICHARD
Jane is easy to talk to, listens and is concerned about everyone regardless of caste.

SANTA
Social, polite and humanistic.

RICHARD
Mildred Easthouseman's name carries prestige, connections and future investments.

SANTA
Material gains do not invest in love.

RICHARD
'Jane Burton, the Butler's daughter,' the Easthouseman's stated, 'hired help.'

SANTA
Jane lights up a room, people look at the person, and the person defines status, not the linage of a name.

RICHARD
Mildred . . .

SANTA
Cannot cook, nor do manual labour, hates physical sports, leads when you dance, expects wealth to be a priority for existence and a marriage merger.

RICHARD
Jane . . .

SANTA
Struggled and strived for everything gained, considers the worth of others before herself, expresses love and affection as a commitment for lasting existence in a marriage.

RICHARD
Life would be easier to understand if all I had to do is make a list of pros and cons for people, then the person with the most check marks in the pro column wins.

SANTA
Or follow your heart, or you could have listened to my input. A list will definitely give the facts.

RICHARD
Thanks Nick, I am going to make a list. Cold hard facts, that's what I need, cold hard facts.

DIRECTIONS
Richard wanders off in thought, unaware of Nick standing dumbfounded.

SANTA
Nick, my boy . . . love overrides a list . . . love.

DIRECTIONS
Richard continues to walk off with thoughts in a quandary. Nick glances up to see Molly gazing down. Molly comes dancing down the stairs to meet Santa, she takes his hand and they move to the Christmas tree. Santa sits in an arm chair and leans back with dejection on his face. Molly sits on the sofa stool and leans towards Santa's knees. Her head is poised on fists and arms on knees; she is in wonderment.

MOLLY
You have a lot on your mind. Will you be able to fulfill everyone's wishes by Christmas?

SANTA

Too many conflicting wishes. (lean forward and imitate Molly's form) I trust that you have an opinion and a fantasy outcome for everyone.

MOLLY
I do, but it is my happy ending story. After all, I am a child, and all children want stories with happy endings.

SANTA
It would be nice to have a happy story for all, but life has a reality and it is not always happy.

MOLLY
That is why we believe in Christmas, the baby born is a gift to the world, a child filled with all of the wishes of mankind. For the child will change the world by bringing peace and love for all.

SANTA
Who are you child? Is there a one-hundred-year-old wise person in your mind?

MOLLY
Nope, just the innocents of childhood that has a wonderful intended view of the world.

SANTA
And what part do I play within your story?

MOLLY
You have the most important part.

SANTA
Oh . . . I do?

MOLLY
Everybody needs a little help fixing their problems; you provide the magic that solves problems.

SANTA
And you believe in Magic?

MOLLY
I do. You stopped my Dad's bus without getting hurt. We stopped Jane. Martha met Burt and they met Jane. You brought us here. Jane met Richard and Martha and Burt reacquainted with William and Elisabeth.

SANTA
Just a coincident of events.

MOLLY
Of course, but you made it happen for a reason.

SANTA
I do not have a preconceived reason. Please tell me what story you have unfolding in your mind and what ending do you perceive?

MOLLY
Simple; Mom, Martha and Elizabeth are going to start a catering business and are going to create a cook book. Burt is a great singer and William is going to back him musically and manage his friend. Jane is going to represent business interests for Elizabeth and William, and marry Richard, who is the new president of his father's business. On Christmas day I will have a new brother, who will need a big sister to guide him.

SANTA
It all makes sense the way you say it.
(smile bewildered and begin to lean back, pause and lean forward) Have you forgotten your Dad, Fred.

MOLLY
Of course not . . ., my Dad is a writer; someone has to write this story. It will be a great novel, then play, maybe even a movie.

SANTA
And all I have to do is use magic to make sure everything falls into place.

MOLLY
(raise hands, smile a happy child's grin) Yup . . . simple.

SANTA
I see. (slowly lean back into chair and offer a rosy cheek smile) And everyone will believe that I am Santa.

MOLLY
Of course, . . . I do.

DIRECTIONS
Camera focuses on Molly's innocent and determined face. Music builds and fades. The camera slowly pans the interior of the house, focusing on the decorations of the season and the party facilities. Seasonal music is softly

playing. Nick and molly are standing in front of the Christmas tree. William is stiffly standing at the doorway leading to the large gathering area. He nervously eyes Burt standing at the front door, waiting to greet visitors. Jane is busy checking the rooms and making sure that tables are set, and food is presented. Richard is pacing in front of the fireplace, a wandering eye watches Jane's movement, yet eyes flinch and avoid contact when Jane glances over. The camera enters the kitchen where the women are putting final touches to food dishes. Beth continues to grip at her bulging stomach. All eyes continue to dart toward the wall clock. Anxiety is evident in their faces for different reasons; Beth; because of nervous pregnancy pains; Martha because of food presentations; Lizzy because of future in-laws. The camera glances back to the clock showing the time to be 7 P.M..

BETH
It is after seven, do you think anyone will show up?

LIZZY
Richard's future in-laws must show up, though they will be fashionably late. They must; something about etiquette of established old money. The older the money the later one arrives.

MARTHA
If their money is ancient, then they will arrive in time to leave.

LIZZY
If we are to be so lucky!

BETH
I sense resentment?

LIZZY
Bill and I are simple folk that just happen to have money. We want to be simple folk, not to be praised and envied.

MARTHA
Then you approve of Richard and Jane's childhood association.

LIZZY
I do, only Burt displayed intolerance. I did not want you to leave then, or ever again.

MARTHA
Burt is a stubborn man.

BETH
All men are.

DIRECTIONS
All women nod in agreement and then turn heads to the clock.

BETH
When will any guest arrive? (to self, rub stomach) When will this child arrive?

LIZZY
 I do have assurance from Burt that house hold representatives will promptly arrive.

DIRECTIONS
Eyes turn to the clock at the same moment that door chimes ring throughout the house. The women instantly double check the food, uncovering and arranging and set about to carry the food out to the arrivals. The camera moves to the main door where Burt is about to reach for the handle. William motions for Richard to join him and both advance to join Burt. Well dressed servants begin to enter. Though representing prestige and quality, their attire is not of the quality of social old money. Burt begins to introduce arrivals by name and houses represented. Bill is at first apprehensive until his eyes meet Burt's glinting smile. Arrivals warmly greet Bill and Richard then revert to servant status and assist each other to remove coats and store before moving forward to greet Molly and Nick, and Jane who has joined them at the Christmas tree.

BURT
Jack and Sara Shoul, representing the Morgan House Hold . . ., Jill, Janice, Joy and Jackie . . . floor maids representing the Mansfield Estate.

DIRECTIONS
Bill warmly greets with a smile and a light kiss to their hands. Each sister giggles then flushes when Richard greets each by name.

BURT
Sam and Pauline, chauffeur and cook for the Fender House.

WILLIAM
Pauline, a pleasure . . . Sam . . ., what do you think of that new Ford? I've been thinking of a new car.

SAM
(a bit apprehensive, then reply when Bill gives a manly handshake) Master Wentworth.

WILLIAM
Just Bill, Sam.

SAM
Fine car . . . Bill; good sound construction, needs to be used, not well suited
to be cooped up in a garage.

WILLIAM
I need a good working man's car.

SAM
A ford is your best buy, Bill.

BURT
(hesitate . . . somewhat shocked) Master and Mistress, George and Melissa
Hempton, of the Hempton Estate.

DIRECTIONS
A moment of silence looms and eyes of sevants avert contact until the voice
of Mr. Hempton echoes.

GEORGE
Good to see you again Burtrum. (shake his hand strongly, move to Bill) Bill
Wentworth, it is about time we met, we're new to town, couldn't wait to be
invited to a shing-dig.

WILLIAM
Howdy . . . glad to have good folks a-visiting.

DIRECTIONS
Silence evaporates as all mingle. As the women exit the kitchen and begin to
associate and present dishes of appetizers, the trays suddenly are taken away,
out of servant habit the trays are passed about freely. Jill, Janice, Joy and
Jackie rush to meet Nick, Molly and Jane.

GIRLS
(in unison) Hello Nick.

SANTA
Hello ladies, may I introduce Miss Molly, and this is grown up Jane.

GIRLS
(in unison, and each selecting a part of the conversation) You are gorgeous.
You haven't changed. Open your eyes, she has. You are lucky; you got out of

the service. But she is back. We know, we've heard. The whole town has heard. You and Master, Richard Wentworth? The cottage? All night? A storm? Miss Easthouseman walked in. So . . . you and Richard? Yes . . . why not? She's not a servant any more. So . . . Jane tell us?

JANE
(mouth open and drooping, close mouth and smile) We are just friends, old acquaintances, nothing has or will happen.

GIRLS
Of course not. Play hard to get. Richard will chase after you. It will happen. Should happen! Why not? You're gorgeous! Smart! Successful! High class! Not one of us anymore.

JANE
I haven't changed. I am still the same Jane that hung around with you girls doing all those crazy things.

GIRLS
Ooh . . . we were bad. Remember the mud fight? Poor Mildred, covered in mud from head to toe. And, that fancy dress ruined. You started the fight. No, it was Jackie. Heck no! Jackie made the mud pies. I was only six.

JANE
(laugh, huddle with girls, move off with them) We all started the mud fight.

MOLLY
Santa, I feel sorry for Mildred. Were they picking on her for being rich and spoiled?

SANTA
No, oh no, they were all being children, playing. And Mildred tossed just as many mud pies. It is only when children become adults do they distinguish rich from poor, social status and form personal opinions. All was fine when they were children.

MOLLY
I can't wait to go back to school and find new friends . . . lots of friends.

SANTA
Having and being friends is important for everyone.

DIRECTIONS
The party continues as invited servants arrive along with a scattering of social

upper crust people. All seem to mingle, except those of old money and close acquaintances of the Easthousemans. Time duration lapses. Various people perform in various combinations. After a length of time when no new arrivals arrive the door bell chimes and no one pays attention until a prolonged ring gains everyone's attention. Silence encompasses the house as all eyes turn to face the door. Burt rushes to the door followed by Richard, William and Elizabeth. Burt waits until Richard and parents are lined up to greet. Burt opens the door.

BURT
Master Robert, and Lady Louise Easthouseman and Miss. Mildred.

WILLIAM
Welcome . . . it's about time you showed up!

LIZZY
Just in time to sample . . . special horderves, and . . . and . . . champagne . . . to toast Richard and . . . Mildred's engagement.

RICHARD
(reach for Mildred's hand, lead Mildred into centre of room)

MILDRED
(scowling) And where is your little play mate?

RICHARD
(speak to crowd) My I introduce the future Mrs. Mildred Wentworth.

DIRECTIONS
Slight applause is heard until Jane rouses the crowd. The insinuation is already seated in Mildred's mind. The gathered servants pretend to be pleasant, yet expressions are cold. Various social established guests begin to surround the couple to present fake congratulations, or rather to accept new money into the fold. Servant guests mingle among themselves and chatter varies from complaints about employers; the once love affairs of Richard and Jane, the tension between Jane and Mildred, the food, the success of a potential service of a catering service. Fred wanders and innocently listens in on random conversations and secretly takes notes, at times slings random question and innuendoes to feed responses to further his knowledge for a potential story. Santa and Molly are seated by the fireplace watching the crowd and carry on a commentary of events.

MOLLY
I have noticed that rich folks stand stiffly and talk in cold mono tone voices,

and regular people partake of the party and enjoy socializing.

SANTA
True.

MOLLY
I think of Richard as regular folk, but he is also rich and marrying into more money, so is he going to change and be like those stuffy people?

SANTA
I hope not, but the temptation of money and the domineering pressures from Mildred may change him.

MOLLY
Then why can't he see what his future life will be like and dump Mildred and marry Jane?

SANTA
That is not as easy as it seems . . . love is very fickle, love is blind, love is a binding matter that cannot be altered or influenced by external people.

MOLLY
But . . . we can see that Mildred and Richard do not belong together.

SANTA
We may see it, though we cannot tell, or force people to change, individually they need to make a decision to change. Everyone deserves happiness. Though Richard and Jane may belong together; if they were to become a couple then Mildred would be cast aside. Her feelings would be hurt, she would be devastated. Just because we may feel that Richard and Jane should be happy together, we can not destroy Mildred's potential happiness.

MOLLY
I see . . ., there is a saying . . . and it goes like this; for every fish in a vast ocean there is another fish meant to be its one and only. We just need to find Mildred's true one and only fish.

SANTA
That would be a tall order.

MOLLY
Just check your list.

SANTA

My list?

MOLLY
You have a list of every boy and girl, and you check the list for naughty and nice . . ., what if you check the list for potential matches?

SANTA
List?

MOLLY
Who is that man? (point to a slightly older man)

SANTA
Chester Chesterfield, very wealthy, a widower.

MOLLY
He has potential, and, that skinny man with thick glasses?

SANTA
Chester Chesterfield the third, heir to the Chesterfield Steamship Lines. A bit naïve and inexperienced though is willingly aggressive to learn.

MOLLY
So, he has plenty of old money, just what Mildred's family is seeking. There . . . there by the door, the man with a fancy woman on each arm.

SANTA
An old money play-boy; he has money but would rather spend other peoples' money.

MOLLY
What is a play-boy?

SANTA
Let's just say that Mildred would be just one of a dozen women to hang onto his arms.

MOLLY
Does he have new or old money?

SANTA
Never touches his money. They say that the money in his vault is growing mould.

MOLLY
That qualifies for old money and a potential candidate for Mildred.

SANTA
What about love; Mildred may be looking for love?

MOLLY
Over there, who are those two men?

SANTA
The Baily twins, they are the right age, plenty of old money . . . but Identical twins . . . difficult to tell them apart. Mildred may fall for one and yet end up with the other, may be confusing.

MOLLY
Well, they all have the qualifications and the potential. We just need to plant the seed of interest in their minds. Them about Mildred and Mildred about them.

SANTA
I see . . . by manipulating potential scenarios to make them think about new options. If greedy people think that there is a loophole they will attack for the sake of their own benefit. We cannot lie; just make suggestions of what if, because they need to make decisions for them selves.

MOLLY
I do not lie. Just check your naughty and nice list.

SANTA
My list?

DIRECTIONS
Music builds as does the chatter of mingling guests. The camera notices the eyes of people glancing to important people and various expressions of characteristics of characters that are prominent. Richard glances at Jane with hints of affection and Jane at Richard with hesitant interest. Mildred glares at Jane with childish vengeance. Fred stares at everyone with suspicion. Beth grunts and growls at odd times and startles guests. Martha and Burt peek at each other with newfound love then to Jane with hope. Lizzy and William worry and hope for Richard and for the success of the party. The Easthousemans stare with contempt against everyone. Everyone is assessing suitable expressions from each other of which the camera captures at random. The camera focuses on Santa and Molly as their faces develop expressions to suit their devious thoughts. They side glance at each other then move to

mingle. The camera follows each and jumps between them as they spread among the crowd.

MOLLY
(lean against sofa chair containing Chester Chesterfield senior, lean until an inquisitive stare comes from the man) Mildred Easthouseman is quite a looker. I hear that she has oodles and oodles of old money. Do you have oodles and oodles of old money?

CHESTER SR.
It is improper for a man of my age to stare at a young woman. And let's just say that I have extensive oodles, as you eloquently say, of old money.

MOLLY
You don't look old to me. Miss Easthouseman adores men of essence. You have oodles and oodles of essence. What if Mildred changed her mind about marrying Richard; right here tonight? I think she would notice you because of your oodles and oodles and oodles of essence.

DIRECTIONS
Chester Sr. stares at Molly. Molly smiles broadly and pats the man's shoulder then casually walks away. Chester Sr. Leans forward and searches and stares at Mildred.

CHESTER SR.
(tug on the coat of a guest servant) Did you hear anything about a cancellation of an engagement?

DIRECTIONS
The servant and man stare at each other and both nod yes then no. the servant moves away and whispers to another person and so on. The camera follows Chester's stare toward Mildred then the camera passes on to focus on Santa standing between the Baily twins. As if of one thought the twins sense Santa's presence and turn to face the jolly grin of Santa.

SANTA
Well boys, you have been good boys this past year; generous to others, pleasant in manners, and very little sibling squabbling.

TWINS
(blank stares to each other and to Santa)
How do you know?

SANTA

I read my naughty and nice list regularly.

TWINS
A Santa list?

SANTA
You boys deserve to find a good woman. A woman such as Mildred Easthouseman, if by chance something happened that just may break the engagement between Richard and Mildred. Such events do happen and when such things happen it is always best for a single man to jump right in and make themselves visible.

TWINS
(blank stares to each other and to Santa) Mildred Easthouseman, what did you hear?

TWIN ONE
Did you hear something?

TWIN TWO
It is like you to keep information from me.

TWIN ONE
What you can't read my mind?

TWIN TWO
Try reading my mind now.

DIRECTIONS
Santa questions their blank response with a grimace. Santa slowly backs away. The twins mirror each other, and thoughts are of same. Rising on toes they search for Mildred, when locating her they study and advance as if being cats of pry. The camera glimpses Chester 3rd following on the tail of the Playboy and dates. Molly steps between and halts Chester 3rd.

MOLLY
Hello!

CHESTER 3rd
(halt and look down) Excuse me?
MOLLY
My name is Molly. I just had a conversation with your father. A delightful man. He has your best interest in mind.

CHESTER 3rd
He has!

MOLLY
Oh . . . sure . . . he told me that you and Mildred would have made a delightful couple . . . old money merging with old money. Though now that he is a widower, he, well let's just say that if Mildred and Richard were not getting engaged, he would give you a new step mother. You would call her Mother Mildred. Maybe he knows something about Richard and Mildred maybe breaking up. Have you heard anything?

CHESTER 3rd
I say, I would be more suited to be with Mildred than my old father. Wait a minute; this is an engagement party, did my father hear something? He sure was in a hurry to get to this party. He has never associated with anyone in forty years. Little girl, what have you heard about Mildred and Richard, is there a scandal, a break-up?

MOLLY
(lean in, put hand to cover side of mouth) I have heard . . . but I cannot confirm, but something is amiss about old money and new money, they do not mix well, and any association is sure to be doomed from the start. Maybe you should do some eavesdropping.

CHESTER 3rd
Quite right.

MOLLY
It is never too late to be Johnny on the spot.

CHESTER 3rd
Quite right!

DIRECTIONS
Molly urges Chester 3rd with a hand push in the direction of Mildred. Santa crosses paths with Molly and Chester 3rd.

SANTA
Chester my boy, bring Mildred her favourite drink.

CHESTER 3rd
Quite right . . . yes . . . drink?

SANTA

White wine with a spritzer.

CHESTER 3rd
Quite right.

DIRECTIONS
Chester Sr. notices Chester 3rd's movements and he stands and awkwardly advances through the crowd. The camera pops between characters. Molly is seen whispering to the twins who then pick horderves from trays for Mildred. Santa straightens Chester Sr's tie and dabs a napkin on the man's brow. As guests mingle the main characters; Beth, Fred, Lizzy, William, Martha and Burt begin to sense a ploy and begin to watch interested parties advancing. Santa approaches the play-boy as Molly accidentally with purpose steps on the dresses of the two women. Frightened by the little girl trying to brush the dresses they back away. Santa takes up the play-boy's arm.

SANTA
Lovely women, not for you though.

PLAY-BOY
I beg your pardon?

SANTA
They are poor heirs, no endowment, no inheritance.

PLAY-BOY
I beg your pardon?

SANTA
They have the same intent as you, a incentive to latch onto financial stability, a well of deep old money to draw from.

PLAY-BOY
They do posses beauty.

SANTA
That they have, unlike Mildred Easthouseman, both beauty and a foundation of old money supporting an only heir.

PLAY-BOY
Richard, my rival, is a lucky man. His new money will have the backing of an established fortune.

SANTA

You have been on Santa's naughty list all of your life, why would you let Richard better you. You never even put up a fight. Have you become weak? I would have thought that you would fight, never to let an engagement stop you. You have always craved the beauty, prestige and money that Mildred represents.

PLAY-BOY
What is going on? Why are the twins, Chester and old man Chester swarming . . .? I knew that Richard did not have the class to be with Mildred. It must have been that servant girl . . . I heard something about her . . . has she caused a break-up.

SANTA
Go my boy, find out.

PLAY-BOY
My conquest will be a great Christmas gift.

DIRECTIONS
Chester 3rd, the twins, Chester Sr. and the playboy merge upon Mildred forcing others aside. Santa slides beside Richard taking an arm and slowly leading him away while Molly is childishly playing around Jane and guiding her away. All eyes seem to understand what is happening and begin to focus on the gathered men around Mildred. All ears wait abated. Those associated with the Easthousemans are standing at a distance, alienated. Servant guests ring around Mildred and her new suitors. Richard and Jane emotionally stand together while Santa and Molly draw away. Mildred suddenly plays the tease when dawning on the amorous intent of the new suitors. Instrumental music of 'I Shall Return to Kintyre' builds. The camera draws up and away at a 45-degree angle and the scene blurs in soft hues. Approaching a black the camera begins to zoom into the room to show a Christmas scene of the same house, though it is modern times. Santa is sitting in an arm chair beside the fireplace. He is relatively the same though slightly plumper with current fashionable attire. A young couple is sitting together on the sofa opposite of Santa. The girl is a close resemblance of Jane, dressed slightly gothic though clean and fresh without the trappings of extremes. The boy is typical punk with dress and accessories. The girl sits properly while the boy is slouching and pawing the girl.

SANTA
Everyone has differences both internal and external. Opposites do attract to the extreme, as do similarities seek comfort of their own kind. Each one of Mildred's suitors was compatible. It is true love that binds people together and keeps them together throughout the long term.

GIRL

So, Grandma Martha and Grandpa Burt were meant to be together, even though they were separated they found each other again and spent the rest of their life together. Fred and Beth had different personalities yet love kept them together. Grandma Lizzy and Grandpa Bill loved each other for the sake of love, being rich and having luxuries did not mean anything to them. And Mom and Dad were brought together because of love with the help of Aunt Molly and Santa.

BOY

Wild story, man!

GIRL

What about Mildred, did she have a happy ending?

SANTA

Oh, she found happiness of sorts, though it was never true love. She never craved spiritual love.

GIRL

Who did she marry?

SANTA

Let me see . . . Chester 3rd was first then the Play-boy, then finally Chester Chesterfield Sr. Oh there were interludes with each of the twins between and during commitments, but the twins never had a chance for they continuously fought between themselves and Mildred could not tell them apart.

GIRL

If Dad had married Mildred by making the wrong choice . . . then I would not be here, or I would be different, maybe a snob, self-centred, a total b-i—ch, and not love Mom and Dad.

SANTA

Richard and Jane have raised a wonderful young lady.

GIRL

I get it . . .!
(turn and stare with condemnation at the boy) You told me this story so that I will think and make the right choices for the sake of inner love, not for money, riches, prestige, or current fads and for the sake of baulking the establishment for the deprivation of the likes of . . .. (jerk thump at boy-friend)

BOY

HO . . . HO . . .HOLD ON! So . . . man . . . your saying you were there and here now . . . no way . . . (turn to girl) He is the dude . . . Santa . . . no way . . . am I on the nice list . . . no way . . . not the naughty list . . . hey Santa . . . I've been good . . . you need help . . . I'll feed the reindeer . . . they outside . . . on the roof . . . I'll shovel their do-do for you . . . that would put me on the nice list . . . I always thought Santa was a gimmick . . . he is real . . . man . . .

DIRECTIONS
The camera pulls away over the back of Santa's head as it tilts slightly. The girl turns her head away and her hand removes the boy's hand from her leg. The boy continues to rap-on oblivious of the story's point. The camera continues to pull up at a 45-degree angle and softening in hues. A silhouette of aged Richard and Jane is seen staring at each other and swaying their heads in mock disappointment as instrumental music of 'I Shall Return to Kintyre' plays then the instrumental music of 'When Hearts Believe', then when it plays out through the fading of an exterior winter scene the final version of 'I shall Return to Kintyre' plays.

THE END

JUST THE KIND OF MAN I NEED
by
Richard Mousseau
Copyright August 26, 2013

Basic Story
A man, Richard, who has lost his memory, is befriended by a young child, Whitney, who takes a liking to the dishevelled man and feels he will be the best person to meet, date and marry her mother, Sondra. Along the way a cast of characters take it upon themselves to assist, a mother figure, Martha, who overlooks the financial needs of the man, a mall security custodian, Alloyuis, to mentor the man in the ways of social matters, Dora, a friend of Sondra to foil events, a doctor and a judge to mend matters, the mystery estate benefactors aiming to disrupt everyone's life, all acting above the sub plot of a end destiny that was conceived before this story began.

Characters
Male, John Doe, Richard (selected name by Martha), Rickman Bisson (assumed to be), Richard Bisson-Stanfield-Montcalm-Willowby (adopted name).
Description; Age 35 to 45 years, 5 foot 10 inches to 6 foot 2 inches, fit, healthy, well groomed, warm brown eyes, brown hair.
Demeanour; Easy going, always concerned to the needs of others.
Mannerisms; Easy going, graceful and debonair, quick to actions, ahead of

disasters, anticipates disaster outcomes and attempts to counter or prevent disasters, animated and funny when one on one with people, shy, stand-off-ish in crowd, some consider arrogant, rather a quiet, shy, reserved man with compassion for all.

Background; Unknown, suggested background is that of a teacher of some sort, assumed background is that of an heir to a fortune to the Bisson estate, no actual connections made.

Character

Female, Mother (name used by all) Miss Martha Stanfield-Montcalm.

Description; Age 75 to 85 years, 5 foot 4 inches, well shaped, full figured, healthy, well groomed, red hair, brown hazel eyes,

Demeanour; Easy going, suggestive, makes events happen, generous.

Mannerisms; Prim and proper, Queen like presence, puts up no airs, eager and childlike when with children, hides those actions when in the presence of adults. Walks with grace and wears clothes of elegance.

Background; From wealthy family, though self made, successful business woman, now a philanderer. In actuality is the mother of Rickman Bisson. Had a marriage and a child at late age of life and gave up child to father in exchange for a career. At later age found out that father died, and so was living reclusively. Becomes re-acquainted with Richard through an out reach program, knows man's history but does not release information and lets life play out as it does.

Character

Female, Sondra Marie Willowby, mother of Whitney.

Description; Age 30 to 35 years, 5 foot 6 inches, well shaped, healthy, struggles to maintain figure, does not eat healthy, brownish-reddish long hair, green eyes.

Demeanour; Needs to be ruthless, cringes when doing so, really wishes everyone works and receives fair pay, even those that try to ruin her or are lazy at their jobs, tries to be a fair business woman, able to handle job, life, child, single life style and does it, though sometimes messes up constantly, sometimes gullible.

Mannerisms; Slow moving, slow animated actions, always a moment behind the action of disasters, as if seeing events happen and knows events will happen yet cannot prevent. When attempting to correct, actions are slow motion, walks as if stooped, as if carrying the world on her shoulders. Sometimes wares clothes that are frumpy. Does dress up well and elegantly when required.

Background; Dresses front window displays and advertising, promotions, presentations. Self employed, boss of own company. Had a boyfriend that came and went and took her savings.

Character

Female, child, Whitney Willowby, daughter of Sondra.

Description; Age 6 to 7 years, tall skinny for age, bright eyes, long hair, blondish, light brown.

Demeanour; Acts older and more mature than age, is still in wonder of life and its magical possibilities.

Mannerisms; Silent in movement, not rambunctious, talks clearly with adult maturity, talks openly and often walks daintily, often walks with movements of imitation of others, not to make fun of rather to praise with wanting to be like them. Wears clothes elegantly most of the time in contrast to mother, often directs mother to be more fashion aware, tries to be frumpy when required.

Character

Female, Dora Soblick, best friend of Sondra.

Description; Age 35 to 40 years, 5 foot 10 inches, skinny, over board with makeup, dresses for business and differently for social gatherings, a bit off.

Demeanour; Highly motivated, highly dressed, kooky, works but is lazy, needs to be centre of action.

Mannerisms; Actions extreme, exaggerated, fidgety, flirty.

Background; Stole job from Sondra, best friend of Sondra and now works for Sondra.

Character

Male, Judge, Nicholas Stankowskie.

Description; Gruff looking, no plump side, white beard, white hair, resembles Santa Claus.

Demeanour; Hard and cold faced in work area, soft hearted underneath, takes work seriously, soft hearted to charity and children and dogs.

Mannerisms; Acts gruff, frowns and stares when in work place, Santa Claus persona when with children.

Background; Career Judge, associated with the Bisson Estate and long-life friend of Martha. Plays Santa Claus.

Character

Male, Alloyuis Barthomew.

Description; Age 35 to 45 years, 6 feet, 200 plus pounds, chubby face with light expressiveness expressions, almost childish.

Demeanour; Exterior attempt to be mean and aggressive, internal emotions soft hearted.

Mannerisms; Big actions, light on feet, movements flowing, a ballet dancer in the body of a football player, squeaky voice, high pitched voice, uncharacteristic of large man.

Background; Big ex football player, now a mall security custodian.

Minor characters
Cabbie – Cab driver.
Salesman – Clothing store personnel.
Maitre`D – Restaurant waiter.
William – Santa Claus float driver.
Doctor – Richard's physician.
Bartend – Bartender.
Stranger – Bar-room patron
Old Lady – Grocery store person.
Lawyers – Evermore, Poopal, Crookster, Armbender, Monies.
Male parade announcer.
Female parade announcer.

NOTES;
Suggestion, keep flow at a fast continuous pace, do not lull or drag out. Character mannerisms should be prevalent and expressed at the same time that dialogue is presented. Camera multi-view of characters in all scenes stressed to show interaction of characters.

DESCRIPTION
The eyes of the audience flow through the hustle and bustle of a December day in a city eagerly embracing the season and among those that could care less. Seasonal music is choppy as if searching for the correct beat. The camera flow begins quickly in a blurry effect then slowly slows and pans from side to side as if peeking into decorated store front windows through the eyes of the audience as though the camera is searching for someone. Faces of the many, expressing the gambit of emotions, are studied then discarded. Seasonal music speeds up, slows and draws out to match the mood of the people.
The camera's eye stops roving and stares down a sidewalk watching a scene unfold. A hospital front is noticed and a man standing on the top step. Non-descript people are exiting and entering, all avoid looking at the man.
A woman and child are noticed exiting a store front. First the woman emerges with bags hanging from arms, a note pad in hands and talking in a business manner into a hands-free ear device. A coat strap extends out from her back and into the store's doorway. In a tug motion of a horse pulling a load and stretching leather traces the woman drags out an inquisitive child who is caught up in the delight of the season. The woman is concerned about work, packages and child, and is jumbling all. Moving down the street she pauses when the child tugs on the coat strap. The child wants to study the store front windows filled with toys, clothing and books.
The man attempts to button up a long overcoat, there are buttons missing, one shoe seems to flop in a Chaplin style step. He begins to descend steps and

stand in the centre of the sidewalk. The camera's eye begins to focus and advance on the man and woman with child. Music seems to have found a comfortable pace. Background voices and chatter of the city fades. Conversation between women talking on the phone is clear. Expressionless, the man sees the mother and child approaching, only his eyes react to an impending collision of the distracted woman and child staring off into a fantasy world of the season. Music softens.

SONDRA
(talk into ear phone, use hands to describe meanings in an effective frustration, conversation starts from moment of exiting the store)
No Dora, we need the display to entice men to think about the woman in their lives.
Hang on tight Whitney, don't let go, follow your mother.
No, I don't have a fixation that men should cater to women's every emotion. We are selling products, and we want men to purchase them for the women in their lives.
This way Whitney!
No, I did not yell at the man at Zales Department store. It does not matter if he is cute, he displayed the clothing wrong in the window display. Yes . . . yes . . . yes, I did flirt . . ., he didn't ask me out.
(stop, gesture with open arms to self and child staring into store window)
What's wrong with my clothes? Frumpy . . . I am frumpy . . ., what is frumpy? (stare at window display)
See . . ., see what that cute guy did. He had the mannequins posed as if the men and women were in a futuristic battle of the sexes. No . . ., no . . ., wait until I get there. I'm hailing a taxi as we speak. I am not frumpy. No don't set me up . . ., I can get any man I want. Yes, I can, I will, it's a bet.

DESCRIPTION
Man's eyes widen, he does not move. Woman and child approach, woman begins to hail a cab while passing in front of man. Child is walking behind man, staring at decorated evergreen trees and lights sparkling through a light snowfall. Taxi pulls to a stop. Woman rushes toward car door, coat strap tightens and yanks the child, pulling free of child's grasp. Music stops. Child reaches out blindly and grasps hand of man. Man, and child stare at each other. Both smile a greeting.

SONDRA
I'm in the cab. Zales, on . . .?

CABBIE
On booker street!
(stare at woman with interest, do not pay attention to traffic)

254

SONDRA
Yes, Zales on Booker. No Dora, nothing will hold me up. I'll be there in . . .?

CABBIE
Ten minutes . . ., for you five minutes.
(begin to pull out without looking)

DIRECTIONS
Man realizes what is transpiring and reaches out an arm and snaps fingers. Cab halts and stalls. Other cabs blow horns. Child's eyes widen with surprise, delight and wonderment as if the man has magic. Sondra bounces in seat and checks packages and searches as if missing something.

SONDRA
I will be there Dora, just a slight hold up . . ., no, no, I'm not being robbed. Sir, sir . . ., what's the problem? No, he's, he's my father's age.

DIRECTIONS
Child and man approach cab, man bends down and knocks on woman's window. Sondra and cabbie turn heads. The man's slight smile is hidden behind a scruffy beard.

SONDRA
I'm sorry, this cab is taken. What . . ., what do you want?

CABBIE
Don't open the window, he's crazy.

SONDRA
No, he's not, how do you know?

CABBIE
We're in front of a hospital. Sick people and crazy people use hospitals.

SONDRA
(open the window just a crack) Yes, what do you want?

RICHARD
(move eyes from front to side, trying to indicate the child left behind)

SONDRA
Speak up please.
(open window a bit more then quickly close slightly)

CABBIE
He's a Looney, don't open the window.
(try to start engine)

RICHARD
(with free hand point down to child)

CABBIE
He's a pervert, don't look.
(crank key, engine sputters)

SONDRA
(slowly peek)
Dora, he's not a pervert, yes, he has an overcoat. Yes, buttons are missing.

DIRECTIONS
Man's eyes and pointing finger point to side. Sondra and cabbie stretch to look. Sondra notices Whitney then frantically searches the cab.

CABBIE
He wants to sell a kid.

SONDRA
It is my kid.
(frantically reach for the door handle)
Whitney, I'll save you.

CABBIE
He's holding your kid for ransom.

DIRECTIONS
Sondra forces the cab door open, forcing window against man's head several times until man backs away. Sondra reaches out and grabs Whitney's hand and pulls her into the safety of the cab. Cabbie starts engine. Man, and child's hands slowly pull free of each other. Cab pulls away. Man stands bewildered. Whitney stares out of the back window and gently waves. Man returns a slight wave. Music builds. Man pulls up collar and begins walking down sidewalk. Camera pulls back, camera's eye sees the entire street scene and taxi fading.

SONDRA
I don't know if he is cute. Too much facial hair, and a messy head of hair. Single!? He is a weirdo, a trench coat weirdo. No . . ., no . . ., not a chance. Goodbye Dora . . ., I will see you at work.

(hold cell phone at an arms length)
Goodbye Dora . . .!
(trail off voice)

DIRECTIONS
Richard turns head and looks into abyss of a multi-use open air street mall.
He stares about, not anxious to go in, yet slowly steps toward entrance.
Camera's eye moves to inside and looks back out at man. Instantly a
formation of people gathers and enters the mall. The flow of people entering,
seemingly push man along within the wave. Once inside, the group disperses,
and man gathers composure as if now comfortable that the ordeal was not too
traumatic. Man searches surroundings with eyes looking for a person. An
elderly woman standing at a distance waves in an aristocratic gesture. Man
notices, smiles and approaches.

MOTHER
Richard dear, here, Richard.
(continue to wave in an assumption that Richard did not notice, be overly
doting)
Dear, dear, here I am!

RICHARD
Hello Mother.
(approach, place hands on Mother's shoulders, bend slightly and kiss cheek)
I am sorry that I am late for our appointment. There . . .
(pause, point back to street)

MOTHER
(concerned)
What dear? Did you lose your way? Did you have a memory lapse?
(hold onto Richard's arm with deep worry)
Do you know my name?

RICHARD
Miss. Martha Stanfield-Montcalm, Mother dear.

MOTHER
(sigh with relief)
I am so worried that your memory progression will be lost.
(pause, then remember Richard's bewildered pause)
What is the problem dear? What happened on your way here?

RICHARD
There was a woman . . ., I was standing outside of the hospital . . ., this woman

was so distracted with life . . ., she forgot about her child . . ..
(stare down at hand as if child is still there)
Mother, this child held onto my hand . . ., held it without fear. Me!?
(gesture to clothes and features)

MOTHER
(place hands to Richard's worried face frightened by child's abandonment
and pleased that the child accepted and felt a connection to Richard)
What did you do dear?

RICHARD
(surprised by self accomplished results)
I snapped my fingers and halted a cab, received a bump to my head from the
cab's opened door, child was pulled away and I am here.
(open palm as if releasing the child's hand)

MOTHER
Dear, dear, are you alright?
(place hands on Richard's face)

RICHARD
Yes, yes, fine, confused about that woman.

MOTHER
Don't worry dear, you made sure that the mother and child were reunited.
That is what is important. No need to attempt to understand women. You will
have a lifetime to do that.

RICHARD
(nod and walk ahead, look about as if intrigued by a child-like interest, do not
listen to Mother)

MOTHER
Just as we were reunited.
(study Richard as a mother observing the splendour of a child)

RICHARD
Well, Mother, are we going to spruce me up?

MOTHER
(popping out of dream)
Definitely!

DESCRIPTION

Mother takes Richard by the arm and leads him from storefront to storefront, first selecting a clothing store. Richard stands tall above clothing display racks. Mother is unseen by a salesman watching Richard with disgust and concern. Camera is watching from view of salesman then notices Richard and stops to watch with interest. Sondra is inspecting the window displays and talking to Dora.

SONDRA
Dora, take a note. This display at Moe-Be's needs to be fixed. No Dora, it is shabby, we need to highlight the suits, not trashy mannequins seducing the male mannequins. We are not selling porn.

DIRECTIONS
Elderly patrons passing by stop and look, searching for porn. Eavesdropping on Sondra's conversation, Sondra becomes aware.

SONDRA
No mannequin porn. Just, poor wardrobes on the slut-ty female mannequins. Yes Dora, get the display fixed.

DIRECTIONS
Sondra moves to the next window display indicating to patrons that this is a decent display. Whitney watches Richard and Mother through door opening. Camera focuses on salesman approaching.

SALESMAN
Sir, may I suggest the value shop on the corner of Seventh and Bailey Street. A fair selection of garments to suit . . . your needs.

RICHARD
The value shop? In which direction?

MOTHER
I beg to differ!

SALESMAN
(see and appreciate the quality of the woman's clothing)
Madame, may I be of assistance. Are you seeking clothing for your husband? May I suggest . . ..

MOTHER
I wish you to assist this man.

RICHARD

Mother, this gentleman has suggested the value shop.

MOTHER
Indeed!

SALESMAN
(suddenly aware of woman's value and odd connection to man)
Your son? Your son! Madame, we definitely have suitable clothing. May I suggest . . ..

DIRECTIONS
Salesman dances about selecting clothing, asking Mother what occasions are desired. Mother gives orders and shakes head yes or no to selections. Richard pleasantly nods head and goes with the flow. Whitney's facial expression follows suit of agreeing or not agreeing to selections. An adoring smile is reflective of Richard's introduction to life-smile.

SALESMAN
Shall the gentleman require dining wear, casual and business attire? May I suggest silk dress shirts?

MOTHER
Do not be ridiculous. The name is Martha Stanfield-Montcalm, not Versage. Give me quality Canadian clothing.

SALESMAN
Noted Madame, wool blends.

DIRECTIONS
A montage begins of following Richard and Mother through clothing changes. Thumbs up and down by Mother, and at a distance by Whitney. Richard is transformed into a well-dressed man. Sondra is moving about working at inspecting window displays and talking on the phone to Dora and is unaware of the connection between Richard and Whitney. Richard and Mother move into a salon, haircut, beard trim, facial, nails, the works. At a distance, Whitney is amazed by the transformation. Camera speeds about following the fast pace of mall flow then abruptly stops to focus on Richard and Mother exiting store. Whitney is sitting on a bench and is deep into a silent debate about women beginning to notice Richard. Sondra does not.

MOTHER
Well this has been a successful transformation.
(admire man in a motherly way, as a child on graduation day, dab an eye)
Richard, please wait here while I make arrangements for delivery of your

wardrobe.
(walk away, placing a hanky to nose)

RICHARD
Yes, Mother.
(look about, notice bench)
May I have a seat?

DESCRIPTION
Whitney eyes Richard, she is sitting in the middle of the bench. Richard smiles slightly which enhances his debonair essence.

RICHARD
Good day Miss, I believe we have met earlier?

WHITNEY
(smile, move slightly to one slide of the bench)
Yes, you magically stopped my mother's cab.

RICHARD
It did seem like magic, but . . ..

WHITNEY
My mother, Sondra Willowby, is a bit absentminded. She is a very busy business woman. She sometimes loses me, but she always comes to find me.

RICHARD
(concerned)
I see. May I introduce myself, Richard, Miss. Willowby.
(extend hand)

WHITNEY
Whitney.
(extend hand to shake his)
I am seven point seven-five years old.

RICHARD
Impressive, Miss. Whitney Willowby. May I share a seat on this bench, if you do not object?

WHITNEY
(shuffle to end of bench)
Please Mr. Richard . . .
(hint for a last name)

Mr. . . ., Mr. . . .
(inquisitively lean in, in a questioning manner)

RICHARD
(make a connection)
I have the same inquisitive dilemma. Unfortunately, I do not have a last name.

WHITNEY
Everyone has to have a last name. A last name defines your ancestry. Sometimes you carry both parents name. For example; I carry my Mother's name, Willowby. I am a selected child by means of artificial insemination.

RICHARD
(bewildered by the frankness and knowledge of the child)
Indeed!

WHITNEY
Yes, a modern scientific accomplishment in egg fertilization does not require historic matting or the requirements of a father to be involved with the creation of a child's life.

RICHARD
You don't say.

WHITNEY
This is why I use my mother's last name. What is your reason?

RICHARD
Well, (think) based on my age, I would say that I was conceived the archaic old fashion way. Medical complications have removed my memory of parental linage.

WHITNEY
I know, you suffer a form of amnesia and your past has been removed from your memory.

RICHARD
Somewhat a bit more complicated.

WHITNEY
(slide a bit closer, put a hand on back of bench and lean toward Richard to imply wanting to hear complete story)
Go on. My mother, Sondra Willowby, says that it is important to talk about your problems. It is healthy.

RICHARD
Technically, I have had a brain injury, to the extent that complete memory has been removed along with most bodily functions. A man of my age had been reduced to an infant state of being.

WHITNEY
Let me get this straight. You became a baby, unable to talk and walk?

RICHARD
Yes, diapers and all. I needed to learn to walk, talk, wash myself, dress myself and learn to read and decipher math all over again.

WHITNEY
(mouth hangs open in wonderment)
Having to learn math is enough once but having to learn it twice is excruciating.

RICHARD
No big deal. I do not remember learning math the first time.

WHITNEY
Then that's good. I don't mean. I'm sorry. Brain injury is tragic.

RICHARD
Yes. There are people who do suffer. I do suffer migraines.
(turn to face Whitney)
The up side is that life is a new adventure every moment from the instant I open my eyes until I fall asleep, then I dream about my daily adventures.

WHITNEY
Will I be in your dreams tonight?

RICHARD
I do believe that you will, and it will be a pleasing memory.

WHITNEY
What about Sondra Willowby?

RICHARD
Indeed, she will.
(nod with disappointment, then realize the daughter – mother connection)
I'll over look the way she abandoned you and remember her hugging you in the cab.

263

WHITNEY
Is that woman talking care of you, teaching you how to adapt to the world?

RICHARD
In a way, Mother is providing security at this state of my growth.

WHITNEY
Mother?
(excited)
Then you have a mother and a last name?

RICHARD
No, I just call her Mother because she provides care like a loving mother would. She is Martha Stanfield-Montcalm, a wonderful caring woman. I do remain known as John-Doe at the hospital, a name given to unknown persons. Mother suggested the name Richard.

WHITNEY
May I call you Richard? You may call me Whitney.

RICHARD
Please do, though I shall address you as Miss. Whitney out of respect.

WHITNEY
(stick out hand to shake)
Deal.

DIRECTIONS
From a distance Sondra sees Whitney and man touching hands. Bobbing through crowd, Sondra heads in direction of bench while continuing to talk to Dora. Mother is finishing up in store and is beginning to exit.

SONDRA
Dora, call the police, forget about the Zales store. Listen, a man is talking to Whitney on a bench. Ugly, good-looking, doesn't matter. A weirdo is a weirdo. Move, get out of my way, frantic mother coming through. Dora, nothing innocent about it, he is grabbing her hand. Pulling, no, yanking Whitney, stealing my child. He's got an accomplice, an old lady. Move out of my way. Dora, did you make the call? No, not to Zales, to the mall cops.

DIRECTIONS
A mall cop sees a frantic woman pushing her way through the crowd and not going with the natural flow in a correct direction. The mall cop is huge, an ex

football player, mean looking, yet sweet and timid in nature, with a high squeaky voice. Mall cop begins to advance in a direction to cut Sondra off.

ALLOYUIS
Miss., Miss., please stop! You are not flowing with the correct flow. Obviously, you are disturbing law abiding citizens. I must ask you to stop before I have to do something drastic.

DIRECTIONS
Sondra continues to disrupt flow of people traffic, she notices a large form looming closer, yet eyes keep flashing toward Whitney. Mall cop is moving with flow of people while apologizing as he tries to hustle.

SONDRA
Thanks Dora, I see a mall cop, they sent the biggest, meanest-mother of all. What, you didn't call, I asked you to call.

ALLOYUIS
Please stop Miss., you bumped a helpless old grandmother. She has an artificial hip.
(said in a squeaky loud voice)
Sorry Mrs. Strompolpolis, I will scold and discipline that law breaker of mall traffic etiquette.

SONDRA
Dora, Dora, I think the mall cop is after me, he is going to . . ..

ALLOYUIS
Mame, Mame, please!

DIRECTIONS
Mall cop steps in front of Sondra, she bumps into man and attempts to push through with little success.

ALLOYUIS
Mame, you have broken every rule of correct traffic flow. Mall traffic is always in a counter clock-wize flow.

SONDRA
I am in a hurry, in that direction.

ALLOYUIS
Mame, that is not a good-enough excuse.

SONDRA
A man and woman are stealing my child.
(frantic voice, point in direction.

DIRECTIONS
In a slow motion action the mall cop becomes a football player, head turns in direction of pointing finger, wide eyes focus then squint, in a turning motion a large arm grabs Sondra around the back and lifts up under an arm, semi-lifting as if clutching a football, the other hand rises and the mall traffic flow halts, and people part forming a path, the monster bursts toward the bench.

SONDRA
Okay, this is a better way. Under control, Dora, I'll call you back.

ALLOYUIS
No lost child under my watch.

MOTHER
(surprised by sight of a child but delighted to see compatible conversation)
Well, hello dear.
(extend a hand to young girl)

WHITNEY
Hello Miss. Martha Stanfield-Montcalm, so delighted to meet you. Richard has spoken well of you.

MOTHER
Has he?

RICHARD
May I introduce Miss Whitney Willowby.

DIRECTIONS
Mall cop looms over group, a shadow darkening the scene. All eyes look way up into the frowning face of the mall cop, then to Sondra's quirky accusing grin.

ALLOYUIS
Is there a problem here? I have had a complaint from this woman about an alleged abduction attempt f a child.

MOTHER
Ridiculous, Richard would never.

ALLOYUIS
You Mame, have also been accused.

MOTHER
Me! . . ., by whom?

WHITNEY
No, no, there is no abduction, this is the same man who stopped my mother, (point to Sondra) from abandoning me earlier this morning.

ALLOYUIS
(scornfully frown at Sondra)
You abandoned your child? Did you abandon your child in this mall, under my watch?

SONDRA
(shake head comically no and yes)
I was working, and . . . and . . . my daughter . . . Whitney . . ..

WHITNEY
Hello, (extend hand) a pleasure to meet you Mr. . . .?

ALLOYUIS
Alloyuis Barthomew the third.
(shake Whitney's hand with two fingers which smother her little hand)

SONDRA
Really! Please put me down!

ALLOYUIS
I am not sure, abandonment is equally as wrong as abduction.

MOTHER
Please, please, a misunderstanding I am sure.

WHITNEY
Alloyuis Barthomew the third, please meet my mother, Sondra Willowby, and this is Martha Stanfield-Montcalm. Everyone calls her Mother, and this is Richard, also known as John-Doe.

DIRECTIONS
Mall cop lowers Sondra. All shake hands with each other. Mall cop shakes hands twice. A tear forms in his eye.

ALLOYUIS
I am a big supporter of Stanfield cotton briefs.
(said in a whisper to Mother when shaking her hand)

MOTHER
Indeed, my Grandfather designed them in 1923.
(eye the big man)
Extra, extra large?

ALLOYUIS
Extra strength waistband.

SONDRA
(eye Alloyuis and Mother inquisitively)

WHITNEY
See, everyone now knows everyone. We are now acquaintances.

DIRECTIONS
Mall cop sternly stares at everyone, but is ready to burst into tears, everyone nods, Sondra reluctantly nods.

ALLOYUIS
Okay, fine, situation stable . . ., I must go.
(waddle away, tearful emotion building, regain firmness, high voice does not deliver fear, turn to Sondra)
Miss. Willowby . . . this is your first warning, follow mall traffic flow, no more hysterics. Grandmother Strompolopolis just got her new hip, we can't have any accidents.
(shake limp finger then sniffle with a hand rubbing under nose while walking away)

DIRECTIONS
All eyes turn to Sondra. Sondra shakes off displayed accusations.

SONDRA
You . . . Mr. Doe . . . just because you look different . . . I . . . there are weirdoes of all kinds . . . ah, we must go . . . sorry . . . thank . . . nice to meet you.
(shake Richard and Mother's hand and even Whitney's hand then turn and walk away, realize forgetting Whitney, turn and take her hand)
Whitney needs to go with me.

MOTHER, RICHARD, WHITNEY

Goodbye.
(wave to each other)

DIRECTIONS
Mother and Richard shrug shoulders, Whitney waves as she is being dragged. Mall cop is seen assisting Mrs. Strompolopolis.

SONDRA
(talk on phone)
Yes Dora, it is the same guy, I think. New clothes, spruced up. A man . . . I don't know.
(turn to take a peek through the crowd)
Not bad . . . yes, good looking. Not my type. Dora, we need to concentrate on the Zale Display. No . . . no . . . I am not going to look back.
(sneak a peek back)
No!

DIRECTIONS
Mother and Richard enter a restaurant and wait at door. At a distance the Maitre`d is moving a chair at a table and notices the entering patrons and rushes to greet.

MAITRE`D
May I offer a table for two?

RICHARD
I think we would prefer a meal for two.

MAITRE`D
(stare questionably)
A party of two?

RICHARD
No, I do not think we will engage in a party.

MAITRE`D
A seat for two at a small table?

RICHARD
(slightly nod)
A small table would be fine, but I do believe Mother and I would prefer individual seats.

MOTHER

(slight smile, amused by Richard's learning process of what is logic, offer a smirk to the Maitre`d)

MAITRE`D
(think deeply before saying)
Sir and Madame, may I suggest an intimate table with two chairs and provide a meal for two?

MOTHER
Yes, that would be fine.

MAITRE`D
(begin to lead Mother and Richard through restaurant)

RICHARD
Unless you have a party in progress that you would wish us to join? I have no memories of ever having or attending a party of any description.

MAITRE`D
(quizzically stare at Richard)
Sir, we do not entertain parties in this establishment.
RICHARD
I do believe you suggested a party for two?

DIRECTIONS
Maitre`d bumps a chair moved previously and side-steps several people. In a single motion Richard grasps chair and moves it to its proper position as a lady begins to sit without looking. Maitre`d seats Richard and Mother and hands them menus. Meal scene unfolds.

MOTHER
Richard, dear, how is your memory, is there any bits of a past that you recall?

RICHARD
Not one incident. At the moment I am filling my brain with current information at the same time trying to logically analyze meanings. I believe that 'party of two' does not mean to engage in a party.

MOTHER
Quite right, the English language is declining into double entendre innuendoes.

RICHARD
Double meanings with a snide intent.

MOTHER
Correct drear. Yes, life can be that way. For example; at the moment you feel like a nobody, yet in reality you may be important, rich, and famous. You may be Richard Rickman Bisson.

RICHARD
The recluse, industrial heir, that has not been seen in ten years and is presumed missing for over seven years, or I may be a commoner, Richard Edmond Alcid, the recluse writer and hermit.

MOTHER
Where did you find that name?

RICHARD
I have a book I have been reading, the author Richard Edmond Alcid is a recluse. The only picture of him on the cover is of a five-year old child.

MOTHER
No . . . no . . . you would be more like a Richard Rickman Bisson.

RICHARD
What facts do you have to make such a connection? Wait Mother, let me try something. Let me use the imagination of a writer, Edmond Alcid.

MOTHER
(amused)
Please, entertain me.

RICHARD
Once upon a time.
(frown at mother's objection)
Too mundane? Fine. Devastation lingered in the woman's eyes when abandoning a child, Richard Rickman Bisson to the solitude life surrounded by luxury and wealth. Her own pursuit of power in the fashion world overshadowed the motherly affection she secretly preferred to pursue. In the autumn of aging years, Martha Stanfield-Montcalm pursues an inclusion in the life of her abandoned child, only to be shunned by the tragic memory loss suffered by Richard Rickman Bisson.

MOTHER
(sudden shook of the similarities to the truth turns your face sullen, yet an eagerness to say, 'yes, it is true')
Cliché of every Disney movie ever made to teary eye the emotions of sentimental old women.

(brush moisture from an eye)

RICHARD
Mother, you will conclude that I may have an association to Edmond Alcid, rather than Rickman Bisson?

MOTHER
A far-fetched story indeed.

MAITRE`D
I beg your pardon, for overhearing you mention Mr. Rickman Bisson. Our chef was employed by the Bisson household.

MOTHER
Would the chef recognize Mr. Bisson?

MAITRE`D
Chef Andre has only had rare, very distant sightings of the reclusive man. A very sad state, this man, being a prisoner of wealth and vanity.

RICHARD
Would I rather be a poor hermit or a rich hermit?

MAITRE`D
Rich!

RICHARD
Poor!

MOTHER
Neither, people need people. Despite indifferences we need each other.

RICHARD
True, without Mother I would be a medical hermit being studied by intern eyes at the hospital.

MOTHER
Dear, you have had enough of that. We will find you a place to live and vacate that hospital.

DIRECTIONS
Meal continues and concludes with flashes of tasting, smiles and laughter. Richard and Mother begin to leave the restaurant. Small banter continues. Richard in motion adjusts a chair for a woman struggling to rise without

acknowledgment or observation by anyone. Maitre`d escorts clients to the exit.

MAITRE`D
Merci, and please return.

RICHARD
When?

MAITRE`D
(shrug, tongue-tied)

RICHARD
An innuendo?
(nod and smile)
We shall.

MOTHER
(see mall cop, point)
Dear, you need to experience more in life. A person to assist you. Come dear.
(begin to walk faster toward mall cop, calling out)
Alloyuis Barthomew, Alloyuis!

DIRECTIONS
Camera's eye speeds towards mall cop looming above a group of elderly people, soft eyes peer out from a stern face expecting trouble. Black out.

DIRECTIONS
Camera lens brightens. An interior apartment is nice, seems well lived in, not organized, a neat messy atmosphere. In the apartment of Sondra and Whitney, they are busy preparing a meal. Sondra finally tries to get off the phone and quit working. Whitney is giving disapproving eyes.

SONDRA
Dora, the work day is over. Stop looking at me that way. No Dora, not you . . ., my concerned mother, Whitney! Dora, I have to go, goodbye.
(remove ear phone)

WHITNEY
(talk with adult intelligence)
I must agree with Dora, though I think she is a back stabbing, job stealing, man stealing, corporate traitor. She is your friend and I do like her and I hate having to agree with her.

SONDRA
But . . ., there is a but in there.

WHITNEY
You need to have a life, go out and meet a man. It is a fact as stated by the medical establishment that a father figure is essential in a child's formative years. In several years I will be too old to benefit from a father's insight and parental strictness.

SONDRA
So . . . this is not about me finding a man, you are shopping around for a father.

WHITNEY
(pause and think about facts)
Yup!

SONDRA
What? Do you have a catalogue of available fathers to choose from, and do I have a say?

WHITNEY
I have several possible fathers in mind, and you should have a say. You will need to live with my father too and should get along well together.

SONDRA
Thank you for allowing for my input.

WHITNEY
Mom, you do have the qualifications, after all you picked a suitable sperm donor from a catalogue.

SONDRA
(squint, shiver)
Ooo . . . that sounds too cold and clinical . . . though very true. Sperm donor 469654-UN displayed all of the artistic and educational qualifications.

WHITNEY
How tall is he, fat, skinny, a muscle man, what . . .?

SONDRA
That is what the letters UN after the file number means. Unknown . . ., I did not want to know. I wanted to be surprised that you were going to be unique.

WHITNEY
And am I?

SONDRA
You are, artistic and superbly smart and look like me and sperm donor 469654-UN.

WHITNEY
Then if I am superbly intelligent then you should take my advice . . . go out with Dora and cruise for a man.

DIRECTIONS
Sondra's ear phone begins to buzz. Whitney and Sondra look at it and at each other. Whitney is nodding yes, Sondra is nodding no. Whitney pushes earphone toward Sondra who is shaking head no. Whitney's face pleads with the charm of a pouting 'Shirley Temple'. Sondra melts, slumps and begins to slowly pick up the ear phone. While answering, music dominates the scene and fades into a comparison scene.

DIRECTIONS
Within a silent film presentation actions unfold beneath music. Music is used to drive actions of characters. Mother and Richard walk down hallway of an apartment complex and stop at a door and knock. Alloyuis opens the door, greets Mother while she pushes Richard in and then waves goodbye.

Whitney selects outfits by pointing to clothes in Sondra's closet. Sondra piles onto arm then is pushed into walk-in closet by Whitney who then scurries to bench seat at the end of the bed full of excitement and anticipation, waiting for Sondra to emerge.

Alloyuis begins to pantomime ways of standing and walking into a room and towards a woman. Alloyuis uses every stereo typical type of style form, debonair, bum, working man, gangster, hip hop, jock, gay and straight. Richard imitates, mixes styles with little success.

Sondra parades out to smiles, laughs, frowns, thumbs up, thumps down from Whitney. Sondra's expression is always a dumpy frown. She attempts different modeling stances that all look cold and mannequin like.
Alloyuis begins to pantomime ways of greeting women, using Richard as the intended woman. Facial expressions are important, the Clark Gable squint, Cary Grant semi-smile, John Wayne frown, James Cagney gangster look and various hand greetings. The lean in, the gentle hand touch, the limp and masculine hand shake unfold.

Whitney conducts with hands, directing Sondra to stand tall, head up, shoulders back, chest out, hips to sway, to walk sultry, to tilt head down, eyes up, seductive smile, hand greetings, polite laugh and loud laugh. Sondra goes through the gambit of hilarious to serious and always completely exaggerated gestures.

Camera focuses on Whitney finally smiling and giving a thumb up.

Camera follows Dora walking out of elevator and to Sondra's door. Knocking lightly the door opens. A jealous smile comes to her face. Camera shows back of Whitney pushing Sondra out through the door.

Camera has a long shot of hallway and of Alloyuis consuming entire hallway. He is motioning for Richard to follow. His arm reaches in and pulls Richard out into the hallway.

DIRECTIONS
Camera circles around a club from a ceiling view. A variety of groups occupying various areas are energetic on the dance floor. Cougars are to one side, gigolos are hovering, women bunched together, first timers being timid or over enthusiastic. Music caters to all from big band, swing, rock, classis rock, hard rock, hip hop, rap and dancers change to suite the music. Music surrounds though allows voyeurs to eavesdrop on conversations. Dora and Sondra are sitting at a quiet bar. Sondra is slouched over a fancy drink, not enthusiastic about being there. Dora is searching for action.

DORA
So, this man, your kid befriends is first a bum then magically stops your cab then is magically transformed into a prince and you reject him as you did the bum?

SONDRA
It was not like that.

DORA
And, what about the mother?

SONDRA
Mavis . . ., no, Martha Stanfield-Montcalm.

DORA
(not listening, concentrate on men then realize knowing the name)
Stanfield? Martha Stanfield. Sondra are you serious. Don't you remember, your first job interview was with Stanfield Clothing Company.

276

SONDRA
(perk up)
Oh yeah, the interview I was late for, the interview you showed up for and got the job.

DORA
Lucky for me.

SONDRA
You were there to tell them I would be a little late.

DORA
A wonderful lady, and a great interview. It was going so well, I just forgot about you.

SONDRA
Forgot?

DORA
You got a better job, and now I work for you. It all worked out.

SONDRA
(stare in bewilderment)
As a friend you are great, as an employee you are killing me.

DORA
Friendship is forever and you always forgive me.

SONDRA
(gesture with hands and face to mock self)
I do.

DORA
Now if Mr. Magical is Martha Stanfield-Moncalm's son then he is linked to old money and name.

SONDRA
Nope . . . nope . . ., according to Whitney, Martha is just his benefactor and he just calls her Mother.

DORA
So?

SONDRA
So . . ., no old money and no famous name. He is John-Doe, lives at the hospital and lost his memory from an accident.

DORA
Perfect, just the kind of man you need. Train him your way, just like a puppy and he will always be at your beckon call.

SONDRA
Puppies become dogs and eventually will go sniffing for a bi . . ..

DORA
If you don't want him, I'll . . ..

SONDRA
Dig your claws into . . ., he's here, don't look, turn this way, hide me.

DORA
(instantly search bar for man)
What does he look like?

SONDRA
Ah . . .
(wishy-washy gesture and facial expression)
Normal bum turned into a Prince Charming.

DIRECTIONS
Alloyuis enters room first, Richard is following, lost in the large man's shadow. Both are dressed in casual suits. Alloyuis surveys the crowd then decides on character mood to pursue. Noticing women dancing together, Alloyuis swaggers in. Richard is uncomfortable though is intent on imitating Alloyuis. He takes one step then decides not to. Incoming patrons' herd him towards the dance floor. He backs away towards the long bar, bouncing from the bar and people like a pin ball. Dora is stretching her head looking over patrons entering and only notices a large man, the only one dressed in a suite.

DORA
Would he wear a suite? Of course, he would. Martha Stanfield-Montcalm would not settle for anything less. Would he stand out in a crowd? Of course, he would.

DIRECTIONS
Dora steps away from the bar and edges closer to the dance floor. Richard suddenly falls into a vacant spot and stays there. Dora dances toward Alloyuis,

thinking that he is a real man and is not listening to Sondra searching for words to describe Richard.

SONDRA
Well . . . somewhat good looking . . ., fit, good natured . . ., I mean not in your face, 'here I am full of masculinity' . . .! He did clean up well, exceptionally well . . . and tall . . . not too tall . . . about . . .

RICHARD
(listen in then recognize Sondra)
Six foot one and three eights of an inch tall . . ., sounds better than quoting in Metric measurements.
(pick up napkin and dab at a smudge of a drink on Sondra's face)

SONDRA
(not over reacting)
You are a bit forward, though very diplomatic.
(look into bar mirror to inspect appearance)

RICHARD
We would not want people mistaking your appearance of that of a slob, unhygienic, homeless person, or of a person that cares less about a personal appearance or does not want to impress others.

SONDRA
Okay . . . I get your point. This . . .
(gesture to dress and appearance)
Is not of my doing . . . well the dirty face okay. My daughter Whitney, you already know Whitney . . . she selected this outfit and accessories . . . and Dora . . .
(point to Dora dancing with other women vying for the attention of the large man)
The tall woman battling those other women . . . she did the hair and make up. Beneath all of this is plain old me.

RICHARD
The raw essence of you is natural beauty in its view of nakedness.

SONDRA
(close hand over cleavage)
Excuse me? What kind of pick-up line is that? Eloquent, but a bit too personal. I am not advertising.

DIRECTIONS

A stranger sitting on the far side of Sondra is listening, a man on the search for action, he turns and leans in.

STRANGER
Fancy talk ain`t what women in this place are looking for. They want action, dancing, heat of the moment, no talking, wham-bam and the man gone before morning.

SONDRA
Not me . . . maybe those . . .
(gesture to the women on the dance floor)
Definitely Dora, but not me.

STRANGER
That's what they all say until hooking up with me . . . angel of the night.

RICHARD
Mr. Angel, despite the primate mating rituals you believe is mutually exhibited by all, Miss. Willowby has advanced beyond the Cro-Magnon stage of evolution.

STRANGER
I know what primate means, but are you calling me a monkey?

RICHARD
Primate varies between the great ape, orangutan, chimpanzee and various assorted monkeys. A chimpanzee would be insulted with considering you a close relative.

STRANGER
Fancy-talk all you want, but I know when women are begging for action and I can deliver.
(touch Sondra's arm)

SONDRA
(raise fist closest to Richard with an intent to punch the stranger)
Monkey . . . you are a rodent.

RICHARD
(gently cover Sondra's fist with a hand)
Such a gesture is warranted. I do fear that the result will be your painful hand and maybe with broken fingers. Just allow the . . . as you stated, rodent to scurry to his hole.

STRANGER
(stand and lean against Sondra to glare at Richard)
Join me in the alley and I will settle this matter.

DIRECTIONS
Dora's grip on Alloyuis' arm leads the way toward Sondra, though she is unaware of the relationship between the Alloyuis and the man standing by Sondra. Alloyuis notices the situation unfolding and sneaks up behind Richard and bulks up and glares down on the stranger. A sudden loom of a shadow halts the stranger's banter. Looking up, the stranger's face pales.

RICHARD
(said in a informative manner, not in an aggressive way)
If you have extended an invitation to a confrontation of fisticuffs, I would suggest refraining. The results would definitely create bruising and the release of blood. Your night of seeking a companion willing to engage in a brief relationship would be compromised.

STRANGER
(blink and cower)
You talk too much with fancy double talk, a waste of my time to pound on you.

DIRECTIONS
The stranger slouches away into the crowd and darkness. Sondra and Richard study each other's eyes then their clasped hands. Richard releases hold as if releasing a dove. Dora leans in. Alloyuis moves to the side.

DORA
Who was that creep? You and this delicious man were holding hands.
(turn to Alloyuis)
This is Alloyuis . . . Sondra and . . .?

DIRECTIONS
Everyone mentions their name as they shake hands. Alloyuis and Richard shake several times pretending not to know each other. Richard and Sondra shake hands limply though they do linger.

DORA
This is the bum? A pretty fancy, good looking bum. Whitney knows class when she sees it.
(ohh and ahh and lean in until hearing music)
Dance music, come Alloyuis.
(turn to Sondra)

Sondra . . . what a name, Alloyuis is mysterious.

DIRECTIONS
Dora and Alloyuis disappear onto the dance floor. Silence envelopes around
Richard and Sondra awkwardly staring then gradually stare away. Both seem
at a loss for words. Sondra downs a drink and then Dora's drink and orders
another. While sipping one, orders another. Politely observing, Richard stays,
noticing how quickly the alcohol is affecting Sondra.

RICHARD
I take it that Dora is your best friend?

SONDRA
God-Mother of Whitney, stole my first job working for Martha Stanfield-
Montcalm, tried to talk me out of artificial insemination. She prefers the 'do
it the old fashion way' and that any man is good enough.
 Dora was right there though, right through my labour then stole my second
job when I was on maternity leave.

RICHARD
Friends are true.

SONDRA
She now works for me . . . worst employee ever. She did a nice job with my
hair.

RICHARD
True.

DIRECTIONS
Slowly the camera circles the room from Sondra's position. Camera rises and
the room and timeframe speeds up then suddenly stops to show the image of
Sondra in the bar's mirror then the camera jerks to a cockeyed angle. At the
same time Sondra attempts to stand and crumbles into Richard's arms. He
instantly saves her by supporting from under arms. Un-expectantly his hands
perfectly cup her breasts. Camera sees this view through the mirror. Both
characters react, Richard opens hands and lifts Sondra onto feet though she
has a problem balancing on the heels of her high-heel shoes.

SONDRA
Good night, it has been a delight despite the collaboration of all to make this
night a fairy tale ending.
(kick off heels and begin to walk toward exit)

DIRECTIONS
Richard picks up high heel shoes and stares at them, then at Sondra, then to the bartender, Richard's bewildered eyes seem to be questioning the proper procedure.

BARTENDER
You now follow her, she left the shoes for a reason.

RICHARD
Yes.

BARTENDER
Subconsciously she wants you to bring her the shoes and escort her home.

RICHARD
Oh, yes, she needs shoes. It is dangerous to walk outside without . . .

BARTENDER
That is when you carry her to a cab, deliver her home, help her unlock the door.

RICHARD
Because she is a bit un-coordinated, due to alcohol impairment . . . then?

BARTENDER
Then escort her to the sofa, or bedroom, or in some cases directly to the bathroom.

RICHARD
Assistance in the lavatory is inappropriate.

BARTENDER
(express convulsion actions)

RICHARD
I understand, hold hair back, cold compresses, dab at lips and chin delicately.

BARTENDER
Correct.

RICHARD
Then?

BARTENDER

(shrugging)
Then, man, the rest is up to you.

RICHARD
Up to me?

BARTENDER
(point)
Your date is almost at the door.

RICHARD
Technically, Miss. Willowby is not my . . .
(turn to bartender, but no one is there. With shoes dangling in fingers of hand
held out, head toward the door)

DIRECTIONS
In a sped-up speed, where applicable advance the scenes, not too fast, do not
exaggerate slapstick. Richard reaches the doors, holds the door open for
Sondra until she takes a deep breath of cool night air. The instant inhaling of
oxygen brings her to the fainting faze of passing out. Richard cradles her at
the last moment and begins to follow instructions of the bartender and carries
her to a waiting cab.

CABBIE
Yoh . . .
(notice woman's condition)
Fare will cost you extra is she hurls . . . and you clean the cab. Checker Cab
Company rules.

RICHARD
Acceptable, a reasonable rule.

CABBIE
(surprised)
Thanks! Where may I deliver the package?

RICHARD
Package? Yes, a comparison of a postal service, delivering an inanimate
article. You wish to deliver an inanimate person, the package.

CABBIE
Yeah . . . your package. Where to?

RICHARD

284

(pat Sondra's arm)
Miss. Willowby . . . your address please? The bartender did not tell me what to do in this situation.

CABBIE
Check her purse!

RICHARD
Definitely a source of information.
(read ID card)
4697 4th Ave. South.

DIRECTIONS
Cabbie gears cab and jerks away. Camera speeds up. Cab stops at apartment building. Richard carries Sondra out and into lobby, she is in and out of a daze and in a happy mood and greets and waves to people. Richard approaches lobby concierge, then chit chat then move to elevator, they go up, down, up and then stops. Richard carries Sondra to apartment door. Concierge opens the door, talks to elderly baby-sitter then they leave. Richard searches for the bedroom, finds it, changes mind, heads to sofa. Sondra imitates bartender's convulsion actions. Richard heads to the bathroom, holds Sondra's hair back as she bends over the toilet. He puts cold compress on forehead, dabs at lips and chin. Lifting Sondra, he stands in hallway deciding where to go. Heads to bedroom, places Sondra on bed, pulls covering from beneath. Sondra rolls to opposite side. Richard floats covering up and covers her then moves to end of bed, reaches under and begins to pull off various pieces of clothing. Nylons stretch then snap off. Blindly reaching under a sound of a zipper is heard along with clipping sounds. Richard moves to side then the other side of bed then back to bottom and begins to pull dress off along with under garments. Richard is somewhat proud of accomplishment and surprised by the quality of items removed. Thinking, Richard retrieves a bucket and places by bed. He pushes Sondra's hair away and turns her head toward the bucket then tucks coverings around head. He begins tidying up, hanging dresses, putting shoes away, organizing the room, bathroom, even runs the vacuum, organizes the cabinet of clothing by size and product application, does the same for the makeup table. Satisfied, Richard closes the light and bedroom door, eyes the remainder of the apartment, shakes head before beginning to clean up the main rooms.

DIRECTIONS
Camera rises from end of the bed, suddenly camera and Sondra meet, she springs to a sitting position exhibiting a variety of facial expressions while she thinks of past events. Looking beneath the covers she becomes startled and begins inspecting the room, noticing its neatness, then remembers a

pounding head. Searching for a personal covering, a house coat is found neatly folded at the end of the bed, she covers up and begins to get out of bed, steps into the bucket and hobbles to the bathroom with an urgent need to pee. Sitting comfortably on the throne she contemplates, becomes worried then pleased that someone took care of her. Wondering who, she inspects the organization of the room. Opening the organized cabinet, she takes down a container of headache pills and leaves the container open and on the counter then turns to leave. In thoughtful ponder she turns, replaces the cap and puts pill bottle back in its location. Approaching partially open bedroom door she peeks out and listens to the sounds of voices. Camera turns to the kitchen.

WHITNEY
Mother never drinks to excess. She told me that there are people that take advantage of others when inebriated.

RICHARD
Would you like Canadian St. Joseph Island maple syrup with your flap-jacks?

WHITNEY
Thank you, please. Did you take liberties with mother's situation?

SONDRA
(look beneath robe, mouth drops open)
Yes? NO?!

RICHARD
Of course, if the opportunity presents itself, one must use care in the arising situation.

WHITNEY
So, you took care of mother?

SONDRA
(touch hair and face, make various expressions, gag with slight distaste of being a possible object at the hands of Richard)

RICHARD
Would you prefer coffee, tea, or milk with breakfast?

WHITNEY
Milk please. You brought mother home?

RICHARD
Yes.

WHITNEY
Did you have to carry her?

RICHARD
Yes.

WHITNEY
Did you hold her head and hair when she was sick?

RICHARD
Yes.

WHITNEY
Did you wash her face?

RICHARD
Yes.

WHITNEY
Did you put her to bed?

RICHARD
Yes.

WHITNEY
And it was you that folded and put away her clothes, and cleaned the room, bathroom and the whole apartment?

RICHARD
Yes.

WHITNEY
(exasperated and amazed)
You are Just the kind of man we need around here. Where did you sleep?

SONDRA
(clutch house coat, peak beneath, turn to look at the dishevelled bed coverings)
(whisper to self)
No . . . no . . . don't tell her you slept in my bed . . . you did not sleep with me.
You took advantage of my condition and had your way with me.

RICHARD
I did not want to leave, it was late, you were here, the baby sitter was gone, and your mother probably would not wake if you needed her, so I slept . . .

SONDRA
(rush out of bedroom to stop further information form being leaked)
I'm alright, in perfect condition. I am here for you Whitney . . ., Mr. . . . Doe has places to go.

RICHARD
(glance at Whitney, shake head no)
Nothing of importance, Mother and I . . .

SONDRA
Yes! Your mother may be worried about you.
(head is spacey, weave and hold onto counter)

RICHARD
(in anticipation hand a cup of coffee to Sondra)
Fluids, plenty of fluids are required to counter excess consumption of alcohol.

WHITNEY
Mother, where you drunk? Did Richard have to take care of you?

RICHARD
Whitney, your mother was of no trouble, actually quite easy. I had no trouble having my . . .

SONDRA
No . . . no, I am not easy pickings and I was not inebriated.
(lower head and sway, drink coffee)

RICHARD
(pour more coffee, nod head yes to Whitney)
I had my way with her, she did not object to me taking care of her needs.

SONDRA
My needs! I don't have needs!

WHITNEY
(glance about the apartment)
Obviously, you do. Richard took care of you, cleaned the apartment and made me breakfast. You should hire him as a house care person. He can't live at the hospital forever and he needs a job and a place to live.

SONDRA
We have a house keeper.

WHITNEY
That quit two months ago.

SONDRA
(think)
She did? I just thought that she was a lazy house keeper.

WHITNEY
Mr. Richard Doe . . . you are hired.

SONDRA
No . . . no . . . no!
(begin to display signs of gagging)
No . . . I'm going . . . I need help . . .!

WHITNEY
Deal is done.

DIRECTIONS
Richard anticipates Sondra's relapse and supports her while directing her to
the bathroom and toilet and holds head and hair back.

SONDRA
Out . . . out . . ..
(begin to gag)
I'm alright, please go.
(gag)

RICHARD
(place towel around her head to hold hair back then back out and begin to talk
through closed door)
Mother is sponsoring a float in the Santa Claus parade.
(child like emotion)
She said that I could drive the float. I've never driven before, as far as I know.
Mother suggested that I invite you and Whitney.

SONDRA
(emit gagging sounds)
No . . . no . . .ah!

RICHARD

I take it that you will not be up to such an outing at this time, understandable. The invitation has been extended to Whitney by Mother. Shall that be alright?

SONDRA
(gag)
What?
(hearing a tap at the door, decide to cover up in the blanket and lay on the cool floor)
Alright . . ..
(point to self and wave)
Alright.

DIRECTIONS
Whitney is leaning over chair staring at Richard at the bathroom door. Richard turns and gives a thumbs up. Whitney becomes excited and returns the gesture. Richard begins to clean up as Whitney is excitedly getting ready for a day out. Camera looks past Richard to light snow falling outside. Pulling back, the camera watches Richard writing a note. Whitney and Richard peek into the bedroom to see Sondra snoring in bed. Camera watches the two exit. Camera turns to the window and exits into the lightly falling snow.

DIRECTIONS
Camera falls the height of the apartment building, turns to the front door to see Richard and Whitney exiting and meeting Mother at a limousine. They settle into the car.

MOTHER
Whitney dear, have you seen the Santa Claus parade before?

WHITNEY
Oh yes, just from a distance, I use binoculars and watch from the apartment window.

MOTHER
Well, that is, well this year you will see the parade in close-up action.

WHITNEY
Will I be able to meet Santa?

MOTHER
I think I can arrange a meeting. I am a sponsor of the Santa Claus float.

WHITNEY
I have a few matters to discuss with Mr. Claus.

(excitedly stare out of the window)

MOTHER
Richard dear, you did not return to the hospital last night. Alloyuis said that you and Miss. Willowby disappeared.

WHITNEY
Richard brought my mother home. He now works for us. Mother hired him to take care of us.

MOTHER
Richard?

RICHARD
Apparently, a verbal agreement was made.

WHITNEY
Mother was a bit inebriated last night and not too healthy this morning. She is in bed snoring like a truck driver.

MOTHER
Oh . . . I see . . . I should visit your mother today and see if she is alright.

DIRECTIONS
Camera flows through organized mayhem of people getting floats ready. Whitney is in awe of the commotion of clowns and float characters. Richard and Whitney make their way to the Santa Claus float. Whitney is amazed by the float and animated reindeer and the massive empty float, and she moves to inspect every detail. Richard and Mother talk to the driver of the float.

MOTHER
Richard, please meet William, William is the driver and will accompany you.

WILLIAM
(grouchy face)
This is against my better judgement. I have been the sole driver for twenty-years.

MOTHER
William, Richard needs to explore the world and learn as much as he can. I have explained Richard's condition to you.

RICHARD
I will listen intently, and I will not break anything.

(inspect float and cockpit at the front of the float)

WILLIAM
Why not another float . . . maybe one of those small cars?

MOTHER
Do not be ridiculous William, I sponsor this float. Richard has never driven before so please teach him well. What can go wrong? The top speed of this float is slower than a toddler in a peddle car.

WILLIAM
Never driven before . . . this is a three-ton float with front and rear steering axels . . . it is not . . . a tin peddle car.

MOTHER
Enjoy yourself Richard, and smile once in a while William . . . your are suppose to be a happy elf.

WILLIAM
Hum-bug . . .!

MOTHER
(turn to Richard without hearing William)
We must meet Santa, and introduce Whitney, then I will visit Miss. Willowby about matters of mutual interest.

DIRECTIONS
Santa emerges from a tent and in the eyes of Whitney is cloaked in an aura. Whitney is slack jawed with eyes wide.

SANTA
Ho . . . Ho . . . Ho . . . Merry Christmas!
(notice Whitney)
Well, well, well . . . how are you Whitney? Merry Christmas.

WHITNEY
You . . . you know my name!
(cautious)
What's my last name, what's my mother's name, what's my mother's best friend's name?

SANTA
Whitney Willowby, Sondra Willowby, and I think . . . yes, your mother's best friend's name is . . . Dora.

WHITNEY
(mouth stays open with delighted surprise, inspect the details of the Santa suit and beard, begin to reach up to pull)

SANTA
(lean down)
You are doubtful . . . please tug, but not too hard, it will hurt.

WHITNEY
(gently give the fluffy beard a pull)
Wow!
(turn serious)
You are not doing a good enough job, kids in the hospital can not come to see the parade. You need to hang around longer and visit them.

SANTA
(see mother listening in and understand her nodding head)
Well, I will, and you and Richard can bring me.

WHITNEY
Do you know Richard? He has no memory of his past . . . do you know his real name, did you know him as a child?

SANTA
Ho, ho, ho, do I ever, a nice boy.
(look to mother who gives a shush finger to lips)
If I told you, it would be against the rules. Richard needs to discover his own history for himself and we need to be there to support him.

MOTHER
Hello Santa.

SANTA
Ho, ho, ho . . . hello Mother.

MOTHER
A pleasure to meet you Santa, we have a mutual friend.
(change subject to throw off Whitney's interest)
Alloyuis Barthomew, he is a friend of Richard's.

WHITNEY
Santa knows everyone, Mother, and who is good or bad.
(turn to Santa)

Is Aunt Dora on the good or bad list?

SANTA
Ho, ho . . ., I can honestly say that Aunt Dora is good and bad at the same time. HO, HO?

MOTHER
Santa, Richard is driving with William and if you don't mind, may Whitney be your elf assistant while I deal with other matters. I will have a limousine available later for your visit to the hospital.

DIRECTIONS
Richard tries on a little hat, it does not stay on head, William selects a larger one that is too big for his head and it falls over his eyes while he points out the controls to Richard)

WILLIAM
The speed is fixed for a maximum of five miles per hour, the steering is front axel when in the normal position. In the dual position both front axel and rear axel turn. This is only to be used when needing to move side ways. Gears are forward, reverse, and neutral. I will tell you when to stop and go, understand?

RICHARD
(excited, anxious while turning steering wheel to the limit in both directions) Your instructions are very clear.

WILLIAM
I'll do the waving to the crowd. You keep both hands on the steering wheel.

RICHARD
Do you smile when you wave?

WILLIAM
No!

DIRECTIONS
Music ends bluntly, scene blacks out.

DIRECTIONS
The door bell of Sondra's apartment rings and the camera bursts into the bedroom as Sondra explodes from the bed. Dressed in oversized pyjamas she lets her mind clear before rushing through the apartment searching. A thumping returns to her head and she presses hands to temples and attempts to push out the pain. Rushing, Sondra checks the kitchen, living room,

bathrooms and Whitney's bedroom. Panic sets in as she picks up a note left by Richard. She studies it but does not comprehend the words. The door bell rings again and Sondra grimaces and hobbles to the door and flings it open to view a pleasant and calm Mother.

MOTHER
Good . . . morning dear.

SONDRA
Miss. Martha Stanfield-Montcalm!

MOTHER
Sondra dear, just call me Mother.

SONDRA
(attempt to be angry, but head pain prevents true anger)
Well . . . Mother . . . your Richard has kidnapped my daughter and you are here to negotiate a ransom.

MOTHER
I sense a hang over . . . and Richard did not return to the hospital last night.

SONDRA
Don't change the subject . . . what's your demands?
(shake paper until it unfolds)

MOTHER
Is that a note? Have you read it yet? I trust that Richard and Whitney would not leave without informing you.
(begin to enter, close door, take Sondra by the arm and lead her to the sofa)

SONDRA
(try to focus, turn paper to satisfy viewing and read aloud)
Dear Sondra Willowby. It is addressed to me. Having noted your declined condition by the consumption of fluids and foreseeing a need for you to gain rest in order to regain the lustre and animation of gaiety that you pleasantly display, we, Miss. Willowyby and I, will allow you time to moult into the butterfly that you are.

MOTHER
Most eloquent in his description of your hangover. Richard is expressing an admiration for you.

SONDRA

(slight grin, then frown)
I can see right through sweet talk.
(pause, focus on the note, find place)

MOTHER
Go on dear.

SONDRA
Mother and I have invited Miss. Willowby to partake in the Santa Claus
parade. Please view from your window. We shall be on the last float.
(turn to window and notice binoculars on window sill)
We shall wave and hope to see your enthusiastic return wave. Anticipating a
recuperation, undoubtedly your glow and radiance shall return. Despite your
frumpiness . . .
(frown)
. . . this morning, I relished in the beauty that you have retained, the finesse
of fine wine that you displayed in the glow of reflected light of the bar mirror.
Tantalizing is your . . .
(fall silent in mid word, with mouth wide open bring paper closer to eyes and
read silently, only lips move)

MOTHER
My . . . my . . . a Harlequin romance novelist in the making. Read aloud
Sondra dear. I do believe Richard is attempting to court you. Go on dear.

SONDRA
(blushing)
No . . . no . . . this part is personal, private, strictly business details.

MOTHER
I would say he means business.

SONDRA
(fold up paper then rush to the window, grab binoculars and search up and
down the street below for the parade)
There's nothing . . . I missed it . . . it's over.

MOTHER
No dear, it has not started yet.

SONDRA
(turn to mother, stern face)
What's wrong with Richard? I mean, something is strange about him.
Whitney says he has a brain injury . . . and who are you, are you his mother?

296

MOTHER
Well, Sondra, you are direct and to the point. I could be his mother. I am old enough, and when younger have dabbled in romance, but at the moment I am a concerned person acting as a benefactor, just assisting in his reintroduction into society.

SONDRA
You are good. One business woman to another, I know when someone is just giving superficial information. There is more to this story.

MOTHER
Yes, you are right. There is. I have been successful in business and now dabble in philanthropy, and just took a fancy to Richard's case. Sel- serving, I guess.

SONDRA
(swallow the explanation)
But, but is he all there . . . I mean is he dangerous?

MOTHER
No, no, dear. Brain injuries do affect people differently. Some may become violent or very submissive. In Richard's case the injury, seven years ago, erased his memory and rebooted with a blank slate. Every bodily function had to be developed and abilities learned. A new memory was installed every moment. Good people and positive inputs will formulate a good person. Being unable to produce anger or confront anger with anger may hurt this man.

SONDRA
Sounds like science fiction. How can you be sure . . . that some government department did not take a criminal and erase his mind in order to create a decent person, but implanted an evil side that will explode on a specific day and create world wide havoc.

MOTHER
(laugh)
Dear, dear, you have been watching too many science fiction movies. This is just an accident and a rehabilitation of a person in need.

SONDRA
He is a bit too . . .
(wiggle note paper)
Nice, knowledgeable, perceptive, yet weird about plain everyday things.

MOTHER
Exactly, that is why I am here to help him. Alloyuis is helping him, Whitney

is helping, and I am here to ask you to help him.

SONDRA
By going on a date?
(pause, think, become startled)
You want, you want, expect me to teach him about . . .
(whisper)
Sex? Let him learn like all men, in the street with . . .. There are movies in grade school health classes. I'm not . . . don't expect me to . . .

MOTHER
Richard is well versed in knowledge. He has been reading for the past seven years and devours books and visual knowledge readily. That is not the problem. Mixing with reality is the problem. Only through the past year have we been venturing beyond the confines of the hospital.

SONDRA
(nervous, search the street for the parade, give quizzical looks at Mother)
So, I was a guinea pig for your dating experiment?

MOTHER
Yes.

SONDRA
At least you are honest.

MOTHER
Whitney made a connection with Richard, something that I can not explain, but this brief connection is at a level only they understand. The mother in me thought that you also may be able to help through a connection with Whitney.

SONDRA
I have nothing in common with Richard . . . John Doe.

MOTHER
Definitely not, complete opposites, so this way you may help.

SONDRA
(shake hands in air, exasperated)
You are persistent. That is why you are a billionaire, a famous business woman. I am going to regret this statement. How can I help?

MOTHER
Richard needs to be introduced to domestic life and all of the situations that

develop in domestic life.

SONDRA
I am not even good at domestic life.

MOTHER
So, I have been informed.

SONDRA
(angry, concerned)
By who? Dora? She stole my job interview with you. You hired and fired her then I hired her. Dora, my best friend stabs me in the back again.

MOTHER
(confused)
Dora Soblick?
(shake head)
Dora Soblick is your friend? Never hire friends. I fired her years ago. It was Whitney that divulged a complete story this morning on the way to the parade. Apparently, this apartment was not in its current condition yesterday. You have been without domestic help for months. Whitney is often late for school, and you miss school meetings. Obviously, you need a home coordinator. This is a perfect introduction for Richard, he cleans, cooks and organizes all aspects of his life and can do that for you and Whitney.

SONDRA
(shake head no and yes, reluctantly agreeing, knowing that Mother is going to talk you into an arrangement)
I can assume that Whitney told you about the private maid room that is vacant. I've never lived with a man . . . well brothers and a father does not count.

MOTHER
(nod with agreement)
I will have Richard's belongings delivered this afternoon.
(before Sondra reacts, change the subject to the parade with excitement)
The parade, hurry, hurry, this is Whitney's big introduction to the city. Binoculars, don't forget the binoculars.

DIRECTIONS
Sondra puts the note down on the coffee table, picks up the binoculars and heads to the window. Mother leans up to look at note and attempts to read. Sondra turns in time and grabs the note. Both nod and smile at each other. Mother teasingly smiles and Sondra blushes with staunch deniability. Sondra searches the parade for Whitney on a float. The camera looks through the

erratic movement of the binoculars to focus on people, clowns and floats until highlighting the last float. The massive float carrying Santa's sleigh and reindeer is weaving in and out of the binoculars frame of view. Sondra notices animated reindeer in action then a large excited Santa and Whitney overly enthusiastic. The float is weaving, going from side to side, moving closer to the sidewalks and the pleasure of spectators. Only Sondra seems overly excited and nervous, she searches for the driver. The binoculars zoom in on Richard driving, his interest is on waving to the crowd, looking back at Whitney and nodding to a frustrated William giving manic instructions to turn, not turn, use locking gear, breaks, throttle, all to the acknowledgement of Richard who ignores instructions.

SONDRA
(turn to Mother)
Does Richard know how to drive a vehicle?

MOTHER
He has read the motor vehicle hand book. I do believe this is the first time being actually behind the wheel.

SONDRA
He may be book knowledgeable but lacks ability.

MOTHER
Practice makes a person perfect. What damage can be done at five miles an hour?

DIRECTIONS
Sondra reaches for a remote control and turns on the television and searches channels until a parade is selected showing the float weaving along the street. An insert on the screen shows two hosts, the female host is politely smiling, unanimated, a male host is on the verge of a breakdown, as if announcing a formula car race in exaggeration of what is actually happening.

MALE ANNOUNCER
There is ultimate mayhem at the thirty-seventh Santa Claus parade. Mass hysteria among the thousands of spectators and multiplying as the out of control float weaves dangerously down the street. Oh the horror . . . Santa's little helper . . . can you see her?
(shake arm of female host)
The child is frantically waving, begging for help. Oh, the shame, no one is helping. Santa, the man of Christmas magic is unable to control Prancer and Vixen, where is Rudolph when you need him. The float is twisting, mere inches from the crowd. A roar of fear rises from the spectators. Where are the

300

cops when needed?

DIRECTIONS
Sondra bounces from the television to the binoculars and to the smiling faces of Santa, Whitney and Richard.

FEMALE ANNOUNCER
Thank you, Bill, for your emotional interpretation of the thirty-seventh Santa Claus parade, sponsored in part by the Stanfield Clothing Company, the home of the everlasting, stretchable waist band, the ultimate satisfaction in underwear comfort.

MOTHER
Grandfather Stanfield designed and patented the stretchable waistband.

SONDRA
Excuse me?

MOTHER
So, this matter is all settled. Richard will be your home domestic assistant. He will adjust to the reality of life and you, well, we will see. I am off to do what I do best.

DIRECTIONS
Camera moves quickly away from Mother exiting then to the television hosts in drastic differences, to Sondra stretching to see the parade, to see the Santa Claus float weaving down the street and behind the passing float to the people filling up the street and following the exiting parade. Music builds and scene fades.

DIRECTIONS
Camera focuses on inside of Sondra's apartment. Sondra and Whitney are dressed in their best dresses and standing, waiting with anticipation, staring at the main door. A knock at the door startles Sondra and exciting Whitney.

WHITNEY
He is here, and he is just what we need. Richard is perfect for us.

SONDRA
(unimpressed)
We will see! Richard is here to be a domestic assistant and to learn about life. We need to help him.

WHITNEY

I will.
(walk lady like to the door, face bursting with pleasure and excitement)

SONDRA
A man,
(look about the apartment)
living here, a man,
(sigh)
With problems!

WHITNEY
(open door)
Good evening, Richard.

RICHARD
A pleasant good evening to you, Miss. Whitney, Miss. Willowby, as per Mother's instructions, I am at your disposal.
(slightly bow with an expressed smile, balance two paper bags under arms containing personal belongings.

DIRECTIONS
There is an awkward pause as the three look from one to another. The clock chimes indicating the early evening meal hour. All turn to the clock.

RICHARD
(anxious to get started)
Shall I whip up a meal, perhaps a tender chicken stir fry on a bed of wild rice garnished with crisp vegetables marinated with olive oil and seasoning.

DIRECTIONS
Richard looks at Sondra who is thinking, her tongue licking lips gently in anticipation of the meals taste. Whitney nods slightly and gestures with a hand that the meal is 'so-so'. Richard lifts eye brows in thought.

RICHARD
With an impressive finality of deep-fried ice cream snow balls lightly coated with chilled Canadian Maple syrup from St. Joseph Island's Thompson's syrup farm.

WHITNEY
If you must insist.
(take a hold of Richard's arm and begin to lead him toward the kitchen)

SONDRA

Ah . . . that sounds . . ., would you like to settle into your room first, arrange personal belongings?
(stare into the hallway expecting to see luggage)

RICHARD
(follow stare and look into hallway)
Are you expecting someone, a date, shall I prepare a bath for you?

SONDRA
No, no preparing baths, no date, no man. I was searching for your luggage.

RICHARD
(lift arms to indicate bags)
These bags contain possessions.

SONDRA
Okay then!
(surprised, bewildered)
Your room, your room . . .
(limply point)

DIRECTIONS
Whitney tugs on Richard's arm and leads him away. Sondra stares into the hallway then closes the door. Stands in open area of entrance and is unsure of what to do.

WHITNEY
Do you put sparkles on the ice cream snow balls?
RICHARD
Of course, sparkles are mandatory.

DIRECTIONS
Camera follows Whitney and Richard and reluctantly following is Sondra. Scene fades on Sondra's quizzical expression.

DIRECTIONS
Camera has a tight shot of aged judge seemingly sleeping with head on supporting arm of a judicial throne. Thick eyebrows hide eyes that are reading documents. The judge has an appearance of Santa though with a shorter beard and less bulk, the glint in the eye is the same. Slowly lifting his head, a sour face seems prominent. A false front presented to hide the emotions of a grandfather persona. Camera turns to take in a sea of lawyers and scribes to one side of the room and Martha and a single lawyer to the other side. Silence in the room prevails until the judge clears his throat.

LAWYER ONE
Your honour . . .!

JUDGE
(slam gavel)
I cleared my throat, I did not ask for a statement from members of the assembled peanut gallery.

LAWYER TWO
(raise a hand and begin to open mouth)

JUDGE
(slam gavel louder than first time)
An interesting case we have before us. On one hand we have the state of affairs of the Bisson Empire.
(hold a hand open the beginning of showing an impression of balance scales)
On the other hand, a herd of power controlling, money devouring lawyers.
(stare down at lawyers, both hands being balanced as scales, when lawyers' close mouths and lower objecting hands continue)
On the other hand,
(look at hands)
on one foot we have the disappearance of the only heir of the Bisson Empire, Rickman Bisson. On the other foot we have Martha,
(turn to Martha, smile slightly)
Martha Stanfield-Montcalm, the ex wife of the late Rickman Bisson senior and a current share holder in the Bisson empire.

DIRECTIONS
Judge lowers head onto supporting hand. Silence grows. Lawyers stretch necks in assumption that the judge is sleeping, lawyer one begins to rise. The judge slams the gavel and lawyer one sits.

JUDGE
With deep regret, I must accept the submission from Evermore, Crookster, Armbender, Poopal and Monies, Evermore and bla, bla, bla associates that,
(lift head and stare at lawyers)
due to the lapse of seven years and the exhausted attempt to locate the vanished Rickman Bisson, I grant confirmation of a death certificate for Rickman Bisson.

DIRECTIONS
Lawyers, Cookster etc; begin to smile as camera pans down the line from oldest to youngest. The judge's one eye lifts towards the lawyers then to the worried expression on Martha's face.

JUDGE
In effect there is no living heir, thus, control of estate affairs falls under the control of Crookster and bla, bla, bla associates.

DIRECTIONS
Lawyers pump up chests and glance smugly to each other. The judge turns to Martha.

JUDGE
Unless Miss. Martha Stanfeild-Montcalm can present proof that she is the Mother of the stated heir, Rickman Bisson, thus will be considered an heir.

MOTHER
(deep in though, slowly rise to reply)
Though once married to Rickman Bisson Senior, and our relationship was fruitful in many ways, I was selfish in my pursue of being a successful business woman, I can not take any credit in the raising of the heir, Rickman Bisson.

JUDGE
I take it you do feel regretful?

MOTHER
(nod and sit, shame and regret on face and in actions)

JUDGE
Though you do have a single majority of shares, I trust that you will seek a position to head the board of governors?

MOTHER
(slightly rising)
I do.

JUDGE
Then all applications by Crookster, Evermore Associates to oversee all actions of Rickman Bisson's will is denied.

DIRECTIONS
All Lawyers in order begin to object, stating case studies. The Judge patiently listens and approvingly nods head in agreement. Lawyers eventually run out of steam and become silent and advert looking at the judge. The Judge raises the gavel slowly and brings down to a light tap.

LAWYER ONE

Your honour, objection on the facts we were hired to represent Rickman Bisson's matters.

LAWYER TWO
Papers were signed and sealed in the presence of a notary.

LAWYER THREE
Legal representation supersedes that of the governance of share holders and a governing board.

LAWYER FOUR
      I quote Sears verses Robuck . . . eighteen-thirty.

LAWYER FIVE
Lawyers representing Sears' founder held authority over Sears' decedents.

LAWYER SIX
Robuck had no authority though holding control of business affairs of Sears-Robuck Enterprises.

LAWYER SEVEN
Objection must be noted.

LAWYER EIGHT
Objection to these proceedings.

JUDGE
Objection to these proceedings? You must be a minor associate. Court scribe, take note that I also object to the esteemed councillor's objection. I do agree with Lawyer number three.
(point finger)

LAWYER THREE
(a big robust lawyer stands, huge arms bulging through suit)
Armbender, your honour.

JUDGE
I trust that you are who you say. I quote Mr. Armbender, 'Legal representation supersedes that of governance of share holders and a governing board.' Legally a governing board may oversee the activities of representation and govern the direction and oversee outcomes. I, the Judge will rule based on my satisfaction of all outcomes that the will intends. This session is now concluded until Miss. Martha Stanfield-Montcalm has assumed a position on the board and has instructed Evermore . . .,

(gesture with a hand to lawyers)

Poopal and associates to carry out legalities. I shall put my stamp of approval at a future session.

DIRECTIONS
Camera pans the line of lawyers, bounces over to Martha seemingly satisfied and relaxed. Camera zooms in on the judge waiting for objections. Scene blacks out at the strike of the gavel.

DIRECTIONS
A montage begins in the life of the new arrangement of living in the Willowby apartment. Snippets of scenes in a pantomime presentation are backed by emotional music reminiscent of silent film scores. Sondra and Whitney are seen madly getting ready in the morning as Richard hands over articles, a sweater, shoes, toothpaste, school books, business files and makes sure meals are consumed, faces clean, he accesses a taxi, halts the school bus and greets them when thy arrive home, helps with school work, answers the phone, takes messages and greets visitors. Sondra is constantly watching Richard caring for Whitney and secretly expects him to care for her. Richard is the only man at Whitney's dance class, he claps the loudest at Whitney's plays, recitals, stands for an ovation, despite Sondra shrinking with embarrassment. When trouble occurs at Whitney's school and Sondra is overboard, Richard calms the situation, seduces the teacher with charm. Richard cares for the females when sick, has a bucket ready, scolds them when not willing to eat vegetables, convinces them to try and stares with undeniable charm until they swallow.

Richard gives thumbs up and down when the women select clothing to wear, thumbs up even when the outfits are not the best. Each night Richard kisses Whitney on the top of the head and gives a hug, always shakes Sondra's hand. Sondra continually locks the bedroom door and over time begins to leave it unlocked. One night in a repetitive action of hugs and kisses of Whitney who is reluctant to go to bed after watching a scary movie, Richard leaves the door ajar and a nightlight on, absentmindedly he kisses Sondra on the head and leaves her door ajar. Whitney observes this and notices Sondra standing bewildered in the room. Slowly Sondra reaches for the door handle then leaves the door as is and backs away, she gently touches the spot where Richard kisses her head. Suddenly stopping in Hallway, Richard cocks head in thought, turns to look at Sondra's door left ajar, a smile crosses his face as he hangs a fallen scarf on a coat rack.

The camera focus is fuzzy as in a dream state of Sondra's mind. Richard is kissing the top of Whitney's head as she steps up onto a school bus. Behind the bus a taxi is waiting for Sondra. In an awkward stance Sondra is continuously eyeing Richard, at times dreaming of his affection on her. Suddenly Richard leans in and moves a strand of hair from her face and begins to passionately kiss her. Camera jumps to view Sondra and Dora eyeing a store display as Dora chatters away.

DORA
He kissed you? What did you do to . . ., you didn't . . ., you were wearing a sheer nightgown?

SONDRA
Nothing . . ., no, he, Whitney would not go to bed after watching a scary movie. He just got caught up in kissing her on the top of the head over and over and just kissed me too. That is all.

DORA
He kisses you . . . on the top of the head?

SONDRA
Yes, on the top of the head!

DIRECTIONS
Camera spins to frame Richard and Alloyuis sitting on a bench in the mall.

ALLOYUIS
Did she slap you, did she jump away, did she close and lock the bedroom door?

RICHARD
(silently shaking head no throughout)
No!

ALLOYUIS
She loves you.

DIRECTIONS
Camera jumps to Sondra and Dora.

DORA
He loves you!

DIRECTIONS
Film splits with Richard and Sondra facing each other.

RICHARD / SONDRA
NO!

DIRECTIONS

Camera follows Richard back to hospital and the doctor and a battery of cognitive tests. Camera follows Richard down a hallway as he enters one room after another. Camera acts as a human waiting while Richard is in each room. Camera eyes the door, pans the hall, eyes door handle, eyes the clock at the end of the hallway, nods off to sleep. At the end of the hallway the camera follows Richard like a puppy into the doctor's office. In the spacious meeting room, the doctor is at a desk browsing through the various reports. Mother sits quietly and motions for Richard to sit in chair.

MOTHER
(to Richard)
Doctor Geini is reviewing your tests. I am hopeful that all is well.

DOCTOR
Physically and mentally you are healthy, no hindering effects, other than a void of memory prior to your admission here seven years ago. You are free to create a new life.

MOTHER
That is it?

DOCTOR
That is about it.

RICHARD
That is it.

MOTHER / RICHARD / DOCTOR
(all shrug and lift upturned hands)
That is it.

DIRECTIONS
Black out. Fade in. Camera follows Mother through the hollowed halls of justice as she pauses before knocking on a door below a name plate of Judge Nicholas Stankowskie. Mother takes a deep breath and walks in. the judge bounces from a chair with the excitement previously shown when portraying Santa Clause to Whitney and during the parade. Eagerly the Judge claps onto Mother's hand and leads her to the sofa. They sit comfortable in a familiarity that has lasted for forty years.

JUDGE
I am still crazy over you Martha. Marry me.

MOTHER

Oh, Nick! You are sweet. This is proposal number . . .?

JUDGE
Sixty-nine. For the first fifty you defiantly said no.

MOTHER
Well, you must be breaking down my resistance with your charm.

JUDGE
Then what do you say now?

MOTHER
We must settle this current situation with the Bisson estate and Richard,
(pause, become playful)
then ask me another ten times and I will give in out of sheer weakness to your
overbearing charm.

JUDGE
I am a judge and must warn you that your statement is legally binding in a
court of law and in my heart.

MOTHER
(blush, do not object, remove gloves, place a light touch on the judge's hand,
a subliminal sign of agreement)
What have you found out and what will the public be able to dig up?

JUDGE
Very little in the public eye. The Bisson family, for generations have been
very private. If not for my association with you, I would be in the dark and
would not know where to search for information. Only you and I know that
Richard Bisson is your son and that our Richard Doe is Rickman Bisson.

MOTHER
In a way it is a shame that a child has lived in recluse in the same manner as
his father. I should have been stronger and forced myself back into my son's
life and exposed him to the world.

JUDGE
You have the opportunity now, present yourself and give the man the
substance of the lost memory of his life.

MOTHER
No! Absolutely not, that could do more harm than the burdens Richard has
currently endured. He has made such strides, he is open, engaging with people

310

and society and wants to contribute. He has no dependency on wealth. He is free to live. Bombarding him with wealth and the remembrance of seclusion may trap him within the void and I will lose Richard again. He accepts me now as a surrogate mother, more than a failed mother through his entire existence from birth to the day of his accident.

JUDGE
You will need to be on the board of governors of the Bisson Estate in order to make sure the estate is not squandered, and that Richard is able to earn a living.

MOTHER
I trust that you will make the contents and stipulations of the estate crystal clear to the governors and Evermore, Poopal and Associates.

JUDGE
I shall. Since you are not willing to come forward to state that Richard Doe is Rickman Bisson and your son, I must rule, that after seven years that this application from Poopal and Associates to declare Rickman Bisson deceased, is declared. It is only your majority shares in the Bisson Company that gives you a slight power of authority, and you must be a formative presence on the board of governors.

MOTHER
It may sound selfish, yet I have been given a second chance to be a mother and maybe a grandmother. The current state of Richard and his future is important. The past plays only a minute duration in life's timeframe.

JUDGE
No laws have been broken. There is no law forcing a person suffering amnesia to accept being forced to accept an unknown past. No one can force you to declare that you are the mother of Rickman Bisson.
(pause, lean in with compassion)
I have accounted for a timeframe of events, and I am the only one retaining DNA comparisons between you, Richard, Rickman Bisson and Rickman Bisson senior.

MOTHER
Of which you will keep secured.
(said with a demanding manner of a mother informing a child)
Now, tell me what you have uncovered about my son's past behind the wall of the Bisson compound.

JUDGE

From the day you exited the doors of the Bisson mansion, the doors were locked. I have provided a continuous report of events to you throughout the years, and the content had not changed. Father and son were reclusive, lived within the walls, never venturing out, catered to within the darkened walls. Richard continued this same existence after Rickman Bisson Senior died. Until . . .!
(pause in reflection)

MOTHER
Until? What have you failed to inform me about seven years ago?

JUDGE
I was not going to inform you that Rickman was seeking sexual gratification on the streets under the cloak of darkness.
(halt mother's indignation)
This was not the case. I have surmised that Rickman realized that a normal relationship, which might entail a wife, children and a normal existence, would not happen behind the rock walled enclosure and his reclusive life. He was well enlightened to his own existence. In every man there is a need, a desire to sew the seeds that would carry the essence on one's self toward future generations.

MOTHER
(repulsed)
Playing the field is one matter, but to randomly . . . with . . . who?

JUDGE
No, no, Martha, you are off track. Rickman left the estate to fulfill a pre-arranged appointment at a medical sperm bank, one that is aware of privacy and stresses only the genetics, not names, nor wealth status. After leaving the premises, Rickman was just a victim of a mugger. In a brief scuffle, Rickman was pushed from a bridge walkway and suffered head injury. Having no identification, no valuables prior or after, he became a John Doe with brain damage.
(pause)
And here we are.

MOTHER
And who was the recipient of the clinical sperm donation?

JUDGE
That, my dear, will take some cloaked sleuthing.

MOTHER

If a child is the result, an ingrained desire to find a birth parent is paramount. They will find each other, as Richard has found in me in a round about way without knowing the facts that connect all of the dots.

JUDGE
Shall I continue to search?

DIRECTIONS
Martha slightly nods as Nicholas gently reaches for her hand. Scene becomes fuzzy.

DIRECTIONS
As if eyes are slowly opening, the camera sees the fuzzy faces of Dora and Whitney waiting for Sondra to wake up from a deep sleep.

WHITNEY
Mother, are you awake?

SONDRA
No, I am sleeping and dreaming that my daughter is learning bad habits from my so-called-best-friend.
(open eyes wide)

DORA
So-called-best-friend? I am your only best so-called-friend!

SONDRA
Because you scare people away.

WHITNEY
Concentrate, we are here to convene an intervention.

SONDRA
A what?

WHITNEY
Intervention!

DORA
We need to get you on track in your life.

SONDRA
My life is on track.

DORA
Your love life.

WHITNEY
Yes, Mother, from one woman to another, your love life sucks. You need a
man, a husband and you owe me a father figure.

SONDRA
No, I don't!

DORA
You do, you are emotionally and sexually suffering. Look at me, always
happy, always satisfied, always craving the next encounter.

SONDRA
That is because you are a floozy.

WHITNEY
What is a floozy?

DORA
A woman that test drives a variety of potential men in order to find a suitable
mate, suitable husband and future father.

WHITNEY
Mother, you need to be a floozy.

SONDRA
No, I don't. I date respectfully. I have dated plenty of men.

WHITNEY
How many? You have never brought anyone home for me to meet.

DORA
I will show you them and give your mother's list of rejection notes.
(pull out cell phone and begin to scroll through pictures of men)
Take Andre, your mother stated, 'too short, moustache reminds her of a
walrus'.

SONDRA
He does!

WHITNEY
(squint eyes at pictures)

Yes, I see the resemblance.

DORA
But look at his abs. Next, what do you think you said about this hunk?

DIRECTIONS
Whitney and Sondra press heads together to view the picture then smirk at each other.

WHITNEY / SONDRA
Schwarzenegger, the terminator.

DORA
(turn phone to view)
Oh, that one was mine . . . a little . . .
(with a finger indicate a small appendage)
Next!

DIRECTIONS
Camera follows Richard and Alloyuis making their way through an indoor market. Richard is selecting fresh vegetable items as Alloyuis pushes a tiny cart, that at times he simply picks up to move. Alloyuis is stumbling over thoughts and words to express thoughts.

ALLOYUIS
Richard, Mother has asked me to have a talk with you, man-to man, somewhat like a father to a son.

RICHARD
Shall I be the father, expounding learned quotations from literary classics? Is there a particular subject that you would wish to discuss?

ALLOYUIS
Yes, there is a subject, but in this case, I am the father. After all, I have the most experience. You may have had, but you cannot remember, so I need to reintroduce you to the facts of sex.

DIRECTIONS
Suddenly there seems to be silence, but only in the mind of Alloyuis. People close by hesitated, turned to view the large man stumbling over the conversation. A little old woman lingers a bit too long, eager to listen to the conversation and its intriguing subject manner.

RICHARD

I have read in-depth of the clinical aspects of both the male and female anatomy and reproduction, and of birth. What would you like to know?

ALLOYUIS
Reading is boring. Have you got down, did some banging, do the deed, humped . . . engaged in sweaty naked sex?

DIRECTIONS
The old woman leans in and stares directly at Richard. Alloyuis waits while Richard's hands squeeze melons for ripeness.

RICHARD
Not that I can remember before my accident. From that point onward I would have to say I have been celibate.

OLD LADY
A virgin?

RICHARD
That is possible.
(said in a matter of fact)

ALLOYUIS
(hunch over the woman and whisper in a soft pleasant voice)
Mrs. Polard, this is a private conversation. I think that Mr. Polard is in a hurry. He just came from the pharmacy. You may get lucky tonight.
(wince and shiver at the thought)

DIRECTIONS
The old lady waves to husband at a distance then she gives a goodbye wave to Alloyuis, then hurries off. Alloyuis picks up a shopping cart and hustles after Richard.

ALLOYUIS
That is a long time to be celibate. Seven years man! Seven years! I have taken you under my wing, introduced you to a social life and you have failed. You are a nanny, house keeper, cook, a father figure and everyone assumes that you are a husband, yet you ain't getting anything, nothing, zilch.

RICHARD
The moment of opportunity for mutual bonding has not presented itself. No female has presented interest. Female pheromones have not been detected as is indicated should occur. This is a study presented by a Doctor Ruth, a highly
. . .

316

ALLOYUIS
Forget Doctor Ruth's hypothesis, listen to Alloyuis' statement of fact. Make a move, instigate your intensions, convince the woman that you are what she needs. Present your complete package.

RICHARD
Exposure!

ALLOYUIS
Eventually, but first, wine, dine, intimate conversation, smooching, light petting, dim the lights and bingo she is hooked. After that you just follow, for she will lead the way.

RICHARD
You make is sound so simple. Who do you have in mind?

ALLOYUIS
Really? Man, really? Whitney knows, Dora and Mother know, and I know that Sondra is the one.

RICHARD
Sondra? As you say, Really? We have been cohabitating and I have fulfilled their needs and I seem acceptable to them, and them to me. I do posses an emotion of belonging to a family and a wanting sensation to Sondra.
(smile with seduction)
Alloyuis, lets make a go of this?

ALLOYUIS
Romance!

DIRECTIONS
Camera zooms in on Dora's cell phone to show a picture of a man in leathers, wearing a prominent dog collar.

SONDRA
Romance, his version of romance is barking at women we passed along the street. He even barked at a poodle.

DIRECTIONS
Dora continues to bring up picture after picture. All three make random objectionable sounds and comments.

DORA
Stanley?

SONDRA
Self serving.

WHITNEY
A mob boss, a stuffy banker, a teenager!

DORA
That was your mother's cougar faze.

SONDRA
I did not date that person, he was your date.

DORA
Twice.

WHITNEY
Mother, Richard has all of the qualifications you need, and you do like him, don't you?

SONDRA
I do not dislike him, and he is nothing like these . . .

DORA
. . . twenty-seven previous candidates.
(raise a finger over the cell phone delete button)
Shall I delete your past?

SONDRA
Definitely.
(pause, swoon, become cautious)
But we know nothing about Richard's past. He knows nothing about his own past. What if he remembers? What if he has a wife, a family?

DORA
It has been seven years, someone would have claimed him by now. If they haven't then they do not want him. Do you?

DIRECTIONS
Dora and Whitney eagerly wait for a response.

SONDRA
I don't expect to be swept off my feet, but I could be swayed by a little romance.

DORA
Alloyuis is coaching Richard.

SONDRA
He needs coaching?

DIRECTIONS
Camera spins around the room as the women get Sondra ready for a date. The camera randomly searches the darkening cityscape for acts of romance; an old couple walking arm in arm, a young couple cuddling on a park bench, an older couple giggling as if they were youngsters, a woman reading to her husband who is in a reclining bed, an elderly man feeding his wife in her hospital bed, two young children watching each other's reflection in a store window, punk dressed teenagers within a group secretly couple pinkie fingers. The camera focuses on a man and a woman sitting apart. As the camera draws back the viewers see a male couple leaning heads and shoulders together, and a female couple nose to nose and whispering to each other. The camera turns to watch a poodle walking slightly ahead of an older male dog. She has a leash in her mouth; the male dog is obviously losing its sight. On a TV screen in a storefront window is a bedroom scene from the 'I love Lucy show', shows Ricky Ricardo bending over to kiss a frustrated Lucy. The 'I love Lucy' heart and title fill the screen. Time passes. The camera follows legs entering an elevator; the legs turn toward each other; the woman's foot rises slightly. The legs exit the elevator and approach an apartment door; the male legs open the door, the female legs enter, pause and then drag in the man. The camera climbs the tangled legs to see Richard and Sondra kissing.

DIRECTIONS
Camera clicks still shots of the unfolding romance of Richard and Sondra on a night out accompanied by Alloyuis and Dora. Richard, Sondra, Mother, Nicholas and Whitney at Christmas at the hospital meeting people and handing out small gifts. Richard and Sondra on a date. Richard and Alloyuis cooking in a hospital kitchen and with Whitney bringing deserts to child patients in cafeteria. Richard and Whitney bonding. Mother and Whitney, Alloyuis and Sondra, Dora and Richard, all random pictures of humour, drama, slapstick, bewilderment. The song 'What are you doing New Years Eve' replaces Christmas songs. Richard and Sondra walk away from a crowd as the clock ticks to midnight. The camera moves to sky and fireworks and a full moon as snow disappears.

DIRECTIONS
Camera follow the night turning into early morning. The camera climbs from the street up the building's walls and enters the Willowby's apartment to see Richard and Sondra kissing in the darkened hallway between separate open

bedroom doors. Dishevelled robes hint at their hastened rendezvous. A sudden noise from Whitney's room distracts the kissing. Their faces pressed together slowly turn, lips pulling apart, cheeks pressed together. Lips are puckered into the air, eyes search for the sounds. Upon hearing another noise, they break apart to arms length.

RICHARD
Under the current situation, will you?

SONDRA
Yes . . ., I guess I should.

DIRECTIONS
At the turn of Whitney's door handle, Richard and Sondra scamper back to the wrong bedrooms, close the doors then open them in a panic to meet Whitney tossing up coloured streamers.

WHITNEY
Merry Christmas!
(greet without consideration of the bedroom confusion)

DIRECTIONS
Whitney tosses up streamers as the camera draws in on Richard and Sondra's blushing faces. The camera fades then brightens to a meal setting featuring the gathering; Richard, Sondra, Whitney, Alloyuis, Dora, Mother and Nicholas. Banter commences as Richard introduces special dishes. Sondra is obviously smitten by Richard and watches his movements. Mother watches Whitney, observing mannerisms that are imitated from Richard. Noticing Whitney chewing gum, Mother holds out a hand, asking Whitney to eject. Dora and Alloyuis begin to sing, an example of their pervious karaoke performance. Mother takes the gum and wraps it in a napkin and then hands it to Nicholas and whispers.

MOTHER
Test the DNA for comparisons.

JUDGE
Martha, do not jump to conclusions. It is only a coincident that Sondra received insemination from the same sperm bank that Richard . . .

MOTHER
Satisfy the curiosity of an old woman.

JUDGE

A demanding old woman.

MOTHER
(smile, pat Nicholas' hand)
Yes.

DIRECTIONS
Laughter erupts when Dora hits a sour note as Alloyuis hits a perfect high
note that demands silence and then applause.

RICHARD
(stand to gain everyone's attention)
A year has ended with many changes and new friends, and new hopes, and a
new year must start with growth, so I must find employment, must select a
name before a marriage takes place.

DIRECTIONS
Silence, all eyes turn to Sondra.

WHITNEY
To my Mother?
(more eager than surprised)

SONDRA
Yes!
(grin at others)
What? All of you contrived to make it so, so why are you surprised.

DORA
Because you are never impulsive, or are you going to say it will be a two-year
engagement?

ALLOYUIS
This is a new year, a new start, get everything started at the beginning. The
Judge can preside over the name change and a wedding at the same time.
Right, Judge?

JUDGE
Yes, I can.
(pause and look at Sondra)
If Sondra is so inclined?

SONDRA
(stare at Whitney, melt from her broad smile, wearily reject the other smart-

ass grins, sigh and smile when looking deep into Richard's eyes)
Yes, no need to delay.

DIRECTIONS
Enthusiastic uproar of pleasure.

MOTHER
All set then. I will have documents ready from the board of governors of the
Bisson foundation naming Richard as chairman for the Judge to validate once
Richard selects a name.

RICHARD
A job, well! What will I do?

MOTHER
What you are good at, organization, charity work, philanthropy and seeing
that the foundation is legally above board.

RICHARD
For that I will need an assistant, someone in the security business. Hiring
Alloyuis would be in the best interest of all.

ALLOYUIS
(glance from Richard to Mother, eager for a positive response, reply in a
squeaky emotional voice)
I would be honoured, Richard. I am honest Mother.
(dab a napkin to nose and sniffle)

RICHARD
A wage of twenty dollars per hour is non-negotiable.

ALLOYUIS
(shake head no a bit and with a hand indicate higher with an upturned hand)

RICHARD
Twenty-five dollars an hour, each!

MOTHER
(surprised by the low amount)
Yes . . . that is agreeable and . . .

JUDGE
I will make arrangements.

DIRECTIONS
Camera takes a close up of Evermore, the lawyer representing the Bisson Board of Governors, then the camera jumps down the line of lawyers, pausing to view the random expressions of each. The camera pulls back to view the entire group of associated lawyers then to the small gathering consisting of Richard, Mother, Sondra, Whitney, Alloyuis and Dora all dressed in their best attire. The camera turns to view the Judge looking over papers.

LAWYER ONE
Your Honour, we object to these proceedings.

JUDGE
(lift head slowly, eyes lifting first)
Do you know what the contents contain?

LAWYER TWO
No, but we need time to prepare an objection.

JUDGE
Do you not think that being informed of information is important before deciding to present an objection?

LAWYER THREE
Yes, but . . .

JUDGE
Then how can you object to these proceedings?

LAWYER FOUR
Because we may not like what we will hear.

JUDGE
(cock an eye of frustration)
Objection denied.

ALL LAWYERS
(all begin to rise and sit as if bobbing puppets in a carnival game, state objections, excuses, make random gestures, flip pages, point to facts, turn and open various sized law books)

JUDGE
(slowly raise gavel, raise several inches each time a lawyer says something stupid, as the lawyers slowly begin to quite when seeing the gavel rising above shoulders and then above the head and stop, when silence prevails and all

lawyers are sitting, slowly lower the gavel until a mute tap of the gavel sounds against the anvil)

Objection denied.

(turn to Mother's group)

Today we are here to confirm the death of a John Doe and the birth of a person and to legally register this citizen's name. Once this is confirmed he will be appointed to the head of the Bisson board of Governors. Then a celebration of a wedding.

(turn to frown at the lawyers when a lawyer attempts to rise)

To be witnessed by the legal association of Evermore Poopal.

(pause and wait for a response)

LAWYER ONE

No objection.

JUDGE

(stand up behind the bench)

Will the party please approach the bench?

DIRECTIONS

The group approach and arrange themselves in an appropriate manner. Dora and Alloyuis juggle to stand beside the correct person. Whitney snuggles in front and between Richard and Sondra. Mother stands slightly to the side.

JUDGE

John Doe will no longer exist once you decide on a name, Richard. Have you decided?

RICHARD

Yes, your Honour, I have. I have become accustomed to the name Richard, that Mother has so anointed upon me, so I shall keep. As to a last name I have placed thought into the benefactors and have selected to be named, Richard Bisson-Stanfield-Montcalm . . ..

(pause, turn to Sondra and smile slightly)

Willowby.

JUDGE

So be it.

(slam gavel)

By the power vested in me by the state,

(glance to Evermore Associates)

and with no presented objections, we are gathered to present the bonds on matrimony between Sondra Marie Willowby and Richard Bisson-Stanfield-Montcalm-Willowby.

324

DIRECTIONS
Camera pulls back and music builds, lips are seen mouthing words, the progression goes through the steps until the marriage kiss and mounting congratulations. After Mother and the Judge make their congratulations they step aside and whisper to themselves. The camera and audience eavesdrop.

JUDGE
Martha,
(retrieve a letter from vest pocket as the camera notices markings of lab company name and the letters noting the DNA analyzing report)
these are the results of your request. It is uncanny that your hunch is absolutely correct, uncanny!

DIRECTIONS
Camera focuses on Mother's astonished and pleased facial expressions, then drifts to the couple taking Whitney's hand and walking down the isle. Before reaching the exit doors, Sondra notices the told-you-so expression on Dora's face.

SONDRA
I hate it when you are right. Yes, yes! He is just the kind of man I need.

DIRECTIONS
Camera turns from the group to face the exit doors and pushes doors open then the scene goes black. The camera is pulling away from an aerial view of the city. Music builds.

THE END

OTHER AVAILABLE TITLES
FROM MOOSE HIDE BOOKS
Imprint of
MOOSE ENTERPRISE Publishing
Visit our web site at www.moosehidebooks.com for complete title listings.

TITLES
    Steeltown
    Steeltown Blues
    Roosevelt Street
    Executor of Mercy
    A Print of a Man
    Sky Flyers
    Assault of a Princess

Assault
Basement Bargain Price Leafs For Sale
Reflection
Guilt in Accession
Déjà vu
Fragmentation of Life
Dodger
My Pecker Ain`t Working
Cowboy Poetry for Sale
Badland Trails
Existence
Opening night (theatre plays)
Part The Curtain (theatre plays)

www.ingramcontent.com/pod-product-compliance
Lightning Source LLC
Chambersburg PA
CBHW031156020726
47499CB00002B/382